"You are too kind,"
Flip whispered as they emerged from the house.

Darcy?! She'd been rescued by Whatever-His-First-Name-Is Darcy? She'd taken his arm not only because he'd offered it but because this dreamworld, already tilting on the edge of total chaos, was starting literally to sway.

He was taller than she would have expected and far more capable. He helped her up the steps to the phaeton's high bench and launched himself easily into the other side. As he adjusted the reins, footmen scuttled around the horses, snapping harnesses and clacking buckles. Flip wished desperately for a seat belt.

He sighed. "I'm sorry. I'm afraid Louisa and Caroline can be, well—"

"Complete and utter bitches?"

He bit back a smile. "The limpidity of your language, Philippa, is ever a delight."

There was a realness to this man she had never found in the pages of *Pride and Prejudice*. The shadow of bristle dusted his cheeks, a scar marred the length of his neatly manicured hand, and his leg flexed against the boot box in a way that made her wish the silk on her bodice wasn't so thin. How was it she'd known the era, the house and the butler, but didn't recognize the most famous man in literature except maybe Hamlet? What sort of poorly planned dream was she producing?

ALSO BY GWYN CREADY

Tumbling Through Time

AVAILABLE FROM POCKET BOOKS

Seducing Mr. Darcy

GWYN CREADY

POCKET BOOKS

New York London Toronto Sydney

Pocket Books
A Division of Simon & Schuster, Inc.
1230 Avenue of the Americas
New York, NY 10020

This book is a work of fiction. Names, characters, places, and incidents either are products of the author's imagination or are used fictitiously. Any resemblance to actual events or locales or persons, living or dead, is entirely coincidental.

First Pocket Books paperback edition August 2008

POCKET and colophon are registered trademarks of Simon & Schuster, Inc.

For information about special discounts for bulk purchases, please contact Simon & Schuster Special Sales at 1-800-456-6798 or business@simonandschuster.com

Illustration by Alan Ayers
Design by Lisa Litwack

Manufactured in the United States of America

10   9   8   7   6   5   4   3   2   1

ISBN-13: 978-1-4165-4116-5
ISBN-10:   1-4165-4116-0

For Lester,
who has given me everything

Acknowledgments

As usual, there are many people to thank: Manuel Erviti, a sterling friend and librarian, who always has the answer; Larry Whalen, who responded to a torrent of detailed questions about Japanese obscenities without blinking an eye; Doris Short, whose design work is spot-on perfect; good friends Katie Kemper and Scott DeLaney, Stuart Ferguson and Gudrun Wells, Craig and Jeanie Barrett, Camille Walton, Elaine Knighton, Fred Lorini, Laura Keserich, Eva Lorini, Emily Lorini, Diana Postlethwaite, Janet Mc-Closkey, Theresa Gallick, Mark Prus, Michael Roe, Jeremy Diamond and Alison Muir, Charlie and Margaret Foppiano, Marnie Unruh, Sharon Wible and Rich Mankovich, Kim and Wayne Honath, Kate and Mark Zingarelli, Doris and Lloyd Heroff, and Liz and Steve Kapur, whose interest in and ongoing support of my writing is much appreciated; Phil Hieber at the University of Pittsburgh, who has the power to unlock all doors; Linda Berdoll, whose vastly entertaining *Mr. Darcy Takes a Wife: Pride and Prejudice Continues* gave me my first taste of what Austen may have missed; friend and coworker Valli Ellis, with whom I have shared, knowingly and unknowingly, many of life's journeys; Marie Guerra, supporter *extraordinaire*, who genuinely seems to enjoy this as much as I do; Caridad Piñeiro for several year's worth of knowledge in a few short hours; Linda Mullens, who inspires me; Mary Parish, for reading an early draft and always being there when I needed her; Donna Neiport, for keeping me abreast of library strategy and understanding what to do when families and friendships get tough; Lynne Crofford and Beverly Crofford, for their support and for helping me remember; the wonderful ladies at Arnold—Rema Chandramohan, Cheryl Loo, Julianna Bogdanski, Nina Warfield and Perry Fleisig-Greene—as well as Gwen Davison, for friendship and good cheer on many creative journeys; Jeanne Lowther and Janet and Lee Parish, for stepping in to fill the void; the inimitable Karen Schade, who not only gave me a better ending for *Tumbling Through Time* but was generous enough to help me improve this book, too; Scott Cready, for his love, even when it wasn't easy; Kate Kruckemeyer, for appeasing a person who, I'm sure, seemed like a deranged stalker; Philippa Brophy's brother, whom I don't even know but who gave me my heroine's name in the course of a sixty-second elevator ride; Diane Pyle and Nick Cole, for enough laughter to last two lifetimes; Richard Holme, for a great title, even though we didn't use it, and for inspiring Magnus's sartorial style, lime green excepted; Teri Coyne, for being there, mom-wise, when my arms wouldn't reach; Linda Dickerson and Laura Ellis at the National Aviary, for running a great shop and giving me a peek backstage; Ninja, for years of charming me—you'll be missed, my little friend; Kathi Boyle, Mary Bockovich and the folks at the Pittsburgh AIDS Task Force, for modeling compassion and determination; Karen Rumbaugh at Borders, who taught me the amazing power of hand-selling; Jeanne Fitzmaurice and the great people at DesignHerGals.com, for raising awareness of the plight of women with Stage IV breast cancer; Jackie Wisner, who knew just what to say and made me cry; Wileen Dragovan, who never minded letting a little bit of cool rub off on me; Dawn Kosanovich, for friendship and sage shoe advice; Tim Gallagher, whose fascinating book *The Grail Bird: Hot on the Trail of the Ivory-billed Woodpecker* served as the basis for all I know about that illustrious creature and the quest to find it; my superhero copyeditor, Judy Steer, for doing her best to keep me from looking like an idiot; the wonderful people at work who act as if they're on the official launch team; my readers, especially those who have been kind enough to write and let me know what they're thinking; Megan McKeever, who likes *To Catch a Thief* as much as I do, which is about the best thing you can ask for in an editor; my agent, Claudia Cross, who scores me one great thing after another and has now actually begun creating extracurricular adventures for our shared enjoyment; my husband, son, and daughter, who, as always, endure it with hardly more than a roll of the eyes; and last but far from least, the incomparable Jane Austen, who I hope can look the other way for a few hours.

Chapter One

"*Did* you say Mr. Darcy's pants?" Dinah asked, choking on her espresso.

Flip tucked a long strand of blond hair behind her ear, happy to shock her more upright friend. "Well, it's more polite than the first thing that popped into my head."

Eve grinned. "Which was?"

"Mr. Darcy's pants and a breath mint."

The women laughed loud enough to turn heads at the outdoor café.

"If I were Lizzy Bennet and the heroine of *Pride and Prejudice*," Flip said in only a slightly lower voice, "and had just bagged Darcy, the hottest man in literature, forget the engagement gift. I'd want his pants, coat, shirt and—well, he could probably keep the boots—for a hardy screw in the hedgerow." She considered the image forming in her head. "Oh, yeah. Definitely keep the boots."

Dinah put on her fiery high school English teacher look, the look that transformed her from a happy, bisexual Julianne Moore look-alike to Magenta in *The Rocky Horror Picture Show*. "Lizzy Bennet is not that kind of girl," she said hotly.

"And that, my dear Dinah," Flip replied, "is the trouble with *Pride and Prejudice*. Not enough hedgerow."

Eve, whose spiky black bob and sleek attorney suit gave her the look of an upscale punk rocker, considered the sandstorm of sugar she was stirring into her iced tea. "I think our friend Flip has a hedgerow fixation."

"You know what they say about hedgerows," Dinah said with a superior smile. "If you're not careful, all you'll end up with is pricks."

"What is it about divorce that takes all the fun out of that word?" Flip tapped a dollop of cappuccino foam from the end of her stirrer. "But it doesn't have to be a hedgerow. I'm just as happy with the deck of a sailboat, the parapet of a duke's castle or the front steps of the New York Public Library. I just like my heroines to get their due."

"Gee, I hope their due includes a pillow." Eve emptied a fourth packet of sugar into the glass. "My ass hurts just thinking about it."

"Gratuitous sex is the refuge of the uninspired writer," Dinah said with the smugness only a few gate attendants or someone who majored in English Lit can muster. "With its figurative blank page on the matter, *Pride and Prejudice* allows a reader the ultimate flight of imagination."

"Oh, is that what we're calling it now?" Flip said. "I wondered why you were going through so many batteries at night."

The women's laughter filled the green space in which the café tables sat, but Eve's, Flip noticed, was more infectious than that of all of them. Once you've faced breast cancer, Eve told her, you never pass up the chance to belly laugh. Flip smiled. It was a wonderful sound, and the first man Eve had agreed to see since her mastectomy, Adam—hold for the laugh—seemed to like it too. Eve had been teetering on the "should I/shouldn't I" line for a month now.

The *Columbia livia* at Flip's feet cooed and flapped happily, bobbing for crumbs. She threw down a bit of her biscotti, then let her gaze slide across the street to the gleaming forty-two-story tower known as the Cathedral of Learning that dwarfed everything else on the University of Pittsburgh campus. The topic of sex never failed to reduce her and her friends from thirty-plus-year-olds with more than a decade of bad relationships behind them to a slumber party's worth of snickering teens. It was just what she needed after a long couple of weeks at the Aviary. She rubbed her aching neck.

"Tough day, sweetie?" Eve asked. Eve tended to mother.

"Ugh," Flip agreed. "And it's only half over. I'm supposed to be working on that damned presentation at the library, but Ninja's got a nodule on his wing, so I swung by work this morning to take a look, and, well . . . let's just say 'Bird Density and Diversity in Clear-cut Oak Forests' is not exactly writing itself." Unsurprising, she considered, given that instead of writing when she'd returned from the Aviary, she'd spent an hour daydreaming about the book she was reading—specifically, a sink top sex scene in which, for once, the hero was the one who ended up with tile marks on his knees. Venice, she thought fondly. Who needed a gondola?

And now she'd have to tear herself away from what happened next to reread *Pride and Prejudice* for their book club on Thursday.

Not that she didn't enjoy Darcy and Lizzy's long, fitful submission into love. It was like waiting for two strongly repelling magnets to flip over and snap together with a bang. But given her own current state of carnal deprivation—two years, three months, one week and 2,437 laps in the YMCA pool, but who was counting?—what she really needed from her reading material was not a flight of imagination, but an intricately detailed charter excursion into cool sheets, silky boxers, and the snap of panty under insistent fingers. Darcy and Lizzy simply lacked sufficient detail.

Her Venice hero, sure to be literally spouting detail in the next scene, would have to wait, though Flip couldn't help but wonder in what form his reward would come. She tipped the chair onto two legs and let the various options curl through her thoughts. . . .

Stop! her industrious side commanded. Clear-cut forests. Winter migration. Biodiversity. These are the thoughts you should be thinking.

But nothing even faintly ornithological popped into her head. Instead the Cathedral of Learning transformed itself from a stolid skyscraper into what could only be described as the largest literary device ever conceived, with the gently swaying trees at its base pillowy curls of hair, and Forbes and Fifth, the wide boulevards that ran on either side, a pair of creamy, muscular thighs.

Flip dropped the chair back onto four legs and took a deep breath.

She assured herself these spells would be entirely natural in a woman who hadn't experienced the real thing in over two years—six if one were inclined to charge her ex-husband Jed with heroic underachievement in the area, and, in this case, one certainly was. Entirely natural, she repeated. Why fight it? The tower pulsed with gleaming, pent-up—

"Don't you agree, Flip?"

She jerked her attention back to the table, nearly toppling her cappuccino in the process.

"Hmm, what?"

A plain-faced young woman in a wrap skirt and a PANIC! AT THE DISCO T-shirt stood next to the table, smiling. Two mouse-colored pigtails snaked down the straps of her bright orange backpack, and she clutched an organic yogurt.

"I was saying the best stories appeal to our more noble desires," Dinah repeated, smiling encouragingly.

"Oh, sure," Flip agreed. "Like *The Economist* . . . or beets."

The young woman chuckled. If she were a bird, she'd be a killdeer, Flip decided, spindle-legged and slightly nervous.

Dinah said, "Flip and Eve, this is my friend Beth Olinsky. She's a senior in history at Pitt. We're in the choir at church together. Beth this is Flip Allison, an ornithologist with the Aviary, and Eve Bloomberg, a lawyer at Pilgrim Pharmaceuticals."

Beth gave everyone a lopsided grin. She bloomed when she smiled, Flip thought. Not quite a peacock. An oriole, perhaps.

"Flip?" Beth said. "That's an unusual name."

"Short for Philippa," Flip admitted. "Blame it on my older brother, who couldn't pronounce it. He also called elephants 'elphiniums' until he was about fifteen. You a *Pride and Prejudice* fan like your choir colleague here?"

Beth nodded, rubbing her nose vigorously. "I loved the book. My sister gave me the DVD for Christmas, but my boyfriend never wants to watch it."

"Uh-oh. Time for a new boyfriend."

"Yeah, well, I guess that's what he thinks too." She shifted her weight from one Teva sandal to the other. "We're, um, breaking up."

Flip shook her head. "Oh dear, idiocy starts early. Well, at least you can watch the miniseries now. Believe me, it's a worthwhile trade. Say, would you be interested in coming to our book club Thursday? We're discussing *Pride and Prejudice*."

Beth brightened. "Sure."

"We're not as old and wizened as we look," Eve assured her. "Some of us even text instead of having meaningful in-person relationships."

"Hey," Dinah said, "there's nothing wrong with a little text sex, I always say."

"Yeah." Flip gave her friend a gentle poke. "Why should your first two fingers be the only digits getting any action?"

"Thursday would be perfect, actually," Beth said. "My history paper's due Thursday, and I hate doing things at the last minute. This'll give me just the impetus I need to get it knocked off by Wednesday."

"Clearly you need to give Flip some pointers," Eve said. "She seems to be stalled on her particular assignment."

"God, it's true," Flip said. "This part's always the challenge for me. I like to be out in the field doing the stuff, you know, but writing about it?" She made a sour face. "I've been working on this presentation for two weeks now, shut up in that sterile library. I was also sidetracked by a fellowship application—not that that's going to matter much now. So I'm—"

"Not matter?" Dinah interrupted. "Why?"

Flip tossed more crumbs from her biscotti to the ground and groaned. "Jed applied too."

"That bastard," Eve said. "I thought he was absolutely convinced the ivory-billed woodpecker no longer existed. I thought you'd nearly had a shouting match over it on your birthday a few years ago."

Flip rolled her eyes. "We did, and he is. But that doesn't

stop him from trying to get in on the most important bird expedition of the century. And Cornell's only looking for one more person on the search team, which means I've got no chance. You know his résumé is as long as my arm."

"I know it's the one thing of your ex-husband's to which the adjective *long* could be applied," Dinah said.

Beth laughed again, and Eve gestured for her to sit down.

"Don't give up," Eve said, patting Flip's arm. "God only gives opportunities to tromp around in the mud and cold for weeks at a time to those who really deserve it. Isn't Jed afraid he'll get his hair dirty?"

The corner of Flip's mouth rose. Jed bore a strong resemblance to Matthew McConaughey, from his tequila Texas accent to his athlete's frame and golden Adonis–like waves. It was a resemblance Jed eagerly fostered, and without his blow dryer, he was unmanned. "Oh, no, didn't I ever tell you? When he's in the field he wears a beret."

Dinah's jaw dropped. "You're joking. Military or French?"

"H&M. He's very in touch with his inner urban hipster."

Dinah put her chin in her hands and let out a long, satisfied sigh. "Darcy would never wear a beret."

"I think we can all say our thanks for that." Flip grinned. "Now if we could only get him into handcuffs and black cotton bikinis."

The women chortled into their drinks.

"I'm sure Lizzy and Darcy have a very satisfying physical relationship after they marry," Dinah said.

"Right," Flip said, "because we all know that's when the really hot stuff happens."

Eve frowned. "C'mon, Flip, I thought you liked *Pride and Prejudice.*"

"I do, I do." She held up her hands. "It's just that . . . how do I say it? The book I'm reading now is filled with high-tension longing, just like *Pride and Prejudice*. But there's also hot sex on the bathroom sink in Venice to pay it off. Darcy strives to be a better man for the love of a great woman. Catnip for a woman's soul, right? But where does all that sublimated desire go?"

Eve lifted her cup. "Incredible hard-ons?"

"My point exactly," said Flip. "Where's the catnip for a woman's nether regions?"

Eve stopped mid-sip. "Say, you don't suppose that's why the house where Darcy stays is called Netherfield, do you?"

"All I'm saying," Flip continued, "is that Darcy is all about mannerly silence. I happen to like the bathroom sink better. Look at *Gone with the Wind*. Ashley Wilkes, mannerly silence. Rhett Butler, sink."

"How about *Casablanca?*" Beth offered. "Victor Laszlo and Rick Blaine?"

"Thank you. We all know who we'd want to end up with."

"Darcy," Dinah said pointedly, "is no Ashley Wilkes."

"No, better breeches to be sure." Flip put down her stirrer. "But it isn't just in books, either. I honestly believe real men fall into those two camps too. And you don't even need to talk to them to figure it out."

"No way," Dinah said.

"You don't think so? Okay, look at that guy over there, the one with the thighs."

The women swiveled in unison to follow the easy stride of a shirtless fortysomething jogger in abbreviated yellow running shorts and abs so quilted they'd make a Chanel bag envious.

"Sink," Flip said definitively. "There's only one reason you develop thighs like that."

"One-hundred-thirty-pound leg lifts?" Eve grinned.

"You got it, girl."

Dinah tapped her finger on the table, unmoved. She lifted a thoughtful brow and tilted her head. "What about that guy?"

Flip turned her head. Two tables away, in a thin, black V-necked sweater and stone-colored trousers, was a dark-haired man in his midthirties. A scuffed backpack sat at his feet and a stack of journals lay on the table beside him. He removed the pair of Elvis Costello glasses he'd been wearing and rubbed the bridge of his nose. He had the body of a pass receiver, tall, with an easy agility to his movements, and fine-cut features that reminded her of the barn owl with its piercing, knowing eyes. But he was clearly all intellect and no action. He probably had a thesaurus next to his bed.

"Oh, please." Flip waved away the challenge. "Definitely mannerly silence. He practically screams 'underemployed graduate student.' You know they're not getting any."

Beth laughed, then covered her mouth.

"Actually," Dinah said, triumphant, "if he screams at all it's *at* underemployed graduate students, and he's actually getting a lot. He's a visiting scholar in literature and the reputed Lothario of the Rare Book Room."

Flip's eyes cut back to the man in question, stunned. She'd passed the high-security Rare Book Room in the university library dozens of times without the faintest spark of carnal inspiration. Had she lost her touch? How had this, this . . . seeming academic, this man who had all the manner of a theorist to him, managed a record of action worthy of, well, her?

The man in question returned his glasses to his nose, flipped open the journal and sipped his drink. As she watched his large, steady hands shape the pages into pliable submission, an unexpected shiver shot up her spine.

"The Rare Book Room?" Flip repeated abstractedly, still lost in this astonishing reappraisal. "There's no place to sit."

Eve cleared her throat meaningfully.

"Oh, right." Heat crept into Flip's cheeks. Good God, she'd forgotten real people can actually live like they do in novels. After the last few years with Mr. Missionary, it was like she'd been neuralized.

"Yeah," Dinah went on, "and the provost fought like hell to get him here too. He's a genius in the world of literary criticism, apparently. I forget his name. Something Knightley."

"Thrice?" Flip murmured. The women's laughter filled the courtyard again, and the man's commanding gaze immediately cut to her. She dropped her eyes in a flash, like a schoolgirl caught passing a note. Knightley? Kingly would be more appropriate. And forget the barn owl. This guy was an eagle.

"His name is Magnus Knightley," Beth said, rising. "I heard him speak last semester. He's an Austen scholar, actually."

"I'll be damned," Flip said.

"Are you off, Beth?" Eve rose, too. "I've got to get back myself. I can only make a meeting with outside counsel last so long." She winked.

Flip looked at the time on her phone and jumped to her feet. "Cripes! Me too. The library beckons. Hey, don't worry about that," she said to Beth, who had begun to pick up the cups. "I'll take care of it. Garbage can's on the way."

"Don't forget the book club Thursday," Dinah added. "We'd really love to have you. I'll give you the address at practice tonight."

"Sure." Beth smiled.

"Will Claudia be coming?" Eve asked Flip.

Claudia was the absent fourth musketeer. Flip nodded. "She'd better be. She asked me to pick up the book for her."

"Pick it up? The book club's three days from now. How's she going to read it by then?"

Flip busied herself with the rumpled napkins. "That's more than enough time—I mean, for some people."

"And she *is* going to read it, right? Not just watch the movie like she did the last time. I mean, who thinks watching *Shakespeare in Love* is the same thing as reading *Romeo and Juliet*?"

"Gosh," said Flip, who had watched it with Claudia, "no one I can think of."

Beth lifted her backpack over her shoulder and paused. "You guys are really funny. It's like watching an episode of *Sex and the City.*"

"Better," Dinah declared. "They never discussed the classics."

"Oh yeah," Flip said. "We're nothing if not erudite."

Magnus sipped what passed for tea in the States. It would take a good deal longer than one term as visiting scholar here to learn to abide the overloud, underdiscriminating ways of Americans. But the university here had been willing to pay his salary—enormous, just the way Americans liked things—whilst he finished his book of criticism, and all he had to do in return was give a couple of lectures. A fair trade, he thought, given that his book was likely to put both him and the institution generous enough to underwrite him on the map.

A shriek of outrage cut through his solitude like a

Howitzer, and the women at the table from which this annoyance arose dissolved into a cacophony of equally annoying giggles.

An odd lot, he considered as his eyes swept the group,
with two dressed neatly and the third looking a bin woman
of some sort in T-shirt, work trousers and scuffed trainers.
She was an admittedly attractive bin woman, though, with
high tight breasts and the blond hair of a Botticelli and
whose unorthodox manner of screwing herself into a chair—
could that be bird shit on her shoes?—gave her the look of a
precocious and slightly naughty child.

He found the paragraph he'd been reading in *The Cambridge Quarterly* and returned to Macalister's mildly mis-
guided analysis of gender roles in nineteenth-century British
novels.

A moment later another round of hoots blasted him from
reading.

This time he distinctly heard the words "Lizzy Bennet."
His ears pricked up, and he caught "Darcy" followed by
"*Pride and Prejudice*," and, most curiously, "hedgerow."

" 'Hedgerow?' " He was virtually certain the word did not
appear in *Pride and Prejudice*. Perhaps he'd misheard. The
women laughed again.

He bristled. What could be so amusing? *Pride and Prejudice* was the crown jewel of the last two hundred years of
objective representationalism, not the latest episode of
Blackadder. He tried to pick up where he'd left off in Macalister, but just as he'd found ". . . Wollstonecraft's insistence on
the female archetype as . . . ," the bin woman bent her long
legs against the arm of the chair beside her and tilted her
seat back. The movement was earthy and unself-conscious,

and something twitched at the base of his brain. The journal slipped from his hand.

She cocked her head, looking into the distance, and he found himself following her gaze up the length of the Cathedral. Her face—an interesting confection of confidence and curiosity—dissolved into . . . what? He sat up straighter. He'd seen the look before, but never in the observation of architecture.

"Excuse me, young man," a voice interrupted, "are you using that chair?"

"Pardon? Oh, yes, please. Help yourself." Magnus made an accommodating gesture to the elderly man carrying a waxed bakery bag and returned his attention to the blonde, but a student had joined the party now, and the woman's chair—and expression—had returned to earth.

He sighed and returned to the article.

He was deep in Wollstonecraft's mechanics when the phrase "incredible hard-ons" rose above the conversational din. Well, there wasn't much to misconstrue about that. He gave the group a preemptory look—wholly unnoticed—and redoubled his efforts at concentration, but when "nether regions" and "Darcy" followed in quick succession, his blood began to boil.

There were few things worse than the sophomoric lunacy of some women on the topic of Darcy. As far as he was concerned, the damned BBC should have had their license revoked for reducing a complex socioliterary masterpiece into a pantalooned version of *When Darcy Met Lizzy*.

He considered making his way to the table and saying a word on behalf of the nineteenth-century literature class he'd seen on the university's adult ed schedule so these woman could begin to appreciate something farther north than Darcy's breech buttons, but when four heads whipped on their axes like spinning tops to ogle a passing jogger, he'd had enough. He threw down the journal and pinched the bridge of his nose, fending off both a headache and an overwhelming urge to turn one or all of them over his knee.

One for certain.

After a moment of relative quiet, he growled and reopened the journal, determined to complete what he'd started. But the raucous laughter rose again. He looked up, and this time the blonde was staring right at him. Her open, unabashed appraisal surprised him, as did her stunning Nordic eyes, and he managed only the barebones version of his famously lethal lecturer's glare.

Oh, yes, he thought. Definitely that one.

He realized his attempt to absorb Macalister here was going to be an utter wash. He unzipped his pack, stuffed the journals in and grabbed his unfinished tea, looking for the waste bin.

Cups and napkins in hand, Flip was headed for the garbage when a flapping flicker of white at the edge of her vision brought her to a complete stop.

No, she thought. Impossible. Instinctively she fell silent and turned slowly in a circle, letting her eyes trace the edges of the trees. At the same time her ears sorted through the different streams of input, easily filtering out the irrelevant urban soundscape and leaving only the critical notes for categorization: the *dee-dee-dee* of *Parus atricapillus*, the *keedle-keedle* of *Cyanocitta cristata*, and the familiar mocking *caw* of *Corvus brachyrhynchos*. It was everything one would expect in the middle of a city neighborhood, but nothing from a bird even marginally white.

She paused, catching the questioning eye of a gray-haired man several tables away. She realized she must look somewhat ridiculous, turning in circles, transfixed.

"I heard *go-out go-out*," she called to him in explanation. "It sounded like *Lagopus muta*—er, a rock ptarmigan."

He smiled blankly.

He has no idea what I'm talking about, she thought—and clearly neither do I, for one does not find an Arctic bird like a rock ptarmigan in the middle of southwestern Pennsylvania.

But whatever she'd seen or heard was gone, so she waved the old man a polite good-bye. She needed to get to work, and the laptop bag was making the crick in her neck sing with pain. She resettled it on her shoulder, which was not easy with her arms full of dirty cups, and swung back toward the garbage can, bumping hard into someone.

"Gosh, sorry!"

Oh God, it was Mr. Rare Book Room, and she'd spilled his drink all over his hand.

"Wow, throwing that out?" she said nervously. "You've hardly drunk it." She dug the cleanest napkin from the mess in her hand and offered it to him. "Hey, I hear you're an Austen expert, eh?"

He tossed the cup in the can and took the napkin with obvious reluctance. "Yes, I am."

A Brit. *Hmmm.* Dinah hadn't mentioned that. He sounded a bit like that guy on *Blackadder*. His eyes were the color of topaz, and he was a head taller than her, at least. What was it about that stare?

"You must pick up a lot of women with that." God, she felt like an idiot, and now she sounded like one too. "Not the accent, I mean," she said, speaking in the hurried tones of the criminally idiotic, "though I suppose that doesn't hurt, but the *Pride and Prejudice* stuff. Go to dinner with the man who can channel Mr. Darcy, that sort of thing." What blather! She dumped her garbage and rubbed the base of her skull. Say *some*thing intelligent, will you. "Hey, we're actually discussing *Pride and Prejudice* at our book club this week. Any suggestions?"

"Only one." The man's gaze was unwavering. "If your interest in Austen rises only so far as—I do hope I've captured this correctly—Darcy's 'nether regions,' I suggest you apply yourself to *The Thorn Birds* or Jackie Collins instead."

He deposited the napkin in the can, gave her a brief bow and walked away.

For a long moment, Flip stood unmoving, feeling enough heat in her cheeks to steam her own cappuccino. Then, with growing fury, she decided if anyone was going to feel like they'd just been frothed into submission, it ought to be him.

"Trouble, young lady?" the elderly gentleman called.

She was confused until she realized her hand was still rubbing the base of her skull. "Yeah. A big, freakin' pain in my neck."

Chapter Two

The bastard.

Flip marched toward the Pitt library, furious.

The irritatingly smug, butler-voiced jackass of a British bastard. How dare he?

How dare he what? her inner voice asked. *Overhear what you and your friends practically shouted at the café? Is that what you're blaming him for?*

She cringed. Had he heard the breath mint comment too? Oh God, and the one about hard-ons? She supposed she couldn't really blame him for what he'd heard, but she certainly could for repeating it, especially in such an ungentlemanly manner.

She banged through the entryway, fuming while the chubby young man with the red beard and crew cut at the desk, who always vaguely reminded her of a tall, overfed cardinal, stopped his work to scan her ID. She was still mad as she strode across the floor and madder still when she jabbed the button for the elevator. It wasn't until she lowered her finger that the volume in the nearby display case caught her eye.

She'd gazed at it, of course, dozens of times in the last few weeks. The leather cover was brown and cracked, and the paper yellow with age, but somehow the moment captured on those open pages struck her more forcefully today than ever: Darcy making his marriage proposal to Lizzy, and Lizzy, to his very great surprise and embarrassment, turning him down with hardly a moment's consideration. She could almost hear Lizzy's voice, choked with anger, as she read.

" 'Do you think that any consideration would tempt me to accept the man who has been the means of ruining, perhaps for ever, the happiness of a most beloved sister? . . . I have every reason in the world to think ill of you.' "

Go, Lizzy! Flip thought. Give that snake his due. Imperious, high-handed, stick-up-his-ass—

"Excuse me?" The clerk was standing next to her now, a stack of books in his hands.

Flip colored again. Had she been muttering out loud? Great. Maybe next she'd be pushing a cart of empty soda cans and shouting the theme song from *Pimp My Ride*. "No, sorry. Bad day."

She only wished the page would turn, so she could witness the culmination of Darcy's humiliation—his reduction from pompous blue blood to mere rejected man. But, alas, the case was locked.

"It's a first edition," the clerk said.

"Pardon?" Flip said absently, savoring the scene of satisfying retribution.

"The volume you're looking at," the clerk said. "It's a first edition. Only fifteen hundred were printed, and far fewer have survived. Austen's handwritten manuscript for *Pride and Prejudice* no longer exists, so that's as close to original as it gets."

"Hey, maybe I should borrow it," she joked weakly.

He held up his arm across his chest like a Roman soldier. "Not on my watch, ma'am."

Flip laughed, and her neck zinged her again. It was as if a small arc welder were pinpointing a spot just below her shoulder. She touched it gingerly, wincing, and rolled her head, but the pain only deepened.

"Hey, maybe you should take a look at this," the clerk said. "I was just going to take it down." He pointed to a paper pinned on the bulletin board next to the elevator. It was one of the photocopied ads with strips of phone numbers at the bottom one sees posted around campuses, though this one had only one strip left. The ad read: LOOKING GLASS MASSAGE THERAPY. IMAGINE YOURSELF IN YOUR FAVORITE BOOK. 138 *CHESTERFIELD STREET*. $45. NO APPOINTMENT NECESSARY.

Flip checked the time on her cell phone. Chesterfield was only a five-minute walk down Forbes Avenue. Ten minutes round-trip; thirty minutes for a massage. She could be back by two thirty and still get in a solid hour on the presentation. She headed to her locker on the fourth floor, dropped off her bag and headed out, certain this was the distraction that would allow her to return to her paper, totally focused.

Forbes, as usual, was crowded with students and hospital workers. She saw a woman in scrubs leading a toddler out of the Original Hot Dog Shop. The toddler held his arms up to be lifted, and the mother grabbed both hands and swung the boy in an exuberant circle. Both erupted in peals of laughter. Flip felt a pang. How could Jed not have wanted that?

Halfway down Forbes she heard the *go-out, go-out* again, and this time she saw the bird, too, darting from tree to tree in front of her, its distinctive white plumage and black tail fanned against the green. A rock ptarmigan, here in Pittsburgh, she thought. Strangest damn thing.

Her cell phone rang. She looked at the ID and brought it to her ear. "Don't tell me you're not coming to the book group."

"What sort of greeting is that?" Claudia asked.

"The sort only your oldest friend can give you. I've already picked up a copy of the book for you."

"Has anyone read it yet?"

"Everyone in the world's read it, Claudia. Several times. It's *Pride and Prejudice*. Jane Austen. You know?"

"Sounds familiar."

"I'm glad to hear it."

"As it stands, my Thursday has cleared up and—hold on for a second, Flip." Then Flip heard her friend's muffled voice say, "Would you be a doll and see if you can find this in a nice chocolate brown and the other in a bottle green?" Claudia's voice returned full strength. "I'm back. My Thursday's cleared up, and I can be there."

Bottle green? "Claudia, where are you?"

"A place called—let me see—um, Designer Shoe Warehouse? Have you heard of it?"

"Yeah, it's like Payless for rich people."

"Payless?"

"Never mind."

"No, no, more of a Belgian chocolate," Claudia said, muffled again. "With just a hint of Amaretto. That's it. You've got it. Sorry, Flip. I'm back."

"Hang on. They don't have personal service at DSW. Who are you getting to do your bidding?"

"My bidding. Flip, dear, you make me sound like a princess or something. Oh, yes, yes, that's it," she called. "I can almost taste the truffle insides." Her voice lowered. "No personal service? Are you sure, Flip? Gosh, they're absolutely great."

Flip shook her head. Claudia was a person to whose will people automatically and happily bent. No wonder they loved her on the charity fund-raising circuit.

"So, this *Pride and Prejudice,*" Claudia went on. "It's not another major Oprah downer, is it? I can't take an abandoned child or quadriplegic. I've got Bikram that day."

"Nope. A love story."

"Excellent. Sex?"

"It was written in the nineteenth century," Flip said.

"Oh, boy. I'm falling asleep already."

"Yeah, well, it's not exactly up my alley, either. But you'll live. It's romantic."

"High points?"

Flip paused. "You *are* going to read it?"

"Oh, definitely. C'mon, Flip, be a bunny."

Flip sighed. "Darcy, our hero—"

"Darcy?" Claudia interrupted. "That's a girl's name."

"Er, it's not his first name. His first name is . . ." Flip stopped. What was his first name? "Well, anyway, Darcy is a rich, proud man—exceptionally proud—who declines a dance with Lizzy Bennet, a spirited young woman, at their first meeting. The Bennet family is firmly middle-class, so a good distance below Darcy in rank. Lizzy overhears his dismissal of her as 'not pretty enough to tempt me' and takes an immediate dislike to him. No surprise there. Their mutual dislike, played out with wry barbs and teasing, captures Darcy's heart for he is used to only reverence and flattery from the women in his life."

"And you're sure there's no sex?" asked Claudia. "I think

I read this last year. In fact, didn't you lend it to me? The hero and heroine meet at a masked ball. He's the bastard son of the Earl of Landsmere, she's the talk of the *ton,* and they end up on a bumpy carriage ride to Bath with her straddling his—"

"*Written* in the nineteenth century," Flip put in firmly. "Despite their difference in rank, Darcy swallows his pride to follow his heart—"

"Hoping the heroine will be swallowing something equally as large? Yes, I'm sure this was the same story."

"No, honey," Flip said. "Try to focus. Darcy asks Lizzy to marry him. She refuses instantly and is not shy about telling him why. Not only has he acted as if he's chosen her against his better judgment, the prick, but he's convinced his also-wealthy friend Bingley, who happens to have fallen in love with Lizzy's sweet older sister, Jane, to abandon that relationship, leaving Jane with a broken heart. So Darcy's back to square one, spending the second half of the book attempting to pull his head out his ass and actually earn Lizzy's respect and love."

"Wow, sounds like a total bastard."

Flip frowned. "Oh, well, perhaps I've overstated it a bit—"

"And there's no sex at all?" Claudia said.

"Offstage only, and not the hero and heroine. Lizzy's intemperate youngest sister, Lydia, runs off with the book's official rogue, Mr. Wickham. Wickham tempts Lydia with . . ." Flip finished in a cinematic tone of horror. ". . . the attractions of premarital carnality. Enormous social disgrace will befall Lizzy's family if Wickham and Lydia aren't found and made to marry immediately."

"But they get together in the end, Darcy and Lizzy?"

"They do."

"Great. Let's see if I have this right. Lizzy has two sisters: a good one, Jane, and a wild one, Lydia. Darcy is rich; he insults Lizzy then falls in love with her—usually it's in the opposite order, so he has a problem. At the same time he talks his rich friend Bingley out of marrying Lizzy's good sister Jane because of class differences. Jane is heartbroken, and Lizzy turns down Darcy's proposal because of it. The turn-down fuels Darcy's desire even more—typical man—but he has to become a better man to win her. And, let me guess. The two couples end up happy in the end?"

"That's it."

"Great. That saved me about six hours."

"Okay, you still have to read it."

"I don't know. Is the wedding night scene hot? Gosh, thanks," Claudia added to what Flip presumed was the helpful DSW waitperson. "You were right. The black leather is better than the bottle green."

"The wedding night is fabulous," Flip said. "Darcy in nothing but boots. Lizzy in nothing but carriage floor burns on her knees. Sadly those chapters were lost. You'll have to settle for a simple double wedding ceremony at the local church."

"Carriage floor burns?" Claudia tsk-tsked. "My dear, you need to upgrade to a better class of husband. There are some too gentlemanly for that sort of thing."

"Really? Jed treated me like a goddess the first year of our marriage, and I had all the nectar of the gods I could drink."

Claudia laughed.

"World's most effective birth control, after all," Flip added, and immediately wished she hadn't. The fact that she'd ended four years of marriage without a baby was an open wound that never seemed to heal, which in itself wouldn't be so bad if her friends didn't act like overprotective deer caught in the headlights whenever the topic of babies came up around her. Claudia fell into one of those awkward, sympathetic silences.

"Flip, honey—"

"Wasn't exactly nectar, either," Flip noted wryly, and was relieved to hear Claudia snicker. "Hey, speaking of black leather, is your ex still seeing that New Wave architect of his?"

"Yep. Now she's dyed her hair blond and wearing baby-doll dresses. She's channeling Sienna Miller."

"Jeez," Flip rolled her eyes. "Why would you want to channel someone whose only claim to fame is getting dumped by Jude Law?"

"Sienna acts too, dear."

"Apparently you didn't see *Casanova*."

"As long as we're doing the ex report card," Claudia said, "anything new with Jed?"

Flip hung her head. "I found out he's applying for the same fellowship as me. At Cornell."

"I see," Claudia said coolly, and Flip could feel her friend expand like some ancient Greek Fury. "It's not enough to cheat on you, break your heart and ruin your marriage. He's got to outgun you at work. Gee, maybe he could shoot Scruffy too."

"Yeah, well . . ." Jed was Jed, Flip thought. The past didn't really bother her anymore, but the Cornell thing was going to hurt. Her neck pinged.

"Honestly," Claudia said, "I don't know how you can do it. Bernie and I still have a decent relationship, but I'd rather have my eyelids nailed shut than work with him."

"We mostly stay out of each other's way."

"He should have left," Claudia said. "When you two broke up, he should have left the Aviary."

"We're both field researchers. We're only there a little part of the year. We just happen to be overlapping right now." Flip shrugged. "Anyway, he was there a long time before me."

"Yes, and now he's got a new, underage protégé. Pig. Oh, speaking of food, I'll be stopping at Mad Mex before I drop by. Can I pick up something for you? They do a great wrap."

"Mm. Wraps. The culinary equivalent of edible burlap. No thanks. How about some wings?"

Claudia sighed. "I don't know how you do it. Eat wings and still have an ass someone could hammer silver on."

"I just keep waiting for my Thor."

"And it's okay for me to drop by?"

"Yep. I'll be home after five."

Flip turned onto Chesterfield and stopped in front of the little row house at 138. It was a mock Tudor with a tiny front porch and one off-center window, in which a satisfied marmalade cat sat next to a hand-lettered sign that read: LOOKING GLASS MASSAGE THERAPY.

"Hey, Claudia," Flip said, "what's your favorite book?"

"I don't know. Something with a bumpy carriage ride, I guess."

"My thoughts exactly. I'll see you later."

Chapter Three

"Dees eez bad. Many toxins."

Flip sat in a high-backed chair in the middle of the cozy waiting room listening to a softly playing concerto. The stout, gaudily dressed owner, who had introduced herself as Madame K, was now standing behind Flip, gauging the tension in her shoulders. Madame K looked nothing like the masseuses Flip had seen before. In fact, she looked nothing like anyone Flip had seen before. She wore a large Pucci-esque caftan trimmed with jingly foreign coins, and her makeup appeared to have been applied by Jackson Pollack.

The woman lifted Flip's left arm and then her right, squeezing and rolling as she went. "You are in need of an adventure, *ja?*"

The light, roving pressure felt wonderful. Flip closed her eyes. "Actually yes."

"At vurk and in bed, I think."

"Well, I . . ." What kind of question was that?

"There eez a man."

"No," Flip said.

"Ja. A man who represents adventure."

Ugh. Jed. "No."

"*Ja.* A man who has recently made you consider reavakening to the world."

Flip frowned. Darcy? No. The Venice hero in her book? Mmmm. Yes!

The woman bent Flip forward and checked her spine. "You vill bring him next time, *ja?*"

Along with her good friends Wallace, Grommet and Harry Potter. "Sure, whatever." The woman was totally nuts but had fingers to die for.

"Vee are ready. Go into the therapy room, remove your clothes and wrap yourself in a towel. You vill let me know vhen I can enter."

The therapy room was softly lit, and on a table in the corner a citrus-scented candle burned next to a folded towel, a bottle of water and an ornate round mirror—perhaps the "looking glass" of the establishment's name? This at least looked like Flip expected it to. There were two massage tables in the room, each with a padded oval opening at one end to hold the patron's face while the rest of her body was kneaded into submission like errant bread dough.

Flip picked up the bottle as she kicked off her Pumas. DRINK ME SPRING WATER the label read. "Cute." She twisted off the cap and took a long draft. The water was cool and tinged with the faintest taste of grass. For some reason it made her think of bunnies and Easter.

"You like the vater?" Madame K called.

Flip frowned. The door was closed and there was no window in it. "Er, yeah."

"Eez from my country. Many rabbits."

Flip put the water down.

Slipping off her clothes, she caught a glimpse of herself in the mirror. Her breasts might be on the small side and her legs a tad knock-kneed, but she'd been blessed with the Allison musculature and her ass was a good one—high, tight and firm—and in her work cargoes, a perfect vision of two caramel lollipops. She tossed her T-shirt on the chair and dropped the khakis beside it. She stared for a second at the matching cobalt panties and bra. Alternately sheer and lacy, they were a bit like carrying the complete North American birding guide for a trip across the Kalahari Desert given her ascetic, man-free life, but Flip was nothing if not prepared. She dropped them on the khakis and picked up the towel.

It was toasty warm. She clutched it around her and called, "You can—"

The door opened.

"—come in."

"You vill stretch out on the table, *ja?*" Madame K commanded. "And clear your head."

But what Flip wanted to clear was her nose. The mellow orangey scent wafting from the candle was making her a little woozy. Madame K tucked her in on the table, covered her with a warm sheet and snapped off the towel like a magician doing the tablecloth trick.

She worked in small circles, from Flip's shoulder blades to her hips, folding back the sheet as necessary to ensure every muscle got its proper workout. Flip felt like a tube of recalcitrant toothpaste.

"Vhere do you vurk?" the woman asked.

"At the Aviary."

"Ah. You like?"

"Usually it's great, but today—ugh. Don't ask."

The woman made a sympathetic clucking noise and continued her Nobel Prize–worthy kneading. Flip felt the tension begin to trickle out her fingers and toes.

"Are you clearing your head?" Madame K asked.

"Mmmm-hmmm."

Flip considered the flowered carpet visible through the table's porthole, and watched the suede tassels of Madame K's odd little booties flop around as she worked. But then her eyes grew heavier and her lids began to flutter. Clearing her head was not easy. Whatever Madame K was releasing in her back seemed to come pouring up her neck into her brain in a soft-focus, home-movie sort of way: her girlfriends and their over-the-top fascination with Darcy, *Pride and Prejudice* and that whole weird historical romance thing; Jed jogging up the stairs of the Cornell ornithology building like Rocky; a black and white ivory-bill woodpecker soaring through the forest top; the things she'd wanted during her marriage that Jed hadn't; that asshole Brit from the café with the interesting topaz eyes; that asshole Brit from the café in a pair of ivory breeches and an open linen shirt, turning her over his knee—

What?? Flip started. *No.*

Darcy in a pair of ivory breeches and an open linen shirt, tugging the laces of her chemise. There we go. Or better yet, the handsome Venice bathroom hero, who'd been only too happy to serve his heroine on his knees, his shiny dark head of curls bobbing up and down between her—

"Hey." Flip, who had gone two years without any head bobbing, shiny, dark or otherwise, lifted herself on an elbow. "What about the imagining-yourself-in-your-favorite-book part? That's part of your advertisement for the massage, right?"

Madame K gave her a fish-eye. "Indeed it is. Have you cleared your head?"

"Oh, yeah, absolutely."

"Very vell. There are two very important rules. You cannot imagine something that vould not naturally happen in the book. King Lear, for example, cannot fly a plane."

King Lear. Flip snorted. Like that's what she'd be imagining. "And?"

"And you cannot imagine the same book twice. Both rules observed or big trouble."

Flip waited. "That's it? That's the value-added favorite book service? You don't hypnotize me, or play the book on tape, or give me a crown and princess dress or anything?"

The woman slitted a frosted blue lid. "Our clients are very happy."

Well, I could've done that in my own bed, Flip thought, and the only rule there would have been D cells give out in about thirty minutes. "Okay. Sure." She rested her head again.

The palms maintained their tireless efforts, bringing warm, healing heat to Flip's shoulders and neck. Her thoughts tried to drift to the sexy scene atop the bathroom vanity, but the tile marks, the steam, even the cool, hard marble under the hips of the heroine kept slipping away from her mind's eye, like sand through open fingers. She wondered for a long moment if Darcy had topaz eyes, too, then she was gone.

An instant later—had she fallen asleep?—the scent had changed, from citrus to a heavy floral, roses or honeysuckle. *Yes, honeysuckle, that was it. Like my Grandma Thompson's powder room. God-awful.*

Flip drew her eyes open, a momentous effort, to say as much to Madame K, and stopped, shocked.

The massage tables were gone. The room was gone. At least *that* room was gone. The room Flip found herself sitting alone in was easily eight times its size. And the quaint furniture of the massage studio was now enormous, expensive Georgian furniture. Brocade sofas as long as an Airstream. Curlicue table legs. Impediment-topped sideboards, and silk-tasseled drawer pulls. She was resting on a chaise, her head inclined.

Oh, I get it. I'm dreaming. This must be the lobby of the hotel in the romance novel. Very Room with a View. Flip smiled. At the point she'd reached in the book, there hadn't been any scenes in the lobby, but, hey, she thought, one's sexual escapades had to start somewhere. But if this was Venice, and Mr. Iron Knees was about to whisk her up to the bathroom, why was she feeling a strange niggle of unease?

She looked down, eager to see what sort of slinky outfit she'd provided herself for this dreamy adventure, only to discover her skirt covered her knees. In fact, her skirt reached to the floor. In fact, her skirt reached to the floor, and the bra she was wearing was so uncomfortable, she felt like she was wrapped in a picket fence.

I sure hope the hotel honor bar has wire cutters, she thought.

She grabbed an armload of the voluminous violet fabric and pulled it up before her eyes, examining the stiff satin and heavily beaded hem.

Cripes, no wonder I'm uneasy. I'm a freakin' bridesmaid!

She dropped the skirt and found herself looking straight into the embarrassed gaze of a bald servant in tails. Definitely not her Venice hero. Too curl challenged.

He cleared his throat. "Lady Quillan?"

"Yes?" Flip answered.

Isn't it strange, she thought, how you automatically

accept what happens in a dream: you're a one-legged avocado designer from Tunisia; the sky turns plaid at sunset; an English butler addresses you as Lady Quillan, and, boom, you're Lady Quillan. Weird.

"There's news." He tilted his head toward the hall. A long, sad note from a violin quavered, then fell away.

She felt the shiver of the minor key. "What was that?"

Mild confusion rose on the man's face. "M'um?"

"The music. Is there someone here who plays?"

The servant's forehead creased. He looked left, then right, then back at her. "No."

"But there is a violin."

"No, m'um. A messenger has arrived."

The words hit her like a bucket of ice. There was something in his tone, or perhaps it was the uncomfortable look on his face, that made all hope of an evening rendezvous disappear.

"He's been instructed to give the note to you directly."

"Thank you." Flip stood, feeling like a heavy weight had been dropped on her shoulders. Whoever she was, Lady Quillan was not looking forward to this message.

"You look unwell," the man said. "May I call for something?"

"A bathroom vanity?"

His forehead creased. "Bathroom?"

And then Flip saw it. Outside the room's intricately paned window. A carriage and horses at the top of a long treed drive.

Oh, hell. There wasn't a bathroom vanity in the house because there wasn't even a damned bathroom. It was freakin' England, before freakin' plumbing! She was absolutely not paying anything extra for this massage.

"Nothing, Samuel."

Samuel, is it? Another plaintive violin note filled the room. She looked around the room and again saw nothing. Things were coming to her but in bits and pieces—and the oddest bits and pieces. She knew Samuel's name just as she knew her right slipper was missing its second button, just as she knew this wasn't her house, just as she knew her hostess and her hostess's sister were in the room next door. But why this yet unseen letter was making her feel like she'd taken a belly punch, she didn't know.

Samuel bowed and gestured toward the door. Flip stepped tentatively into the cavernous hall. Tall and square and built to showcase the looming double-doored entrance, the hall housed a staircase that curved elegantly to the upper floor, a massive silver chandelier and doors leading in every direction.

"There you are, Philippa," a concerned voice said as she rounded the corner.

The man who had spoken was tall and expensively dressed, in a midnight blue coat, cream waistcoat and breeches, and gleaming black boots. Philippa, was she? Despite a disappointing lack of curls, the man's striking brown eyes, dark hair and strong patrician profile were oddly familiar. A footman stood next to him holding a top hat and pair of riding gloves. *Was the blue-coated man the owner of the carriage?* The man accepted the items, but his eyes stayed on her.

"Has Jared arrived at last?" he asked.

"No," she said. "A messenger, it seems." Embarrassment throbbed in her like a fresh bruise. But why?

Samuel called, and a dusty-faced youth fiddling with a pouch emerged from a doorway. He scratched his nose unself-consciously and extended the note. Flip accepted it with unsteady fingers.

The note was written in a neat, masculine hand. The violin began again, this time in a flood of notes, forbidding and dark, that repeated over and over. Like Samuel, this man seemed deaf to the music as well.

She bent her head to read.

> *Clearly I have not made the supper. Nonetheless, I had thought I would be able to arrive in time to accompany you to Abbott House, but I find my business keeps me longer than I expected. Secure an invitation for the night from Louisa. I feel certain she would be pleased to keep you. I shall fetch you in the morning, and we can arrive at Abbott House as our servants do, which shall be more convenient in any case.*
>
> *—Q*

Flip felt a black stone settle in her gut.

"Bad news?" the gentleman asked, oblivious to the footman who stood poised, waiting for the signal that would prompt him to open the double doors.

"No," she said. "Not at all."

Across from them, beyond another door, the sound of quiet female talk had been apparent for the past moments, but now, from the indistinct hum, a clear snippet rose. "Business, my foot," came a bemused woman's voice. "Quillan's with his whore in Stourton." Another woman tittered. "Ah, the poor, oblivious girl. Do you suppose she even knows?"

Flip stood rigid, drowning in the all-too-familiar waves of shame and humiliation. Husbands hadn't changed much in two hundred years.

The youth was the first to break the uncomfortable silence. "Is there a reply, m'um?"

"No." Her voice was barely a whisper.

The gentleman pulled a coin from his pocket and placed it in the hand of the boy, who immediately trotted to the back of the house.

Interpreting this as closure, the footman placed his hand on the knob.

"Sir, your phaeton is—" Samuel began, but received an unspoken signal from the phaeton's owner and stopped.

The hall was silent now, save the pounding in Flip's ears.

"Has Jared been held up?" The gentleman held his tone even, as if he hadn't heard the women, giving Flip every opportunity to collect herself, though it was clear from the mild disgust in his eyes the women were not people whose claim on him was strong.

Flip heard the violins ease and, as often occurs in a dream, conceived instantly the meaning of the words in the note and the part she was to play, though it hardly seemed like playing when the feelings struck so close to home.

"Yes." Flip folded the note. "My husband will not be arriving until tomorrow. I-I must ask Louisa if I might stay. I am a bit of trouble," she added with forced laugh. "I'm sure Louisa didn't expect a simple supper invitation to stretch into an overnight stay."

"Is there anyone else in Wiltshire to whom you owe a visit?" the man asked carefully. "A cousin, perhaps? You have so many. I should be happy to drive you anywhere you'd like to go."

The footman waited, motionless.

"No," she said. "No one." Wiltshire felt like a vast, lonely place.

The man nodded, understanding. There was no more to be said. He placed his top hat on his head and bowed a regretful good-bye. The footman clicked his heels and opened the door.

Flip gathered her skirts, full of dread. Sadly it looked as if the only person on his knees tonight would be her, deep in humiliation, asking the Wicked Witch of the Wiltshire for an extra bed.

She took a deep breath, entered the room and found the women seated at a table playing cards. The first was reed thin and brunette, too recessive to be the owner of this home. The other was horsey, plump and blond. That one, Flip knew, was Louisa. Though her face bore the mask of polite concern, Louisa's eyes were lit with the spark of recently shared amusement.

"Oh, Lady Quillan, you look hardly more rested than when you lay down. Pray, do not fear. I was just saying to Caroline I'm sure your husband is merely detained and—"

"I have heard from my husband," Flip said. "And I shall have to beg your indulgence. It seems—"

"It seems," interrupted the blue-coated gentleman who had appeared unnoticed at Flip's side, "my phaeton shall require an extra cushion, Louisa. My old friend Lord Quillan sent his man just now to ask me to give her ladyship a ride to Abbott House."

The man pressed his elbow very lightly against Flip's, a gesture invisible to their hosts.

"Abbott House," he went on, "is quite close to my destination, after all, and Quillan has arrived in Wiltshire more tired than he expected."

"Quillan is in Wiltshire?" Louisa repeated, unbelieving. "At Abbott House?"

The gentleman's eyes flashed cold, hard iron. "At Abbott House."

For a moment, the women sat silent under his chilly gaze, then Caroline broke into a coquettish giggle. "Oh, Darcy, will you be always the knight who rescues the fair maiden?"

Darcy?! Flip's gaze shot to her savior, and her knees began to buckle.

Chapter Four

"You are too kind," Flip whispered as they emerged from the house. *Darcy*?! She'd been rescued by Whatever-His-First-Name-Is Darcy? She'd taken his arm not only because he'd offered it but because this dreamworld, already tilting on the edge of total chaos, was starting literally to sway.

He was taller than she would have expected and far more capable. He helped her up the steps to the phaeton's high bench and launched himself easily into the other side. As he adjusted the reins, footmen scuttled around the horses, snapping harnesses and clacking buckles. Flip wished desperately for a seat belt. The bench on which they sat appeared to be hovering about a hundred and fifteen feet above the ground.

He sighed. "I'm sorry. I'm afraid Louisa and Caroline can be, well—"

"Complete and utter bitches?"

He bit back a smile. "The limpidity of your language, Philippa, is ever a delight."

"That's not what Jared would say," she answered, and knew without thinking that it was true.

"Might I observe that Lord Quillan's tastes are, perhaps, too prosaic to appreciate your gifts fully."

And then it struck her. If he was Darcy, then their hostess had been Louisa, the sister of Darcy's friend Bingley, the man who had fallen or would eventually fall in love with Lizzy Bennet's sister Jane, and the second woman had to have been Caroline, Bingley's other sister.

The footman snapped his hands against his thighs and announced, "The horses are ready, sir."

Darcy tested the lead. "Yes, thank you, I see everything is as it should be."

There was a realness to this man she had never found in the pages of *Pride and Prejudice*. The shadow of bristle dusted his cheeks, a scar marred the length of his neatly manicured hand, and his leg flexed against the boot box in a way that made her wish the silk of her bodice wasn't so thin. How was it she'd known the era, the house and the butler, but didn't recognize the most famous man in literature except maybe Hamlet? What sort of poorly planned dream was she producing?

"Are you braced?" he asked.

"Pardon?" she said, and *ooph*-ed as the horses leaped into action. Darcy drove quickly and confidently, conveying his commands with subtle flicks. If Magnus were an eagle, Darcy was a black swan—elegant, proud, and not to be crossed. Flip was very glad he had intervened on her behalf.

The moment they put Louisa's unpleasant abode behind them, the early evening sky seemed to banish its clouds, dappling raspberry light across the hills and fields. The suffocating honeysuckle perfume was gone, replaced by the scent of lavender, fresh-mown hay and, when the carriage made a turn, the faint sandalwood of Darcy's clothes.

"Indeed," Darcy said, returning to their discussion, "when Bingley finds a country house to take, I'm afraid I find myself hoping his sisters will be otherwise engaged."

"Yes, perhaps a nice voyage to the Far East, shipwreck optional." If Bingley hadn't yet moved into Netherfield, the house he has just taken at the start of *Pride and Prejudice*, then Flip's dream was taking place before Darcy meets Lizzy Bennet. It is Bingley, after all, who brings a horrified Darcy into the circle of occasionally uncouth country folk in his new neighborhood, a circle that includes the Bennet family.

At the same time Flip was calculating a timeline, the violin returned with a lighter song. While still not quite to be described as happy, it was certainly not the woeful dirge of a few moments before.

I guess, Flip thought, smiling, my dream's got a sound track. Cool. And as the melody played, she felt the pieces of Philippa's world tumbling into her brain like the notes of a birdcall she couldn't quite identify. And every piece was making the picture a little clearer even though she didn't exactly know where the pieces were coming from.

"I cannot go to Abbott House," she said, dead certain, and the violin made three quick pizzicato notes of warning. "The house is closed, and the doors are locked. And, in any case, Jared would not care for it."

Darcy pressed his lips in a thin line. "Jared may be damned."

"Jared," she said, "may be there."

She watched the realization pass over him. The horses slowed.

"Oh, Philippa," he said, sorrowful. "I have done you no service in removing you from Louisa, have I? I apologize."

"You have done me a great service, Darcy. I should prefer sleeping in a bog to spending a night in Louisa's grasp—though the comparison is not without merit. Come, let us not despair. You shall drive me to Abbott House, and if Jared's carriage is there, we shall leave him to his liaison, and I shall find a nice haycock under which to make my bed— like Little Boy Blue."

Haycock? Flip thought. Where is this stuff coming from?

Darcy smiled and geed the horses back to regular speed. "And when Jared finds hay in his entry hall?"

Flip raised a brow. "I shall tell him 'tis better than finding a cock in his bed."

Darcy laughed. "Ah, Philippa, you are a breath of fresh air. I can see why Jared is in awe of you."

"In awe of *me*?"

"You run rings around him. You were always the center of our circle back then. Your wit, your enthusiasm, your curiosity. Jared was drawn to you—"

"Like a moth to a flame?"

"Like a bee to a rose, I was thinking. You do not have any of the lethal about you, Philippa, though perhaps you should. It might protect you. And I had thought, once"—he paused—"that you grew and thrived under Jared's care."

The violin reverted to its melancholy trill. Darcy was right about the early days of her marriage. Whatever she might feel now for her husband in this dream, her relationship with him had sprung out of a mutual and agreeable dependence. But what exactly had her relationship been with Darcy? That piece had not fallen into place yet. And what about Lizzy Bennet?

"He has taught me much," Flip admitted, and this time a waterfall of notes brought with it a very clear picture of the early days with Quillan. "It was he who urged me to follow my art. It was he who first took me to Florence and Paris. It was he who allowed me to return there again and again on my own to do my sculpting. But," she added with a wry smile, "there is but a fine line between an act motivated by love and one by indifference. And I fear neither of us noticed when that line was crossed."

Darcy considered this, silent.

"Then these four years of marriage," he said, "have not brought you great sadness?"

"No. That would be unfair." The music made a dramatic swell and stopped, and a flood of details filled her head. The music, Flip saw, wasn't the sound track to her dream. It was the soundtrack to this dream life, or rather what accompanied the bits and pieces of Philippa's life as they came to Flip. "Yes," she said. "He has taken a lover. But he is dutiful and kind and, at most times, discreet."

"I-I think . . . I think I should have done something to avert this."

"Why is that, Darcy? Because you are all-powerful?"

Darcy harrumphed. It was easy to tease him.

"Do you remember the games of vingt-et-un?" he asked, stealing a sidelong look.

Her cheeks bloomed with heat, but the emotion evoked was pleasure, not shame. Flashes of a darkened bower rose in Flip's head—and warm, soft kisses, though the man's face was indistinct—and . . . cards? And much, much laughter. It was like skipping backward on a DVD at high speed. She could almost make out the story, but not quite.

"Your card skills have always been regrettable, Darcy. 'Tis a blessing for you your property is entailed."

"Some games are not so bad to lose."

This time the violins, a host of them, sung out their urgent, full-bodied rhythm—*Boléro* with strings—and the memory hit Flip with a blush-inducing wallop.

"I was but sixteen," she said. "One cannot hold a sixteen-year-old responsible for what she proposes."

"You were seventeen, I was twenty-three, and you seemed to have an excellent grasp of your proposal. For God's sake, you had already cleaned me out of every bank note I carried. But tell me this: if Jared had not come upon us, and if in fact you had held twenty-one in that hand, for if I recall, your bluffing skills were world class—"

"I most certainly had twenty-one."

"—then would you have held me to the bet?"

"I-I—" And there it was, the sketch she'd needed for the bronze, clear in her mind. "One can hardly sculpt an Adonis in frock coat and breeches. I needed a sketch of a true artist's model."

"It was March, and we were outside."

"It was April, and in half an hour I should have had what I needed."

His eyes met hers. "In half an hour, I would have had what I needed, and I would have never let Jared near you again."

Her gaze dropped to her delicate slippers, and she thought about how life changes on a single, misplayed hand. "You are kind."

"I think I ought to have made you an offer of marriage then."

His eyes had returned to the road, and in his profile she saw genuine regret. Ah, she thought, there is no good to come of that. That much I have learned.

"I think you should have, too, Darcy," she said with a smile. "Would have saved you the embarrassment of that unfortunate Cornelia Grant interlude."

He laughed.

Their conversation returned to the ordinary. Flip felt the

great pleasure one feels in laughing with a friend, and an hour passed without notice.

Darcy slowed the horses and made a turn. Without warning, the sky darkened and thunder rumbled in the distance, but it was the birds that flew into view which caught Flip's attention.

"My God," she whispered.

These were not just any bird. These were—could it be?—passenger pigeons. Slate blue head. Long pointed tail. Distinctive reddish chest.

"Stop the carriage," she cried. "Stop!"

Darcy jerked the horses to a halt, and Flip scrambled from the vehicle.

"Philippa, what is it?"

Darcy, too, had jumped to the ground.

"The pigeons!" she said. "Look at them."

At once a blast rang out from a field to the west, then another, then another. A handful of the beautiful birds fell from the sky.

"No," she cried. "No!"

She set off through the field, heedless of the uneven earth beneath her slippers. She could hear Darcy's unlabored stride behind her.

"Philippa, what on earth . . . ?"

And then she saw them, spread across a stream bank, their lifeless ruby eyes unblinking. "Oh, no." She dropped to her knees and examined one, a male.

"They're passenger pigeons," she explained to Darcy, who had bounded up beside her.

A thrilling shiver ran through her. Flip had studied pictures and paintings and even seen one stuffed in the Smithsonian, but she had never seen one this close and so . . . recently alive. They were not native to England, but Flip knew noblemen had tried to breed them there. With a bird as popular as a source of food and sport as the passenger pigeon had been in America, that would have been hard to avoid. In fact, she remembered reading that Audubon himself had tried to introduce them to England.

"Freakin' wingnuts," she cried. "At least Cheney only popped off wrinkled old Republicans."

"Wingnuts?" Darcy dropped to a knee beside her.

"The men shooting. We have to stop them. These birds are a treasure. They must be saved. They're extinct."

"No, Philippa, no. Dead. Not extinct."

She caught herself. They were not extinct in Darcy's day. In Darcy's day, they had been among the most numerous birds on the planet, the only meat some families ever saw. Until they began to be hunted for sport in the 1800s. Flip had read that in one shooting match the victor had won with a total of thirty thousand pigeons killed. Thirty thousand! The last passenger pigeon in the wild died in 1900. The last passenger pigeon on earth died at the Cincinnati Zoo in the early afternoon of September 1, 1914. It is the only bird extinction whose details are known so precisely. Flip knew more than one ornithologist with that date pinned over their desks.

Another shotgun blast fired. Darcy eyed her with serious concern.

"There are places I've been," she tried to explain, "where these birds have completely disappeared."

"Where? Not in their native land, surely. And even here I know of several men who are breeding them, my friend Bingley for one." His eyes narrowed.

Oh, boy. "Have you ever been to Florence?"

He shook his head.

"There. In Florence they used to cover the countryside. But hunters killed them off. Hunters like those men." She gave him a plaintive look. "Please, we have to stop them."

Darcy regarded her thoughtfully. Then he stood and dusted off his breeches. "Come." He offered her his hand. "Let us see what we can do."

"Wait. I-I—" She pored over the bird, thinking this might be her only chance to observe one.

Darcy patted her shoulder. He whipped out a handkerchief and wrapped the bird in it, creating a little carry knot at the top. He handed it to her with a formal bow. "For you, madam. The accessory de rigueur for country outings."

She grabbed the kerchief, lifted her skirts and leaped across the narrow stream. However, the bank was more slippery than she expected, and she teetered for an instant before Darcy caught her firmly and righted her.

The hunters emerged through a break in the wood. There were three or four gentlemen accompanied by their servants and dogs.

"Hmm. I do not recognize them," Darcy said, "do you?"

They raised their guns to the sky. "I certainly do not," she growled.

She had started directly for the group when Darcy caught her arm.

"You will, I think, remain here."

"What?" She considered bolting anyway but there was something in Darcy's stance that made her imagine he would brook no resistance.

Darcy approached the men, hands clasped in a lordly manner behind his back. Despite the men's shared rank, Flip could see Darcy assume easy command. As he spoke, the men's eyes went from Darcy to her to the birds wheeling overhead and back again to Darcy. In a moment, the men looked at each other, shrugged and handed the guns to their servants. One man even shook Darcy's hand. Flip gave a sigh of relief.

Darcy returned, smiling.

"They understood?" Flip asked.

"Well, as you might imagine, the notion of extinction was beyond their understanding." Darcy cleared his throat, and another mass of birds rose behind him. "However, a complicated woman was not. I told them I had high hopes for this evening and their sport was making you a devil to manage."

Flip's jaw dropped. "You-You—" She gave him a push.

"Now shall we try this for a note of realism?" He hoisted her over his shoulder, and she squealed.

"Perfect." He hopped across the stream bank and toted her to the carriage, unloading her on the step.

"If I return you any more disheveled, Jared will have me arrested as a cutpurse or worse." He drew himself onboard in a single movement and untied the reins. "Do you think you can sit still now until we make Abbott House?"

Flip harrumphed. Nonetheless, the shooting had stopped, and her bird sat in her lap. With a cluck from Darcy, the horses broke into a trot.

As they approached the town of Stourton, which sat some ten miles from Abbott House, the home Jared had recently let, Flip began to grow uneasy. Flip—or Philippa as she had clearly become—had hoped Darcy would avoid the town somehow, and he probably would have if she hadn't led him to believe Jared would be at the country house. The trouble was, Philippa, apparently, could never be reasonably certain where her husband would be, and his lack of discretion had been growing. Flip's understanding of Philippa's life had grown as sharp and crystal clear as a jagged wedge of glass.

They passed Saint Peter's and the Spread Eagle Inn, where a handful of workingmen labored outside, and there it was, parked in front a large brick house on the far edge of town: Jared's unmistakable maroon carriage with the 2 in gold script on the side. Flip said nothing, but she saw Darcy's hands tighten around the reins when the carriage came into view.

"Is that his mistress's house?" he asked.

Flip nodded, and Darcy said no more.

Once past the town, they rode in silence for several miles, and a few light raindrops began to fall. As the drops grew more frequent, Darcy sighed. The phaeton didn't have much of a roof, and after searching for a thick overhang of trees and finding none, he pulled the carriage onto a smaller drive, where they found a magnificent grove of pines. The horses made a gentle turn under a thickly leaved oak, and Darcy pulled the beasts to a stop.

Flip drew in an appreciative breath. They had pulled into a considerable estate, whose beautiful, lush landscaping stretched as far as the eye could see. Before them was a sapphire lake, dappled by the rain, surrounded by stands of foliage in lush emerald, jade and lime. A charming bridge bisected the water, and the sharp scent of pine filled the air.

"Oh, look!" At the far side of the water, a Greek temple nestled among the trees. The pink-red glow of the fast-falling sun was reflected in its pale stone. "Is that someone's home?"

But Darcy had no eyes for his surroundings. He sat brooding, gaze fixed on the reins in his hand. "It is appalling," he said at last. "He does not scruple to hide his licentiousness. Will his carriage remain there all night?"

On the DVD of *Pride and Prejudice,* Flip had seen Darcy simmering before, when he dove into a pond fully clothed to cool his ardor for Lizzy and again when he tried to lose himself in a fencing lesson for the same reason, but never like this, from a distance of a dozen inches. It was a little like sticking her hand in a lion's cage.

But how could she explain? Philippa, like Flip, had grown so used to her husband's behavior she hardly gave it a second thought. "You must remember, Darcy, the woman in question is the recent widow of his younger brother. Jared is guardian of his brother's estate. Even the worst gossip could find nothing in his being there that would be officially worthy of comment."

A crack of lightning lit the world around them, and the rain began to fall harder. The sky appeared to match Darcy's ever-darkening mood.

"Hell." He urged the horses once again into motion. "I know a place. We'll have to run." The drive forked into two, a lower road that circled the lake and an upper one that scaled a small rise. Darcy took the upper one.

The rain came down harder. Flip's dress clung to her. In a moment they had reached the summit. Darcy held her arm as she jumped from the seat, and they ran through booms of thunder to another white temple, this one circular, with a domed top and a columned porch. Two, four, six steps they climbed, and they were out of the rain at last.

Darcy flung his coat over her shoulders. His warmth still clung to it as did the faint scent of sandalwood. There was nowhere to sit, except perhaps the recessed alcoves, perhaps once meant for urns, which circled the inner structure at waist height. Darcy stood with his hands behind his back, and while he gazed out at the lake and drive below, he did not seem to see them.

She touched his cuff, and he roused himself from his thoughts.

"Forgive me, Philippa. I have forgotten my manners. We are on the grounds of—" His eyes fell upon her, and he inhaled. "May I say the rain compliments you? Between the flush from our run and the sparkle of the drops in the setting sun, you look like a dew-kissed rose."

She flushed, and Darcy adjusted his cuffs, self-conscious. "Er, I was saying we are on the grounds of Lord Hoare's estate. This is Stourhead Gardens. Have you not been here before?"

"No," she replied. "Abbott House has been ours but a season. Jared's friends are mostly in town, and we leave for Paris again in a month."

"The squarish building there"—he pointed—"the one we first saw, is Hoare's version of the Parthenon, and this"— he made a broad gesture about their current abode—"is the Temple of Apollo. They are Hoare's follies, I suppose, though they're undeniably pretty. The gardens attract many visitors."

"I can see why."

Flip asked a few questions and Darcy answered, but their earlier frivolity had been erased. He fell silent, and she could feel him wrestling with something as he paced, lion-like, oblivious to the lightning that now crackled and hissed around them.

"What about the brother's son?" Darcy asked. "He is how old? Three or four?"

Flip saw the adorable boy in her head, his shock of brown

hair and those curious Quillan eyes and the adoration with which he gazed upon his mother, and for an instant the longing nearly undid her. "Four," she answered.

Darcy frowned. "Would Jared's brother be comforted to know his only child bears witness to his mother's debauching?"

"He would not," Flip said, "were the child his."

Darcy's eyes widened, and a dangerous sort of fire exploded in them. "Do you mean to tell me that Jared's liaison with this woman has gone on throughout your marriage?"

"Even before." Flip sighed. "What I was told when I found out last year was that Jared has loved her since the first year of her marriage to his brother, before Jared and I even met."

"My God! The child is Jared's heir!"

"So long as I remain childless." Flip felt an even deeper pang and had to bite her lip. "Convenient, is it not? Which is why Jared has recently informed me—how shall I put it?— that he shall no longer partake of the marriage bed. He has promised his love her son—their son—will inherit the title and estate."

"Profligate blackguard, I have a mind to—" Darcy stopped when he saw her face.

"Come," she said. "It does no good to wallow in it. My wallowing is complete. I have quite come to terms with it. I have my sculpture, my friends, my family and the money to do as I please. And," she added with a rueful smile, "one must consider the happier side. After all, Jared has kindly arranged things so that I may sleep in my own bed tonight."

But Darcy would not be sidetracked. "And you are reconciled to this?"

A suffocating sadness welled in Flip. How had he plucked at the one hurt she wished to bury? "Darcy . . ."

The lightning flashed, and he stared distractedly into the distance.

"Do you remember your little niece, Lisette?" he said after a pause. "You held her so much back when I knew you that I—" He threw up his hands. "For a year Lisette was literally attached to your side. I didn't think the babe would ever learn to walk. Her feet never touched the ground."

"Darcy, please." Neither Jed nor Jared had been willing to budge on the matter, Flip thought, and the ache she felt reminded her of how much that had hurt.

"I fear you cannot be happy without a child."

"I can," she said, throat tightening. "I-I— Can't you see that I am?"

"What I see is that your husband needs to be horse-whipped."

The emptiness burned inside her, the emptiness she wished to deny, but she would not give in to it. Make him stop. Make him stop, she told herself. Not a single word more. She lifted her hands to her eyes, which had blurred with tears.

"Philippa—" He paused, frantic at her anguish.

"Do not urge me as if I have chosen this path," she cried angrily. "He will not give me a child! Don't you see? I have no choice!"

"The hell you don't."

He brought his mouth to hers, and the emptiness imploded. His kiss was hard and searching. She struggled against it—the longing, the need to be whole—but the fire had gone untended so long, she could not stop.

He tasted of brandy and Seville oranges, and he brought her roughly against his hips, characterizing his desire unashamedly. The kisses were not gentle or cajoling, like the ones Flip had glimpsed in the past. They were demanding and insolent, and if Flip's arms were not crushed against his chest, she would have slapped him. But her body did not feel the insult. Her hips twisted and bucked until he hardened into steel against them.

She pushed herself free. "No. Stop. He will disown a bastard. I will not do that to a child of mine."

"How will he know? When did he last take you to his bed?"

"I cannot. I will not."

"When, Philippa? I will not have it. He cannot take everything from you. When did he take last take you to his bed?"

"He took measures—"

"Measures fail. When, Philippa, when?"

"A week ago."

"Then if he insists on leaving your marital bed, we have a month, no more. How long are you at Abbott House?"

"A month."

She wanted to be wanted, wanted to be needed. She clung to his shirt, listening to the thump of his heart, afraid to think about what he was unleashing.

"A month," he repeated.

"Yes," she said. "Yes."

After a long, questioning kiss, he lifted her onto the shelf of an alcove. The marble felt cool against her fevered flesh, and her nipples tightened under the damp silk, an event he observed with gleaming eyes.

"These will haunt me no further." He drew his thumbs roughly over the stiff flesh, and she arched. "I shall have you now, just as I should have had you five years ago."

"I was a girl."

He rucked her skirts onto her lap. "You were a bloom whose thorns I should have braved. I should have plucked you then and there and had you for my own. Then you would have had this"—he pressed himself against her, savoring the shock in her eyes—"every night. And I"—he lifted her breasts and nuzzled them through the silk—"this."

Flip squirmed against the dizzying pressure, anchoring her fingers in his thick hair. The exquisite burn in her belly had to be extinguished. Darcy caressed her bare thighs, from buttock to hip, now taking full measure of what he would possess.

"Not here," she whispered.

"Here. Now." He reseated her roughly, then lowered the straps of her dress and threaded her elbows through them. With a flick, her breasts were free.

"The road," she warned.

"Damn their eyes. They shall see you as you should be seen."

The picket-fenced undergarment around her waist thrust her breasts aloft and toward his frank gaze. He stripped the links from his cuffs and threw off his vest.

"*Les cerises d'amour,* eh?" He took one of her nipples in his mouth, and she made a noise she barely recognized. He alternately nipped and suckled. "They say it takes a woman's peak to produce a son," he whispered. "I should like to see a son in Quillan's house."

He slid two fingers between her legs, releasing a charge that nearly unseated her.

"Oh!"

"Has he brought you there?" Darcy demanded as his

fingers worked. "To a peak?" His eyes gleamed gold in the lightning flashes. "Has he made you cry out?"

"No." She was like a fish on a hook, gasping for air. "Yes. Perhaps. I don't know."

"Well, you shall know now." He began to undo his trousers, and the unfastening of each button by one hand was timed neatly to a quake-inducing movement of the other. In truth, Flip had never known such heat. Jared, it seemed, had been eager, curious, kind, but apparently unschooled. Darcy's breeches dropped in a smooth *hiss,* puddling around the polished leather of his boots.

The linen of his shirt billowed around his bare thighs. He undid his tie and drew the shirt carelessly over his head. He *was* an Adonis, with muscular hips and wide, proud shoulders. Outside, the lightning flashed like fireworks, each burst rendering the extent of his desire in stark relief.

"Philippa, you have won your bet at last."

He gripped her by the small of the back and entered her roughly. Despite her readiness, his size slowed him, and every inch made her gasp. She clasped his hips, feeling the tight muscles contract under her palms.

He began to move slowly, bringing a thumb to dance across their joining. She fretted noisily, the stricture around her waist only serving to bring more focus to the place their bodies met. The marble stung, so she tightened her legs around him, and he groaned, losing his rhythm for an instant. The stumble titillated her, and she bore down on him with every muscle, hoping for more. With quickening breaths he took the challenge, ramming her to a disorganized beat.

White-hot fire licked her belly. His thumb tormented her

mercilessly. He'd found his cadence now and pounded more steadily, pulling back enough each time to replumb her with the hammerhead of his cock.

On the road below a coach appeared, its twin lanterns casting narrow circles on the darkening road. Their faces were too distant to be recognized—she hoped—and in any case Darcy's back was to the carriage, but there would be no mistaking the primitive joining laid bare with each crack of lightning.

"Darcy, stop."

"Is it Quillan," he asked, thrusting deeply, "here to suffer his penance?"

"No, no." She could barely focus, the tide of pleasure driving her well beyond reason. "It's not him, but, for God's sake, it's *someone*. What will they think?"

"Just another country maid," he said, "succumbing to her gentleman's pleasure."

The carriage slowed to a crawl. Around them the hill lit as bright as day. Darcy reared back like a satyr, drumming her so hard her breasts beat against her chest.

"No, please." She no longer cared about the coach. She only wanted release. Hotter and hotter the gathering spasm grew. She gripped his hips hungrily, riding the jackhammer pulse.

"Cry out," he demanded. "Let them hear you."

"No."

"Cry out or I shall strip you to the skin and bend you over the railing like a six-shilling whore."

The flames engulfed her. Every muscle quivered. There was no stopping now, no matter her scruples. She clutched the sill beneath her. Just as her back, iron-arched and aching, was about to break, he caught both nipples and twisted.

A fireball ripped through her, and Darcy plunged into the heart of the conflagration, pinioning her at the fiery peak. Again and again she cried out, an urgent, primitive squall that echoed down the rise, and again and again he poured himself into her, until they collapsed, weak-limbed, his head on her shoulder, hers against his chest.

"A son, then," he declared.

The coach driver clanged his bell merrily.

"Reckless fool," she whispered, and ducked as the carriage drove on.

"We shall be the talk of the county tomorrow," he murmured, kicking free of his breeches. "Though unless someone recognizes my boots, it shall be the act which is notable, not you or I. Thank God for a cobbler whose designs are elegant but indistinguishable."

She kissed him hungrily, laving his tongue with hers. A shiver ran through him, and he arched again.

"Strumpet, stop. I am empty."

"And I am nearly full." She teased her hips back and forth.

"Nearly, is it?" He thickened inside her. "But you shall not have me again. Not tonight. You shall come here again tomorrow, at moonrise. I will bring a coach."

"Jared will be at Abbott House. I could not leave."

"Have you not separate rooms? Surely the man who exhorts marital celibacy cannot endure a shared bed."

"Darcy, I cannot. Slip from the house like a common fishwife?"

"Slip from the house, or I shall come to you. Is that what you want? To have me possess you in your husband's home?" He lifted her chin. "Tonight was for the child. Tomorrow—and every night until you leave—shall be for us."

She drew a thumb under each of his buttocks, and the length inside her sprang to life. "Convince me," she said, grinning.

He lifted her bodily from the alcove, still joined to him, and carried her halfway down the steps. He sunk to sitting, then leaned back on his elbows. The rain ran down her shoulders as she loomed over him, running in rivulets off each nipple. She felt as if she were straddling the temple itself.

"I think," he said, stirring his hips slowly, "the time has come to convince yourself."

Chapter Five

Flip opened her eyes slowly to the muted scent of oranges and limes. Madame K's oddly flowered carpet shimmered below the massage table's porthole.

Holy moly. That had to be the best freakin' massage in the whole damned world.

She tried to raise an arm. It was like the bones in her body had turned to vanilla cream, yet she felt as light as air. She had literally become a Twinkie. Somebody could just pop her in his mouth and—

Oh God, don't mention it. They'd done that too.

Nothing below her waist had an iota of feeling. Claudia would have to toss her into the trunk of her BMW like last week's haul from Saks to get her home.

"Vould you like some vater?"

"Vhat? I mean, what?"

"Vould you like vater, or a cookie?" Madame K sounded pleased with herself.

Flip lifted herself slowly. She was sure she'd have cushion marks around her face for days. "Wow. That was some dream."

"Not dream so much. Imagination."

If that was imagination, Flip was glad she wasn't in the

storytelling business. She checked to see if she had teeth marks on her nipples.

"Vorm compresses vill help."

"What? Oh." The masseuse gestured toward Flip's chest. "Thanks. I've a . . . never felt so involved in a book before."

"Vun likes to encourage literacy."

"Oprah has nothing on you."

"Vill you come again?"

"Do you have heart paddles nearby?"

"Where are you?"

The sky seemed twice as blue and the day twice as pleasant, so pleasant in fact Flip was feeling as if she might fly when her phone began to ring. It was Claudia.

"On Forbes," Flip said. She waved at the cop at the corner of Atwood.

"Jesus, are you *humming?* I thought you were at the library."

"Yeah, um, got a bit sidetracked. Had a massage. Best forty-five dollars I ever spent. You imagine yourself in a book, and, trust me, it's just like you're there."

"Is it like Cliffs Notes? Can I skip reading *Pride and Precipice?*"

"*Prejudice.* And, no, you can't skip reading it."

"Even if the hero's a dud?"

"Er, dud may be a little strong. He's actually not so bad."

"I thought 'not bad' was the problem. No sex, right?"

"Ah . . ."

"Is there or isn't there? This could affect my evening."

"Well, no, technically. But, believe me, the guy's capable of it. *Definitely.* I mean, really. Not like I know, of course. That would be crazy. You can't actually know what a character in

a book would do, right? It isn't like I slept with him myself."
She laughed nervously. "It's just, well, all signs point to 'Go,'
if you know what I mean?"

"Have you been drinking?"

"Nothing but water. Good for the soul, right? Full of
bunnies."

"Two words, Flip: more sunscreen. I'm calling because I'm
going to be a little later than I expected. Five thirty or so."

"No prob."

"And mild, wild or Pass the Tums?"

"What?"

"The wings I'm picking up for you."

"Oh, Pass the Tums, definitely."

"Great. See you in a couple hours."

"What? I thought you said five thirty."

"I did. It's three thirty."

"It's *three thirty?!*" Flip yanked the cell phone from her ear
and looked at it. There, just above the photo of Scruffy, the
display read 3:30. Holy hell, she'd been gone three hours!

"Flip," Claudia squawked through the little speaker. "Are
you all right?"

"Gotta go."

Flip changed direction and jumped on the downtown
bus. She had to be at the Aviary by four to check on Ninja.
Cripes, she'd missed the whole afternoon. Had she been
drugged? She felt her purse. No, her wallet was still there.
Had she been molested? Okay, yes, but it wasn't like she was
going to bring charges. God, she'd have to hurry at work so
she could head home to meet Claudia.

Downtown, she jumped off the bus and jogged the last
mile across the river to the Aviary. Huffing and damp, she flew
through the entryway. Vera, the organization's community

outreach ornithologist, read a tabloid behind the welcome desk.

"Slow today?" Flip asked.

"Not with Britney and K-Fed." Vera flipped a page. "Jed's in. New girlfriend in tow."

"Rental car, voting card or driver's license?"

"Voting card, I'd say."

"Really? That old?"

"Oh yeah. And straight airhead ticket."

Great. The only thing more embarrassing than being dumped by your husband is seeing the third-stringers with whom he replaces you.

Flip dumped her purse on the floor next to her desk, one of the two desks the Aviary had jammed into the minuscule space she shared with the evening coordinator, and checked her messages. Except for their security system, the Aviary was behind technology-wise and still relied on individual answering machines. Only a message from her mother, reminding her about dinner on Sunday. Nothing, she noted, from Cornell. The decision was due next week.

Then she popped into the more expansive hospital area and spotted Jed. He was unloading Ninja from his finger onto the pink-nailed finger of his latest squeeze. Golden-haired—they always had to be blondes—and wearing a Clash T-shirt she'd somehow reconstructed into a halter, the girl had tits the size of emu eggs. Her nipples were literally in another zip code.

"Careful with him," Flip said. "The antibiotics he's on give him the runs."

The girl regarded the titmouse nervously.

"Sorry. I meant Jed."

"Flip," Jed said, "We're doing an interview here."

"Really?"

"On the ivory bill. She saw me on CNN." He turned to the girl. "Io, this is Flip Allison, one of my colleagues here at the Aviary. Flip, this is Io. She's a journalism student at Carnegie Mellon."

"Eye-O," Flip repeated, confused. "As in E-eye-E?"

Jed gave her a piercing look, but Io's face crinkled. "What? No," she said. "It's a moon of Jupiter."

"Nice to meet you," Flip said. "I'm also one of Jed's former girlfriends—ex-wife, actually, but why fixate on technicalities?—seven or eight back. I don't know, Jed. Do we count Beatrix, the intern from Amsterdam? It was only a single dinner party, after all."

"Wow." Io dimpled in Jed's direction. "Must have been an amazing party."

"Jed is nothing if not the perfect host."

"Flip," Jed said, "surely we're keeping you from something."

"Only Ninja," Flip ducked her head in the direction of the bird, who had now flown to the edge of a bookcase. "I need to remove his stitches."

"Done." Jed slouched against an examining table. "I did it at lunchtime."

Gee, thanks for letting me know.

"Well, I can see I'd better let you two kids get back to the interview," Flip said. "And I have to get back to my presentation, anyhow. Make sure you get that story about the party. Oh, and you might want to ask him about the aftereffects too. I mean, it is only an STD, but the fact that it's still around after two years has the doctors thinking mutation."

She marched back to her office. The only thing on her

desk was a half-finished time sheet. She opened her drawer, deposited the paper and pulled out a small glass bottle. She unscrewed the top, sprinkled the powder inside onto the desk and returned the bottle to the drawer. Then she strode into the main demonstration area, where she ran into Vera, checking the viability of an office umbrella.

"Well, that was certainly worth an extra bus trip," Flip said.

"Yeah, and get this. He's charging their lunch to the PR budget." She pulled car keys out of her purse. "How's the presentation going?"

"You know the smell of penguin shit? Oh, hell! I have to go back to the library. I left my notes there."

"Want a ride? I'm heading in that direction. And it looks like it might rain."

The last thing Flip saw, through the sliding glass window of the hospital area, was Ninja in flight, dropping a green-gray slurry on Jed's head.

Uh-oh. Beret time.

Chapter Six

Vera pulled to a stop in front of the library.

"Oh, *crap,*" Flip exclaimed.

"What?"

"I left my purse at work." Flip checked her pocket. She still had her phone, some cash, and her house key.

"Maybe you can con your way in."

"Oh, I'm not worried about that. But my wallet's in my purse. So's my checkbook. I'm going to call."

She checked her phone. Four o'clock. Jack, the evening coordinator, occasionally arrived early. She called up his number and pressed it.

"Hi," the recording answered. "This is Jack Kosanovich. Leave a message at the tone."

"Jack?" Flip paused, knowing there was a chance he'd be screening the call and would pick up when he heard her voice. "Jack? Are you there? Pick up. Dammit. Listen, when you get this message, can you lock my purse up? I left it in the corner. Please. It's important."

She punched off. "Thanks, Vera."

"You want the umbrella?"

"Nah." Flip looked at the cloud-streaked sky. "It's not gonna rain."

* * *

Flip ran down the sloping entryway into the library. The red-haired grad student was busy with a cart of books, so another attendant issued her a temporary pass. She joined the grad student at the elevator.

"Pigeons are at QL696, right?" she said conversationally, though she knew exactly where everything in the ornithology section was.

"Uhhh, yeah, I think. Fourth floor."

"I wanted to check out something before I left today." She sighed, thinking longingly of that beautiful dead bird. The dream had seemed so real. . . .

Her gaze came to rest on the copy of *Pride and Prejudice* in the display case. She chuckled. "Get over it, Lizzy. You have no idea how good you're going to have it." The bell announcing which elevator was about to arrive dinged, and she was just about to step closer to the appropriate one when the word *bastard* on the page caught her eye.

Bastard?

Lizzy had been mad, but as far as Flip knew, profanity did not play a part in any of Jane Austen's books, certainly not in the famed rejection scene. She gazed at the page curiously.

The door slid open, and a handful of flip-flop-shod students *slip-slapped* out. Flip and the grad student entered. He pressed 3 and Flip pressed 4.

Bastard? she thought again. In Jane Austen? More likely to be an illegitimate child, knowing dear old Jane—

Holy crap!

She slapped a hand against the closing door.

The grad student narrowed his eyes.

"Sorry, sorry, sorry. Gotta check a reference." She shoved

her way through the opening, yanking her trailing elbow through its pincerlike squeeze. Then, in a move that would have made "Mean" Joe Greene proud, she flung herself over the case and began to read.

> ". . . do you think that any consideration would tempt me to accept the man who has been the means of ruining, perhaps for ever, the happiness of a most beloved sister? . . . I have every reason in the world to think ill of you. Even were I to forgive you that, your intemperate conduct this past year would utterly preclude it."

Intemperate conduct? Flip's neck twinged sharply.

> "Intemperate conduct?" Darcy repeated. "What possible charge could you lay at my doorstep?"
> "I dare not say it. That woman and her . . . bastard."
> "Bastard?" Darcy spoke with heightened color. 'I urge you to tread lightly, madam.'
> "And I urge you to recall your honor, sir. Fully half of London is aware that—"

Oh no, it couldn't end there.

But there it was: the end of the page. Flip surreptitiously banged the case with her hips. No go. The pages barely moved.

Had she possibly forgotten this element of the story? It had been years since she'd read the book. Perhaps it was Lydia, the reckless youngest sister, and her blackguard suitor, Wickham? But, no, Flip had just read this particular passage this morning. If she could only get to the next page.

She checked the back of the case. Locked. Geez, she thought, where are we, in a war zone? Ever heard of trust?

She noticed a slender gap between the top of the display glass and the side. She looked around. No one was watching. She kneeled and blew. The page fluttered. Encouraged, she tried again. This time it actually moved a little and held. She filled her lungs and really let it rip. The page mounded in a half-turned position. Okay. All she needed now was a little gravity to fall in her favor. She stood up and summoned her best moves. A bang, a shake, a *thumpa-thumpa-thumpa*.

"You must be looking for the *Pride and Prejudice* pinball machine," a butler-voiced man drawled. "I'm afraid that's downstairs."

Flip swung around, panic-stricken. The asshole from the café had just exited the elevator. And the look he was giving her could have melted kryptonite.

"Um, someone must have moved the case from the wall," she said. "I was trying to move it back."

"Good of you. You're aware that's an almost two-hundred-year-old copy with which you were doing the bump, are you not?"

"Two hundred years, huh?" She made a high-pitched laugh. "Can't just pick up one of those on eBay, can you?"

"Mirthless" hardly described him.

He sighed, dropped his backpack and bent to grab the case.

Flip sucked in her breath. Why do jerks always seem to have the best asses?

He walked the case back into position against the wall. The page relaxed into its original position.

"Super," she said.

He picked up his pack and hoisted it over his shoulder. His gaze lit on the pages. She slid in front of the case. "Slogging through the rare books?" she asked.

He frowned.

At this angle, he could see right down her shirt, though she dared not move. *That'll teach me to wear "fuck me" lingerie to work.*

"We haven't met," she said, "at least not officially. I'm Flip Allison." She held out her hand.

His grip was surprisingly cool and firm—a hand that gave the impression it was perfectly at home on a woman's body. In fact, Flip noted with an electric tingle, she felt as if he'd just run his hand up her thigh. She gazed at her palm.

"Flip?" he asked.

"Short for Philippa."

"Ah. Like Philippa of Hainault."

"Huh?"

"Wife of Edward the Third? Mother of the Black Prince?"

"No. It was our neighbor's three-legged poodle, actually. My mother loved the name."

"Ah." He gave his head a small shake. "I'm Magnus Knightley."

That's an odd coincidence. His eyes are exactly the same golden-brown as Darcy's. Gee, she thought with a sudden internal giggle, how many women get to say that? Then she remembered the proposal scene, and the giggle died an immediate death.

"Yeah, well, thanks so much." She grabbed her bag and made a motion toward the door she hoped he'd be swept into as well.

He shrugged his shoulders and turned to go.

"Hang on." She held out her hand. He paused, took it again, and the same frisson ran through her. *Amazing.*

"Watch the banging," he said. "You'd be surprised how much damage it can do."

Oh, baby.

Chapter Seven

"*Oh*, darlin', that's right," Jed said. "Just like that. Oh, *yes*."

Man, he loved the way fake tits moved when you pronged a woman. He could watch that tight, unnatural bounce till the cows came home. He also loved the way the really rich college girls came outfitted with fake tits, belly rings and a baby Benz. Thank the Lord for solicitous, obliging parents. And there was nothing better on God's green earth than pronging a babe on a former babe's desk—unless it was pronging one in a former babe's bed. Not that he had any sort of score to settle with Flip. She had excused herself without too much bother when the time came. But there was just something goddamned wonderful about getting his rocks off exactly where he shouldn't be.

The phone across the little office rang.

Io stopped moaning and sat up on her elbows.

"Don't worry, baby." He squeezed her knees, keeping his pounding steady. "The door's locked."

He blew out his breath. The beret was making him warm, but he felt it added an impressive touch of "global explorer." God, he wished there was a mirror here.

The answering machine kicked on.

"Jack?" It was Flip. "Jack? Are you there? Pick up. Dammit.

Listen, when you get this message, can you lock my purse up? I left it in the corner. Please. It's important."

Jed spied the purse in the corner. Poor Flip. Always so disorganized. Wonder what she had in there she thought was so important? The presentation she never seemed able to finish? He chuckled.

"Was that your wife?" Io asked breathily.

"Ex-wife. Yup."

"She's kind of a bitch, isn't she?"

"Oh, darling, no need to talk like that. You've got all of big, bad Jed right now. And big, bad Jed's gotta finish. C'mon, baby." His blood was starting to tingle.

"I'm trying."

A drop of sweat rolled down his face and landed on his belly. Two decades of beer drinking was beginning to leave an impression even the ab machine couldn't erase. "C'mon. Jed's at the finish line. Half a lap left. Let's bring this big ol' race car home."

"Go faster," she moaned.

"Baby, I've got the pedal to the metal. You've gotta pop the nitrous."

He palmed a tit and thought quickly of the Nolan Ryan baseball his dad had given him for his tenth birthday. Then his own balls started their hallelujah chorus. "This is it, sweetie pie. I'm seeing the checkered flag. It's gonna be a photo finish. Oh, yes, yes, *yeeeesssss!*"

Two more thrusts, and he stretched his arms over his head, let out a whispered rebel yell and slid out. She looked happy enough. He'd probably nailed it. Peacock time.

He snagged Flip's purse and leaned against the file cabinet to give Io The Pose. This is when he looked his best—casually erect; obliviously heart-stopping. He wondered if the purse detracted. He put it down for a moment, but curiosity prevailed.

"What are you doing?" Io twirled a lock of hair. She seemed to be focusing on the purse, not The Pose.

"Nothing, baby." He unsnapped the bag. "Just trying to help. Go ahead and get dressed." He looked inside. It was divided down the middle. He fished in one side. There was a wallet, of course, and a lot of loose gear—tampons, a lipstick, a roll of Life Savers, a checkbook. He opened the cracked leather and looked at her last entry. Forty-five dollars at Looking Glass Massage? What was that? No papers, though. He checked the other side.

Holy hell!

Something large and dead was wrapped in a white hand-kerchief. He lifted the flap of the handkerchief and nearly lost his balance.

She had a goddamn passenger pigeon in her bag! A passenger pigeon! His heart started to race. This was an unbelievable find. This was the sort of find that would put you on top of the birding world. Goddamn! How? Where? And why the hell would she have shot it? His brain raced in a thousand directions. Then he had it. Cloning.

Flip Allison had somehow figured out a way to crack the puzzle. Ornithologists had joked about it, though they knew even now the process could likely cause as many problems as it solved. It had been officially dismissed as scientifically difficult, biologically dangerous and ethically wrong. Though, truth be told, it wouldn't be too hard to find the DNA required. Even though the last passenger pigeon had died almost a century ago, there were numerous bits of ones in museums around the world. And if any of the bits had been kept cold enough to preserve the cells . . .

But if that's how Flip thought she'd get to the top of the ornithology world—his ornithology world—she had another thing coming.

"What?" Io said. "What did you find?"

Jed let go of the flap and shoved the purse aside. "Nothing, baby." With a casual groan, he slipped into his briefs and pants and put a foot in each huarache. That must be what Flip had been working so hard on at the library the last few weeks. He'd get to the bottom of it. One way or another. He'd be there too. He tossed on his shirt and buttoned two buttons.

"Baby," he said, "get a move on. We've got to go."

Goddamn. A passenger pigeon.

The door clicked as Jed disappeared out of Flip's office.

Io sighed. Sometimes even the cute ones were disappointing. She brought a hand between her legs and with half a dozen quick tugs finished what Jed had started.

She wiped her fingers on Flip's chair, found her jeans on the floor and pulled out her phone. Then she grabbed Flip's purse, backed against the door in case Jed returned and peered inside. There was a large cotton-wrapped bundle, like a lunch. She undid the top.

Eeeuuuwww. A dead pigeon. Totally disgusting.

But there'd been something about this bird that had fascinated Jed. She'd seen the look on his face. She wasn't the only Gordon Scholar in her journalism class for nothing. She laid the bird and fabric on the file cabinet, flipped open her phone and took a picture. Then for good measure she took out the wallet and placed it in her pocket.

Jed tried the door and hit the blockage. "Io? Are you all right?"

She stuffed the bird in the hankie, the hankie in the purse and tossed the whole thing back on the file cabinet. She grabbed her thong off the desk chair and slitted the door.

"Coming," she said with a grin, dangling the lace off her finger.

"Just the way I like it," he whispered.

"You know it, Hercules."

The minute Knightley disappeared out the library door, Flip flung open her phone and called Dinah.

"Hey, you," Dinah answered cheerily. "How's the presentation going?"

"Don't ask. Listen, I've got an important question."

"Mm?"

"Is there a bastard child in *Pride and Prejudice?*"

Dinah laughed. "I think you have your Jane Austen mixed up with your Thomas Hardy."

"Dinah, seriously," Flip said, trying to keep the terror from her voice. "Is there any woman anywhere in the book that has a baby?"

"Hmmm." Dinah considered for a moment. "Honestly, Flip, I can't think of a single baby in the whole thing. There are the kids of Lizzy's aunt and uncle, of course . . . and there are babies in *Sense and Sensibility* and *Emma.* But I can't think of a single baby, legitimate or otherwise, in *Pride and Prejudice.*"

"What about Lydia, the ne'er-do-well sister?"

"Unless she and Wickham were even more wicked than we thought, no. Why?"

Oh, crap. "I'm, um, looking for a good opening joke about genetic diversity for my presentation. You know, 'Today I crossed an owl with a goat and got a hootenanny.' That sort of thing."

Slightly worried silence. "Uh, sorry, Flip. Can't help you. Why not use that one?"

"This year's theme is Regency England."

"At an ornithologists' meeting?"

"Last year it was *Lord of the Rings*. You should've seen the cloaks. Look, I gotta run."

She shoved the phone in her pocket. This is insane, she thought, there's got to be something unusual about the book in that case.

At the checkout desk, she gave the grad student a warm smile. "Hi, me again." She eyeballed the ID he had around his neck. "Bob, listen, um, that book over there, the one in the case?"

Bob held his arm up like a Roman again.

"No, no," Flip said. "No checking it out, I get it. I was wondering, though: Is it like a special version or something?"

Bob opened a book and picked up the scanner. "It's a first edition, like I told you."

"But is it different from other, later versions?"

"Actually, since the manuscript is not extant, the first editions are considered the best source available. It's what all the other editions of *Pride and Prejudice* are based on."

This couldn't be happening.

"And you're sure," Flip said. "It's not like, oh, I don't know, a parody or something?"

Bob's scanning hand froze mid-sweep. "Like in *MAD* magazine?"

She winced. "Yes."

"No." His smile disappeared.

"Maybe you could come over for a minute? Just to see if everything looks okay to you?"

Bob sighed. He laid down the scanner and walked around the desk toward the case.

"It isn't that I think something's wrong—really wrong, I mean," Flip assured him when they stopped. "It's just that—what the *hell*?!"

"Excuse me?"

She gasped, unable to form words. The scene had changed again!

"Do you think that any consideration would tempt me to accept the man who has been the means of ruining, perhaps for ever, the happiness of a most beloved sister? . . . I have every reason in the world to think ill of you. Even were I to forgive you that, your intemperate conduct this past year would utterly preclude it."

"Intemperate conduct?" Darcy's color heightened. "I suggest you choose your words with care."

"Would that you choose your women with equal circumspection."

"Is your tongue always employed so improprietously, or do you waste your incaution only on words?"

Blood sang in her ears. "Profligate cur."

"Perhaps your pique would not be so full-blooded if the attentions you accuse me of bestowing so irresponsibly had been lavished . . . elsewhere." He took frank measure of her. "Such high-spiritedness suggests the proper investment, regularly applied, would be returned tenfold."

"Abhorrent man. Leave me at once. Go back to that woman and her child."

"Your green eyes betray you, madam."

"Your foolhardy dissolution betrays you. Fully half of London is aware that—"

"I have to get into that case!" Flip cried.

"What?" Bob said, alarmed. "No. It's curated."

"Did you notice anything wrong with that scene?"

He frowned. "It does seem a little . . ."

"Lurid?"

"I'm no expert on Jane Austen, of course, but I don't remember—"

Aaaarrrrggghh. "No, me neither. Thanks, though."

He left, shaking his head.

Flip slipped around the elevator bank and pulled the Looking Glass flyer out of her pocket. She dialed the phone number.

"Good afternoon, Flip," Madame K said cheerily. "Vee are feeling better, *ja?*"

Flip looked at the phone. She hadn't had time to say her name. "Listen, something very strange is going on." Two students in study carrels lifted their heads. Flip turned her back and lowered her voice. "The book has changed."

"Vhat?"

"The story I imagined. It's different now."

Madame K chuckled. "My goodness, you vur in deep during the massage, vurn't you? You vur in Venice, I think? Something about a sink?"

"Well, um . . ." Flip debated. Venice, Wiltshire. "Does it matter?"

"Not really. As long as you vur in Venice book, you do not vurry. Effects vill not last long."

"And if I wasn't? I mean, just out of curiosity?"

"Voof!" Big trouble then.

Oh, man. "I thought it didn't matter which story one imagined."

"It doesn't, if the imagining fits the story. Remember rule number one? Sink activity good for some stories, not for others."

"Yeah. Um, have you ever, um, had a client with big trouble? You know, postimagining?"

"Once, *ja*. Very bad." Madame K clucked her tongue.

"Really? And, ah, what did this client do? I mean, what happens exactly?"

"Oh, *ja*. Book changes to mirror imagining."

"And then it changes back?" Flip said with fervent hope.

"Oh, no. Book never changes back."

"*Never?!*"

"Never."

Holy hell. She'd undone *Pride and Prejudice*! She'd taken one of the world's most famous love stories and turned it into her personal sex blog. Dinah was going to kill her. Dinah, hell. A mob of *Pride and Prejudice* lovers would batter her to death with their tenth-anniversary DVD cases.

"Ah, but it gets vorse," Madame K said.

"Worse?" Could it get worse?

"*Ja*. Character's name changes to client's name, and book reveals client's innermost secrets."

"*What?!*"

"Oh, *ja*, spread on every page. Fortunately the book this man was reading vuz a little-known thriller. In it he became the upright businessman who—oof!—does some very saucy things to boss's vife before framing boss for embezzling money from the company. Unfortunately it vuz his real boss's favorite book too."

Oh, crap! There were a gazillion copies of *Pride and*

Prejudice. Every high school student, every literature major, every college prof—her mother!—would see her homage to Apollo!

Flip felt faint. "And there was no way for him to fix it?"

"Too late for him. I've heard there is a vay but . . ."

"But what?"

"Very risky. And I cannot believe it vurks. Vun must determine the full extent of the current damage—names, places, people affected. Not a detail can be overlooked."

"And what? And what?"

"Return to the story and fix it. The whole enterprise must be concluded very quickly. Vithin a day at most."

Flip's mind raced in a hundred different directions, none of them inviting. "Well, that doesn't seem so hard."

"Ah, but the trip back to fix is not possible, you see. Breaks rule number two."

Flip laughed nervously and stole a glance at the case. "Gee, who knew two little rules could cause such problems."

Chapter Eight

Details. She needed the details.

Flip hopped on the elevator. Fiction was on the second floor. She raced by the stacks, reading the signs as she flew by—DO–EL, CE–DO, BE–CA—and finally stopped at AA–BA. Austen was near the end. Flip grabbed the first copy of *Pride and Prejudice* she could find and paged wildly to the proposal scene.

> "Do you think that any consideration would tempt me to accept the man who has been the means of ruining, perhaps for ever, the happiness of a most beloved sister? . . . I have every reason in the world to think ill of you. Even were I to forgive you that . . ." Lizzy's voice trailed off and she said no more.

Forgive him what? Forgive him what? I need every blasted detail. She flipped the pages. Neither *b* word anywhere. This version seemed entirely *bitch* and *bastard* free.

Her phone vibrated. *Not, now.* She looked at the display. It was Jed. She snapped it open. "What?"

"Now what kind of a way is that to say hello to your dear old ex-husband?"

"What is it? I'm busy here."

"Yeah, and that's what you and I are going to have to talk about. Cloning, babe. Highly unethical."

She pulled the phone away and stared at the display, blinking, before returning the phone to her ear.

"Are you out of your freakin' mind?" she asked. "Has our favorite little diphthong slipped a Mickey in your wheat germ?"

"Flip, we're going to talk, and we're going to talk now. Are you at home?"

"Good-bye, Jed."

She clicked off.

Now why, Flip thought, does this book only show a little change and the fancy old first edition plays like *Dynasty* in corsets? She tried a second one. This one was nearly the same as the first, which buoyed her spirits until a third one read far more like the one downstairs. She stretched, considering, when the first one dropped to the floor and fell open to the front. The words printed at the bottom of the first page, "Foreword copyright © 1986 by Simon & Schuster, Inc.," caught Flip's eye.

1986.

And the first edition was 1813. Flip remembered what she used to do with her collection of pennies when she was eight. She pulled all the copies of *Pride and Prejudice* the library had, and arranged them by date, the oldest on the left, the most recent on the right. Then she opened each one to the proposal scene. The older the copyright date, the greater the variation from the real *Pride and Prejudice*. The one downstairs in the case had every change—well, every change that had shown up so far, Flip thought grimly. The one dated 1947 had about half the changes. The one dated

1986 had a hint of the changes. And the ones she'd purchased for the book club—Oh, cripes, the book club!—might show nothing at all.

She had to get into that case. If she needed every detail, she needed the oldest version she could find.

In a moment she was back at the checkout desk.

Bob laid down his scanner. "You know, it's almost like we're dating."

"Listen, I have a really important thing to ask."

"Let me guess. It's about the case."

"Good one, Bob. See, the thing is I'm doing some research—I'm a researcher—and my specialty is wood pulp, you know, paper. I was just talking to a colleague—Magnus Knightley, maybe you've heard of him—and he told me that the paper in that book was made from a rare stand of, um, Truffula trees—*Truffula loraxa*—in the Azores. And they don't exist anymore. Haven't for a hundred and fifty years. But if"—she held up a finger—"I repeat, *if* I can get the tiniest scrapping from the paper—no more than the head of a pin—we may be able to, well, graft new ones."

Bob weighed the improbable story.

"Not that we'd do the scraping now, of course," she assured. "But if I could just examine the paper closely to see if it has the distinctive Truffula ocellus markings . . . ?" She gave him an encouraging smile.

Bob shifted from one foot to the other.

"C'mon, Bob. Ten minutes is all I'll need."

"It's not a matter of me letting you," he said at last. "The case is locked. I don't have a key."

Dammit. "Who does?"

"Betty Scott, the curator."

"Can we ask her?"

"She's not here. I'd have to call."

"Truffulas, Bob. It could be a breakthrough."

Bob took a deep breath and disappeared into the windowed office behind the desk. Flip saw him consult a list, then begin to dial. She looked at her phone. It was 4:45. She'd arrived at Looking Glass Massage at 12:30. That means she had a little less than twenty hours left. Where was Jack Bauer when she needed him?

Bob returned. His dour look told her everything.

"Bob—"

"It's not as bad as you think. Betty says you can look, but you'll need to file a request with Archive Services that includes a note from your home institution first. Then they'll review it and in a day or so—"

"A day or so? Bob, we're talking Truffulas."

"Gee, after a hundred and fifty years, could another couple days really matter?"

"Bob, can I talk to Betty?"

"No. Absolutely not. I had to call her at home. She'd kill me."

"Does anyone else, anyone, have access?"

"Well, I can tell you who's accessed it before. That doesn't mean they necessarily have access now, though." Bob sat at his workstation and typed a handful of keys. "Okay, there's been two. Seymour Rafflestein in the History Department."

Flip thumbed this name into her phone.

"He's on leave until next semester," Bob added.

Flip dutifully cleared the entry. "And?"

"Oh, this should help. The other is Magnus Knightley."

Chapter Nine

Flip looked at the number Bob had written on the piece of paper for her and bravely dialed.

"Professor Knightley's office," a forbidding female voice answered. "Hold, please."

What was this, Pizza Hut? The woman probably had a good game of Minesweeper going.

After a protracted length of time testing nonmine squares, the woman clicked back on the line. "Professor Knightley's office."

"Yes, I know," Flip said. "Can I speak to him? My name is Flip Allison."

"May I ask the reason?"

"Tell him it's about pinball."

No reaction. "Professor Knightley is out of town."

"No he's not," Flip said. "I just saw him at the library."

"I see. Hold please."

A split second later, the woman clicked back. "Professor Knightley is not in the office today. If you'd like to make an appointment for next week . . . ?"

"Is he in the office, just not taking calls?

"Ma'am, if you'd like to make an appointment, you can. Otherwise, I can't help you."

Flip rolled her eyes. "Sure. Does Monday work?"

"The professor is out Monday."

"I'll tell you what. Why don't you let me know when he'll be available? I'll rearrange my calendar."

"All right. Let's see. Would Thursday at two ten work for you?"

"Yes. My mother can find another ride to dialysis. Where are you located?"

"Are you familiar with the Cathedral of Learning?"

Flip chuckled. "Intimately."

"The professor is on the thirty-second floor. Room thirty-two seventeen."

Bingo.

Flip looked at her phone. It was four fifty. If Knightley was there, he'd probably only be there till five. She hurried to the exit, slipped by Bob, who was busy with another patron, and came to an abrupt stop. It was pouring.

Perfect.

Well, nothing to be done about it. She grabbed a copy of the university newspaper, put it over her head and began to run.

Jed rolled the Porsche into a rare free space and looked out the windshield. He didn't think umbrellas were compatible with the image he wanted to project, but it was like Noah time out there. With a sigh, he grabbed the portable one he kept in the glove compartment, popped it open and jogged toward the library.

* * *

Io watched Jed park. The trouble with a bright red Porsche, she thought, was that it wasn't very discreet. Not that Jed placed a lot of value on discretion, of course. After all, it was his observation that the sixty-four-story elevator ride to the top of the USX Tower downtown was just the right length for the tits-to-the-wall-gotta-have-you-now screw that had first brought them together.

She flicked the wheel of the iPod and brought up "Fall Out Boy" on the Benz's speakers. A car behind her honked. She gave the driver the finger. She'd double-park until she knew exactly where Jed was heading.

She watched the pedestrians unlucky enough to be caught in the rain pelt across the crosswalk, water pouring down their necks and filling their shoes. Pathetic losers. "Pig people," her parents called them. Jed was almost to the entryway when he stopped and turned his back, nonchalantly, like he had seen something. Io looked but only saw more pig people heading to the crosswalk—a man with a black garbage bag over his suit and a woman with a newspaper pasted over her head.

Jed waited another few seconds, then ducked into the entrance.

Io squealed forward, spraying water in every direction as she made an illegal right and pulled into a handicap space. She slapped her grandfather's handicap driver pass onto the rearview mirror, pulled out her father's golf umbrella out of the backseat and made her way into the library.

Bob leaned against the office doorway watching Manuel, the assistant library head, at the monitors.

"Look, look, look," Manuel said gleefully. "This one's picking his nose."

Bob chuckled. Manuel called his pastime of scanning the security feeds for embarrassing activities when he was bored "Patrons Ain't." "Patrons ain't classy. Patrons ain't cool. Patrons ain't got any idea we're watching," he'd say, and laugh.

"God, I wish the camera came with a speaker. Imagine the guy's face if a voice came on and said, 'The table is not a Kleenex, buddy. Pick that damned thing up.' " He hooted, then stopped and tilted his head toward the counter. "Uh-oh, Bob. Check-in for you."

Bob turned. A movie-star-handsome man in a beret, shaking an umbrella, stood at the desk. "I don't know, Manuel," he said. "Looks like he might be your type."

Manuel gave the man an appraising glance and shook his head. "Trust me, you aren't ever going to see a gay man in a hat like that."

Bob stepped to the counter. "May I help you?"

"You sure can. Listen, I left my wallet at home. Is that going to be a problem?"

"No, we can give you a temporary pass to get in, but you won't be able to check out any books. Is that okay?

"Sure."

"Name?"

"Flip Allison."

"Flip?" Bob raised a brow. "That's unusual."

"Short for Philip."

Bob keyed the letters and looked at the screen. "Say, were you already in today?"

"Yep. Big paper."

Bob wrote the ID number on a temporary pass and

handed it to the guy. "I can't help you with your locker, though," he said.

"Pardon?"

"If you don't have the key to your rental locker, I can't help you."

"Oh, no," the man said quickly. "I still have that. What was that number again, though?"

Bob looked at the screen. "Forty-six thirteen."

"Super. Thanks. Oh, and one more thing. Where will I find what you have on passenger pigeons?"

Pigeons again? That's a little weird. "Well, pigeons are at QL696. Fourth floor. That should get you pretty close."

Io burst through the library entrance and scanned the floor. Jed was just entering an elevator. That probably meant the third or fourth floor. She smiled for a moment, thinking of the USX Tower. Even Jed probably couldn't get the job done in four floors. She started toward the elevators.

"Hang on. Can I see your ID?"

She turned around and gave the red-haired attendant behind the desk a killer smile.

"Oh, sure." She dug in her back pocket. "Say, I'm looking for books on pigeons."

The man laughed. "Gee, the next thing you're going to tell me is your name's—" His eyes widened as he looked at the ID. "Flip Allison."

"It's not a very good picture," Io said. "It was taken before the corrective surgery." She smiled again.

The man handed the ID back hesitantly. "Er, QL696. Fourth floor."

* * *

Bob swung into the office. "Question for you," he said to Manuel. "Exactly how concerned should I be about the fact there are three people here with the same name, including at least one without an ID?"

Manuel kept his eyes on the security monitors. "Any of them packing heat or a leaky chocolate milkshake?"

"Not that I could see."

"Then I wouldn't worry. Oh God, ya gotta see this. There's a woman in the music stacks sniffing her pits."

Chapter Ten

Flip poked the cross button and hugged the newspaper a little closer to her head, waiting in the monsoon for traffic to slow.

A single massage, and not only had she destroyed a classic, but every intimate detail of what should have been a private encounter was going to be laid out, well, like an open book. Madame K said the book would change, and, worse, that it would eventually change to include the visitor's own name. The pornographic bits were bad enough, but she'd die, she'd absolutely die, if Jed saw her in Darcy's arms crying about a baby.

The crossing light turned to WALK. She took one step and yelled, "Nooooo!"

A Mercedes plowed through the puddle, against the light, drenching Flip with a bathtub's worth of water.

Muttering every oath she knew, Flip raced across the street, up the stairs and, with water squishing noisily in her Nikes, shot into the base of the Cathedral. She wrung out her hair as best she could. The air under the soaring stone arches of the Commons Room, the building's lobby, was freezing, and she ran to keep from breaking into a shiver. She prayed Knightley would be in his office and willing to help her get inside the case.

Not exactly the way I thought I'd be scaling this, she

thought ruefully as the elevator whisked her to the thirty-second floor. When the door opened, a sixty-something woman with a sour expression and a key in her hand was standing there, nearly blocking Flip's exit. She gave Flip a deeply suspicious look as the elevator arrow clicked to down.

"Can I help you?"

Definitely the three-headed Cerberus, Flip thought as she slipped by. She recognized the voice. "I'm, ah, looking for the restroom." She lowered her voice to Kathleen Turner levels and tried to sound vaguely French.

"That's on twenty-nine," the woman replied with all the warmth of a nun correcting an incompetent fourth grader. "I'm going there now. I'll show you."

Shit.

The woman stepped into the elevator and put her hand on the door to keep it from closing. She waited for Flip to join her.

Flip glanced to the left. There, beyond an unoccupied outer room, was a doorway to a thickly carpeted office in which the edge of a massive wooden desk was visible.

The woman's gaze hardened. In another moment she'd step out and there'd be a race to Knightley's door. Not that Flip had any doubt about taking her—a well-placed foot could probably snap that hip like a matchstick—but it was unlikely that would help her case with the woman's boss.

The elevator dinged in compliance. Flip shuffled into the car.

The door started to close.

In a single movement, Flip rolled her arm over a half-dozen buttons under twenty-nine and slipped out just as the doors edged shut.

She shot toward Knightley's office, pausing only when she reached his door. The office was clubby and large, filled with overstuffed bookcases, expensive-looking oriental rugs and ceramic-potted ferns. The rain sheeted down the gorgeous floor-to-ceiling trefoil-shaped window. A well-worn leather couch hugged the far wall. *Hmmm*, Flip thought. I wonder how many rare books get reviewed there?

Magnus was gazing intently at something on his credenza, his back to her.

She scuffled a foot.

His eyes flickered for a split second in her direction, but the focus on his work never wavered. "Go ahead," he said absently. "Don't mind me."

"Go ahead and what?"

"The plants. You can water them."

Flip colored. He'd taken her for someone from the university plant service. "I'm not here for your plants."

"Oh." He turned to take her in. The moment he recognized her he tilted his chair back, hands behind his head, and placed a foot against his desk. The bemused look turned to something more complex, and Flip realized the detailed libido-provoking nuances of her sheer-paneled demibra as well as the cold-tempered flesh straining against it were visible through her shirt. She also realized every inch of real estate from her shoes to her hips was splattered with mud. At least the bird shit was gone. But how was it that Philippa looked like a dew-kissed rose when she got rained on, but Flip looked like a wanton sewer rat?

"Sorry." He gestured vaguely at her clothes. "The uniform."

"It's not a uniform," she said testily, crossing her arms. "I work with birds."

"Children's birthday parties, that sort of thing?"

"I'm a bird researcher. At the Aviary." Damn these work cargoes. What she needed was for him to get an eyeful of the caramel lollipops in back. That never failed to settle any man's hash.

"Oh. I do apologize. What can I do for you?" he asked. "Pinball machine broken?"

He stretched his legs, and Flip started. Despite conservative shoes and conservative trousers, his socks were an outrageous shade of lime. For some reason this threw what little she knew about him into complete disarray, and her train of thought did a total Casey Jones.

"What? Oh, I was wondering if—hoping, actually—you could help me." She found herself trying to guess what he had on underneath the trousers. After all, a man who wore lime socks might wear Pucci boxers or chocolate bikinis. She loved chocolate.

"Help you?" he said. "Again?"

"Yes."

"How?"

There was something about the man that told her the Truffula story wasn't going to fly. She turned slightly, to give some good ass profile. "I, um, want to see the book in the case."

"Ahhhhhh. That explains the Waring blender dance at the library." He smiled. "And why might a bird researcher need to examine a first edition *Pride and Prejudice?*"

Was that a note of condescension? The hair on her neck prickled.

"There's a reference to a bird in it I would like to review," she said.

"The word *bird* occurs twice in *Pride and Prejudice*. Once in chapter fifty-one, when Lydia is certain Wickham will shoot more birds than anyone else, and once in chapter fifty-three when Mrs. Bennet encourages Bingley to shoot birds in Longbourn Park after he's shot all the birds on his own estate, which I think you may recall is named Netherfield." He gave her a long look. "And *that* you could have ascertained from any edition of *Pride and Prejudice.*"

"Please. I just want to look for a few minutes." She took a few steps forward. "The attendant at the library said you might be able to help."

He brought his feet to the ground. "The truth is, I couldn't help you even if I wanted. I have looked at the volume, yes. But I don't have a key to the case. It's not like a key to the Playboy Club. One doesn't get it permanently."

"But you could call Betty Scott . . ."

"Why don't you tell me why you're really here."

The elevator dinged, and Flip winced. She ducked out of sight into the corner of the office just as the three-headed watch dog emerged.

"In here, officer," the woman said.

Officer?!

The woman stopped at the doorway. "Professor Knightley, are you all right?"

Knightley leaned back in his chair. "Yes, Miss Clarkson. Why?"

"A woman shoved me out of the way as the elevator doors were closing and ran toward you."

Shoved? Flip mouthed and crossed one arm past the other in a "no touchdown" signal. *No way.*

"You must have seen her," the woman went on. "Disheveled hair, filthy clothes. Probably one of those crack addicts. And," she added in a disgusted whisper, "you could see through her bra."

"Oh, her. Yes, I do recall something like that. Ran by babbling about trousers and breath mints. I assumed she was a university plant person. A menace, is she?"

"Well, I'm fairly certain she was the woman who called a little bit ago."

"Concerning?"

"She said pinball. I didn't believe her."

"Very intuitive."

"And she shoved me."

Flip turned her palms skyward and mouthed *no* even more emphatically.

Knightley tapped his fingers on the desk. "Well . . ."

"Mind if I take a look?" said the security guard.

Knightley looked at Flip, then let his eyes trail pointedly to the tall window directly behind her. She saw it was actually a door to a tiny balcony. He stood and made his way to the door to the outer office, throwing her a beautiful pick that covered her exit onto the balcony to a spot out of sight of anyone who might be in the office.

The balcony was three hundred feet up and about eighteen inches deep. Flip hugged the building, buffeted by the wind, and wondered how much worse her life could get today. The rain ran in bucketfuls down her back.

Note to self, she thought. Never turn down an umbrella.

At last the door opened. Flip prepared to be thrown into the waiting arms of the local gendarmes, or at least the hosts of *What Not to Wear.*

But it was only Knightley, smiling. "I think the peregrine falcon nest is on the other side." He handed her a blanket.

"Funny."

"Try not to get it too wet. It's cashmere."

The door to the outer office was closed. Knightley directed her to the couch, and she saw the work he'd been laboring over when she arrived was a Scrabble board. *Nice. I can see why he was too busy to take my call.* The words on the board were ones like *exegesis* and *leitmotif.* She rolled her eyes. On his credenza sat a picture of three young girls in elementary school uniforms. The girls had the same dark chestnut hair and feline eyes as Knightley. *Father of three and the reputed Lothario of the Rare Book Room? Totally uncool.*

"Listen," Flip said, "how about this? How about if I show you something you'll find very interesting in the case at the library."

He cocked his head as if he were observing his first great auk. "I don't think so."

"But why—"

His cell phone rang and he held up a finger. With a quick glance at the display, his body language changed from smug superiority to smooth operator. "Hello, Kendall," he said in a low, pleased voice.

Kendall? Flip groaned. Sounded like a college student with a trust fund and big tits—either that or another moon of Jupiter.

He turned a quarter turn toward the board, trying to shield the conversation. "What? . . . Oh, I like that. . . . Where?" He nodded once. "Uh-huh. . . . You got it." He seemed to remember Flip was there. "Look," he said into the phone, "I'm going to have to call you back. . . . Okay, bye." He flipped the phone closed, and the romp through dirty phone sex was over. As an afterthought, he laid a word on the Scrabble board—nice to know he had managed to ignore both of them—then it was back to cold, hard facts.

"Right. Where were we?" he said. "Oh, yes, visiting the case. No. I'm busy, and you haven't given me a reason yet."

The clock on his desk chimed. It was five fifteen. He rested on the edge of the desk and crossed his arms. "I expect you'll want to get to that about now."

She bit her lip. Who was going to believe this? "Well . . . I know this is going to sound weird—"

"Weird? I'm hiding a secretary-shoving, case-banging crack addict on my balcony. How much weirder could it get?"

"Oh, you'd be surprised. Here's the thing. I think something in *Pride and Prejudice* has changed, but only in that first edition, and I want to look at it." She held her breath.

"Changed? You think someone has changed the book?"

"Someone. Yes."

"How did this feeling come to you?"

"In a dream, actually. Okay, I know this is bizarre but I had this dream about something in the book—well, not really in the book, but in the book now."

"And it involved *Pride and Prejudice,* that edition specifically?"

"Yes."

"Where did I read about this?" he said with growing engagement. "I was reading something just like this recently, where there was a dream and something in a first edition changed."

"Really?" *My God, maybe there was hope. Maybe this had happened before and there really was hope.*

"Oh, yes. Now what did they do?" He tapped his lip. "That's right. I need to ask you a question. Just one. But it's very important, and it just might help us figure this out."

"Okay, shoot."

"Did this dream, in any way, involve Darcy's nether regions?"

Silence.

"You know what?" Flip said. "Go to hell." She threw down the blanket and stood. "There are amazing things that happen in the world every day. A boy lifts a car off the ground to save his brother. A woman with stage four cancer survives. The ivory-billed woodpecker has been extinct for seventy years. It's been seventy years since the last humans laid eyes on it. Then, boom, out of nowhere, it's back. Half a dozen confirmed sightings."

Knightley made a small grunt of skepticism. "From the bits I've read in the newspaper, the confirmation you're talking about is a picture so blurry it could have been Sasquatch on spring break or possibly even Lindsay Lohan. It's not that easy telling them apart sometimes, especially if they're getting out of a car."

"No. These were experienced field researchers who knew their stuff. It's one of the most important ornithological findings of the last hundred years, and Cornell's putting together a team to search and—oh it's true. I just know it is." She felt the same emotion rise that always overtook her on this subject. "Oh, God, you sound just like my ex—ready to disbelieve—no, insistent on disbelieving. How does the objective change, I ask, if one approaches it with hope? Or even more than hope? A determination that it has to be. What did Saint Augustine say? 'Faith is to believe what you do not see; the reward of this faith is to see what you believe.' And now my ex is snatching that Cornell assignment right out of my hands—just when what they need is hope and determination, not pragmatism and . . . Jed. Aaarrrrghhhh." She caught a glimpse of Knightley watching her critically, eyebrow raised, and she threw up her hands. "Why am I wasting my breath? I need to get into that case. It's very, very important."

He shook his head. "You arrive in my office like a madwoman, after either shoving my secretary or not—reports conflict—and tell me this came to you in a dream. Frankly I'm more inclined to call Western Psych than the library curator. Perhaps you'd like to try the truth?"

"This is the truth."

"A dream?" he said dismissively.

"Yes."

"You dreamed the book changed?"

Flip squirmed. "Well, no, that happened later. After the dream. Well, after the massage, which is where the dream happened. See, I was at this little place called Looking Glass Massage Therapy on Chesterfield, and the masseuse said I could imagine myself in a book—"

"No, it can't be." Knightley began to rub his temples.

"—and I didn't think anything of it—I mean, who would? So I thought about a book. And there was this man . . ."

"Here it comes."

"And I didn't even recognize him. Why would I, after all? But he was good enough to rescue me from my hostess and her sister, who were being so cruel. And it turns out it was Mr. Darcy."

"Oh, God, you're one of them!" he moaned. "One of those crazed women with the Pemberley stationery and all the DVDs, and it's 'Colin' this and 'Darcy' that, and, you come into my classroom with your mooning and starry-eyes and try to reduce the greatest socioeconomic observational novel ever written into romantic mush."

"I am not!" she replied fiercely. "I wasn't even a big fan of Darcy's until he, ah"—she felt her cheeks grow hot under Knightley's searing gaze—"befriended me."

"Befriended you, did he? What a noble gallant."

Flip felt her anger rise. "Look, all I'm saying is I had a dream about Darcy, and he certainly behaved differently than you might expect. And now the volume at the library seems to be reflecting that and—"

"Darcy will never behave against one's expectations," Knightley lectured. "That, my dear, is the sublime beauty of Austen's prose. Darcy is a man of his times, a perfect man of his times, which you might be able to appreciate if you were to upgrade your reading material."

"What, and read your books?"

"It couldn't hurt. No hedgerows, though."

"You know. It is possible you don't know everything there is to know about *Pride and Prejudice.*"

"You may want to advise the *New York Review of Books,* which has already described my latest work as 'the definitive analysis of Austen and her times' as well as the National Book Critics Circle award committee who have short-listed it for the criticism prize based on the first six chapters, even though it won't be published until December."

"There's a difference between what you know about something here"—she pointed to her head—"and here"—she pointed to her heart. *"Pride and Prejudice* is a love story, not a dry 'socioeconomic observational novel.' God, does anyone stay awake in your classes?"

"I don't teach classes anymore."

"I can understand why. Look, believe me or not, but your precious treatise is in trouble. There's more going on beneath the surface than you or I or anyone knew. Darcy is not a mannerly metaphor, he's impassioned and angry and capable of . . ." She paused.

"A swim in a pond?"

She wondered if a Nike to the balls would wipe that look off his face.

"A sexually charged fencing lesson?" he offered.

"No!"

"What then?"

"Try a steamy tryst at the Temple of Apollo in full view of the Wiltshire countryside. Sans trousers," she added with a triumphant chin-raise.

He barked a laugh and relaxed, as if he realized she was beyond insane.

"The full extent of what Darcy is *in*capable of," he said, "I forbear to think. But I can assure you that anything outside his meticulously formed character, particularly involving his trousers, is at the top of the list."

"So you think I'm making this whole thing up?"

"No, I think it's real to you. I just don't know if it came to you through an antenna in your tinfoil hat or a crystal ball held at arm's length as you ran through a ring of standing stones naked—oh, pardon me, sans trousers."

"He did jump in the pond, you know."

"It wasn't in the book!"

Flip's cheeks reddened. "You're a jerk."

"And you, madam, are the worst sort of reader. The one who will see only what she wishes. *Pride and Prejudice* is a love story only to the most unsophisticated. It is a story of manners and change."

"It is a story of desire—fulfilled and unfulfilled," she said, flinging the door open to a very surprised Miss Clarkson. "And anyone who doesn't get it in *Pride and Prejudice* probably doesn't get it much of anywhere."

Chapter Eleven

Magnus watched her storm past Miss Clarkson and jab the elevator button with such savagery he wondered if it might hurtle into the shaft like one of Zeus's thunderbolts, and his thoughts traveled not to *Pride and Prejudice* but to a much earlier work, *A Midsummer Night's Dream*. " 'I never heard/ So musical a discord, such sweet thunder,' " he quoted, reflecting on the provocative display of fireworks he'd just witnessed, though as she bent to brush mud off a sodden pant leg, it was another of that play's lines that figured prominently in his head: "Bless thee, Bottom, bless thee!"

He made his way back to his chair and imagined the weighted heft of those orbs filling his palms as he channeled the fireworks into something far more interesting, though a few well-placed cracks of his palm in the same general area might satisfy him just as much, and who knows what else they'd attempt after he'd got her properly sprawled across his lap.

His hands tingled in pleasurable anticipation, and he rifled the top drawer of his desk absently, looking for the box of candy his father had sent him for his birthday. He'd hardly touched it since it had arrived, but he suddenly had an odd but unmistakable urge for a caramel. He found one and bit the morsel firmly, letting the sinful sweetness ooze through his mouth, only to have the joy of the moment erased by the sight of a visibly furious Miss Clarkson.

"That woman . . ." She could barely form the words. ". . . was here!"

"Yes, she was. Hidden on the balcony, which is why none of us saw her, I suppose. Minor nutter. Feminist theory, that sort of thing."

"Do we need to talk to security, maybe have someone posted?"

"I feel certain she won't be returning."

Knightley templed his fingers, considering Flip's story. *Pride and Prejudice* changed? Bosh. Literature was immutable. That's the beauty of it, he thought, especially his beloved Austen. And because of a dream of all things? Ha. Why not solar activity or a vision of the Virgin Mary on the book jacket? He snorted.

Damn shame about that ass, though.

He scavenged another caramel and returned to the Scrabble board, but his mind floated.

That was it, he thought. What had seemed so familiar. Her pique. Exactly the same as Lizzy's after Darcy makes his generous but ill-presented proposal. Magnus leaned back in his chair. The scene had never been his favorite—he'd found the rich context of early nineteenth-century life Austen had laid out like a Canaletto landscape more to his liking: Mr. Gardiner's business in Cheapside, the commission Wickham must purchase then sell in the army, the changing relationship of clergy to gentry exemplified by Mr. Collins and Lady Catherine de Bourgh—but now he wondered if he'd given the scene its proper due.

He reached for the finely tooled leather spine that sat

just behind his desk, the second edition he'd purchased
when he'd won the Capote prize, and flipped the pages until
he'd found the scene, almost precisely in the middle of the
book.

> "Do you think that any consideration would tempt
> me to accept the man who has been the means of ruin-
> ing, perhaps for ever, the happiness of a most beloved
> sister? . . . I have every reason in the world to think ill of
> you. Even were I to forgive you that, your intemperate
> conduct this past year would utterly preclude it."

That's odd, he thought. I don't quite remember it that
way.

> "Intemperate conduct?' Darcy repeated. "What pos-
> sible charge could you lay at my doorstep?"
> "I dare not say it. That woman and her . . . bastard."

"Bastard?" Magnus stood, knocking his chair halfway
across the floor.

> "Bastard?" Darcy spoke with heightened color. "I urge
> you to tread lightly, madam."
> "And I urge you to recall your honor, sir. Fully half of
> London is aware that you and that woman . . . Decency
> prevents me describing it, the wanton, scandalous dis-
> play—"
> "Enough, madam. You have made your point. I have
> only myself to blame."

Knightley turned the page and found another passage.

"He quitted the room and, with a nod to the servant, the house as well, undone by the destruction of his hopes. But even in the scorch of Elizabeth Bennet's words the burn of a more distant brand rose in his memory: that of Lady Quillan's lips.' "

" 'Lady Quillan's *lips*?!" Magnus shouted. "What the bloody hell is going on?!"

Miss Clarkson appeared instantly.

"Get me that woman's phone number," he commanded. "Flip Allison. She works at the Aviary."

He paged furiously past the scene and before it, and noticed a few more changes, though these were only nuances. He flipped to the front and scanned the early chapters, as familiar to him as his family, and saw there nothing amiss and certainly no mention of a Lady Quillan. It was as if someone had taken a glass of cheap wine and flung it into the middle of the book, letting the cloying stain spread slowly to each side.

What had she said? The book changed after a massage—no, after a dream after a massage, when the masseuse had said she could imagine herself in a book.

Whatever mischief this had been, he'd make her pay for it. That edition was worth a thousand dollars, and the one in the library was practically priceless.

"They wouldn't give me her number," said Miss Clarkson, who'd reappeared in his doorway. "They said it's against policy. She'll be in tomorrow. But there's a Robert Allison listed in the phonebook—in Cranberry.

Robert? he thought, irrationally indignant. Robert who was unimaginative enough to live in Cranberry, a soulless tract of wretched McMansions in the far suburbs, and yet still capable of attracting a firebrand like Flip Allison? Robert, the deadly dull little squit who probably couldn't—

"Sir," Miss Clarkson said, evidently for a second time and considerably louder. "There's a second Allison, sorry. It was at the bottom of the previous column. A P. Allison in Mount Washington."

"Oh." He relaxed. "Clearly that's her. Philippa, you know."

Miss Clarkson gave him an odd look. "No, I didn't know. Do you want me to give you the phone number?"

"Yes, actually." Then he looked at the desecrated book in his hand and the spell broke. "No. Give me the bloody address."

Io scanned the pages, careful to ensure the walls of the library's study carrel kept her hidden from the rest of the room. She didn't know much about pigeons except that they shit everywhere, ate garbage, and that she wasn't very good at plinking them off the pool patio in Sewickley with her father's rifle. Her phone was on the desk in front of her, with the picture of the unusual red-tinged bird on the screen. If she leaned slightly, she could see the back of Jed's beret six tables over, looking at the same sort of book. He hadn't spotted her.

She had an odd sensation on her ass, like burning, and wondered if the maid had washed her clothes in the wrong detergent again. *Stupid slut.*

From what she could tell the picture she'd taken was of a passenger pigeon, but she didn't know how that could be possible since the book she was looking at clearly said the passenger pigeon was extinct—extinct, in fact, since 1914. And she might not know a lot about birds, but she knew enough to know the bird in Jed's ex-wife's purse had not been dead a hundred years.

Christ, she thought, fidgeting, the detergent's killing me.

She dug a discreet hand in her jeans and scratched her right ass cheek, then she did the same with her left. A fat, curly-haired guy caught her doing it and snickered. She gave him the finger.

Jed snapped his book closed, which caused Io to lean back. She watched him stand and wander back into the stacks. She followed, keeping her distance. He lounged for a moment in front of a stack nowhere near the bird section. Now what? She found a good observation point, between two deserted shelves, where she could see him over a stack of books.

Christ Almighty! What the fuck was going on?

The itch was getting worse. It felt like acid eating into her flesh. She tried scratching but her jeans were so tight she could barely maneuver.

Jed selected a book and tucked it under his arm, strolling into the men's room with a hand on his belt.

Great, Io thought. This'll be a ten-minute wait easily. Holy hell! The itch was getting unbearable!

She had to reach the bottom of those cheeks.

Jed finished his business.

The Historical Sites of the Windward Islands was not exactly his choice of reading material for a good, relaxing crap. He preferred either *Sports Illustrated* or *Jugs,* but since both were back in his office, he grabbed what he could. At least there'd been pictures.

He washed his hands and dropped the book on a shelf by the door. Then he reached into his back pocket and pulled out a utility knife. The longest blade was only about four inches, but still he thought it would do the job.

He tucked it under his arm and headed toward the rental lockers.

With a depressing feeling this shift might never end, Bob dug diligently in the bottom drawer for any remaining copies of the Graduate Student Room permission forms. Manuel was at the counter trying to settle a recall dispute with a history prof who thought fifteen months was a perfectly reasonable amount of time to keep the only copy of *The Roots of Evangelical Christianity in Colonial America* east of the Mississippi checked out.

It had been one of those bizarre days. First the woman and the case, then the passenger pigeon stuff, and now the online form system had gone on the fritz. He'd be glad when ten o'clock rolled around. Not that he had anything better to do at his apartment, but at least he'd—

What the . . . ?

He cocked his head, unable to believe what he was seeing on the security screen. Some blonde deep in the fourth-floor stacks was bent over a table, jeans down to her knees, scratching her bare thonged ass like she was possessed. He'd now officially seen it all.

Bob shook his head. "Manuel," he called.

Manuel was still deep in the allocation-of-shared-resource argument with the professor, but turned and lifted a brow.

Bob inclined his head meaningfully toward the screens. "There's an issue here you're going to want to take a look at."

Jed loped toward the lockers and found 4613. The book on passenger pigeons had mentioned nothing about potential cloning, though it had been published four years ago and a lot had changed in that area since. He'd thought about taking the time to check periodicals, but decided he'd give that assignment to an intern. They ate that sort of shit up. But if there was something important to be found, he'd find it in her locker. Flip had been hiding out in the library for weeks.

It was close to dinnertime, and if there was one thing he knew about students it was they never missed a meal, so the library was pretty quiet. Nonetheless, he scanned the ceiling until he found the video cameras and casually adjusted his position so that his body blocked the view of the flimsy combination lock built into 4613's door.

He pretended to examine an ancient framed print of Fort Duquesne, and when the last visitor had passed, he jabbed the blade into a space between the circular lock and the door, lifted up his heel and kicked.

The bolt made a *crack*. He kicked it again, the knife fell to the ground, and the door opened. He looked inside. She had a stack of books here as well as a couple legal pads, two mechanical pencils, a water bottle and a Gap bag with running shorts and a T-shirt in it. He sniffed. Flip's scent—a combination of vanilla and sweat—still made his balls do the cha-cha-cha. After five Long Island iced teas at last year's holiday party, he'd offered to resume the fucking part of their relationship whenever she wanted. She'd looked at him with those smoky gray eyes of hers, all grateful and shit, and told him to go to the storage room and "get ready, if you know what I mean." Oh, he knew what she'd meant. She said she'd be there in five minutes. He'd waited twenty before passing out in the broken office chair, and the cleaning crew had found him two hours later with his pants unzipped and a fifty-pound-test-line boner waving in the wind.

Babes. He'd never figure 'em out.

He carried the books, legal pads and photocopies to the closest empty table. He was just about to examine his findings when a movement in the stacks caught his eye. The profile of a magnificent bare ass was sticking just into view, wriggling for all it was worth. Ah, he recognized that movement. Some lucky guy was getting his knob polished.

Well, I suppose these books can wait, he thought, leaning back to enjoy the show. At the rate this babe's working, that poor bastard isn't going to last another thirty—

"Excuse me. Do you know where the restrooms are?"

A blue-haired old lady with a face like a bagel stood over his shoulder. He toyed with the idea of sending her in the direction of the letters-to-Penthouse stack, but a fraternal sense of loyalty kept him from ruining this guy's party. He pointed around the corner and turned his gaze back to the Cinemax After Dark channel, but the wriggling ass was gone.

Hell's bells.

Flip's books spanned an interesting range: Rachel Carson's *Silent Spring*, a gazetteer of Pennsylvania, the writings of Charles Darwin, *Conserving Biodiversity*, and one of those ridiculous romances she was always reading. He opened it to the earmarked page and scanned a few paragraphs. The hero strips while the heroine watches. What was the big deal? Flip had gotten to see The Pose whenever she wanted.

He abandoned the book and looked at the legal pads. An outline of the presentation she'd been asked to make at the Association of Field Ornithologists conference as well as the first couple pages of a rough draft. He snorted grudgingly. She'd made some interesting points. Nothing on the passenger pigeon or cloning, though. Then he paged through the photocopies. There were several articles from *Studies in Avian Biology* and *The Auk,* even an article he'd authored on the red-tailed hawk. And of course the latest article on the ivory bill. He rolled his eyes. She lacked the objectivity of a world-class birder. He was about to give up when something folded in the back of the legal pad caught his eye. He opened it.

It was a copy of an application for that Cornell position. *Her* application. Goddamn. She'd never said a word about applying, not even after he'd told her he'd applied. Not that it would matter, of course. Why hire the apprentice when you can hire the master?

He sat up straighter.

Unless she'd told them about the passenger pigeon. In fact, maybe that's why her presentation for the Association of Field Ornithologists conference looked like it was barely begun. She'd probably abandoned that idea and begun writing up the cloning experiment.

The conference would be the perfect place to announce these kinds of findings. But no, that didn't make sense. Cloning was completely unethical. She'd be censured, booed out of the auditorium. That wasn't ornithology. Hell, it wasn't even conservation. It was crass exploitation. Where was the win for your career in that?

Unless . . .

Unless you weren't going to tell anyone the bird was cloned.

Shit. He needed a piece of this action.

Chapter Twelve

Flip fumed the entire way to her apartment—from the bus ride from Oakland to downtown, where she alternately froze in the air conditioning and suffocated in the fug of wet, warm bodies, to the short train ride across the river, where not only did no one offer a muddy, soaked woman a seat, but one man actually had the gall to snicker when her soaking shoes farted, to the glorious climb up Mount Washington on the Monongahela Incline, where a tipsy businessman openly ogled her wet T-shirt. Charming.

Knightley was a prick. There was no doubt about that, and those single-malt eyes weren't going to change it. If he wouldn't get her in to see that book, she'd find someone who would.

But first she was going to get out of these disgusting clothes, take a quick hot shower and toss down a drink.

She was climbing the outside side stairway to the attic apartment her landlord had carved out of his turn-of-the-century house when her phone rang. *Christ Almighty.* Jed again.

"*What?*"

"Calm down, sugar. I'm going to be doing you a big favor."

Flip groaned. The last time Jed offered to do her a "favor," the cleaning crew at work had ended up reporting him to HR. This favor didn't sound any more attractive than the last one. She hoisted the phone to her shoulder as she worked her key in the lock. "Really?"

"You bet. I found your purse at work. I thought I'd drop it off."

"You know what? Let me save you a trip. Just leave it in my drawer, okay?" She swung open the door and kicked off her wet, socially tactless shoes.

"I'm already in the Porsche, babe. It's no problem."

"Really, Jed. You can give it to me tomorrow." The A/C was killing her. If she didn't get these clothes off soon, she was going to go mad.

"You know what else, Flip? I found out you and I have something else in common—an uncommon interest in Cornell."

Her heart stalled. How the hell had he found out about that?

"Oooh, kinda quiet on your end," he said. "Guess you forgot to mention it to me."

"Didn't realize I had to get your permission."

"No, but now you're going to need my cooperation. So why don't I drop by, give you the purse, and we can talk?"

"Forget it, Jed. I'm not even home tonight."

She clicked off the phone and threw it into the closest chair. Off came the T-shirt, which she flung to the floor. Scruffy began to scrabble in the back bedroom. Some people had dogs. She had a bird. "Be there in a minute," she called. "I'm going to shower first."

She peeled off her socks, which were disgusting, and kicked off her cargo pants. At the bathroom door, she dropped her panties and her bra. The bathroom rug felt warm and lusciously dry under her feet. She was just about to turn on the water—good and hot—when her cell rang again.

"Christ!"

She cranked the water up high and marched into the living room. The place was small, but the ceilings were high and the far window in the living room provided not only a sweeping view of the city skyline but a literal bird's-eye view of the hawks that floated on the updrafts along Mount Washington. After her divorce, this apartment represented pure freedom to her. She hoped no one in the PPG Tower across the river had his binoculars out today.

"What, what, what, what, *what?*" she demanded after jerking open the phone.

"That's pleasant," Claudia replied. "I can't imagine why anyone would think you have an attitude problem."

"Oh, sorry." Flip bit her lip. "I've had a lousy afternoon. I thought it was Jed. What's up?"

"What's up? I'm on my way, remember? I've got the wings. I'll be there in two minutes, then it's off to my board meeting."

"Oh, cripes." Flip considered the wet clothes strewn about the floor and the enchanting *shhhhhh* of the shower. "Look, I'm filthy and freezing, and I gotta take a shower. I'll leave the door unlocked, okay?"

"No prob. See you in a flash."

Magnus parked his Audi on the street and looked at the address he'd written down.

Flip, he thought absently, the perfect sort of nickname for a woman who upends everything she touches. Sort of like a WMD in running shoes.

The squat, turn-of-the-century two-story with the wrap-around porch was on the low-rent side of the street. Mount Washington was an interesting mix of ethnic groups and socioeconomic levels, perched on a hillside overlooking Pittsburgh's downtown, and Grandview Avenue, which ran the length of the ridge, was made up of million-dollar condos and town houses on the side with the view and small blue-collar homes on the other. The yellow traffic line down the middle of the street might as well be Hadrian's Wall. Come to think of it, Flip Allison had a lot in common with the blue-painted barbarians Hadrian had been trying to deter.

Immediately an image of that wispy bit of blue lingerie floated through his thoughts. Even barbarians had their finer points, he considered.

He tucked his volume of *Pride and Prejudice* under his arm and made his way up the walk. The front door had little plastic signs beside it: DIBARTOLO/DOWNSTAIRS and ALLISON/UPSTAIRS. The latter had a hand-drawn arrow on it pointing left and up. He walked over and looked around the edge of the house. Hugging the side was a narrow black metal staircase weaving its way up to the top floor. A pot of fat pink geraniums sat at the top landing, and a black letterbox hung at the base. It definitely had the look of a separate apartment. He mounted the stairs and found birdfeeders filled with sunflower and thistle seeds. There you have it, he thought. It has to be her.

He knocked. The watery sounds of a dishwasher filled the space beyond, but no one answered. He knocked again, this time louder. Still no answer. He tried one last loud *rap-rap-rap*.

"Come in!" she bellowed. "Your book's on the table."

He frowned but turned the knob, hoping she'd be standing there to greet him. It made him uncomfortable to enter the place without her knowing it was him.

The hall was empty save a coatrack and table. His discomfort grew as he realized the sounds he'd heard were not the dishwasher, but the shower, which thundered in the distance, and he almost retreated before he remembered "the brand of Lady Quillan's lips" and any hesitation disappeared.

He gazed into the living area. The room held a small sofa, bookcases and a coffee table at one end, and a round dining table with four chairs at the other. A galley kitchen overlooked the dining area. The apartment, he noted with definite interest, looked too small for two.

"Miss Allison?" he called tentatively, then stopped. On the floor in the middle of the living area lay her trousers. And directly beyond that was a provocative trail of dark blue satin. She'd shed her clothes like a snake. The panties were a good ten feet from the bathroom door. In his mind he saw those final breathtaking steps toward the shower. . . .

He blew out a long stream of air.

"It's Magnus Knightley," he called.

"Can't hear you! Sorry," came a bellow from the shower. "Christ, Claudia, what an awful day. You wouldn't believe it if I told you."

"Miss Allis—"

"I met the world's biggest blowhard."

Magnus stopped.

"An Englishman," she called in a labored accent somewhere between Winston Churchill and Dick Van Dyke in *Mary Poppins*.

Americans, Magnus thought with a shudder. An unperceptive breed, the lot of them.

She added, "Ass like Brad Pitt, though."

Well, perhaps he'd been a tad hasty. He stole a glance at his reflection in the window.

He was unsure how to proceed. The woman clearly had no plans to end this outpouring, and nothing short of opening the bathroom door was likely to stop her. And while there were certainly pluses to that idea, it was unlikely to move them toward the constructive end he desired.

The doorbell rang and he started. How had he missed a doorbell?

"If that's my ex," Flip shouted, "tell him to drop dead. He calls me today to complain that I'm applying to Cornell. What an asshole. Worst part is, I really wanted that job. I haven't had a date in two years, he has to rub my nose in the fact that he's boffing some worthless bit of blonde undergraduate fluff in a Clash T-shirt she probably stole from her mother, and of course he and his damn curriculum vitae are gonna trump me out of a fellowship he has no business even applying for."

The bell changed to a more aggressive knock. Magnus shrugged and made his way to the door. He opened it to a well-dressed woman of just under forty with reddish blonde hair pulled into an artful knot. She held a take-away bag, and when she saw him, her eyes widened and a corner of her mouth lifted with innuendo.

Magnus gave her an unreadable smile. "Your book's on the table."

She walked into the living area, head angled to continue the inventory she was taking of him. When she noticed the trail of Flip's discarded clothing, she stopped the surreptitious observation and moved to unabashed visual assault.

Magnus crossed his arms, attempting to fend off the

gamma-ray level of question marks coming at him. She dropped the food on the table and picked up the book. It was, he noticed, *Pride and Prejudice*. The plot, so to speak, thickened.

"Interesting book choice," he said. "Are you and Flip working on something together?"

She squinted an eye at the admittedly odd question. "Only if you call a book club working on something."

He scanned her face. Nothing suggested subterfuge. Everything, on the other hand, suggested white-hot curiosity. He wished he'd thought to bring a lead apron and goggles.

"What about you?" she asked. "What exactly are you two working on?"

"Nothing to speak of."

The silence grew heavier. The shower roared on.

"You know," she said, tapping her finger on her thigh, "Flip's ex-husband Jed was a real jerk. Put her through hell. I mean, like, fourteen months before toast stopped making her cry. You're not a jerk, are you?"

"Er, Magnus Knightley." He put down his book and extended a hand. "Visiting scholar at the university."

She shook it. "Claudia Talbot. Best friend. What sort of scholarship?"

"Jane Austen, actually."

"Wow. Now that's the sort of book club preparation I like to see. Will you be coming on Thursday?"

"Not," he said pointedly, "if my life depended upon it."

"Well, consider yourself invited nonetheless. The party's at Eve Bloomberg's. Gateway Towers, eighth floor, six o'clock."

"You're too kind."

Magnus waited. Claudia reshouldered her purse and headed for the door. In the hall, she paused. Her eyes flicked once more to the bra and panties, and she smiled. "You'll make sure she's all buttoned up by then, will you? It's been a long time since she covered this kind of material."

Magnus gave her half a bow. Claudia chuckled and left.

And still the water ran. Magnus slumped onto the sofa. A jerk, was it? A jerk was one thing. A lot of men got accused of that. But a jerk who made her cry for fourteen months? That was something else entirely. Flip seemed as tough as nails. It had to be something more than professional competitiveness over whatever this much-longed-for Cornell assignment was. Cheating, perhaps? No. A man that cheated on her would be more likely to be rewarded with a butcher knife between his shoulder blades than tears. What on earth could make Flip Allison cry? He felt an inexplicable sense of protectiveness rise within him.

Protectiveness and . . . something else. Something admittedly less protective.

His thoughts trailed to those bits of silk on the floor and then farther back to the very wet, very clingy shirt of this afternoon and even farther to the provocative tilt of a café chair and that heart-stopping, gorgeous round ass. Then he remembered his damn second edition and still another feeling, equally as potent, stirred. He couldn't imagine what action he could take that would satisfy all three urges. Anything he thought of—and he let a number of interesting options play out in his head—seemed to fulfill him in one area but leave him wanting in another. He wondered if all American women were like this.

He also wondered what sort of mischief this so-called book club might be involved in and whether it was connected to Flip's interest in the library's first edition or to the changes he'd seen in his second edition. The latter wasn't impossible to imagine, after all. He'd once heard of a woman who'd bought an early edition of *Gone with the Wind* and paid an expert archivist to change the ending so that Rhett and Scarlett ended up together.

Another knock came at the door. Good God, it was like rush hour at Paddington Station. He decided Flip could answer her own damn door. The visitor knocked again, but it was the curious *che-che-che* that followed that made Magnus sit up. Whoever it was, was using a key. He unfolded himself to full height.

A man in an egregious beret slipped silently into the hall. He was holding a woman's purse. The man had not noticed him.

Magnus was tall, a good four inches taller than the new visitor, and had learned early in life that height, properly employed, not only offered an effective threat but established an immediate male hierarchy. And there was something about this man that called for immediate hierarchy establishment. Magnus squared his shoulders and cleared his throat.

The man jumped. "Holy crap! You scared the shit out of me. Where's Flip?"

"In the shower." Magnus invested the words with as much probable cause as he could.

The man did not try to hide the mixture of prurient interest and shock with which he now observed Magnus. Magnus could almost see the little beret-covered wheels turn as the man tried to put two and two together. He reminded Magnus of his former brother-in-law, Dougal, the high-powered ad exec with the Northumberland accent who'd charmed his younger sister out of her knickers, then her self-respect. He felt his blood begin to simmer.

"You're a Brit, huh?" the man said.

"Indeed."

"You a friend of Flip's?"

"A friend? No, I wouldn't call it that." Magnus smiled. "Does Flip know you have a key?"

Terror flashed briefly across the man's face before the Southern smoothness resettled itself. "She and I have an understanding." He gave Magnus his own suggestion-filled smile. "She does what she wants. I do what I want."

Behold the jerk ex-husband. "You must be Jed."

"She mentioned me?" A spark of adolescent pleasure appeared in his eyes.

"In a manner of speaking. You're her colleague, correct? We were talking about potential references."

Jed narrowed his eyes. The wheels were really turning now. "Yeah, sure, I can provide one, I guess."

"Actually, we decided it wasn't necessary. Her résumé can stand on its own."

Dubious amusement rose on the man's face, and Magnus felt his fist tighten. He had the guy's number. Just like Dougal, he depended on subtle but relentless condescension to keep his women in their place.

Jed extended a hand. "Jed Hughes."

Magnus had to concentrate to keep from snapping it off at the wrist. "Magnus Knightley. Cornell."

Jed's jaw dropped to his sandals. "C-Cornell? You here for a conference?"

"Actually, I'm here for dinner. Oh, I see, you mean 'here' in general. No, not a conference." It was juvenile and he'd probably regret it, but Magnus felt a deep sense of satisfaction as Jed's face filled with uncertainty.

"You, ah, here about the fellowship?" Jed asked.

"Fellowship?" Magnus could almost see the smoke curling up from the beret. "About the ivory bill, you mean?"

Jed nodded slowly.

"Yes, I suppose you could say that's the case." He laughed. "We're supposed to be doing the interviewing on the QT."

"Interviewing?" Jed's eyes bulged. "You're interviewing Flip?"

"Yes."

"Have all of the interviews been set?"

"There are very few, actually. And yes."

Jed turned a quarter circle, rubbing his temples, clearly frazzled. He was still trying to deal with this grenade when his eyes came upon the discarded lingerie.

Ka-boom.

Jed brought his horrified gaze to Magnus, who did nothing to shrug off the unspoken accusation.

"Drink?" Magnus suggested.

"I-I—"

"You look like you could use one." Magnus stepped into the narrow kitchen and put his palms together like a gracious host. "What'll it be?"

"I—Anything, I guess."

"Super. Let's see." He opened the refrigerator door with the bluff assurance of someone who'd already spent untold hours here. "I think there might still be some wine . . . er, tequila in here." Tequila. Jesus Christ. Apart from that the refrigerator held three yogurts, nail polish and something that looked like it might once have been an orange. All at once he had a vision of licking a dollop of yogurt out of Flip Allison's navel.

Whoa!

"Yeah, a shot of that." Jed dropped onto the stool on the

other side of the kitchen pass-through and eyed Magnus with incomprehension. "Is she likely to get the fellowship?"

"I probably shouldn't be saying this"—well, that was certainly the case—"but yes."

"Wow." Jed looked like he'd swallowed a boulder.

"It wasn't so much her credentials," Magnus went on as he attempted to guess where either the shot glasses or the salt would be. "We see dozens of assholes with credentials as long as your arm. You know the type: self-important; recognition more important than the subject matter itself; not happy unless every student in the room is fawning all over them."

"Blowhards," Jed affirmed, head in his hands.

Magnus frowned. "Er, perhaps that's overstating it." The cabinet over the dishwasher held cereal, two mugs and a bowl, and the one next to that held six bags of birdseed, a can of WD-40 and a chipped wineglass. "Flip's scholarship is, of course, impeccable, but more than that, she has a passion . . ."—he let his eyes drift over the clothes on the floor—"that's simply remarkable." Try that on, you irritating little prick.

Jed chewed at a nail, pinched with raw insecurity. After a moment he said, "And how would you feel about a candidate that's done something unethical?"

Magnus snagged the wineglass. He pushed the bottle and glass toward Jed. "Depends what you mean by 'unethical.' Are you suggesting something like undermining a friend or cheating on a spouse?" He gave Jed a long look. "Things like that would be contemptible, of course, but would hardly merit being dismissed from consideration. We're talking about one of the most important potential findings of the last hundred years, after all."

Jed poured himself a good three fingers of tequila and downed half in a single gulp. "Try cloning," he said, wiping his mouth.

Was the man institutionable? A woman who couldn't manage to carry an umbrella in a rainstorm involved with cloning? "Ah, yes. Long rumored and little evidenced. Has Flip been cloning?"

"I think you might be surprised."

"I think I might be as well." Magnus was starting to get nervous. Flip would finish soon and this was going to stop being fun and start being seriously embarrassing. "You know, I doubt Flip's going to want to find a colleague here when she steps out of the shower, so if you could wait outside . . ."

Jed slitted an eye and gazed at Magnus skeptically. "You know, you don't really strike me as Flip's type."

"Really? Perhaps you don't know Flip as well as you think."

The shower stopped. Jed made no move to leave. *Hell.*

Magnus grabbed a mug and poured himself a generous portion of tequila, waiting for everything to blow up in his face.

Chapter Thirteen

Flip cracked the bathroom door, letting a cloud of steam escape, and felt the crisp, cool air swirl over her body. She leaned down to straighten the rug and, as an afterthought, tightened the thick white towel around her body. She felt like she'd exiled half her problems down the drain. The other half she'd face with renewed strength and, more important, dry clothes.

She opened the door and nearly shrieked. Magnus Knightley was standing in the middle of her kitchen!

"What the hell—"

"Flip," Knightley said with exaggerated care, "your colleague Jed was just telling me he didn't know you were being interviewed for the Cornell fellowship."

She spun her head and saw her ex-husband standing there too.

Knightley went on, "I told him how excited we were to receive your application."

Application? Cornell? Knightley? What the freakin' H was going on? She felt almost dizzy and distinctly underdressed.

Knightley held her gaze hard. "You are still interested in the fellowship, aren't you?"

"Of course I am."

"I thought so. Your colleague offered to write a recommendation. I told him we didn't need one. Your résumé stands on its own."

She looked at Jed. He looked like little Karen after she'd watched Frosty the Snowman melt in the hothouse. Magnus walked to her and put a mug in her hand. "Tequila," he said, smiling.

She took a big gulp.

"Baby," Jed said, "we gotta talk."

Flip narrowed her eyes. She'd deal with Knightley later. "I'm busy, Jed. And I believe I told you not to come."

"You also told me you weren't going to be home. I have your purse." He held up her bag.

"Leave it at the front door on your way out."

Jed tilted his head toward Knightley, who was pouring a second mug of tequila. "I need to talk to you in private. Why don't you ask Romeo to take a walk?"

Romeo? Flip looked at Knightley, who gave her a weak smile and shrugged.

"No," she said to Jed.

Jed's cell phone rang. He looked at it and answered. "Hey, baby, listen, I'm kinda in the middle of something."

Under cover of Jed's conversation, Knightley sauntered again to Flip's side and tapped the mugs. "He broke in," he said under his breath. "He thinks I'm from Cornell and you're our top candidate—oh, and for some reason he seems to be under the impression we're sleeping together."

"*What?!*"

Jed snapped his phone shut, and Knightley broke away.

"Don't blow me off, Flip," Jed said. "Or any chance of you getting that fellowship is gonna be whisked away."

God, she hated that smug, imperturbable confidence. How had she ever found that attractive? She wished, just for once, she could do something to knock that bastard completely off his superior feet.

"Her fellowship," Knightley put in coolly, "is exceedingly secure."

Go, Knightley! Total lie, but go!

"Cut the crap," Jed said, cheeks flushing. "Tell me you don't have candidates better qualified than Flip."

Uh-oh. Jed was going day care. Flip's toes curled in pleasure. In another minute he'd be beet red, pounding his fists and feet on the floor.

"Better candidates?" Knightley swirled his mug casually. "Like you, for example, Mr. Hughes?"

The red spread to Jed's ears. "Yes, like me," he said belligerently.

"Let me make myself clear," Knightley said. "Cornell is not looking for someone with the longest résumé. We're looking for someone who approaches the ivory-bill project with hope—more than hope, in fact. We're looking for someone with a determination that it has to be. What did Saint Augustine say? 'Faith is to believe what you do not see; the reward of this faith is to see what you believe.' "

Flip swung around. Was he mocking her?

"That is the most idiotic thing I've ever heard," Jed cried. "That's not science. That's, that's . . . Oprah! Listen, you. I know exactly what's going on here," he said, shaking the purse in Flip's direction and taking a step forward.

It was like someone had thrown a switch. Knightley snapped an iron fist around Jed's wrist, and his single-malt eyes sparked golden fire.

"I'm certain," Knightley said with dangerous precision,

"you do not mean to be making a threatening gesture toward our hostess. Now hand her the purse." He jerked Jed a half step forward and twisted. Jed squealed, spilling the tequila in his other hand, and the bag dropped at her feet. Knightley released him.

Jed rubbed his wrist. "Relax, buddy. I only want to talk."

Knightley slouched against the doorjamb, keeping his eyes hard on Jed. "Do you want to talk, Flip?"

"No."

Magnus crossed his arms. "Good evening, Mr. Hughes."

Jed stood, nostrils flaring, and looked at Flip. "Maybe the words 'passenger pigeon' will change your mind."

The words hit her like a Mack truck. The only way Jed could possibly know about that would be if it now appeared in *Pride and Prejudice*. For God's sake, the man never read anything that wasn't either about birds or printed on glossy paper with a foldout in the center. He'd hardly have picked up Jane Austen.

Panicked, Flip looked at Jed and back at Knightley. "Why don't I just talk to him for a minute? We could get this out of the way and him out of our hair. Please."

Jed gave Knightley a triumphant look. "Alone, if you don't mind," Jed added.

Flip didn't know why she felt such a stab of disloyalty. She'd known Magnus Knightley for all of six hours. But it was with considerable regret she pointed him in the direction of her sleeping area at the back of the apartment. Knightley held up his hands in surrender and walked where she pointed.

Since she used the apartment's only real bedroom as a playroom for sick birds, the little area was really just a large hallway outside the storage room, separated by a curtain from the rest of the apartment. But in it she had arranged a single bed on a platform, a small chest of drawers with a mirror and her grandmother's slipper chair. Ugh, she thought, embarrassed, as Knightley settled onto the mauve silk seat. Nothing says you've got nothing going on like a single bed. At least she'd remembered to make it this morning.

Jed led her past the corner of the hall and the living room, out of sight of Knightley.

"Listen, babe. I want a piece of this," he said in a low voice. "You don't have the sway to get a buy-in from the ornithology world on your own. Add Jed Hughes as your coauthor, you may have a chance. It's your only hope. Otherwise I go to the AFO, and you'll get that pretty little ass of yours kicked out of ornithology forever."

"Jed, have you stopped taking your meds again?" She wanted to slug him, but she also wanted to find out how the hell he knew what he seemed to know.

"Oh, no, baby. I see the big time, just like you. And we'll be side by side, just like you always imagined. I'll give you twelve hours to make up your mind. Call me to tell me you're making me lead author or I'm going to the AFO."

"Lead? You said coauthor."

"My price went up." He tweaked her nose. "But you know it's always negotiable."

Her fist prickled. "Get out."

"And what's up with Prince Charles in there? There's no way you're balling that guy."

"So you're the expert on whom I'm balling now too?"

"It's not like it takes a lot of research time."

Flip felt the infamous Allison temper taking hold. It wasn't so much ferocity as stone-cold insanity. It emerged about once every seven years, like the locusts, and, like the locusts, produced intense localized destruction including at various times the end of her relationship with the best-looking veterinarian in western Pennsylvania, her ejection from the 2002 American Birding Association Northeast Regional Conference awards dinner and a Toyota Camry with a front end so badly damaged the body shop manager still used a picture of it as his screen saver—in short, the sorts of things you remember with a wince.

"Then I guess," she said to Jed with a slightly fanged smile, "you'd be surprised to discover that today's interview, which began in the library coffee shop, evolved to a hot striptease in the stacks before I found out why the tables in the Rare Book Room have to be bolted to the floor."

Jed looked like he'd been sucker punched. It was a good look on him. She hoped he'd sport it more often.

"Today?" he said, paling.

"Yes, today."

"Fourth floor?"

Didn't someone once say it's the details that make the lie? "Yes. Fourth floor."

"No," he said after a long internal debate. "I ain't buying it."

"Really?" Flip felt her sanity depart. It made the same you-got-it-nailed rumbling a bowling ball makes after it leaves your hand, and unless Jed dropped the Alabama asshole routine this was going to be the strike to end all strikes.

"Sorry, sugar. I think you're lyin'."

The pins blasted in every direction. "Magnus," she called.

He appeared at the corner in an instant, ready for action.

Which was a damned good thing, for she walked to him, put a hand on his cheek and dropped her towel. Magnus needed no further invitation. He pulled her taut—one hand fanned across the base of her back, the other twined deeply in her hair—and kissed her. His mouth was demanding and crisp, and he tasted faintly of caramel—exactly the way she'd imagined he would in the split second she'd had to imagine. Every nerve on her body jumped with the intensity of a pistol shot.

Magnus relaxed his hold but trailed a hand down her hip. "You called?"

She ducked under his arm, still inhaling his soapy, fresh scent, and snagged the towel. "Bye, Jed," she called over her shoulder and sauntered down the hall. The last thing she saw before pulling the curtain closed was Jed's astonished face and Magnus in a satisfied slouch, chivalrously nodding toward the front door.

Chapter Fourteen

She checked her lower back in the wardrobe mirror. Nope. No burn marks there, though it felt like Magnus's hand had left a permanent scorch.

The front door slammed. Jed. Good riddance.

Her insanity had shown itself in a variety of ways before but, she had to admit, retying the towel, never in so satisfying a way. Damn, that had felt good. How had Knightley known exactly where to press, so that she'd bend without thinking? Between the kiss and the dropped towel she was feeling more than a little adventurous. It had been the most glorious day she'd had in two years.

So don't stop, her inner voice said.

"Shut up," she whispered.

Chicken shit.

"Am not," she said. "Did you just see me, for God's sake? I was naked."

"Are you saying something?" Magnus asked and she jumped. He must have stayed where she'd left him, slouching in the hall on the other side of the curtain.

"No, just mumbling."

"You know," he said in a huskier voice, "that, ah, was rather nice."

"Yeah, thanks. Nice on this end too." *Oh, baby.* "I kinda hate to bring this up, seeing as how well things went and all, but, ah, do you mind telling me what you're doing here?"

"I want to talk to you. About the book."

"Oh?"

"We can talk when you're dressed," he said. "I'd rather do it face-to-face."

"But when did you arrive exactly?" She was trying to piece together the sequence of events in her head.

"Er, with Jed, essentially." Magnus cleared his throat. "Right before you came out."

She frowned. "But . . . did you see my friend, Claudia?"

"Ah . . . briefly. Flip?"

"Yep?" She grabbed a brush and pulled it through her hair. She hadn't washed it, so it was only damp from the rain, not soaked.

"Where are the dishtowels? I'll clean up the tequila."

"Gosh, sorry. First door on the right."

She heard the doorknob turn when it dawned on her. "I mean the left! Oh, wait! There's a bird in there—"

Magnus let out a blood-curdling yelp.

She flung back the curtain.

He was backed against the hall wall, hugging it, wide-eyed. "That's not a bird. That's a bloody blue emu!"

Scruffy strutted into the hall, head bobbing. He wasn't anything like an emu, Flip thought, though he was fairly dramatic for a pigeon. Two and a half feet tall with a cobalt blue body, maroon breast, piercing red eyes and a stunning mohawk of seven-inch-long lacy white-tipped feathers, Scruffy was a Victoria crowned pigeon, the largest and, to Flip's way of thinking, the most beautiful species of pigeon in the world.

Scruffy stopped at Magnus and cocked his head.

Magnus held the wall firmly. "Is he going to eat me?"

"Don't be silly. Pigeons don't eat vertebrates."

"He looks like he could eat an antelope."

"He's a Victoria crowned pigeon. *Goura victoria.* He's here for rehabilitation."

"Assault and battery?"

"He had a fungus on his foot. I keep him in the spare room there. He's separated from other birds, and I can still keep a close eye on him. The foot's almost healed, but I think we're going to have to send him back to the Philadelphia Zoo, which is where he came from."

"Why?"

She made a sad face. "He doesn't mate."

Magnus's squinched an eye. "Please don't tell me your work at the Aviary includes sexual surrogacy."

A bass drum–like *boom-boom-boom* filled the hall. If you haven't heard it before, the call of the Victoria crowned pigeon can be quite surprising. It was the sound of a symphony orchestra timpani drum coming out of a squat blue bird not much higher than your knee.

"My God!" Magnus said. "Is he going to explode?"

"Don't move."

Scruffy *boom-boom-boom*-ed again, this time flapping his wings and violently thrusting his head toward Magnus's feet.

"That's his mating call," Flip said, excited. "Look, it's your socks. He's attacking them!"

Scruffy continued his thrusting and flapping, pacing around Magnus's feet. Magnus shook his pant legs to hide the provocative bits of color.

"Oh no, don't," Flip said.

"I'm afraid I'm inciting him."

"You *are* inciting him. That's the whole point. Go, Scruff! Get him."

Scruffy boomed and flapped against Magnus's shoe.

Magnus managed a stoic smile. "May I say I find your hosting skills somewhat lacking?"

"Sorry, this is the first sign of mating we've seen in him. It has to be the color. He likes the lime green."

"I see. Er, I have to ask. Am I being wooed—or attacked?"

"Oh, wooed. If he saw you as a rival, he'd be trying to gouge you with his talons."

"Ah. Another day, perhaps."

Scruffy raised his head and let his feathers unruffle. The booms stopped. He raked Magnus with an intense ruby eye.

Magnus gave him a beseeching look. "Will you call me in the morning?"

Flip laughed. Scruffy hopped twice and flew to the top of the dining room radiator.

"He'll be okay there," she said. "I, ah, better get dressed."

Magnus held up his hands. "Not on my account."

Flip grinned. She ducked behind the curtain and closed it. Giddily, she opened the bottom drawer of the chest and scanned the contents for something nice. She didn't dress up a lot.

Maybe, the voice inside her said, *you won't be needing clothes.*

Well, that will certainly make getting him to open the case easier, she thought. Though it might cause some commotion in the library.

With a tug, she freed the towel and tossed it over the headboard. She heard Magnus daub up the spill. She wondered if he'd stay in the hall or retreat to the living room. The hall would definitely indicate more interest.

"Your ex is, uh, interesting," he said.

Still in the hall. She let out an inner cheer. "That's one word for it. By the way, I want to thank you. Even if it's only for one glorious night Jed Hughes will think I aced him out of a Cornell fellowship. That's worth a lot."

"I couldn't help myself. He's just such a bloody wanker."

"Don't take it personally. He has that effect on everyone. I know college girls are impressionable, but, honest to God, sometimes I wonder what it is they see in him."

"He's a professor?"

"Predator. Of rich, nubile young women, preferably with tits out to here, preferably covered with a T-shirt paying homage to some retro band Jed can claim an affinity for—in this case, The Clash."

"You're saying your ex-husband has a college-age girl-friend?"

"Oh yeah. Always. Currently named Io."

"Io?" Magnus cocked his head.

"Io."

"As in the moon of Jupiter?"

"Or E-eye-E-eye-O, depending on how you look at it."

"Rather a burden."

"I think the Mercedes makes up for it."

"So she's probably not losing sleep over it."

Flip grinned guiltily. "Well, possibly tonight she is, but not over her name. Jed likes to have sex in my office when I'm gone. He thinks I don't know, but, well, the cleaning crew at work are buddies of mine. Anyhow, long story, but I think Io probably won't be resting too comfortably tonight."

"Trouble in paradise?"

"Only if you call powdered poison ivy trouble."

"Ouch."

"Exactly."

"And spreadable by contact. Oh, dear, that's awkward."

"I know. I feel awful."

There was a long, companionable silence before Magnus added, "Anyhow, I enjoyed our little adventure tonight—all of it, actually."

The last words made her pulse boom almost as loud as Scruffy. "Yeah. Me, too."

She could see a sliver of Magnus's body beyond the curtain, and she realized with an electric shiver he could just as easily be seeing her. She should move, she considered. A step to the right would put her completely out of sight if in fact he was looking, though there was certainly no evidence he was.

If he's not looking, the voice said, *make him.*

No.

You're a chicken shit, and you never finish what you start.

When is enough, enough with you?

I'll know it when I see it.

"Fine. See this." She took a step to the left. If Magnus was looking—and, again, no evidence—he'd have a perfect view of her back, from shoulders to heels. Her heart pounded, but she held herself in place. She kept her eyes off the mirror, knowing her courage would fail if she saw him.

Hands shaking, she opened an upper drawer and chose a pair of sheer pink bikinis with three tiny pearls over her left hip. She wriggled the pair up her thighs. He'd seen her totally naked—well, glimpsed her—but this felt worlds different.

She thought she heard him move, but she wasn't sure.

She reached for a handful of bobby pins. This would be harder. Her breasts were her least favorite part of her body.

She forced herself into a quarter turn, giving him a perfect upturned profile. She wanted to melt, to disappear between the cracks in her oak-planked floor, but she remembered the fingers spread across her back and the buttery-sweet taste of his tongue and let the feeling push her past her fears.

She lifted her arms over her head, and slowly twisted her hair into a loose knot. One by one the pins went in, despite her quaking fingers. She swore she could feel the warmth of his gaze everywhere—her shoulders, her belly, the rise of her hip—and the heat rose to her cheeks. She felt tipsy, like she should giggle out loud, and she almost wished she had a nipple ring to tempt him with.

Then she saw it. Her shimmering pot of finishing powder.

She hardly ever wore it. She rarely wore makeup of any type except a little lipstick and a touch of mascara, but there it was, just waiting for her.

She reached for the brush. It was thick and wide, like a fan, and the hairs caught the loose powder like a bough of a fir tree catches flurries. The powder had a scent—she'd forgotten its name—but it reminded her of an island in the South Pacific with notes of jasmine and hibiscus. She brushed the powder over her shoulders. It left tiny sparks of light in its wake. Then she brought the brush around the curve of a breast. Immediately her nipple hardened. She flicked it, too, with the brush, enjoying the tickle in her belly. She dusted the other just as slowly and with equal effect.

You're an idiot, she thought. He's probably not even looking.

His loss.

She found the strapless bra that matched the panties, a confection of delicate pink lace with more pearls on its demicups. She wrapped it around herself and fastened it in the space between her breasts. There. Now it was no more than letting him see her in a bikini. She put on a pale blue A-line skirt, a white off-the-shoulder peasant blouse, and a pair of ankle-tie espadrilles in navy with tiny bugle beads.

Show's over, she thought, but she was still smiling.

She looked fabulous. Sun-kissed and man-kissed. Better than makeup. Now she'd be able to convince him to open the case. There was no doubt in her mind.

With a casual tug, she opened the curtain. If he'd been in the hall, he wasn't there now. She sashayed into the living room. He stood by the window, watching a rosy twilight stain the evening sky. When he heard her enter, he turned. Those topaz eyes betrayed nothing.

"Pretty," he said with feeling.

"Thank you." She curtsied. "Where's Scruffy?"

"I escorted him back to his room. Well, to be truthful, he walked back into his room and I closed the door."

She gave him her biggest smile. "I'd love for you to take me to the library now."

The corner of his mouth rose. "You think one kiss buys you that?"

"It was a bit more than a kiss, if you'll recall."

"Indeed. Almost a brand, I'd say."

There was something in his tone that made the hair on her neck stand up. "Brand?"

"Yes, apparently Lady Quillan's lips leave quite a memorable impression."

Flip's cheeks burst into flames. The only way he could know about Lady Quillan is if he'd seen a changed book.

"Lady Quillan's lips?" she said.

"I believe Darcy refers to them as a 'brand'."

Magnus knowing *Pride and Prejudice* had changed might be just what the man needed to get his ass in gear and get them into that case in the library, but the absolute last thing she wanted was him knowing any of the details of her dalliance with Darcy or, worse, Darcy's reasons for it.

"H-how do you know . . . ?" she stammered.

"My much-treasured second edition seems to have been tampered with," he said, and from out of nowhere what looked like a copy of *Pride and Prejudice* appeared in his hand. "If you're not careful you're going to owe me considerably more than you'll be able to repay with a kiss."

"Y-you have a second edition?" Flip felt like the air in the room had evaporated.

"I'll play along. Yes, I have a second edition. And I don't appreciate Darcy trotting about like a staghound in heat."

Flip held her breath, waiting to hear his horror over the Temple of Apollo scene, but nothing more came out.

"I've got to get into that case," she whispered. "Just take me there."

He gave her a thorough look, pursing his lips. "It's not that easy. There's a restriction on how often the book can be taken out of the case. Effects of handling, etcetera. I'd have to bend the rules pretty hard, and to do that, I'd have to be pretty motivated. Which in my mind would include hearing exactly what this escapade is really about."

She gulped.

Then something in her bookcase caught her eye. Her salvation. She hadn't been four-time champion of the annual Allison Family Thanksgiving Day Tournament for nothing.

"Scrabble," she said.

"What?"

"Scrabble," she said, marching over to the box. "You fancy yourself a player, I imagine. I'll play you for access."

"You'll lose."

"Then there's no risk, right?" She pulled the box out and set it on the coffee table.

"And what's in it for me?" he asked.

"What do you mean?"

"You win, I get you into the case. I win . . . what?"

She crossed her arms. He had an unnervingly wolfish look to him. "I don't know. Something."

"What could a woman like you offer, Flip?"

She shifted in the heat of his gaze. She wanted him to go for the wager. That meant what she risked had to be equally attractive. "Well . . ."

"Watering my plants for a month?"

The ass. "No," she said pointedly. "Better."

"Better is in the eye of the beholder. Have you ever been spanked?"

Her belly did a cartwheel. She never had and until this moment would have sworn she'd hate it, but the thought of submitting even briefly to those large capable hands while those knowing eyes drank her in made her nerve endings buzz. She tried to form a reply but only a breathy "Ah" came out.

"I'll take that as a no," he said. "Set up the board. First one to one hundred wins."

"Deal. But, please," she said with real feeling, "don't look at the book anymore."

Magnus hesitated for a moment, but handed it to her. She placed it on the table.

Magnus set up the game and drew a letter. T. Flip drew a C. Flip's letter came before his alphabetically. That meant she was first. She drew six more letters—R, P, I, K, O, and S—and added them to the C already on her rack. She handed him the bag.

Magnus paused. "Let's make it interesting, shall we?"

More interesting than getting spanked? Clearly Flip needed to get out more.

"What are the odds of making a bingo right out of the gate?" he asked. "Pretty low, right?"

"Yeah."

"Let's say if you make a bingo, game's over; you win; it's off to the library. If I win, well . . ." He twirled the bag in his hand.

Flip's mouth dried. Spanking? What had she been thinking? His lap was wide, and the more she stared at that hand, the more unforgiving it looked. She glanced at her tiles. She hadn't had time to think, but the mixture of letters—some vowels, a handful of workable consonants, and a high-value K to protect the C—looked good. "Yeah, sure."

Magnus picked his tiles, not one at a time as she had, but in a handful. *Handful.* She swallowed. He placed the first seven on his rack without looking and threw the remaining tiles back in the bag.

"Time per turn?" he asked.

She needed that edition fast. "Five minutes."

He nodded. "Ready?" he asked.

"Yes."

He looked at his watch and wrote down the time. "Go."

With a new underlying urgency, she went to work, moving

the tiles around the rack with clinical intensity as she waited for patterns to emerge. Magnus raised a brow at the *clack, clack, clack* for an instant but quickly returned to his own letters.

A bingo is a word that uses all seven tiles. Flip was comforted by the fact that it was easier to make a bingo on the first turn since you have that beautiful blank canvas in front of you, and, in any case, she knew it was going to be a helluva lot easier to reach a hundred before Mangus with the advantage of the first turn.

She stared at her letters. Jeez, what sort of man chooses a spanking? Then she had her answer: PRICK. It gave her a very respectable thirty-two for the turn and a fine editorial comment on the competition besides.

She laid it down, anchoring the K in the center, and picked up the S on her rack. PRICK or PRICKS? PRICKS only gave her two extra points but that S could be a lifesaver later. She brought the tile halfway to the board, then pulled it back. No, she decided. Save it.

She looked at him and smiled. "Prick."

He didn't bat an eye. Damned British reserve.

"Done?" he asked.

"Yes."

"Not a bingo."

Bite me. "No."

He wrote "32" on the score pad, crossed off her start time and wrote his.

"Wait!" Her heart fell. She should have put the P on the center tile, extending it from there which would have left the K for the double-letter square on the other side of the board. "I just need to move it," she said, miming a gentle shove.

"Turn's over." He looked at her as if to ask if she had the honor to abide by the rules or not.

Well, the answer was she did, and he could take his look and shove it. She leaned back in the chair, silent but definitely feeling the sting of those four missing points.

He picked up his rack with unsettling confidence. Her blood began to tingle. She couldn't decide if she wanted to be spanked or not. No was the obvious answer, but yes had some unexpected merit as well. Looks like you'd better make up your mind soon, Flip thought, given the way he had suddenly stopped looking at his tiles and was only scanning the board. A surprisingly simmering heat spread through her as she thought about being stretched out across his hips and clutching the frame of the couch as he rucked the fabric over her—

"Flip."

She leaped to her feet. "Yes? What? I thought I'd get myself a refill."

"Don't be long. This'll be fast."

She froze. Fast was bad. It was bad in sex, and it was definitely bad in Scrabble if describing the speed of one's competition. He picked up the first three of his tiles—all one could practically put down with one hand, even if one was going to play all seven—and stopped. He gave her an unreadable smile.

"Another thought," he said. "A sub-bet. A quickie, as it were."

"What?" she asked suspiciously.

"I'm about to play. Could be three letters. Could be seven letters. We know, of course, what happens if it's seven. But I can offer you a bit of insurance. Small premium, big protection."

"I don't need any protection." She was relieved she'd managed to keep the tremble out of her voice.

"Quite the boast from a woman who's established her credentials with nothing more than a tiny 'prick.' " He smiled.

"I suppose yours will be established with something far more impressive."

"That, of course, is the million-dollar question. My offer is this: take the chance I'm about to lay seven—"

Had she noticed a tiny emphasis on the word *lay*?

"—or be relieved of your panties."

"What?!"

"Your call." He settled back on the couch, arms extended along the back. She could almost feel herself wincing, waiting for that first *crack*. But the removal of her panties? Right now? With 100 percent certainty? A place deep in her belly was doing a very energetic rumba.

"No," she said. "I'll take the risk."

"As you wish." He leaned forward, rack still in hand, and *click*ed the first tile against the board four spaces above the P. God, that meant a word at least five letters long!

"No, wait!" she cried.

He drew back the letter and looked at her. "Wait?"

"Yes."

He reached for his mug of tequila and emptied it. God, she wished she had hers. He waited. She didn't move. Couldn't. It was like her arms and legs had turned to stone.

He sighed and clicked the next letter onto the board.

"No!"

His gaze cut to hers.

"Panties," she said in utter submission.

He dropped the letters onto the board. STRIPPED, built right onto the P in PRICK. Without a word, he leaned forward, ran his hands up her skirt, hooked her panties with his thumbs and tugged them over her ass. When they fluttered to her ankles, he stepped her out of them, snagged them with a finger and dropped them on the table beside him, like Bobby Fisher retiring a chess piece. Then he handed her the mug.

"I'd love a refill myself."

It was as if she *had* been spanked. Her cheeks burned—all four—and the trail of his touch felt like the smoldering remains of a lightning strike. Nonetheless, the risk had paid off. STRIPPED was a bingo, and she was still viewing the board from an upright position.

In the kitchen she found her mug and drained it, the smooth, spicy heat doing little to put out the internal fire. She poured more tequila into each mug and returned. The tile bag was on her seat. She handed him his drink, picked up the bag and sat down—carefully.

"Your turn to draw," he said.

She eyed the score. He'd gotten seventy-six including the fifty for the bingo. Christ, he was one turn away from breaking one hundred. She'd better make this turn count.

The first pull was a Q. Excellent. Then a blank. Better yet. A blank could be any letter, and a Q definitely benefited from a U. She needed sixty-eight to make a hundred.

"Do we need to make a hundred" she asked, giving him a cool, I'm-going-to-kick-your-ass look, "or break it?"

"Given the relative difference in our scores, is it really going to make a difference?" He took a sip. "Make is fine."

With a Q and a blank for a U her luck was picking up. She pulled a U and a Z. Wow. Maybe QUIZZING? Then she remembered the O and S still on her rack and the hope whooshed out of her like the air out of a balloon.

No QUIZZING out of these letters, and, worse, no other seven- or eight-letter word she could think of. Time to punt. But this guy was a player. No regular punt was going to do. She needed to put him on the defensive, and do it fast.

She opened her hand to show him the Q, Z and blank. "Pretty fine letters," she said with a big smile. "I've got one more to draw and QUIZZING is looking like a shoo-in to me. That leaves me with a win and you, well, empty-handed. So I'm willing to drop all my tiles back in the bag and draw again for a price."

"Not the case in the library, I hope. That's the game."

"QUIZZING *is* the game, pal."

"But you have one more letter to draw. Q-U-I-Z-Z-I-N-V"—he stressed the V—"gets you nothing."

"Ah, but QUIZ is good for sixty-one. That puts me within seven of a win."

"And me within twenty-four. And, somewhat significantly, I have a turn first."

"But you haven't drawn yet. You could end up in vowel town. A-E-I-O-U-U-U ain't gonna buy you much. You've been there, and so have I. I'm a tile away from a win. You're seven tiles away from God only knows what."

He pursed his lips. "And the price?"

She had to choose one carefully, she thought. Low enough to get him to agree and high enough to keep him from getting suspicious. A fine balance—she needed to be on and he needed to be thrown off. "The answer to a question."

"What question?"

She swirled the tequila in her mug and leaned back on an elbow. "What is it about you and the Rare Book Room that has so many people talking? Simple, huh?"

She watched the calculation behind those gold-brown

eyes. He knew exactly what she was asking and the answer he'd have to give. A little discomforting, yes, but in the scheme of the game, not much. She'd struck the perfect balance. And not only would she get to see him squirm, if she were honest, she was more than a little interested to hear the answer.

He tapped his fingers, debating. "I . . . don't think so."

"What was I thinking? Brits are far too reserved to talk about such matters."

"Yes, we lack that charming American openness that makes places like the waiting room at the DMV and Friday night at the shopping mall such a delight."

Tucking one leg beneath her and crossing the other over the first, she drew her skirt into a second skin over her unpantied ass and shrugged. "Your choice."

He licked a lip, visibly rethinking. "Um . . ."

"Um? Is that a yes?" She bent toward the table that was juuussssst out of reach.

"Yes." He sighed.

"Oh, goodie. Do tell." She put her elbows on knees and clasped her hands under her chin. "I'm all ears."

"Well . . ." He cleared his throat and appeared to consider his approach. "It seems the Rare Book Room offers men and women with a certain, well, taste for adventure the opportunity to satisfy that desire."

"Adventure?" she said guilelessly. "Like hang gliding?"

He refused to be baited.

"Not that," he said. "A two-person effort."

"Flag football? Charades? Quake online?"

"No," he said carefully, but hairline cracks were appearing in his composure. He searched for the word that would characterize the effort without fanning further prurient interest. "Coiting."

"Coiting?" she exclaimed. "Goodness, how quaint. I can just picture Ma in her kerchief and Pa in his cap. And what is it, might I ask, that brings such a sense of excitement to the undertaking? Is it the time of day, the position, the surroundings?"

"All of those things. Look," he said quickly, "I think I've answered your question. Are we done?"

"Almost." God, this was heaven! "And you yourself have partaken in this adventure?"

"Yes," he said with laser clarity.

"But I'm just not understanding the mechanics. Perhaps if you drew stick figures—"

"That'll be all, I think. Toss in your letters and redraw." He shoved the bag in her direction.

Ta-da! Clearly unbalanced, she thought happily and disposed of her letters. A quick shake of the bag and she drew again. Dammit. No high-point letters and no obvious bingo.

She shuffled the letters quickly as he drew his own. She could make UNLACED, using the C from PRICK. Cripes! Was there nothing better?

Magnus Knightley, hell's timekeeper, looked meaningfully at his watch.

Her eyes raced over the board: east, west, north, south. Nope, nothing else better.

Aaaarrghhh.

She put on her best "cares-be-damned" face and laid the tiles down. At least she'd nearly emptied her rack. That gave her some hope for the next turn—if there was a next turn.

"Twelve," she said, toting her points.

He looked at the word. "UNLACED? Foreshadowing my next prize, are you?"

The lace bra she'd recently donned immediately popped

into her head, and she wondered if he'd been watching her little reverse striptease. She looked into those eyes but as usual nothing was there but wry good humor at her expense.

She said, "It's hardly gentlemanly to make mention of something that was meant to be received in confidence." She crossed her arms over her chest. "Have you learned nothing from Darcy?"

The good humor turned to blank confusion but not, she swore, before she'd seen a flash of merriment.

"I was talking, Miss Allison, about your shoes."

Insufferable man.

"And," he said with a self-satisfied nod, "may I add to the theme?" He put down his letters, one at a time, starting with the K already on the board. K, N, E, E, L, I, N, G.

All of his tiles and on top of a Triple Word space, she thought. It was, like, a seven-hundred-point play. She was fucked. Literally.

"KNEELING," he said.

The terror rose from her toes, turning every muscle into quivering strawberry Jell-O.

He uncrossed his legs.

Honor was honor, but bare-assed on the lap of a man she'd just met? Her belly was saying yes, but her mind was running screaming for the fire escape. Between Darcy this morning and Magnus this afternoon, this day was going to be one for the record books.

Oh, Christ! Darcy! She'd nearly forgotten about him and the damned book. All this, and she'd still not have access to the library case.

Magnus took her hand. That damned tingle again. If she wasn't careful, she *would* forget about the book, and then where would she be? Sore bottomed and suffering the slings and arrows of global reader outrage, neither of which looked good on one's MySpace page.

"Look," she said, "let's deal."

"We dealt." He drew her toward the couch. "This is it."

"But a spanking is—"

"What I won," he said.

"Yes, but it's a lot. It's a pretty big prize." Shut up, she cried to her belly.

"I'll second that."

"And don't you want to show me the library, anyway?"

"Check with me in about two minutes. I'll be better positioned to answer the question." He made a broad Vanna White-type flourish across his lap.

The phone rang, and half of Flip knew for the first time what a prisoner on Death Row must feel like when the governor calls. The other half, however, was chugging margaritas and dancing the macarena.

"I should get that," she said.

"The machine will pick up."

And, in fact, the answering machine lurched to life. Flip prayed for something urgent—a break-in at the Aviary or nuclear disaster, for example—anything that might delay the inevitable. Magnus held her hand firmly.

"Hey, I'm out," said Flip's voice on the machine. "Leave me a message. I'll get back to you." The beep sounded.

"Hello," said a woman, uncertain. "I'm sorry to bother you, but Magnus Knightley's admin gave me this number. I already tried his cell phone."

The color drained from Magnus's face. He leaped to his feet and pelted toward the phone.

"Anyhow, this is Betty Scott. Please tell him I've had *Pride and Prejudice* moved to the Rare Book Room for him. It was no problem. He can come in anytime. Thanks."

The caller clicked off just as Magnus reached the receiver.

He lifted his shoulders sheepishly. "Apparently the restriction has been suspended."

Chapter Fifteen

"Just so you know," Flip said as she sailed past Knightley and into the library. "Darcy would never have lied about the difficulty of gaining access. Unlike some people, he is too well-bred."

"Oh, I see," Magnus said as they stopped at reception. "But bartering one's own spanking is considered the height of deportment?"

"One's potential spanking. After Betty Scott's revelatory phone call, that offer was moot."

Bob the librarian, who had been kneeling behind the counter, stood. Flip pinkened.

"Back for more wood pulp?" Bob asked. *"Truffula loraxa,* right?"

"What? Oh, that. No. I mean, yes." Flip smiled. "Rare Book Room for us."

Bob gave Magnus, who was already displaying his faculty ID, an appraising look. "Yes," Bob said. "Betty Scott gave us a call."

Flip waved the temporary pass from the afternoon. Bob gestured them through.

"Truffula loraxa?" Magnus repeated as they walked toward the elevator.

The case in front of them was gratifyingly empty. Flip maintained the air of a seasoned researcher. "Yes. From the Azores. Possibly connected to the extinction of the Biffer-Baum Bird."

"Hmm. You may want to cross-reference that with *Catina hata.* I believe there may be a connection."

Flip jabbed the Up button. Smart-ass.

The elevator was empty. The library was open until ten, and early evening represented the lull before the late-night storm of gunner students arriving for one more hour with their beloved primary sources. Flip kept her eyes on Knightley's polished leather brogues with the glimpse of lime cotton above them and drew in a lungful of his clean scent. He stared at the numbers above the door, though there was something in his manner that made her certain he was reliving her de-pantying. By the time the elevator opened on 4, a crackling electric charge had so filled the small space, Flip felt like she'd been blown out the door by a rocket launcher. She hoped the Rare Book Room came with fire extinguishers.

The thirtyish woman with her nose in her backpack at the Rare Book Room entry desk said automatically, "I'm sorry, we close in five—" then saw Magnus and gave him a sultry smile. "Professor Knightley, hello. Dr. Scott called. I'll set you up on two-A."

The woman said it with such devotion Flip wondered what else she'd set up for him there.

Magnus's ID disengaged the electronic lock and they entered the deserted room. With its bar-height tables, ascetic carpet and lack of chairs, it didn't exactly scream honeymoon suite at the Four Seasons, but, as she firmly reminded herself, that wasn't what they were there for, in any case.

She did note the table marked 2A was off the main room, tucked between two floor-to-ceiling bookcases that were stacked with ancient fat encyclopedias. Lights from the law school across the courtyard shone through three tall windows, parallel to which the table, with its slightly angled surface—kiss your pens good-bye—stood. Curlicues of wrought iron bolted across the windows served as decoration and security. A Merriam-Webster dictionary lay open on a decidedly unrare book stand under the center window.

No seating, no cushioned surface, and only the most bare-bones idea of privacy. Bare bones. Heh. She shifted nervously. Flip's imagination was broader than that of most, but not even Pamela Anderson and Tommy Lee could conjure this into a place for a quickie.

Magnus put a hand on her arm, and she started.

"The volume's here," he said.

The woman from the entry desk carried the book on a velvet-covered display to Magnus like she was delivering a scepter and orb to a Roman emperor. She jerked a thumb toward Flip. "Does she know how to do this?"

Flip sniffed. She wasn't sure to which "this" the woman referred, but Flip could assure her, her skills were both broad and well developed, thank you.

Magnus smiled. "I'll keep an eye on her."

Ah, condescension personified.

The woman placed the holder and book carefully on the table and dimmed the lights to their after-hours setting. "I'm heading to the main floor. Will you return the book to the table in the front and make sure the door clicks shut when you go?"

"We will," Magnus promised, and she left casting an admiring glow in his direction.

"The padded holder is to keep the spine from cracking," Magnus observed.

"Yes, thank you," Flip said snootily. "My last paper on Audubon would have been impossible without them." Flip had looked at Pitt's priceless John James Audubon folio here, but it had been for her own pleasure, not any paper.

Magnus reached for the volume. Flip threw herself in front of him.

"What are you doing?" he asked, though he appeared to have no objection to being temporarily diverted by Flip's special spine-protective padding now jutting his way.

"I would like to view the manuscript in private."

" 'Manuscript.' *Manu scriptus.* Latin noun. Masculine. Means 'written by hand.' The manuscript for *Pride and Prejudice,* which Austen wrote painstakingly in longhand at a small mahogany writing desk off and on over a period of seven years, is, sadly, not extant. This, my dear colleague, is an edition, a book or a volume. It is not a manuscript."

"Fine," she said curtly. "I would like to see the edition, book or volume in private."

Magnus snorted. "You expect me to allow the woman who has done irreparable harm to my second edition a single moment alone with a first? I'm afraid you have deceived yourself."

"It is apparently a night to be deceived, then, for I was also deceived in a most ungentlemanly manner in my apartment as well."

Magnus recognized the rebuke and shrunk a bit. "Nonetheless, I have given my word the edition will not leave my sight."

Flip pointed to a distant table. Magnus grabbed a book whose cover art looked like a cross between an anatomy text and an auto parts catalog, and adjourned reluctantly in the direction she pointed.

"You know," he said, "my theory is you paid an archivist to change my edition, and now you're trying to change this one too."

Of course she was trying to change it—change it back—but he didn't need to know that. "I told you, I had a dream and the book changed."

"So I've heard." He turned a page slowly. "All the same, I'm sure you won't mind if I keep you from taking it out of the room."

She opened *Pride and Prejudice* with a deep-seated fear that was quickly validated. Not only had Lizzy refused Darcy's marriage proposal, the book ended not with their romantic double wedding alongside Jane and Bingley, but with Lizzy getting pregnant by the rogue Wickham and being cast out by her father and society. Flip's knees began to tremble. She had nursed a minor desire for recognition in the world, but not as the infamous destroyer of the world's most-beloved novel. Lizzy pregnant with Wickham's child! Good God, she should be horsewhipped for this.

Flip's eyes cut to Magnus, who continued his perusal. Yes, perhaps she would deserve such a thing if she couldn't fix the troubles she had accidentally created, but Flip had every intention of restoring Lizzy and Darcy to their happy end. What had Madame K said? Twenty-four hours to right what had changed? Flip looked at her cell phone. Seventeen hours and change was all that remained.

Madame K had also said Flip needed to gather the details relating to everything that had been altered. Without those, Flip couldn't even hope to return the story to its original form, and even in that case hope was all it would be. As

Madame K reminded her, it had never been done before successfully. Well, what had Flip's mother always said? A journey of a thousand miles yadda yadda yadda. Flip leaned in and turned the book back to the beginning, scanning every page as fast as she could.

Magnus lifted his head to watch this improbable exercise, "For what do you search?"

"Ah, it's hard to explain."

"So much of you is."

She grinned. Inexplicable. That was her all right.

"It's not like everything about you is so easy to understand either," she pointed out.

He made an indecipherable British noise.

"See."

On page forty-one Flip noted some gossip concerning Sir William Lucas's dalliance with a servant that definitely didn't jibe with her memory of the story as well as an errant chambermaid on page fifty-seven.

"You know," Magnus said, "I've looked through that volume a dozen times, and I don't believe I've ever looked at it as intently as you are right now."

Yeah, well, you only had your professional reputation riding on it. "I thought for what you do with *Pride and Prejudice*," Flip said, "an easy-to-carry paperback would do just as well." She met his gaze. "Nothing personal."

"No, you're right. It's just that . . ." His face took on a faraway gleam. "I don't know, there's something quite remarkable about that first 1813 edition. Austen had written *Pride and Prejudice* seventeen years earlier but hadn't been able to find anyone to publish it. You can tell; there's little acknowledgment of the war with France, which hadn't begun when Austen wrote the book. It wasn't until she'd written

Sense and Sensibility and that had been published to critical acclaim that she sold *Pride and Prejudice*. Look at the title page there. You'll see Austen is listed as 'The author of *Sense and Sensibility.*' Nothing more. In *Sense and Sensibility* she is listed only as 'A lady.' "

"Wow, that's even worse than the coauthor credits Jed gives."

"When I hold that volume," Magnus said, "I think of her in the world in which she lived, unable to receive credit for her masterpiece, that impossibly perfect snapshot of time and place. There is some belief, never verified, that these volumes were hers. They were purchased at auction in 1987 from a family descended from a deacon in Bristol. The relationship between Jane's father, a deacon himself, and this man has been documented. It is possible Austen herself was at the home."

"Even so," Flip asked, "why would anyone assume it was Austen's copy and not the property of the family, buying a friend's novel?"

"Because there was a letter in it when it was sold, a letter addressed to Austen from her brother James," Magnus said. "The address to where the letter was sent is lost, but in the letter James asks her about her visit to Bristol, the town where the deacon lived."

Flip looked at him, and he smiled.

"No proof," he admitted. "But when I hold it . . . I don't know. It feels like Austen's. Which is why I wanted to do my writing here instead of in England."

England, eh? Where those lovely schoolgirls in their uniforms live. What the hell? Go for it, Flip. "Do you miss your family?"

He paused. A heavy pause. Hmmm, she thought. Divorced?

"Frankly," he said, "yes."

God, worse, she decided. A reconciliation. No, a reconciliation *and* the ex-wife's pregnant again. A sticky "will they, won't they" reconciliation that eats up all his emotional availability but, given the photo of those three smiling schoolgirls, one that only a heartless bitch would hope to fail. *Have I shown you my "Heartless Bitch" tattoo?*

"Yeah, that's gotta be rough," Flip said. She looked at the volume, with its cracked brown leather and narrow spine. Could she feel Austen's touch? The book did seem to have a certain magical quality. Or was it just the room and the company?

"And you know," Magnus went on, "Austen was almost exactly Lizzy's age at the time she wrote *Pride and Prejudice*."

" 'I am not one and twenty,' " Flip repeated, and Magnus nodded.

"That's right. Austen never experienced the love of a Lizzy or the lust of a Lydia. If she knew above thirty families in Steventon, her birthplace, I'd be deeply surprised. She lived under her father's or brothers' care, a spinster, all her life. She may have loved, but her love was never requited, so all that she wrote, all she portrayed so effortlessly was based on what she observed or created in her mind. Anne Milbanke, who later married Lord Byron, referred to *Pride and Prejudice* in a letter as 'the most probable fiction.' It is my theory that Austen's lack of experience *in* the world led to the sharpening of the powers of her observation *of* the world. And that is, at its heart, the central argument of my book."

"The one you're winning the award for."

"The National Book Critics' Circle prize, and I am a nominee. But *Pride and Prejudice* is Austen's story, told within the sociopsychological landscape she created. She deserves to have it told, and she deserves to have her genius celebrated. That is what I hope my book will do."

Just as she deserves to have the stories she created remain the way she created them, Flip thought, and cringed. I'm trying, Jane. If it can be fixed, I'll fix it for you, I swear.

Flip returned to her list, moving quickly through the chapters. Thirty pages from the end, she nearly jumped out of her skin.

"I know a secret about Lady Quillan, Lizzy," Wickham said, "and if you do not pay me the price I name, I shall not tell you."

The lilacs were abloom, Wickham's arm was strong under her hand, and Lizzy thought nothing could dampen the spirit of this fine August morning, not even Lady Quillan. "What is your price, sir?" she asked with a warm smile.

"A kiss, milady."

"You are a rogue."

"A rogue who hopes to be more to you than anyone one day—the best sort of rogue, do you not think?"

"What is the secret?"

"Your part first." Wickham pulled her behind a tree and kissed her deeply.

Lizzy, as usual, found herself undone by the stirring intimacy, though she wished the thought of Darcy at these times was not so vivid in her head. "And now your part, please."

"The story is somewhat wicked."

"I shall bear it, sir."

"The child," he said, "was not simply a by-blow of her wantonness. It seems her husband had removed himself from her bed, unable to stomach her *mésalliances*, and she was desperate for a child. So she lured Darcy to Stourhead Garden to perform the deed her husband refused."

Lured?! I did not lure Darcy anywhere!

Wickham went on, "I have it on good authority—"

Good authority, my ass. You have Caroline and Louisa's jealous guesses— "Hey!"

Magnus, whom she'd left engrossed in the muscle/transmission book, now stood to her left.

"Oh, sorry," said Magnus, who did not look sorry at all. "I needed to stretch my legs."

"Well, I hope they stretch all the way back to that table, because that's where they need to go."

He sniffed, imperious, and sauntered back. "You know, I'll eventually be able to look at that volume."

"Perhaps. But not tonight." She returned to the action.

"—I have it on good authority that Lady Quillan wept and pleaded, that Darcy wanted no part of it, and that she finally tore her clothes off, like the whore of Babylon, to insist on Darcy's quick attentions."

"Which, despite all protestations to the contrary," Lizzy added, "Darcy was not overtroubled to give."

"Neither party discharged themselves honorably, Elizabeth. Lady Quillan's shameless groveling is, of course, pathetic—a husband's abandonment does not excuse harlotry—but I'm afraid Darcy's sin is one which must be shared by all our sex at one time or another."

"Weakness of resolve?"

"Lust. Ah, look, there is Captain Hopkins's cottage. Did I tell you he has the most magnificent Oriental sword? It was reputedly worn by a general in the Battle of Hansando. Sadly Hopkins has been called away for the day, but he has left his key with me that I might have the pleasure of showing you myself. Come, my dear. You look as if a hearty glass of sherry might restore you."

Pathetic? Flip felt the searing sting of the word, like a dagger jerking through her, exposing her secrets to the world. She hated Wickham for talking about her private desires, just as she hated Jed for having known and dismissed them while they were married.

She felt water pool in her eyes but she refused to let a drop fall. She stared at the ceiling as if in thought, gripping the desk and praying the air would dry them.

"Flip?" Magnus eyed her with concern. "Is something wrong?"

"No, not at all. I think the books in here might be bothering my allergies. I'll be fine."

She hurriedly wiped her eyes. *Lizzy, you poor girl, I will not leave you to that fate.* Flip wasn't sure what would be worse in 1813—marrying Wickham or screwing him and getting dumped—but Lizzy would suffer neither if Flip had her way.

She scanned the last pages and looked at her notes for a final body count. Lady Quillan banished from polite society; Lizzy pregnant and abandoned; Darcy betrothed to Bingley's horrible sister Louisa; Jane heartbroken for her sister Lizzy;

Bingley heartbroken for his friend Darcy; and not a single person happy but Wickham, who continued to enjoy his dalliances with regularity.

I'll fix it, Jane Austen! I swear!

Flip scanned the book one last time, just to ensure the list of horrors was complete, and it was somewhere in the middle she realized Magnus's eyes were once again upon her, not with concern or humor. It was with something else; something much more palatable. She felt the heat stir through her like Kahlúa through hot chocolate.

She couldn't blame him, of course. She was bent over the volume, an act that displayed her bottom to fine effect, especially as situated in a loose cotton skirt under which she remained, for better or worse, bereft of panties.

It was for better, she decided, and swayed her hips a bit as she closed the book. This was the Rare Book Room, after all, a bower in which women, inebriated with the crackle of ancient pages and the thoughts of romantic, faraway places succumbed to the—in his eyes, at least—munificent charms of Magnus Knightley.

She heard him rise. Every nerve in her body jumped to attention, like a line of Rockettes, ready to kick into the famed chorus line the minute the conductor's baton went down— or perhaps the appropriate direction in this case was up.

Hey, if she let him make a pass at her, at least she could find out how, in this sterile environment, one actually began the process of achieving carnal embrace. It was an academic exercise, she decided. A field experiment.

And a pleasant experiment it would be. After all, the kiss at her apartment still tingled her lips, and if he'd learned anything from the hero he'd spent so long dissecting, perhaps the carnal embrace here would be just as much a tribute to

Apollo as the one in Wiltshire. After all, they shared the same dark hair, the same large hands, the same hard, flexing thighs—

Oh, God, what was she thinking? Darcy and Magnus, two different men. One man filled the page, and the other? She stole a glance at the commanding, broad-shouldered figure approaching her. The room, the library and most of Oakland. She swallowed.

He stopped behind her. She could hear his intake of breath, feel his rapt attention. She wondered if he'd start on her neck or her lips—or somewhere else entirely.

"Good God," he whispered.

"Mm?" Her knees began to tremble.

"Look at it. That Moroccan leather . . ." He scooped up the book and ran a loving hand over it, sighing as one would when presented with a new baby or a free upgrade to first class. "It never fails to thrill me."

"Really?" Flip unbent and turned, crossing her arms. "Are you done?"

"Seems so."

"I expected it to take longer."

"Yeah, me too. But that's all I needed." Apparently.

He handed the book back to her unopened, sticking to his promise.

"May I ask," he said with quiet concern, "what you found? I watched your face and there was that one moment . . . I don't know. I wasn't quite sure what happened."

That's because your eyes were supposed to be on my ass—followed in short order by your hands and your hips. "Yeah, um. Not good. Er, which is not to say bad," she added quickly, in response to his horrified face. "Just not great. But I have what I need to fix your edition, I think."

"Because there's nothing wrong with this one?" he said with a very large question mark in his voice.

"No, Magnus," she said with reassurance while simultaneously praying she could make what she was saying into the truth. "Austen's story will remain as it should be." She patted his arm, and this time the electric charge was more like the shock of a subterranean earthquake.

He smiled. "That's good."

Yeah. And saying it made her feel like it might even be possible.

He pulled his car keys out of his pocket. "Where to next?" he said, and Flip's heart skipped a beat. *Jeez Louise, what is this, high school? Pull yourself together.* Nonetheless, she found herself unexpectedly sad she'd have to decline his offer. "I, ah, have to do the rest on my own."

His clear eyes immediately turned opaque.

No, don't be hurt! she wanted to scream. *Don't think I'm shutting you out. But I have to get to Madame K and back into that damned book without you ever knowing what's going on.*

She said, "It isn't that it wouldn't be fun"—the word *fun* restored a twinkle of irony to those breathtakingly brown irises, damn him—"it's just that it's a quest I kinda have to navigate on my own, like, ah . . ."

"Alice falling down the rabbit hole?"

"I was going to say Mother Teresa building her leper colony in India, or at least Harry fighting the Hungarian Horntail, but, sure, we can go with Alice."

"You just like Harry because he has a pet bird."

"Believe me, you don't want a snowy owl as a pet. The babies are cute as buttons but, man alive, don't turn your back on the big ones. *Nyctea scandiaca.* They're cold-blooded killers."

"This from a woman who keeps Scruffy the Watch Dragon outside her bedroom?"

"Hmmm. I never really thought about it quite like that, but now that you mention it, you don't think I'm sending the wrong signal, do you?"

"No, I rather like it. The man who actually makes it by Scruffy will feel like he's earned it. Besides," Magnus added with a sly grin, "he likes me."

Suddenly it felt very dangerous in the Rare Book Room.

"He likes your socks," she corrected, "and I, ah, think it's time we got out of here."

Flip dropped the notes into her bag. She opened the book to take one last look, and the page blurred and unblurred. "Lady Quillan" had transformed into "Lady Philippa."

Holy Mother of God! It was just as Madame K had promised. How long would it be until it was just she arguing with Jed on the page and being splayed on that folly ledge with—Turning slowly, she met Magnus's eyes.

Oh boy! She slammed the book shut.

Magnus paled at the unnecessary violence. "Er—"

"Yes, yes, yes. Careful. I know. Sorry. Let's go."

He returned the book to the table at the front and held the exit door. Flip took a final look around their missed opportunity.

"Quite a place, this Rare Book Room," she said.

He gave her an unreadable look. "It is indeed." The door clicked and locked behind them.

They trooped to the elevator then down and out into the purple-black night. Dozens of students prowled Forbes, in pairs or gangs, laughing and talking. The businesses catering to students would be open until at least nine. She prayed

Looking Glass considered itself businesslike enough to follow the trend.

"No ride then?" he said.

Dammit, why did his eyes have to look like butterscotch on chocolate?

"Ah, no. I can walk it. Look, I really had fun tonight. We should do it again."

"Do it again? I'd prefer to finish what we started."

"The book?"

"The Scrabble game. More specifically, the payout on the final bet."

The buzz in her ears sounded like a hoard of African killer bees. Pretty soon Magnus would have to shout for her to hear.

"Disqualified. Remember?" she said. "You bluffed. You had already negotiated access—er, access to the book in the case—before the bet."

"Since when does bluffing disqualify a bet?" He chucked her chin and headed toward his car. "Don't worry," he said. "I'll give you plenty of notice."

The bees were giant, honey-blending helicopters now. She leaned casually on the *USA Today* stand to keep from being blown to the ground. "Yeah, well, bye."

"Why are you shouting?"

"Was I? Sorry."

"Have you your notes?" He pointed the fob, and the Audi beeped and flashed.

Momentarily panicked, she dug in her purse. Then she screamed.

Next to her notes was the half-day-old carcass of passenger pigeon. Her passenger pigeon. The pigeon Philippa put into her bag. Holy, holy Christ! She hadn't just changed the book, she'd freakin' changed the world! That's what Jed had seen! Suddenly it all made sense.

She slammed the bag closed just as Magnus arrived at her side.

"What was it?" he demanded.

"I realized I'd forgotten to mail my father's birthday card. Sorry."

"Wow. Let's hope you never forget your car payment."

"Ha-ha." She was a dead woman.

He paused, looking from his fob to a point a thousand miles into her eyes. "And you're sure that's all?"

"Yep."

"Dammit, Flip. Why won't you tell me the truth?"

"I-I—I am telling you the truth." Why did he have to look at her like that?

"So that's it? That's all the reply I'm to expect?"

She tried to think of an answer that would keep everything from falling apart, but she couldn't.

He screwed up the corner of his mouth and flipped his fob in the air. "Got it. Well, I'd say let me know if you need anything else, but I'm sure I'll be summoned when I'm required."

He walked to his car without looking back.

Damn. This Mother Teresa thing is losing its shine.

Chapter Sixteen

Jed swiveled in the soft Porsche leather, moving the Zeiss binoculars from Knightley to Flip. "That's right, buddy. Get in what passes for a sports car in Limeytown and get on out of here."

He had followed them from Flip's apartment to the library, and now sat parked in a spot a few spaces beyond the Audi. Jed watched Knightley unlock the car, then stop, turn around and race back to Flip.

"C'mon, buddy, how much ya gotta have? The library, her apartment, the library again. Even I've got to recharge the batteries sometime. Tomorrow's another day."

The temperature of Flip and Knightley's exchange cooled.

"Uh-oh. Praying mantis time. She's gonna bite your head off, pal." Of course, he considered with a crooked smile, if she did, there goes the fellowship. Heh.

His cell phone rang. He looked down. It was Io. "Oh, baby, this leash is waa-a-a-ay too short." He punched the Decline button, then Send Text, and thumbed out a quick IN A LECTURE. When he looked up again, Flip was heading toward Forbes. Her bus stop was on Fifth, a block north of Forbes, on the other side of the Cathedral. He was betting she'd head straight up Bigelow. He could quickly circle the

Cathedral on Bellefield, turn left on Fifth, and be the knight in shining Porsche armor who just happened to roll by to offer her a ride.

He adjusted himself so that he faced forward again, then dropped the emergency brake and turned the key. The purr of the car was almost as satisfying as the purr of a woman. It was a toss-up as to which one he'd rather slip into at the end of a day. He glanced into the rearview mirror for a quick look at Knightley's face to gauge how badly things had ended.

"What the fuck?"

The Audi was dark. Knightley was not in the car or anywhere near it. Nor was he with Flip, who, instead of crossing the street toward Fifth at the crosswalk, turned left to head down Forbes.

"Goddamn it." Forbes was one way in the other direction. He'd have to hoof it. He put the car back in neutral, jerked the emergency brake into place and shut off the car. An instant later he was jogging toward Forbes, setting the car alarm as he ran.

She was lugging that damned bag with the passenger pigeon, and this time he was going to find out what the hell she was doing with it.

" 'In a lecture'? What the fuck is that supposed to mean?" Io snapped her phone closed, royally pissed, and watched Jed jog down the street. She'd been watching him for ten minutes, trying to figure out what the hell he was doing. It appeared he was stalking his ex-wife, for Io had followed him from the Aviary to Flip's place and now to here.

She slid off the hood of her Benz and immediately regretted it. The gooey pink calamine lotion she'd smeared on her ass squeezed like grout through her jeans and up her crack, and the movement spawned a lightning round of itching, made infinitely worse by the scissoring of her legs as she crossed the street. If Jed had given her an STD, she was going to kill him. She stopped at the Porsche, debating whether to key it.

"You a Clash fan?"

Io stopped what was going to be a scratched-in word uncouth even by her standards to look at this handsome Brit with velvet eyes emerging from the darkness.

"Actually, yes," she said, smiling down at her T-shirt then up at him. "You like them too?"

"Like them? I did my master's thesis on them. Say, you weren't by any chance hoping to catch Jed Hughes, were you? I couldn't help but notice you watching him."

"The pecker. Yes, as a matter of fact—"

"Then let me be of service."

As if by magic, a sizeable rock appeared in the man's hand, and he hurled it through Jed's window.

Like a pinched baby, the alarm screamed to life, and Io saw Jed, who was halfway across Forbes, come to a dead stop, hesitate, then sprint back toward them.

Or rather back toward her. The Clash fan with the velvet eyes was gone.

"Can't talk now, Claudia. I'm right in the middle of something." Flip juggled the cellphone and her purse as she jogged toward Looking Glass.

"Yeah," Claudia said, "I met what you're right in the middle of. What's the scoop?"

"Not much of one. I just met him today. He's a colleague." Even at this hour, Forbes was filled with the rumble of traffic, student voices and, like the agitated call of an ungainly urban bird, a car alarm in the distance. Flip wove her way through the students loitering on the sidewalk.

"A colleague you bring home when you shower?" Claudia asked.

"It wasn't like he was in the bathroom with me," Flip replied.

"No, it was more like you undressed in front of him. Your bra and panties were on the floor."

Flip bit her lip. "Okay, you're right. There's a little something going on. But he *is* a colleague. We're working on a project together, and, um, yes, he's very cute."

"Cute enough to—"

"Yes."

"Yeah, but what about—"

"That too."

"Oh, Flip, this is great news!"

"Yeah, but don't get too excited. He's married—or separated or divorced, but there might be a reconciliation—and it's possible she's pregnant again. It's messy."

"Jesus, he told you all this? On the first day?"

Flip was almost running now. Chesterfield was the next block. "Well, it isn't so much he told me as much as, well . . ."

"As much as what?"

"I figured it out from a picture."

"A picture?"

"It was a very good picture."

"It must have been. So you haven't really talked about any of these things. You undressed in front of him—silently—and now you're working on a project together while you piece together his life from a sliver of his driver's license photo?"

Sadly that was pretty much it. "Yep."

"And you haven't slept together?"

"First day, remember?" Oh, thank God! There were still lights on at Looking Glass. She ascended the front steps at a run.

"But you were naked in front of him?"

There was no point in lying to Claudia. "A little. It's a long story."

"Sweetie, maybe we need to go over the finer points of seduction again."

"We kissed, okay?" Flip pressed the doorbell and prayed.

"Well, there's something."

"Oh, and he won my panties in a game of Scrabble. Look, I gotta go." Flip clicked off as Madame K opened the door.

Flip grimaced. "Man, oh, man, is my back killing me."

"I didn't break your stupid window," Io said sulkily. "It was some British guy. I have no idea why."

Jed stopped picking the bits of glass off his seat. "A British guy?"

"Yeah. An old one. Tall, dark hair, eyes like John Mayer, liked The Clash. He acted like he knew you."

Jed cleared the rest of the shards away with his arm. "Oh, he knows me. Gimme your car keys."

"What?!"

"C'mon, I need your car."

"Only if I drive."

"This isn't a two-person gig."

"It is tonight. We need to talk. My ass is on fire."

"Sugar, a man's gotta rest."

"Yeah, right there." Flip moaned, mostly out of horror at what she'd gotten herself into, but also in homage to Madame K's incredible fingers.

"Vouldn't you know? I vuz just thinking about shutting down early—and there you vur."

"It's like magic, really."

Flip was stretched out on her stomach, face through the porthole and the fluffy towel spread like warm vanilla icing over her hips. This was much nicer than getting spanked. Almost certainly.

Madame K had not asked about the book or made any reference to their earlier call, which was just as well from Flip's point of view. The last thing she needed was to have to lie more today. Now that she had gathered all the changes in the book, her plan was to return, fix everything, especially Lizzy and Darcy, and have it all done before morning. And some people thought finding the ivory bill was going to be a challenge.

"You found your hero, *ja?*" Madame K asked.

"What, Magnus?"

"Vat Magnus?"

"This Magnus, I hope," said Magnus, who had arrived without Flip noticing.

Flip jerked so hard against the porthole, she thought she knocked a filling loose. "What are you doing here?"

"Good evening, ladies. I hope I'm not interrupting."

"You are, actually." Flip clutched the towel tightly. "I thought I made it clear I wanted to do this alone."

"What you made clear was that you were fixing the problem. Unless fixing the problem involves getting your back loofahed, I'm not sure what's going on here."

"I'm not under the impression you need to know what's going on—"

"Children!" Madame K clapped her hands. "I have never seen so much tension in a room. Mr. Magnus, velcome. I had suggested Miss Allison invite you. Vee specialize in couples massage."

Flip flopped like a fish, trying to push Madame K's hands away. "Oh, no, no, no, no. It's nothing like—"

"You are a couple, *ja?*" Madame K pinned her flat.

"No," Flip said.

"Well . . ." Magnus said simultaneously.

"What the hell does that mean?" Flip strained in the porthole but all she could see were his trousers and feet.

"It means," he said slowly, "you spoke so highly of the massage, I thought I should take a look."

"Which sadly would be impossible," Flip added quickly, "for the therapeutic nature of the treatment requires the utmost privacy and calm."

Madame K giggled happily. "Vhat silliness. You are velcome to join us, Mr. Magnus. Er, not there. On the table."

"The table?" Magnus said, confused. "Oh, I see. No . . . I'm not getting a massage."

"Oh, too bad." Madame K began again the particularly blissful motion she'd been making with her palms. "Miss Allison was just about to imagine herself in a favorite book."

Oh, crap!

Magnus froze. Flip could practically hear his brain shout "Eureka!"

"Was she?" he said pointedly. "Do tell me more."

"If you're not getting a massage," Madame K said, "vould you mind waiting outside?"

"I . . . well . . ." He hesitated. "I'm sure I'll be fine here on the chair—"

"Oh, no, Mr. Magnus. Vee shall have no gawkers. Either step outside or, if you're staying . . ."

"What?"

"Take off your clothes and lie down."

"This," Io cried. "This is what I want you to see!"

"Jesus, what are you doing?" Jed made a hard right on red despite the fact it was illegal on Forbes, and Io was unzipping her jeans. "I can't believe I'm saying this, but can't you wait? I gotta find Flip."

"I don't want to screw you, you idiot. I want to show you something."

"Later, babe. What the hell would she have turned on Fifth for? Her bus stop is in the other direction."

"Look, is this about the stupid bird?"

Jed squealed the car to a stop at the light in front of the Carnegie. "How the hell do you know about that?"

"I know a lot, actually. And I think I might know where your wife is heading."

"Where?"

"Park the car on Bellevue. I told you I want to show you something first."

A frisson that had nothing to do with the massage rocketed up Flip's spine. Magnus undressed? A vision of a British statue of David popped into her head. Ah, the magnificent marble—

"Miss Allison. You're clenching."

"Am I? Sorry."

Flip craned her eyes so hard she thought one might pop out of its socket, but all she could see was Magnus's tentatively drumming foot.

"Choose, Mr. Magnus," Madame K said.

Flip heard him sigh. He stepped out of one shoe, then with a vivid green foot stepped out of the other. His black sweater landed on the chair.

"So this book imagining," he said conversationally, "what's that about?"

"Nothing," Flip tried to shout, though her exclamation was mostly croaked into the porthole padding after a firm readjustment of her head by Madame K.

"Well, the experience is rather magical," the masseuse explained, kneading Flip into submission. "Though it can result in some rather unexpected surprises. I'm sure Miss Allison told you about what happened with her Venice hero and his book this afternoon."

His shirt dropped on the sweater, and he paused. "Venice hero?"

"Vhy, *ja*. I believe he is a—"

". . . scholar who has helped me in my quest to rediscover the ivory bill," Flip interrupted.

"Ah, vell, I did not know about his ivory bill—eez that vhat you Americans call it?—though there was a particularly engaging incident on a sink . . ."

"Hole!" Flip cried. "A sink*hole* in Arkansas that may be where the ivory bill nests."

"Hmm." Magnus did not sound convinced.

Flip heard the clack of the metal tongue against his buckle and felt a fireball blow across her that would have flattened Arkansas, nests and all. If that clack was not the sexiest sound in the world, she didn't know what was. But still the only thing in her vista was lime socks and tan-trousered calves.

"Miss Allison, you must relax if this eez to vurk."

The whoosh of belt through belt loops made her toes curl. The top of his trousers dropped into view as he lifted out one leg then the other.

Flip bit her tongue to keep from moaning. His socks ended halfway up the most gorgeous, muscular calves. This was like the first day of summer vacation or dessert before dinner. Ninety dollars in one day? Hell, she'd sign over her 401(k) for this kind of massage pleasure.

And he had reached the moment of truth. De-panty her, would he? Now he'd get his comeuppance, though she wasn't sure what she liked more about it, the coming or the uppance. Flip strained to lift her head but Madame K held her firmly in place.

He didn't move. Too shy? Oh, poor fellow. He'd better cough up some cotton or he'd never live it down, not if she had anything to do with it.

Flip's mind was racing in so many directions—boxers or briefs as well as length, breadth, and the all-important disposition—she could barely concentrate. The only thing she was certain of was that Madame K needed to be called away or even struck by lightning so that she could raise her head the two inches it would take to get a clear view of what was going on. It was like trying to watch the last inning of a tied-up World Series game from the T-shirt stand in the parking lot.

The underwear dropped, and vengeance was sweet. So sweet, in fact, it was chocolate. What fluttered to the floor were luscious, chocolate brown low-rise briefs.

Oh God, she'd never think of Ghirardelli the same way again. Hell, she'd never think of dirt the same way again. She thought of the hint of caramel in his kiss and wondered if maybe, just maybe, there might be something else on him that tasted as sweet.

The blood rushed from her brain so fast she was light-headed.

"Miss Allison, can you feel that?"

"I'm feeling something."

"Your body just stiffened like a cannon ready to blow. Vhat happened? No, no, no, don't try to sit up. You'll just make it worse."

Madame K *tsk-tsk*ed as she worked Flip's lower back. "A mound of tension."

Magnus hopped on the neighboring table, letting his two green-socked feet sway. Flip saw the hem of a towel drop over his calves.

"Dees, for example." Madame K flung Flip's sheet half away. "Can you see that?"

Flip squinched her eyes, and wished she were dead. The "that" was her ass, and the person whose opinion had just been elicited was Magnus.

"Well," he offered helpfully, "it does seem exceptionally tight."

"*Uff da.* And look, vhen I knead it theez way or theez way nothing moves."

The swaying of Magnus's legs stopped. Flip heard him swallow. "Yes, I can see that would be trouble."

"Dees side is vorse." The entire sheet was lifted. Magnus took a deep breath.

Heat that could have ignited paper flooded Flip's neck and face. Was there a saint of embarrassing moments to make an emergency offering to?

"But see," Madame K instructed, "with some deep, deep massage . . ."

"Right," Magnus said in a hoarse voice. "It's amazing."

"You learn this, *ja?* So that you can do it yourself."

"Consider it done."

Madame K replaced the sheet and moved to Flip's calves.

Magnus's legs began swaying again. "And what about this book imagining? Is it time? I'm sure Flip is eager to find out more about those sinkhole nests."

"Ooooo, very impatient. No good for relaxation. You rest for a moment, Miss Allison. You lie on stomach, Mr. Magnus."

Flip heard the sound of Magnus being shoved flat on the table and the cracking of knuckles as Madame K began her work.

"*Ouch, ouch, ouch, ouch, ouch,*" Magnus yelped. "Good God, madam!"

"Your shoulders are very bound up, Mr. Magnus."

Flip raised a surreptitious eye, then two. Magnus's feet were across from her head. She had an amazing view of his towel-covered ass. The Rockies paled in comparison.

"Meez Allison! Are you lifting your head?"

Flip dove into the porthole. "No, not me."

"Good. Mr. Magnus, stop squirming. Oh dear, look at these thighs." Flip's head shot up. "Vhen was the last time you had your toxins released?"

Magnus cleared his throat. "I, well . . ."

"Have you ever had hot stones?"

Flip snickered. "I don't think the British go in for that sort of thing. They like their stones like they like their country—damp and full of drafts."

"Damp and full of drafts, is it?" he said. "Why, I could swear that was the weather forecast under someone else's sheet tonight."

Postcolonial jerk.

"Vee vill turn on our side now, Mr. Magnus."

"But—"

"Mr. Magnus, turn, please."

Flip curled onto her side and craned her neck hard. With any luck, she might be able to answer Madame K's stone question herself. Madame K lifted the towel and stepped neatly into Flip's line of sight.

"Vhat vell-toned gluteals!"

What?! Flip clutched the table's edge with her fingertips and leaned back as far as she could. Past Madame K's apron, she could make out the barest hint of the plump, shadowy rise. Just a tiny bit farther . . .

Magnus made a deprecating sound. "Actually they've been compared to Brad Pitt's."

Her grip slipped, and Flip crashed to the floor.

"Miss Allison!"

"I'm fine." That bastard! He'd heard what she'd shouted in the shower. Oh Christ, he'd heard everything she'd shouted. She stumbled to her feet like some white linen Tasmanian devil.

Magnus gave her a winning smile.

"Oh dear, you two. This is hardly the atmosphere for relaxation." Madame K marched to an old cassette player on the table and hit a button. Immediately the sound of the Righteous Brothers filled the room. Then she lit a squat white candle, and Flip smelled the familiar tang of lemons. "You, Meez Allison, will lie down—still. And you, Mr. Magnus, will concentrate on more upstanding thoughts. And both of you will keep your eyes shut. Understand?"

Flip stretched out, chastened. "Yes."

"Good. There. We have wasted so much time, we must skip the book portion."

That's what she thinks, Flip thought determinedly.

Magnus began to say something but Madame K must have given him a sharp look for the word died unspoken.

"Now be still while I turn on the answering machine."

When Madame K exited, the room was quiet. Magnus said, "What the hell is going on here, Flip? All I know is my second edition is changed, you're in a panic to see the first edition, and now you're at a masseuse where one can imagine oneself in one's favorite book. I thought you'd hired an archivist to change my book, but now I think something even bigger is going on—something very strange—and I want to know what it is."

She stole a look at him. He sat on the table, towel secured around his waist, staring at his feet. His chest was broad, with a light, mesmerizing sprinkling of mahogany curls that trailed in an arrow down a flat belly and farther south. Her mouth dried.

"Nothing," she tried to say, but all that came out was wind.

"Pardon?"

"W-water," she said, pointing to the bottle on the table. He hopped down and handed it to her. She drank deeply. "I told you I needed to do this alone."

"You weren't going to be alone. Your ex-husband was following you."

"Jed?! How did he know where I was? For that matter, how did you?"

"He must have followed us from your place. I spotted him in front of the library, and when you left he followed. I was concerned. Why is he following you, Flip? What are you really doing here?"

She hated to hide the truth, but there was no way she was going to get Magnus any more deeply involved. "I, ah . . ."

"Lovely. Another lie." He jerked the towel tighter around his waist and hopped back on the table.

"There's nothing going on, okay? Is Jed here?"

"No. He had a bit of an issue with his car. And while I did not have the benefit of a formal introduction, I believe I have met the irrepressible Io. Let us just say I think Jed has found the woman he deserves."

"And you don't think he's coming?" Jed was as determined as Magnus but lacked the scruples that might slow his search.

"Why, Flip? Why would it matter?" Magnus gave her a piercing look.

"It wouldn't."

"Glad to hear it."

"Look, I'm going to fix your book. Let's just leave it at that, okay?"

"That's exactly where we'll leave it, Flip."

She flopped back on her stomach, and Madame K returned, whistling. She stopped abruptly. "Did it get cooler in here?"

Neither she nor Magnus answered.

Madame K clucked her tongue but began on Flip again, making rolling circles and knuckly impressions. Magnus's pique made it hard for Flip to relax, but little by little Madame K's relentless kneading loosened Flip from her worries.

I'll fix the book, and I'll fix us, she thought. I'll fix the book and he'll be so happy he'll reward me with a kiss—an even better kiss.

She closed her eyes, remembering the heady rush of reaching for him today in her apartment and having him instinctively reach back. Cloning? Ha. She thought of Dolly, the cloned sheep. Jed was such a jerk. Magnus had given him exactly what he deserved. She could still feel Magnus's hand across her back and the other trailed across the delicate flesh of her hip.

But those hands were not always gentle, she was certain. She could also imagine them, insistent and hard, hoisting her hips and fitting her roughly into place.

Oh Christ! *Pride and Prejudice,* she reminded herself. Darcy holding Lizzy's hand at their wedding. Lizzy looking sweetly into his eyes. Sweetly, Flip. That's where you went astray the last time. Lady Quillan, forgotten. Jane and Bingley, happy. Wickham, banished to the north. Flip, there to serve. And, oh, what a servant she could be, guiding them all handily toward their goals. Uh-oh. Handily. There he was again with those hands. Holding her; having her; she a servant to those hands, those unforgiving, demanding, hard, hard, artful hands.

She tried to keep her mind on the book, but Magnus was winning, hands down.

"Where, baby, where?" Jed pulled to the curb and left the car in idle. "Where do you think Flip's going?"

"I don't know for sure—"

"Where do you think?"

"Jeez, Jed. She did have a card for a massage place off of Fifth in her wallet."

"You were in her wallet?"

She gave him the finger. "Yeah, 'cause looking for a stupid bird in her purse is so much less an invasion of privacy."

Jed reached for the gearshift. "Then we're going there."

"No! I told you I wanna show you something. And all I can say is, if penicillin doesn't fix whatever it is you gave me, I'm going to be royally pissed."

"Whatever I gave you? Honey, I'm clean. Ninety-nine and forty-four one-hundredth's-percent pure. Like Ivory soap."

"You'd better recheck the label. I got the worst case of crabs I've ever seen."

"No way, baby—"

"Yes way. Look!"

Io twisted until she was on her hands and knees, facing out the passenger window, and pulled her jeans down. "See!"

"Jesus!" Her spectacular and utterly cleavable buns were covered in a sticky, pink mess and waggling about six inches from his face. His gorge and his dick stiffened at the same time. "Baby, you're a mess!"

"Not that! Wipe it off. Look at the skin."

God, he was half hard now, despite her Pepto-Bismol coating. He wondered if he could work in a quick one from this position. Maybe if he stepped out and she put her knees on his seat—

"Now, Jed!"

Christ! He looked around the car for a rag or some Kleenex but saw nothing in the front or the back.

"Jed!"

Fuck. He whipped off his beret and wiped, and every motion brought the color guard in his shorts one step closer to a full rebel charge. He couldn't help it. He clamped his hands over those firm baby melons and felt his balls rumble. Hell, if penicillin was good enough for her, it'd be good enough for him too. He dropped the beret, unzipped his fly and pulled out General Jackson. "Baby, you're about to make a soft landing on a very hard target."

"Jed, for God's sake, would you look!"

He flipped on the overhead light and laughed.

"That ain't crabs, sugar. That's poison ivy!" Jed stopped

mid-guffaw. He gazed down at his hands in horror and looked back at Io.

The car light grew infinitely brighter, throwing her ass into shocking Day-Glo relief, and Jed realized they were not alone.

The officer lowered his flashlight enough to take in Io's ass, Jed's pink-smeared hands and the equally pink beret swaying eagerly over Jed's lap.

"I'm going to need to see some IDs."

Chapter Seventeen

As before, Flip swam through thick layers of consciousness toward the vivid new scent, but this time it wasn't Grandma Thompson's floral bathroom spray. This time it was . . . popcorn?

"I do so love toasted kernels," a pleasant male voice remarked, "though I may not have them."

"Why ever not?" an equally pleasant female voice inquired. "This is your house."

"My sisters cannot endure them. They say they are impious."

"Impious? But why?"

"I believe both the noise and the sudden change in turgidity. But I am glad we have found a quiet spot to share our secret delight."

"Oh, Bingley, as your wife, I assure you, we shall always find time for that."

The lovebirds. Flip smiled. Bingley was Mr. Darcy's friend and Jane was Lizzy's good older sister. Together they are the couple who share a double wedding with Lizzy and Darcy at the end of the real book. Was it possible things were back to normal?

"All right," he said. "Take a handful. It is your turn to count out your kernels."

Jane giggled. "One for you; one for me; one for you; one for me; one for you; one for me; one for you; one for me and—uh-oh—one for you."

"The last one's mine, Jane. That means I shall have a kiss—"

How sweet and Bingley–like.

"—and one more button."

Flip's eyes shot open.

"Mr. Bingley," Jane said with a happy squeak, "I think you are quite aware that is not my button."

Oh, dear! Flip was clearly in a nineteenth-century sitting room, but it was decidedly not the stuffy, dark room of her first visit, which was a deep relief to her. It had an altogether more pleasant feel. This room was filled with the glow of several oil lamps and a small fire, not to mention the diffused light of a spring moon shining through a pair of magnificent French doors. But, despite the voices, the room appeared to be empty, as was the balcony beyond the doors.

"Poor Jane," Bingley said. "Two more of your buttons and you shall be quite undone."

"Poor Bingley," she replied. "Two more of your buttons and you shall be quite overdone."

They laughed, and Flip realized they must be sitting on the floor across the room, behind the green brocade couch in front of the looming fireplace. She herself was curled up in an overstuffed wing chair, facing a corner and turned partly from view. Jane and Bingley thought they were alone. She hoped Jane and Bingley thought they were alone.

The door latch jiggled and Flip froze. A dark-haired woman of around twenty with an open, thoughtful face and a simple cream silk frock strode in and went to the window. Flip held her breath, and she felt quite certain Bingley and Jane were doing the same. The woman brushed back the curtain, peered into the distance and sighed. Then she pulled a flask from her pocket, popped the cork, and drank.

A stray kernel popped at the fire and the woman spun around. In the act of spinning she caught sight of Flip and quickly hid the flask. She pointed in the direction of the noise.

"Did you hear something?" she asked.

The *s* in *something* had the slightest *sh* of inebriation to it. But the good news in Flip's mind was, if this was Lizzy Bennet—and surely it had to be—she appeared to hold no lasting grudge toward Lady Quillan, so perhaps there was hope.

"No." Flip shook her head firmly. She hoped lying was within Lady Quillan's character.

"Not over there?" The woman stepped toward the fire.

"It was my shoe," Flip said. "A button popped."

"Popped?"

"Popped."

"Just now?"

"Yes."

The woman gave her a generous smile. "Well, we can't have you running about with your buttons open. 'Twould be unseemly."

Flip nodded.

A servant entered. It was Flip's old friend Samuel, the butler from Louisa's house. He saw Lizzy and bowed. "Pardon me, Miss Elizabeth. I was looking for Dolly—" He stopped when he saw Flip.

Flip smiled. "Hello, Samuel."

His face clouded. "What on earth are you doing here?"

"Why, I was talking to Miss Bennet and—"

"Dolly, you lazy, good-for-nothing wench!" he cried. "Sitting in your master's chair like the Queen of Sheba?! I'll see that Bingley has you horsewhipped for your cheek!"

Dolly? She was Dolly now? Flip's eyes cut to her clothes. Shit! No pale violet silk with intricately beaded trim. She was wearing what looked like a burlap sack under a stiff white apron. Hell's bells. She wasn't Lady Quillan. She was the little match girl. "I-I—"

"It's all right, Samuel," Lizzy said. "I put her there myself. Dolly fainted." She gave Flip a meaningful look. Flip immediately tilted her head and let her tongue loll out.

"Fainted?" Samuel gave his charge a piercing look. He added under his breath, "It certainly wasn't from over work."

Lizzy said, "You may fetch her some ginger water."

The veins in Samuel's neck bulged. "Ginger water?" He shot daggers in Flip's direction. "Yes, m'um."

Flip squinched her eyes and tried to look swoony.

Samuel exited, closing the door behind him. Flip was on her feet in an instant but had taken no more than a step or two when the latch rattled again. She flung herself back into the chair.

"I beg your pardon, m'um," Samuel said to Lizzy. "I was diverted from my purpose. Your mother asked me to inform you that Mr. Darcy will be arriving at Netherfield shortly."

The curve at Lizzy's mouth dissolved into a chilly line. "Thank you, Samuel."

Uh-oh, Flip thought. Trouble.

He retired once more.

Flip jumped to her feet. "You are too kind, m'um. I don't know how to thank you."

Lizzy's eyes sparked with knowing amusement. "I have been the subject of ill-deserved reproach by certain members of the Netherfield household myself, Dolly. I should not like to see it happen to someone else, even a servant."

A servant, Flip thought. That's sure going to cut down on my dinner invitations. On the other hand, no one was more invisible in a Regency household than a servant.

A toot that could only be Bingley's leather breeks traversing hardwood floor resounded through the room.

Lizzy's forehead creased, and Flip put a hand on her stomach regretfully. "Bad omelet. Er, perhaps a little air . . ." She pointed toward the balcony.

Lizzy pushed open the balcony doors, oblivious to a disheveled Jane and Bingley emerging from behind the couch in a hurried crawl toward the hall. Bingley gave Flip a grateful, abbreviated bow. Unfortunately every step he took was bringing his loosened breeks precariously lower on his hips, a fact he was trying without success to correct.

" 'Tis unexpectedly dull for such a pleasant evening," Lizzy said with a sigh. Netherfield's vast, silent park stood before them, awash in the moon's luminescent glow.

"Quite, m'um," Flip agreed as she arrived at Lizzy's side.

Bingley's breeks had dropped to his knees now, revealing voluminous white drawers and several inches of pale buttock.

"My goodness," Flip said, seizing Lizzy's arm as she began to turn, "is that a zebra?"

"A zebra? In Hertfordshire?" Lizzy strained to see down the long balcony that ran the length of Netherfield's top floor in the direction Flip was pointing. "I hardly think so, Dolly."

"My mistake." Flip turned in time to catch Bingley and

Jane slipping through the door and disappearing from sight. She waited for the violins to start, the accompaniment of the feeding to her brain of dear Dolly's backstory, but none came. Apparently servants didn't rate last names or backstories. "If I may say so, m'um, you must be very pleased about your sister's nuptials. She and Bingley seem to be so very much in love."

"That they do," Lizzy said with forced stoicism. "The house fairly rings with it."

"When was the wedding?"

" 'Was?' " she repeated. "My goodness, Dolly, that must have been a bad omelet indeed. The wedding is tomorrow morning. Have you not seen all the guests?"

Flip's jaw dropped, thinking of the popcorn game. "But . . ."

"But what?"

"B-but I have not had time to choose a gift."

"That is very kind, though they will hardly want for gifts. You will do well to simply . . ." Lizzy's voice trailed off as the distant thrum of hooves heralded a top-hatted man on a magnificent black stallion entering the park gate.

Darcy.

"I think that must be Mr. Darcy, m'um," Flip said with a small hope Lizzy would burst into song and perform a gleeful jig as she confessed their secret engagement.

"Is it? I hadn't noticed," Lizzy said tartly, then added under her breath, "Hateful man." She downed another surreptitious draft from her flask.

Okay, that clearly had the ring of bruised ego to it. But how to get the details so she could formulate the plan to set things to right? There was a carefully delineated relationship in this era between servant and lady, Flip knew, the boundaries of which were never to be crossed. She must proceed with a mixture of delicacy, indirectness and deference.

" 'Tis undoubtedly improper of me to ask this, m'um, but—"

"Oh, he is a villainous, perfidious rogue, of course," Lizzy blasted with enough heat to singe Flip's brows, "possessing twice the mating proclivity of a jackrabbit and only half the moral fiber. To think that he dared propose to me—me, the upstanding daughter of a gentleman!—after disporting with that immoral jade. As if any proper woman would ever receive his attentions again! Ha! He should be driven through the streets with 'fornicator' branded on his chest and forced to answer for himself on his knees to God and polite society."

"He proposed?" Flip said encouragingly.

"After the wedding tomorrow, I shall never, ever have to see the dissolute, degenerate hound's face again."

"Is it possible," Flip asked gently, "that this strong reaction is because you have some feelings for Mr. Darcy and that the attentions he paid to this, um—"

"Harridan with her belly out to here?"

"Not the phrase I was looking for."

"Whore?"

"—somewhat incautious but undoubtedly well-intentioned woman have perhaps wounded your pride?"

"No. Hoare's folly, indeed. Ha."

Flip tried a different tack. "I take it you made your feelings about his behavior clear when he proposed?"

"In no uncertain terms."

"But then later, did you not consider accepting his apology?"

Lizzy gazed at Flip blankly.

"You know," Flip said, remembering the scene in the movie quite clearly, "after the long tortured letter in which he explains the reasons behinds his actions and offers an apology for the ones he has come to regret?"

"Apology?" Lizzy snorted. "Are we talking about the same Fitzwilliam Darcy?"

Fitzwilliam! So that was his first name. Flip snapped her fingers, then caught sight of Lizzy's face. "Er, perhaps not. But I do think you should reconsider. After all, it is a truth universally acknowledged that a single man in possession of a good fortune must be in want of a wife."

Lizzy frowned. "Sentimental rubbish. And I for one wouldn't care how good a fortune a man possesses if he also happens to be a stubborn, insensible stuffed jabot who wouldn't know a moral act if it slapped him in the face—oh!"

An unexpected squeak on Lizzy's part brought this tirade to an abrupt halt. Flip followed Lizzy's gaze.

The top-hatted rider had made his way to the courtyard and was swinging a taut, capable thigh off his steed to dismount.

Lizzy let out a long exhale and gripped the rail for support. "Look," she marveled, "at those magnificent haunches."

Darcy handed his reins to the stable boy and ascended Netherfield's gleaming staircase two steps at a time, stopping only to bend low over the balustrade when the lad called, "Wait, sir! Your satchel."

Lizzy made a noise in her throat like a spigot about to burst and shoved herself back from the railing, babbling something about the heat.

Flip was glad Darcy hadn't been wearing lime socks, too, or she might have had to send for a physician. "Shall we, er, return to the—"

"I think so." Lizzy stumbled into the room as Samuel arrived, scooped the ginger water off his tray and downed half the glass. "Would you mind bringing another for Dolly?" she said to the aggrieved servant, who turned and stomped out. Lizzy added to Flip, "I think I left my gloves on the railing."

Flip didn't remember seeing gloves and was still searching behind a particularly dirty urn when out of the corner of her eye she caught Lizzy pouring what remained of the flask into the ginger water. Flip unbent, brushed her hands on her apron and reentered the room. "No gloves, milady."

Lizzy finished the heroic draft she'd been downing. "Oh dear. Perhaps I forgot to put them on entirely." She held up the glass and nodded. "This is just the medicine I needed."

Yeah, if you were getting your wisdom teeth and a kidney removed, Flip thought. But I've only got until tomorrow morning, and unless Darcy can marry you while you hang unconscious from a coatrack, this ain't gonna work.

"Careful, milady," Flip said, expertly fishing the glass from Lizzy's hand. "Too much ginger can give one the wind."

At that moment, a portly man of sixty in a red velvet frock coat burst into the room, happily breathless, and slammed the door behind him, oblivious to the room's occupants. At once someone on the other side of the door tried to open it. The two tugged and pulled their respective knobs as the old man said through the narrow opening, "Billy's a bad, bad boy. Peg's going to have to give him a crack across his bottom, isn't she?"

A woman—evidently Peg—giggled excitedly. "Indeed I shall—and it will be twice as hard if you do not straighten up this minute."

"Oh, I shall straighten up for you, Peg. Like a yardarm that you shall—"

Flip cleared her throat.

The man started so hard he let go of the knob, and the woman, a buxom, flame-haired serving girl a third his age, toting a soup ladle, was flung onto her backside with enough force to propel her halfway across the heavily varnished hall and into the leg of a table, which immediately broke, disgorging the bushy fern, ceramic planter and cubic foot of dirt it had supported onto the floor.

The man bowed to Lizzy and Flip, clearly flustered. "I, er, we . . . that is to say, there is some talk of a small theatrical for tomorrow's celebration, and Peg, er, Peggy, er, Margaret was just helping me go over my part."

Flip tried to look anywhere but between his waistcoat and his knee buckles.

"I, that is to say, we shall importune you no further," the man said. "We did not realize our rehearsal space was otherwise occupied. Good evening." He bowed again and regally stepped into the hall and closed the door.

Lizzy slumped against the armrest. "I'm the only person in England tonight who shall be reading herself to sleep."

"That's not true," Flip said. "Why, there are lots of people—people in this very house—who are quite happily alone tonight." The sound of the balcony doors of the room next door opening floated in on the night air, followed by a round of giggles from Jane.

"I, ah, didn't realize your sister's bedroom was so close," Flip said awkwardly, running to close the balcony doors of their own room.

"It's not." Lizzy made a plaintive noise. "That's Bingley's."

Bingley's voice rose giddily. "Let's try a different game now. I call it The Last Coach to Maidenhead—"

Flip clapped the doors shut. "I've played it once myself. Too many cards. Worse than double-decker pinochle."

Lizzy dropped her forehead into her palm. "It's been decreed. I am going to die a virgin."

"No, Miss Elizabeth, no. Why, I feel certain love is just around the corner—"

"I do believe the first man that suggests something even vaguely improprietous shall have me for the taking."

"M'um, please," Flip protested, thinking of the evil Wickham. "What sort of talk is that?"

"What about you, Dolly? Is there not some attractive footman here who strikes your fancy? Aaron has very fine shoulders, and I have seen him watching you as you polish Bingley's silver. I can manufacture a need for a bolt of sprigged cotton, you know. That'll have Bingley sending the two of you off before you know it."

"No, no, m'um. Thank you. I am just fine as I am."

"What? There is no beau in whose arms you imagine yourself?"

Flip warmed, thinking of that easily accommodated kiss and the gentle pressure of Magnus's fingertips.

"I knew it!" Lizzy cried. "There is someone. We shall have you married by Michaelmas."

Samuel opened the door, balancing a second ginger water on a tray. He halted when he saw the half-empty glass in Flip's hand. "Feeling better?" he asked, icicles hanging on each word.

Flip swallowed. "A bit."

"I'm glad to hear it. Miss Elizabeth, this is for you."

He set the new glass on a table hard enough to make Flip jump and extended the tray toward Lizzy. On it was a sealed note with MISS ELIZABETH BENNET printed in a masculine hand on the outside.

Lizzy took it carefully by the corner, as if it might catch fire. She looked guiltily from Dolly to Samuel and placed it on the table in front of her. "Thank you, Samuel."

He gave Flip a fiery look and exited.

Flip edged toward the couch, intent on getting a look at the note. She only had until noon tomorrow. How much more complicated was this evening going to get?

But Lizzy made no move to open it. Instead she forced her gaze away from the table and into the treetops beyond the balcony. She began to whistle.

"Lovely night," Flip said.

"Indeed, it is." The tip of Lizzy's satin slipper began to tap. "Dolly, will you see if there's a letter opener on the desk there, please."

Flip sped happily to the desk, found a brass-handled opener under a stack of books and returned to the couch.

The note was gone.

"Thank you, Dolly." Lizzy took the opener from Flip's hand, pulled a loose thread from her gown and used the blade to free it. "Suddenly I'm exhausted. I believe I shall retire."

As Lizzy stood, Flip saw the edges of the now-opened note jutting slightly from Lizzy's pocket. *Aaaarrrrrrgggghhh.*

"Er, shall I bring you some warm milk," Flip asked.

"No, thank you, Dolly."

"Tea? Coffee? Grilled ham and cheese?"

"I'm fine," Lizzy said, and resumed a happy whistle as she sashayed into the hall.

Chapter Eighteen

Flip burst through the doorway, directly into the path of the swiftly moving form of Fitzwilliam Darcy.

Though it had been at least a half dozen months in his world since they'd met, Flip knew no man could forget the acts they'd committed atop that cool marble, no matter what sort of shapeless servant's garb she wore now.

She fought to keep the blood from her cheeks as she lifted her eyes. "Hello."

He handed her his top hat. "A sandwich, please," he said as he cut around her without a glance, "and a claret. I've been on the road all day." His eyes were focused on the lithe form in the cream silk frock disappearing into a bedroom down the hall. As the door slammed Darcy flinched but betrayed no other emotion as he made his way into his own room and closed the door.

"I'm with ya," Flip called. "Pretend we don't know each other. That way Lizzy doesn't get jealous. Good one."

It was then she noticed a carrot-haired servant cresting the stairs with a tray stacked nearly to his nose with candles. He looked at Flip, then down the empty hall in the direction she'd been speaking.

"I'm, ah, rehearsing for the theatrical tomorrow," she

explained. "It's a Shakespeare-type thing. *Twelfth Night* and so forth. Do you by any chance have a sister who works here?"

"Yes, and I don't care if you talk to yourself, channel the dead or levitate so long as you keep one or more of these sodding imbeciles busy long enough for me to sit down for half an hour. It's nearly half past bloody twelve, and I'm supposed to be at a craps game in the stable yard."

A bell jangled once, twice, three times.

"That's you," he said. He snapped Darcy's top hat from her hand and inserted the tray of fat candles on dishes and a pair of brass scissors. "For Louisa."

Flip floundered for a second, then began down the hall. He caught her by the shoulders and spun her around. "That Louisa," he added, pointing to a door directly beside them.

"Codsworth!" a woman's voice called from down the stairs. "My footbath is getting cold."

The man, whose name evidently was Codsworth, shook his head and looked at the ceiling. "Strike me dead, Lord." He raced down the steps.

Flip pushed the door open hesitantly. Though she was fairly certain at this point that no one was going to recognize her as Lady Quillan, she had no desire to reacquaint herself with the pleasures of Bingley's sisters, especially in the guise of someone as low on the food chain as Dolly.

Louisa, the older of the two—and the married one, if Flip remembered correctly—lay sprawled across a chaise longue with a goblet in her hand, and Caroline, the tall, reedy, ostrich-looking one, stood gazing out another set of French doors, her face pinched into a frown.

"Now we'll be stuck with that common, vapor-headed girl in the household forever," Louisa complained to her sister as Flip tiptoed in. "Do you know I smelled popped corn earlier? She's an upstart minx, that one. Not there," she instructed Flip, who was looking for a place to put the tray. "There. And her sister . . ." Louisa held up a hand and made an "I'm at my wit's end" face.

Caroline's mouth smoothed into a coy grin. "Lizzy received a letter this evening."

"Did she now? I hope it wasn't from an officer we both know."

"It did have a certain scent of army tar soap to it."

The women erupted into more raucous titters. Flip's lip curled as she picked up the scissors and began to trim the wicks.

"Actually it really could be from Wickham," Caroline said. "I saw him in town today."

Louisa leaned forward. "Did you now? I thought he had quite disappeared."

"I as well. But there he was. We struck up a little conversation about the wedding tomorrow, and I just might have mentioned that poor Lizzy is quite heartbroken about Darcy."

Louisa laughed. "Oooh, that is quite wicked of you, Caro. You know that Wickham is *persona non grata* after his many misalliances."

"Ah, but Lizzy doesn't know about that. And she is old enough to make her own decisions in such matters—at least, that is certainly what she'd tell us if we dared offer any advice."

They laughed again. Flip felt a terrible pang of foreboding for Lizzy. She thought of the scene she'd read in the Rare Book Room of Wickham walking Lizzy toward that empty cottage to seduce her. Lizzy would be pregnant and abandoned in the blink of an eye. That was an end Flip had to avert, no matter the cost, and to do that she needed to find out what was in that damned note.

"Stop right there," Caroline said, and Flip jumped. Caroline was talking to her.

"Yes, m'um?"

Caroline stepped toward Flip and narrowed her eyes. "Do I know you?"

Flip busied herself with the candles. "I don't think so."

Caroline took Flip by the chin and lifted her face. Every inch came under microscopic observation. Flip would have bitten her if she could have remembered the date of her last rabies shot.

"No," Caroline said at last. "I think not. Though there is something about those eyes . . ."

She said the "something" as if it were clearly salacious, depraved or idiotic. Flip wondered how hard it would be to find powdered poison ivy in Georgian England.

Caroline released her and returned her gaze to the windows. "Darcy has arrived," she said to Louisa. "Did you hear?"

"He certainly took his time about it. Though I suppose since the Stourhead Garden affair he's been forced to keep a low profile."

Caroline sniffed. "Disreputable strumpet. And with a belly out to there."

Hell, it wouldn't even have to be powdered, Flip thought. Just rubbed around the rim of a coffee cup.

"I knew he'd be here, Caro."

Caroline blushed coquettishly. It was a bit like seeing a guillotine sprout flowers.

"Do you really think he came for me?" she asked her sister.

Flip rolled her eyes. She couldn't imagine any man doing that, especially Darcy, who she knew from personal experience had remarkably high standards in the area. She allowed herself a self-satisfied smile as she trimmed the wick and turned toward the door.

"Wait," Caroline said. "Before you go . . ."

Hell. "Yes, m'um."

"I have some laundry to be done. There. In the corner."

Flip saw a heap of sodden stockings and underclothes. She fought back a shiver of disgust. "I will ensure the housekeeper is informed."

"The housekeeper is asleep. I need this before morning."

Flip looked at the mantel clock, which reminded her again how little time she had. "It is after twelve, m'um. This will take a good many hours. And even then it shall have to be hung before the fire to dry."

"Oh, don't worry," Caroline said, smiling. "You shan't disturb me. I sleep like a baby. They're my riding clothes. I intend to get a quick one in before the ceremony."

By quick one Flip hoped she was referring to a bath, for the acrid tang of feet and other, less pastoral body parts rising from the rumpled linen was making Flip's stomach roil. "As you wish," she said as she loaded her arms. "Anything else? A cup of coffee, perhaps?"

"What? At this hour? No, thank you."

Flip bowed and went out. She looked left, then right, spotted a large chest upon which a bronze nude male stood, tugged open the bottom drawer with her toe and dumped the disgusting heap inside. All the more reason to get this story straightened out by dawn. When the drawer was closed, she wiped her hands on her apron and was considering her next step when the bronze caught her eye. The figure was broad shouldered with long, athletic lines and held a stance vaguely familiar to Flip. Everything about it was imbued with an unmistakable gravitas. Flip let her eyes travel down the chiseled chest, past the hard, muscled waist. Everything.

Caroline stuck her head out the door. "Oh, about that washing, Dolly—not too much soap. Last time it burned."

Possibly the only combustion ever associated with that region, Flip thought. "Yes, milady." She smiled until Caroline closed the door. "Miserable old bitch."

"Oh, she's not so bad." Codsworth sailed up behind Flip holding two trays aloft. "Just needs a guiding hand, that's all. Likes the way I help her from the carriage. Calls it 'able and direct.' " He broke into a loopy grin. "And a fine figure, that one."

Flip sniffed his breath for alcohol. "Really?"

"Oh, I've always liked 'em tall." He brought one of the trays down from above his head in a practiced swoosh. "Reminds me of scaling the poplars on my gran's farm. I'm taking the brandy, oysters and a rolling pin to Sir William—"

"A rolling pin?"

"—don't ask—so the sandwiches and claret for Mr. Darcy are for you." He thrust the lowered tray into her arms.

Flip took the handles carefully. The claret nearly sloshed over the rim. "What's that?" She indicated the second goblet on the tray.

"Oh, I forgot. That's a double whiskey for Colonel Fitzwilliam, Darcy's cousin."

Colonel Fitzwilliam—the nice man who tried so hard in the story to mend the rift between Darcy and Lizzy. Then Flip remembered how complicated this story got. Darcy and the colonel were cousins. The colonel was the son of the brother in the Fitzwilliam family, which is why his last name was Fitzwilliam. Darcy was the son of a sister, and he was given the Fitzwilliam family name as his first name. But whatever his name was, Flip hoped the colonel could help where, so far, she had failed.

"And don't be long," Codsworth added. "Bingley has ordered the outside of the house to be festooned with roses as a surprise for his betrothed in the morning."

"Roses? At this time of year?"

"He's had them shipped in special from Cadiz. Three thousand stems. And three thousand bloody copper vases screwed to the brick."

"Wow," Flip said, impressed. "Someone's going to be pretty busy."

Codsworth gave her a look.

"Oh yeah. Us. Right."

"But the buds haven't opened," he said. "It is our job to keep their feet warm to encourage them." He made the motion of someone pouring hot water from a teapot.

"You've got to be joking. Will we have help?"

"Sure," he said. "One-eyed Bobby will be bringing up the kettles for you."

"Do servants last long here? Or are we like long-distance horses, where they just ride us until we drop by the side of the road and hop on another?"

"I wouldn't mention that riding thing too loudly. Might find yourself with more than a rose prick to deal with tonight."

Far down the hall, a peal of laughter rang out behind a door.

"When do these people sleep?" Flip asked.

"In church, I think." He tilted his head toward the tray. "Darcy and Fitzwilliam are in the billiards room."

"Billiards room," Flip repeated, trying to appear as if she knew where this might be.

He sighed and pointed in the direction of a door down the hall.

"Right." She nodded gratefully.

Flip was almost to the door when Lizzy swept around a corner, holding another note. But this was not the earlier one. The paper was distinctly whiter. This had to be the response. When Lizzy spotted Flip, she palmed it.

"Feeling better?" Flip asked.

"A bit. Is that whiskey for someone?"

"Actually yes, and in any case—"

"Oooh!" Lizzy jumped. "Mother, aren't you up late?"

An older woman with a pair of shoes in one hand and three thick volumes in the other reached the top of the stairs, huffing. "My bunions were singing tonight, dear. Positively the 'With His Stripes We Are Healed' chorus. Is that a letter in your hand? I wasn't aware of any letters arriving."

"This?" Panic raced across Lizzy's face. "Why, it's my laundry list, of course. Thank you, Dolly. I believe three pairs of drawers and two cotton chemises will be quite enough." She laid the note on Flip's tray with a strong look of warning.

The word PRIVATE was written in feminine script on the front, and Flip could see writing where the folded paper gapped, but couldn't make out the words.

"Look at these, Lizzy dear." Mrs. Bennet handed her daughter the books. "Bingley said I should make myself at home, though at home we don't have nearly the selection of novels. *Fanny Hill,* if you can believe such a thing. Tsk-tsk. In my day, you wouldn't have found such vulgarity in a decent man's house. I would not have thought Bingley to hold such low interests, though for my part I hold Darcy responsible. That man has certainly showed himself to be capable of a shocking want of manners. But," she added with a put-upon sigh, "I suppose it is a mother's duty to acquaint her-self with the books her daughter may stumble upon in her married life. Come, my dear, bring these to my room for me. I believe I shall review them for a bit."

"I, well . . ." Lizzy looked uncertainly at Flip's tray.

Flip smiled angelically.

"Certainly, Mother."

Lizzy walked backward, keeping her eyes on Flip. At the door Lizzy had to turn for a second to get past her mother. The instant she did, Flip swiveled so that her back was to-ward them, then lifted the tray to the level of her eyes and tried to peek inside the note. The words *meeting tonight* and *balcony* made her heart jump.

Holy crap!

She wanted to put the tray down to investigate, but Lizzy would be back in a moment. Instead she lowered it enough to try to open the note with her nose, which was difficult, since she also had to keep the whiskey and claret from spilling, and resulted mainly in her turning half circles. So she rested the tray against the wall in order to accommo-date a bolder approach. She was bent over the more-firmly-placed tray, flicking the note with the tip of her tongue, when a man's chest came into focus just beyond the tray's handle.

Her gaze traveled up the white wall of linen to Darcy's appraising face.

"Are those sandwiches for me?"

Flip sucked in her tongue and tried to see past the glow of the fireballs on her cheeks. "Um, yes, actually."

"Will you be bringing them in once you've finished your, er, preparation?"

"Yes."

He retreated a step then stopped. "Would you mind terribly if I took the claret now?"

"No. Not at all."

"Thank you." He snagged the glass—"Er, carry on"—and went back into the billiards room.

Flip straightened, blood ringing in her ears, and was just about to ditch caution and put the tray on the floor when the note was snatched away.

Lizzy gazed skeptically at the moistened corner. Flip rolled a shoulder.

"I'm looking for sealing wax," Lizzy said. "Did you see happen to see some in the desk when you were looking for the letter opener?"

"I, ah, would be happy to seal it myself, if you could just wait until—"

"You are too kind, Dolly. But I will attend to this myself."

Lizzy bustled away, and Flip, only somewhat better informed than she had been five minutes before, turned and backed her way into the billiards room with a sigh.

The room was carpeted in a dark green rug of Turkish design and lit by a chandelier and a half dozen crystal lamps. Darcy was bent over the intricately carved table, lining up a challenging shot. His frockcoat lay on a nearby chair.

Flip exhaled. There was something freakishly sexy about that man's ass. And even though she'd seen it up close and personal, it looked totally different in those tight buff trousers, flexing ever so slightly as he found the perfect balance, drew his arm back and snapped—

"You are going to be serving those sandwiches now, are you not?"

Flip's head whipped around. The voice had come from behind her. Darcy wasn't playing. He was leaning against the wall watching the progress of the other man's shot. He drank deeply from the claret.

But if that was Darcy, then who had the world's greatest ass on display?

"I could use a sandwich myself," the man said, unfolding himself and turning. "All this winning is making me famished."

Flip screamed and dropped the tray. It was Magnus!

Magnus slipped slowly into sleep on the comfortable massage table, trying without much luck to keep an eye on Flip's sleeping form. The old woman might be crazy, but she gave a hell of a massage. *Your favorite book,* he thought, snorting. As if there were more than one choice.

The last thing he remembered as darkness overtook him was the breathtaking silhouette of Flip Allison's ass.

He came to not in the small room at Looking Glass, but in an exquisitely detailed Georgian upstairs hall. Only he, he considered, could have summoned something so period perfect. Statuary, ferns, porcelain clock, portraits. This was exactly as he had imagined Bingley's home, Netherfield.

He'd been skeptical of the masseuse's ability to induce a dream, let alone the setting of *Pride and Prejudice,* yet here it was. His scholar's mind went immediately to the water she'd offered him. There must have been a sleep aid in it, he thought. And he knew there were drugs like nicotine that induce lucid dreaming. Nonetheless, he felt in no danger and decided to sit back and let Austen's tale unfold before him if, in fact, that was to occur.

Immediately, a man turned the corner. Dark haired and tall, he wore the elegant tailored clothes of an early-nineteenth-century nobleman.

The somewhat careworn reserve on the man's face broke into a smile as soon as he spotted Magnus. "Cousin," he called. "I wondered if you'd be here."

I'll be damned.

Magnus looked down at his own equally well-tailored clothes and back at the man. That's Darcy, he thought to himself, dead certain, and I must be Colonel Fitzwilliam.

Darcy's appearance shook Magnus more than he'd expected. After fifteen years of careful study, he would have sworn nothing about this man could have surprised him, but fifteen years of drawing conclusions from words, however beautifully constructed, was nothing like standing next to a living, breathing person. For the first time, he thought he might understand Flip's excitement about the chance to find an ivory-billed woodpecker. He had just made literature's equivalent discovery.

A hundred questions popped into his mind. He didn't believe he was really standing next to Darcy anymore than he really felt like he was flying when such things occurred in his dreams. Nonetheless, the man's appearance here was so nearly as it might be in life, he felt as if he could reasonably engage himself for hours with the person he'd known only as a character. Magnus had years of theoretical constructions to be tested.

"Darcy," he said, "is there somewhere we could adjourn? I am most eager to find out how you've been."

* * *

Flip's scream died away as the last piece of broken china skidded to a stop.

Darcy choked and wiped his mouth. "Good God, woman. What is the problem?"

"I-I-I'm so sorry." She dropped to her knees to pick up the sandwiches. In an instant Magnus was by her side.

"Take your turn, Darcy," Magnus called. "You have enough to worry about on the table."

And as Darcy shrugged and moved to appraise the lay of the billiard balls, Flip saw that Magnus's eyes had taken on a slightly terrified glow.

"Why are you surprised to see me?" he demanded in a strangled whisper.

"Jesus, why do you think?"

"Oh God." He clutched his heart. "I was hoping you'd say because Andrew Jackson wears cupcakes or because all trout have hair—something so I'd know this was a dream." Then, as if pleading his case to an unseen jury, he began to reel off his litany. "The nice old massage lady offers me water. I drink it. She says choose your favorite book. I don't ask questions. All I want to do is get my second edition fixed. If that means submitting to the bizarre obstacle course you've laid out for the evening, so be it. I lay down. I choose *Pride and Prejudice*—that is the theme for the day, after all. Abracadabra. I wake up in Austen's masterpiece. It's clearly a dream. I think to myself, Magnus, this is it, the chance you've always longed for, to experience the people, the time, the place. I find myself in breeks. Servants call me Colonel Fitzwilliam. Darcy invites me to a game of billiards, then moons and broods for Elizabeth like a lovesick schoolboy. A perfect dream, right? And it could have been," he added, turning to her, almost desperate, "until you showed up, surprised to see me. When you're a supporting player in someone else's dream, you're not supposed to be surprised." He took a deep breath and looked at her. "For God's sake, can't you be surprised?"

She gazed at him for an instant, totally empathetic, then lifted her hands, fingers spread, to either side of her temples and said flatly, "Omigosh, Magnus what are you doing here?"

He buried his head in his hands.

"We don't have time for this," she whispered. "We need to make sure Darcy and Lizzy get married in the morning."

"Well, at least that shouldn't be too much of a challenge," he said into his palms. "It is *Pride and Prejudice* after all."

Which is when Flip remembered he didn't know about the little problem. Nor did she wish for him to become any better informed. She wanted him to believe matters were well in hand.

"There had to be something in that water," he muttered.

"Water?"

"At Madame K's. You drank it. She offered me some too. I've always been suspicious of bottled water."

"Magnus, I'm going to need you to focus."

"Focus?"

"Yes. Pull that limitless British fortitude into play, please."

He lifted his head. "Right. Got it. Married in the morning."

At that moment Jane stuck her head in the door. Her hair was loose now, and she was dressed in a frilly blue dressing gown that looked suspiciously like an early grab from her trousseau. There was a small piece of popcorn stuck to her check. Darcy and Magnus jumped to their feet and bowed.

"Good evening, Mr. Darcy—oh, and you too, Colonel Fitzwilliam. How nice! I'm right next door," Jane said, pointing past the billiard table to the room's far wall, "and I could swear I heard a crash—" She stopped when she saw the mess at Flip's feet. "Oh dear. I'm sure Dolly will have that taken care of in no time." She stood silent for a moment, then produced a clearly manufactured yawn. "Well, if you'll excuse me, I'll be off. Tomorrow is looming, and I should get my rest. Good night. Oh, Mr. Darcy—" She stopped and turned. "I would like you and Lizzy to do the honor of joining Bingley and me in our carriage on the way to the church tomorrow."

Darcy's face was a constellation of conflicting emotion. Joining Lizzy at this stage of their estrangement would be uncomfortable. "I, er . . ." He bowed. "Yes, thank you. You are too kind."

Jane disappeared in an ethereal train of blue, and Darcy returned to his analysis of the table. Flip got to her feet, gathering what remained of the sandwiches on the only unbroken plate, and gave Magnus a smile that clearly said, See? No worries.

As if on cue, a peal of hushed giggles, soprano interlaced with baritone, came from the direction of Jane's room.

Magnus cocked his head, alert. Flip busied herself admiring the plate.

The giggling ended abruptly, replaced by the start of a slow, rhythmic banging, the sort of slow, rhythmic banging that can only be made by a four-poster bed against a thick plaster wall.

Darcy looked at Magnus. Magnus looked at Flip.

She rubbed a spot off the plate's rim. "My goodness, this pattern is remarkable."

The banging grew faster. Two china elephants sitting on a table against the room's far wall began a migration west.

Darcy cleared his throat uncomfortably and returned to his shot.

The banging increased and began to be punctuated with breathy grunts.

"Tell me," Magnus said through gritted teeth to Flip, "are all of our beloved characters so happy?"

Then the roar of running on the balcony caused all three heads to turn. Codsworth's sister, the flame-haired serving girl, Peg, flew by holding a rolling pin and giggling, followed at a distance by a portly, hypertensive centaur in the form of Sir William, forefingers at his temples. Darcy made an exasperated noise and looked for the chalk.

"Yes," Flip said with enthusiasm. "It's infectious."

"Like a rousing case of gonorrhea. And our hero and heroine?" Magnus demanded. "Has this infection of happiness overtaken them as well?"

"Well . . ." Flip shifted from foot to foot. "Being the more introspective of the two couples, their happiness is, of course, more tempered."

"Of course. But they are marrying tomorrow? I am told there's a wedding."

Darcy asked, "Now where has the chalk gotten to, Fitzwilliam?"

"So sorry," Magnus said, turning. "It's on the chair there— oh, my dear cousin, you're a mess."

"What?" Darcy followed Magnus's gaze down to his shirt. Splattered across the front was a large claret-colored stain. "Hell. I must have spilled my wine when she screamed." He began to unbutton his cuff.

Magnus returned his attention to Flip. "Are they marrying?"

"I would say their plans are somewhat less formed."

His eyes flashed. "How less formed?"

At this point, Lizzy entered the room, "Dolly, I found the seal but no wax—" Lizzy yelped, and the seal dropped with a clack to the floor, followed immediately by the fluttering note.

Flip spun around. Darcy, balled shirt in hand, stood frozen, halfway to the door, in nothing but breeches and boots.

"I do beg your pardon—" Darcy began, but Lizzy turned on her heels as if she'd just been slapped or possibly bent over the nearest couch.

"Miss Bennet, wait." Darcy swooped to scoop up the dropped items. "You've forgotten your letter and—"

Lizzy let out a gasp. She wheeled around, tore the items from his hand and stomped off to the left. Now Darcy, too, wore that just-slapped expression, though without the hint of the just-couched one to make up for it.

"Er, considerably less formed," Flip said.

"Excuse me, if you would." Darcy flung his shirt into the corner. "I'm going to bed." He strode from the room and turned right.

The ceramic elephants hopped around the table like linebackers in an electric tabletop football game. Sir William ran by in the other direction, pausing only to rear up like a stallion as Peg swatted his hindquarters and laughed.

"My goodness," Flip said, "Austen certainly has a keen eye for detail."

Magnus took her by the arm. "We need to talk."

Chapter Nineteen

The waiting room at Looking Glass Massage Therapy gave off a funny vibe, Io thought. Somewhere between The Body Shop and the wagon of Professor Marvel, the carnival huckster in *The Wizard of Oz*. The door to the treatment room was closed, and despite having pressed her ear against it, Io heard nothing except the odd grunt and a muted version of "You've Lost That Lovin' Feeling."

Jed was rifling the papers on the little ornate desk, though the pair of women's winter gloves he wore to hold the hydrocortisone in place—the only sort of bandage they could find at the nearest 7-Eleven—gave a sort of Pink Panther absurdity to the whole thing. The citation from the cop stuck from his pocket like a goldenrod hankie, and he hadn't noticed the long, skunklike streak of calamine lotion in his hair, a fact which had entertained Io for at least the last half hour.

They'd endured a twenty-minute dressing-down by police, then headed straight for Looking Glass.

Jed stopped what he was doing long enough to gape at an unopened box of incense. "Look," he said, reading the name printed on the side. " 'Ylang-ylang' . . . ain't that a beer?" He laughed.

Io rolled her eyes. On certain topics, Jed was like a Wiki for half-wits. "That's *ee-lahng–ee-lahng.*" She pronounced it phonetically. "It's not beer. It's a flower."

"It's not beer," he repeated in her same disdainful tone. "It's a flower. Well, pardon me." He dropped the box back on the desk. "Are you sure this is the right place? This doesn't seem like a place Flip would go."

"You didn't think the guy from Cornell seemed like someone she'd be fucking, either, but you were wrong about that. This is what the card in her purse read, and there's definitely a man and a woman in there."

A man's voice caught her attention. She pressed her ear harder against the door. It was definitely the velvet-eyed guy. She sighed. Flip had certainly upgraded her men.

"What do you hear?" Jed demanded.

"Right now, only you. If you'd shut up for a minute, I might be able to tell you something." She listened. "He's asking about"—she frowned, confused—*"Pride and Prejudice."*

"What the fuck does *Pride and Prejudice* have to do with a massage?"

"Got me." She tried to hear more but the talking had ceased. "But it's the British guy, for sure. I recognize his voice."

"So the guy from Cornell screws my wife, screws me out of a fellowship and puts a rock through my car window? What's his freakin' problem?"

"She's your *ex*-wife—and obviously he thought you were getting too close to the cloning stuff. Maybe he's part of the operation too." Jed had reluctantly shared his theories on the dead bird with Io as they trolled the 7-Eleven for poison ivy treatments. "Okay, here's the deal," she said. "Whatever we find out, I get to break the story and you don't lose your job for screwing a minor."

"Jesus, you should have told me you were seventeen. How the hell did you end up in the honors journalism program?"

She gave him a mischievous smile. "I'm known as a 'child something.' Can you guess what? It begins with *p.*"

"Oh, I've got it. I just didn't know that sort of thing qualified someone for honors."

"Uh-oh." Io jerked away from the door. "Someone's coming."

Jed dropped the papers and slipped into a chair as a woman approximately as large as a MINI Cooper and as brightly clothed as a sixties VW van swept through the door. The woman's gaze went from Io to her desk to the gloves on Jed's hands.

"I didn't hear the bell," she said.

Io said sweetly, "We're here for massages."

"Like those two," Jed said, trying to see over the woman's shoulder.

The woman shut the door with a definitive click. "It's late," she said, "and massages don't help poison ivy."

"But—" Io stopped. That was strange. How had she known?

"We're interested in the pigeon," Jed said with a hard look. "We'd hate to have to see if the cops could help."

"Vhat are you saying?" she asked with concern.

"I'm saying the cops can get kinda particular about licenses and inspections for places like this."

The woman considered her options. She pointed to a smaller room to the side. "You'll have to go in there. It's the only other massage room I have."

Jed gave Io a look. "Yeah. No problem."

"I'll take Dad first," the woman said, and Io snorted.

"We're a couple," Jed said, irritated.

"*Uff da*. My mistake. Vould you like a double massage then?"

He frowned. "So, you're telling me there really is a massage?"

"Vhat else?"

"But we'll find out about the pigeon?"

She lifted her brow. "I think you'll be very surprised vhat you find out. Are you big readers?"

Jed looked at Io. He shrugged. "Yeah, sure. Why?"

"I offer a very special service." she opened the door to the other room and flicked on the lights. "And for you tonight, eez free."

Chapter Twenty

Magnus dropped Flip hard onto the nearest chair. "Talk."

Her throat dried. He looked enormous, towering over her in those knee boots. And the unfortunate placement of his waist directly at eye level didn't help. "I-I—"

"You were here before, yes?"

"Yes."

"As a maid?"

Maid, maiden. Why quibble? "Er, sort of."

"What is going on between Elizabeth and Darcy?"

"I, well, I mean, I assume it's that proposal thing. He didn't ask her very kindly if you'll recall and—"

"Yes, I'm quite aware of Darcy's shortcomings. In the book, however, Austen has this worked out in time for Elizabeth and Jane to share a double wedding."

Flip licked her lips. She wished fervently Magnus would give up this line of questioning and go back to Looking Glass. His appearance was a complication she didn't need when she only had a few hours left, and, in any case, the last thing she wanted was Magnus finding out about Lady Quillan. "I don't know. Maybe Jane and Bingley's wedding gets delayed. Maybe it's one of those behind-the-scenes things that a reader doesn't really even know about before the author cinches things up at the end?"

"Or perhaps Darcy's very public coupling with Lady Quillan in the folly at Stourhead Garden has set Elizabeth's teeth understandably on edge."

Flip made a noise like her father's seventy-two Cadillac on a January morning.

"Yes," Magnus said. "I had an opportunity to have a nice talk with Darcy before you arrived. When I asked how Miss Elizabeth Bennet was, he stammered out a vague reference to Stourhead Garden and immediately changed the subject. Since I recall no mention of Hoare's estimable garden in Austen's work, I used the opportunity when Darcy dashed out to find chalk to ask Sir William for clarification. This was before the start of the horse race on the balcony. The little bit of information he was able to give me before Darcy returned was, shall we say, eye-opening."

"Was it?" *I'm so screwed! Please don't let him know Lady Quillan was me!*

"Yes." He gave her a hard look. "Apparently Darcy's interlude with a woman atop the railing of Hoare's temple is on the tip of every gossip's tongue."

Flip felt the blood creep up her neck. "That Austen. Always another twist up her sleeve."

"The woman wasn't Austen, and it wasn't her sleeve."

Heh.

"Bloody hell." He snagged his goblet from a nearby table. "Gentlemen in this period did not as a rule make love to other men's wives atop a neighbor's favorite garden fixture. And Darcy's scruples would be more exacting than most." He waved his hand. "Hell, maybe it is just gossip. I can't imagine Darcy succumbing to a woman like that."

Flip crossed her arms. "Oh, it happened."

He lifted the drink to his lips. "Is that what Elizabeth told you?"

"Of course not. She barely—" Flip stopped.

He paused mid-sip and looked at her.

"I heard it from the other servants," she said firmly.

Magnus shook his head. "What the hell was he doing? Darcy is neither rash nor incautious."

"They didn't do anything to be ashamed of."

"They weren't exactly admiring the architecture."

"Or the latest acquisition in the Rare Book Room. People sometimes do things with no more motivation than a desire to have fun. Live with it."

Magnus grunted but did not press the point. "What does Looking Glass have to do with this?"

"Well, Madame K clearly sent us here."

"Have all the editions changed?"

Flip bit her lip. He was not going to be happy about this. "Yes. The oldest ones for now, but the others are going to change too—that is, unless I can fix things, which I think can."

"*Think* you can?" Magnus's eyes bulged.

"Focus. Remember?"

"Right." He smacked his palm on his forehead and drank deeply. "Has Darcy even proposed yet?"

"Yes—Listen, do you think I could have some of that?"

He appeared surprised to find whiskey in his hand. He looked around and found Darcy's goblet. Then he tossed down what was left of that, poured half his whiskey into it and handed it to her. "Sorry. Let's take a moment to catch our breath."

"Thanks." The liquid was smoky warm on her tongue—almost as warm as the print his hand left on the glass. She sunk back into the chair, and noticed he was watching as she drank.

He lowered himself onto the seat beside her. "I never realized burlap could be so sexy."

"You're a dick."

He laughed. It was the first time she'd seen him really laugh. His mouth was generous and full, and the lines near his eyes bloomed into inviting branches.

"So, why is it you're a servant?" He stood to retrieve his jacket, which he, like Darcy, had removed for the game. "Seems to me you're more cut out for something fierce and imperious—a dowager duchess or a bear tamer, something of that sort."

"Me, imperious? That's rich." She remembered Madame K's warning about only attempting one visit. If she returned a third time, she thought, gazing at the striking figure he cut in those form-fitting trousers, she'd probably come back as Magnus's washwoman or some sort of other slightly disreputable woman for hire. Oh dear! The whiskey was hitting her fast. "The proposal, you were saying. Yes, Darcy made it, and yes, Lizzy turned him down flat."

"Because of his efforts to keep Jane and Bingley apart?"

He slipped on the coat, which was an elegant dark navy cut to the waist in front with long curved tails in back, and it wasn't until he was buttoning the last button that she caught a glimpse of its exotic lime green paisley lining.

"I-I—" She couldn't take her eyes off him. Between the whiskey, the boots, the paisley and the amazing eye-level view, it was like a curtain had been raised on some amazing Regency peep show, and now she was supposed to answer questions she couldn't even remember and didn't care about in the first place. What she wanted to do was straddle those cream trousers, tear open the coat and make him service her right there on top of that slippery green silk.

He looked at her expectantly, as if he were both waiting for an answer and wondering if she, perhaps, had stroked out.

"Um." She clenched the stem of her goblet. "Could you repeat the question?"

"Elizabeth turned Darcy down because he kept Jane and Bingley apart?" He reseated himself beside her.

"No. Yes. A little, I guess." She looked down at her toes. "Because of Lady Quillan, mostly. But Lizzy wants him. That much is clear. Look, I, ah, appreciate the moment to catch my breath, but I think we should hurry. Who knows how much time we have before we wake up?"

"I think taking the time to formulate a plan would help more than hinder. I know it's probably not your typical modus operandi, but indulge me. Has Darcy explained, sent Lizzy the long letter telling her why he—oh, right." He stopped in response to Flip's raised brow. "I can see where it would be a little awkward to put that in writing."

"He needs to talk to her in person," she said. "He needs to explain and apologize and tell her it meant nothing, that no matter what he was doing or who he was doing it to, all he could do was think of her. There ain't a woman alive who isn't going to go for that one."

He looked at Flip over the rim of his glass, his eyes as clear and deep as twin topazes. "*Do* women go for that?"

"I did with Jed. But no more than twenty or thirty times."

He did not submit to the easy laugh, and Flip felt herself grow uncomfortable under his gentle, interested gaze.

"I expect," he said after a long moment, "most women know the measure of a not-so-good man from the start, and stay with him out of compassion or curiosity or even simple amusement until he's worn out his welcome. There are women, I know, who could never be painted as victims, only experience seekers. Epicures, as it were."

She beamed into her whiskey. That was the nicest she'd ever felt about having fallen for Jed.

"Though I do wonder," he added, "if you found what you were seeking."

What I was seeking, she thought, was an intellectual equal, a partner in crime and a baby. To be fair, Jed had really only failed her miserably in one.

She looked at Magnus, afraid she'd see mocking or, worse, a curiosity she was unprepared to accommodate. But in his soft brown eyes was merely a genuine interest in the answer—the sort that springs out of growing regard.

"No, actually." She felt the tug of the vast volume of tears she'd expended on the topic. "What a surprise, eh?"

"Not a surprise, no." He looked down at his glass, swirling the contents. "But unfortunate all the same."

He might as well be swirling her as that glass, she thought, given the torrent of feelings he was unleashing.

"So, what? A few years of marriage? Not too high a price to pay for knowledge, right? You're a scientist." He grinned. "I'm sure you've got the makings for a paper there. No kids, I suppose?"

A rush of heat went from her neck to her ears. "No," she said, struggling to shake off his narrowing gaze. "With Jed? Are you kidding?"

"Would you have wanted that?" he asked carefully.

"God, no." She didn't even sound like *she* believed it.

"What about you?" she put in quickly. "You've found what you were looking for?"

"I don't know," he said. "Perhaps."

She thought of the photo of those uniformed girls. *Ask*, she said to herself sharply. *It may not change what happens, but you'll at least be making your choice with open eyes.* "And your wife—"

"Did I mention a wife?"

"You were excruciatingly silent on the matter."

He made a small laugh. "I think she'd prefer it that way."

"So you're . . . divorced?" She held her breath.

"Separated, actually."

Hellllll! Just as she suspected—and worse than married, frankly. Married, at least the sex might be great. Separated gave her visions of abstracted dinner conversation and moody ejaculations. If anything should be skippingly care-free, it should be an ejaculation.

Hey! her inner voice interrupted. *He just said he was separated. And the response of a person whose concern extends beyond her own self-interest would be . . . ?*

"That's hard," she said.

"More complicated than hard, really."

Great. Couldn't have gotten my man priorities more reversed if I'd tried.

"Flip," he said flatly. "It's not going to make a difference."

The liquid amber in those eyes was as intoxicating as that in her glass.

"I-I owe you an apology," she said, looking down quickly.

"I hope it's not about that kiss. I rather liked the unexpectedly direct approach."

Damn him, she thought, blushing. How does he make me feel like a tongue-tied teenager? "No, it's about Jed. I didn't tell you why he was following me, and I should have. He was following me because he found a pigeon in my purse."

"Jesus, aren't there enough of those things around to keep him busy on his own? I believe there's a man-eating one in your apartment that might benefit from some careful observation."

"The one Jed found is a special sort of pigeon."

"More special than a man-eater? Does it sing German opera? Or maybe fix small appliances?"

She laughed. "It's *Ectopistes migratorius*. A passenger pigeon. It's extinct in our time."

"Ah. I can see where that might be of some interest to an ambitious ornithologist. But"—his face clouded—"where did you find one?"

She swallowed. "Here. The first time I visited."

"Here?" The realization swept over him like a terrifying wave. "What's happening here can produce extinct birds . . . there?" He jerked his thumb in what Flip assumed was the direction of twenty-first-century Pittsburgh.

"Seems so." She laughed a nervous laugh. "So make sure you empty your pockets before you leave." Then she laughed even more nervously. There was no way those pants could hide anything in a pocket. They couldn't even hide a pocket.

Magnus took a deep drink, collapsed against the back of the chair and put his hand over his eyes.

"Jed found it, dead, in my purse," Flip went on quickly, trying to keep Magnus from pondering too much. "That's what he burst into the apartment for."

She saw a small smile play across Magnus's mouth. "Ah, yes. He did seem to be worked up about something. Though I think," he added, returning his gaze to her, "he ended up with even more information than he bargained for."

"Yes." She flushed. "But in any case, he thinks I cloned it, for God's sake, which would be pretty unethical—and of questionable conservation value, I might add—especially if one doesn't mention that fact when one presents her discovery to colleagues."

Magnus shook his head, never breaking his observation. "Jed doesn't know the first thing about you, does he?"

Flip felt her pulse quicken and finished the last of the whiskey in a hurried gulp. "Jed bulldozes through most situations with his balls or his ego, which doesn't leave him a lot of time for getting to know someone."

"Fortunately he's with someone now whose depth of character isn't going to be a big stumbling block. Would you like more?" Magnus leaned forward and palmed her empty goblet, catching her fingers beneath his.

Flip inhaled, and for an instant neither of them moved. Then he lifted the glass from her hand, bent in close and kissed her. Flip felt a charge rocket through her. He drew back, and she was intensely aware of his achingly clean scent and the light glinting on those dark, loose waves of hair just beyond his ear and the exquisite prickles like tiny charges on her lips and fingers. "I—I would."

He hooked a hand under her knee and angled himself toward her just as someone swept through the door.

Flip jerked herself hard against the back of the chair, and Magnus jumped to his feet, scooping up both glasses and clearing his throat. She could barely raise her eyes to meet the horrified gaze of Caroline Bingley.

The look with which Caroline raked her reduced Flip to a trifling tart. Though not a stitch of clothing was out of place, Flip didn't doubt she looked discreditable. Her lips were apart, her chest was rising and falling like a marathoner's and she knew she wore the pink, upended look of someone very thirsty who has just been interrupted mid-quench.

"Dolly," Caroline commanded, "return to your room at once. I shall be there to speak to you shortly."

Flip stood instantly. "Yes, m'um—"

"*No.*"

Caroline swung to meet Magnus's equally rocky gaze.

"I beg your pardon, Colonel Fitzwilliam," she said coolly, "but we cannot have an upstairs maid behaving like a common—"

"No," he repeated, color rising.

"No, what, Colonel?"

"No, Dolly will not return to her room, and, no, you will not proceed in this attack on her character."

"Her character?" Caroline said in shock, as if servants could no more be expected to have character than a fireplace screen or yesterday's mincemeat pie.

Their gazes hardened into something like two opposing football players an instant before the snap. Flip watched, heart racing, certain she'd hear an audible boom as one or both of their heads exploded off its neck. But Magnus was older, taller and far too used to having his proclamations carry. Caroline broke first, looking away with an aggrieved "You do your service no honor, Colonel." She swept out, vibrating with rage.

Flip let out her breath slowly, still staring at the doorway, then turned. Magnus's eyes met hers with such a look of unconsummated desire that though he was half a room away, the flick of his eyes across her face made her gasp.

"I'm sorry, Flip."

She waved away his concern, trying to find words again

in the barren dust bowl of her mouth. "Don't worry about it. It's nothing."

"It wasn't nothing—and a moment later would have been worse."

This sent a surprising heat in several directions, though most obviously, to her cheeks. She stared at her empty chair, the vision of that unexpectedly diverted future vivid in her imagination.

"Well, this much I can tell you," she said, laughing nervously. "Dolly is going to be having a very bad day tomorrow."

"And for some time to come, I think. That was Caroline Bingley, I take it?" And when Flip concurred, he nodded. "Austen certainly captured the hedgehogian spines of her character with precision."

"You do hedgehogs no honor, Colonel," she said primly, then added with a loopy smile, "I was a big fan of Sonic in high school, you know."

"And I of Mrs. Tiggy-winkle, though at a considerably younger age. I stand corrected."

His elegant bow took Flip's breath away. Taut and sleek, those trousers hugged their not inconsiderable contents with the same sort of subversively proper functionality as chocolate on a frozen banana. God, it had been a long time since she'd had a frozen banana.

"So," he said, rubbing his hands conspiratorially, "what are we going to do to scrub the memory of the easy-virtued Lady Quillan from Elizabeth's mind?"

Flip winced. "Easy-virtued seems a tad strong."

"Pardon?"

"Nothing. Talk to Darcy. You are his cousin and most trusted friend. Get him to tell Lizzy how he feels. Get him to apologize."

"Apologize. Hmmm." Magnus screwed his mouth into a knot. "I find my expert understanding of the precise breadth and depth of Darcy's character a trifle, er, dissuasive in this regard."

"Listen, Sigmund, just because you can quote the number of times the word *pineapple* or *fanny* appears in the text doesn't make you or anyone else an expert on Darcy's character. A character is more than the words on a page. A character's all the other stuff that's in a reader's head too."

"I can assure you, the word *fanny* does not appear in *Pride and Prejudice*—except perhaps in the special edition you've created," he added under his breath.

"All I'm saying is, don't let your conception of Darcy's character shake you. I think he just might surprise you. There's more to him than you might expect." *A fact to which I can readily attest.*

The clock struck a forbidding note, which died into silence.

Flip looked. Twelve thirty! Holy crap! That left them a little more than eleven hours until it was too late to change anything. "And don't wait."

"Talk to him now? At this hour?"

"You know," she said, pulling him toward the door. "The early bird and all. And this is a big worm."

Codsworth marched by, making a tea-pouring motion.

"Oh, boy," she said to Magnus. "I gotta run."

Something at the window caught Magnus's eye and he stopped. "Why on earth," he asked, gazing out into the courtyard, "would a messenger be out and about this late at night?"

"Oh, shit!" Flip clapped her fingers to her temples. She had totally forgotten the note. "Coming or going?"

"Going. As if the hounds of hell are on his heels."

"Dammit! That's Lizzy's reply to Wickham."

"Lizzy's reply to Wickham?!" Magnus purpled. "Hasn't he been banished to a regiment in northern England for his sins at this point in the book?"

She held up her palms. "Would you believe a generous vacation policy?"

"Flip," Magnus said, sharply enough to make her jump, "why is Elizabeth sending a profligate scrub like Wickham a note in the middle of the night?"

She squinched an eye closed, preparing for the explosion. "I believe it might have something to do with losing her virginity."

The purple deepened. "Do you mean to tell me that Elizabeth lost her virginity to Wickham?!"

"Not yet."

His nostrils widened, and he made a noise like a bull in Pamplona eyeing the closest idiot *turista*.

"No time for tantrums, Magnus. If we don't hurry—" She snapped her mouth shut. He didn't know about the deadline—or the awful things that would happen if they missed it.

But he'd caught the import of the word as well as her attempt to swallow it.

He gave her a fisheye. "Apart from the fear of me reaching the end of my patience, what, pray tell, happens if we don't hurry?"

"Um . . ." She swallowed, improvising madly.

" 'Um'?"

She snapped her fingers. "No double wedding tomorrow. One must be true to the book."

"Spoken like the literary purist you are. Fine. You take Elizabeth. I'll take Darcy, and if all else fails, I feel certain Austen could withstand a wedding delayed a day or two."

"Actually," Flip said quickly, " I'm pretty sure we only have until morning to get this fixed. Let me know how that Darcy thing goes," she said, and ran out the door.

Chapter Twenty-one

Magnus tapped on the wide paneled door. "Darcy, it is I, your cousin, Fitzwilliam."

A long moment passed—so long, in fact, Magnus worried that Darcy might be asleep. Then a dispirited "Come" cut through the silence.

Darcy was slouched at his French doors, gazing across the balcony and out into the moon-filled park. He wore a clean shirt, though it hung untucked around his breeches. Magnus was reminded again, even in the midst of this chaos, how deeply moving it was to his scholar's mind to see in the flesh this character he had lived with so long on paper. And whatever may or may not have happened at the Apollo Temple, this brooding, infatuated Darcy remained effortlessly faithful to the man on the page but, at the same time, infinitely more complex. As perfect as the right combination on paper can be, Magnus thought, it cannot hold a candle to life.

"Women," Darcy said glumly.

"Yes," Magnus agreed, thinking of Flip.

"Sometimes I just want to . . ." Darcy thumped the wall with the side of his fist.

"Yes."

"And other times . . ."

Magnus recalled that provocative ass and even more provocative spirit. "Indeed."

Darcy gave his cousin a smile. "I see you have been bitten, too."

Magnus found himself caught off guard. He made a surprised gurgle, and Darcy laughed.

Magnus thought of that kiss and the silky, just-showered skin under his touch and how he'd like to gather that sunbeam hair in one hand and a palm full of breast in the other and break that mouth of its infuriating tendency to curve when he demanded seriousness. In a few short minutes he would cure it of that affliction, and when it tightened as it would into that fretting, deeply satisfying "O" he would—

"Fitzwilliam?"

Magnus jumped. "What?"

"I said, will you marry her first?"

"Marry her?" Magnus blinked. Though the thought had never crossed his mind till that very moment, the image of a slim gold band on a hand flung far over her head, grasping in that swirling eddy of gilded tendrils as he buried himself inside her, excited his libido far more than he ever would have expected.

"They are the ones one must marry, you know," Darcy said thoughtfully. "It is not right to do anything less when one is in love."

That snapped Magnus out of his reverie.

"Don't be absurd, Darcy. You talk as if marrying for love is an everyday occurrence. In this day, not one man in ten marries for love. In fact, statistics show quite clearly that a man of your rank—"

"You are not suggesting," Darcy said, eyes narrowing,

"anything short of marriage for Miss Bennet, I hope? You know how I feel about her."

"Not at all." Magnus thought of Campbell's paper on the complex negotiations often required in wedding arrangements among the upper classes and, given the surprising long engagement periods they necessitated, the rate of failed betrothals. "By all means, marry her if you choose, but you could as easily decide to marry Caroline Bingley or any other of a hundred women for their wedding portions, and just march into Elizabeth Bennet's room right now and"— Magnus's face exploded in pain as Darcy knocked him off his feet with a remarkably capable right jab—"tell her you're through," he finished, wiping the blood off his lip.

"Oh." Darcy dropped to a knee and pulled Magnus to standing. "Sorry about that, my friend." *I thought you were about to say something else.*

"I think you must ask the lady again," Magnus said, taking the handkerchief Darcy offered. "I have it on good authority that she pines for you."

"Pines for me?" Darcy's face lit for an instant, then knitted. "Whose authority?"

"Er, her lady's maid." *Was Flip a lady's maid? In that burlap sack she looked more like something out of Dickens.* "Miss Bennet confided her feelings—reluctantly, of course, and in some amount of tears, I believe—and I, ah, overheard the lady's maid repeat it to another."

"Gossip?" Darcy grimaced. "I abhor such low-minded behavior."

Magnus shrugged. "You know how they are."

Darcy's shoulders slumped. "How I should like it if Miss Bennet were to confide in me."

"You shall have your chance, cousin. You shall have your

chance. But you must act—and quickly, as quickly as you possibly can," he added with emphasis. "I took the opportunity to question the upstairs footman before coming to you. I am told the lady in question has retired for the evening, but that her custom these last weeks is to take a short stroll on the balcony to clear her mind before sleeping. You must wait there, behind the topiary, so that she comes upon you without warning. Then you must make your case. Be firm, though. She will interpret any hesitation on your part as a lack of resolve."

"And you think the lady will accede?" In Darcy's face, humble uncertainty and ferocious pride fought for ascendancy.

Magnus gestured him from the open door and said in a low voice, "Cousin, you and I are men of the world, so I hope I do not have to be more explicit than this: When a man faces the challenge of a woman who is both apparently recalcitrant and—how shall I say it?—less apparently but inarguably *willing,*" he added, raising a blocking arm should his characterization drive Darcy to further violence, "he must carry the moment with action, the kind of action that is likely to force this unacknowledged desire into such an obvious and provocative challenge to her, a sort of Mount Etna to her Hadrian, if you will, that the only way to prove herself master of the situation once again is to scale it and claim the victory as her own. Do you follow me, my friend?"

"Carpe diem?" Darcy's gaze made it clear they were of a single mind.

"You have it in one, sir."

"I think—"

"The time for thought is over. The time for action is

upon us. Do not hesitate. The battle line has been drawn. It started at a small public dance in Longbourn and it shall end at the topiary on the balcony at Netherfield. Go forth, true to your cause!"

"Thank you, Fitzwilliam." Darcy started for the doors, then came to stop. "There was a time, you know, when I wished you would talk me out of it, when I wished you would separate me from her, just as I tried to separate Bingley from her sister. But I must say that I am very glad you never tried."

"I was never even tempted, my friend," Magnus said, taking the proffered hand. "A love like this comes but once in a lifetime." And pressing the handkerchief against his throbbing lip, he watched with satisfaction as Darcy took his first steps into a future envisioned by Jane Austen but facilitated by the timely and judicious intervention of matchmaker extraordinaire, Magnus Knightley.

Chapter Twenty-two

Flip edged along Netherfield's flat, gravel-lined roof, leaning precariously over the short wall that gave the front of the house its final few feet of height. She had tried to find Lizzy but a quick run through the upper and lower floors had been unfruitful, especially unfruitful since she'd run into Codsworth and been immediately handed a brimming tea pot and directed to the roof.

On the balcony below, the light from the lanterns set at regular intervals along the upper floor's length was enough to bring her work into dim view. A seemingly infinite number of rose tins glinted copper in the glow of the flames, and she poured the warm water into the dark reaches of wisteria vines, where the tins had been attached, listening for the metallic jangle that was the only indication of her success in helping to bring Bingley's three-story Valentine to life.

Jesus, Flip thought, what ever happened to just carving one's initials into a tree?

Two nightingales trilled sweetly as they circled overhead. She wished she had a good set of binoculars, hiking boots and about six hours of uninterrupted time in this intriguing country to make it cough up whatever other ornithological treasures it might be holding, but most of all she wished someone, just once, would make a similarly extravagant gesture for her. Jed had once pissed an outline of her breasts in the snow after a particularly foreshortened session of lovemaking on the hood of his Porsche, but since he had immediately followed up with three energetic fist pumps and a shout of "Holy shit, I have one amazing dick!" she felt the gesture probably said more about Jed's feelings for Jed than his feelings for her.

The teapot heaved its last pour, and there was only one way to fill it up.

"Crap."

The steps down to the second floor were so narrow the only way Flip could navigate was by putting the pot atop her head, evoking, she hoped, Keats's Ode on a Grecian Urn, or perhaps the little girl at the end of *The Jungle Book*. She wondered if she could lure any men from their magical world of wild boydom with nothing more than a hypnotic lowering of her gaze.

She balanced the pot with one hand, thrusting her breasts skyward and swished her hips a bit as she emerged into the far end of the upstairs hall.

Darcy strode in from the balcony. She prayed he had already fixed things up with Lizzy, but that uncertain look on his face didn't give her a lot of hope. He stopped when he saw her, and she could feel his gaze as she passed.

Oh yeah, she thought with an inward smile. What did Shakira say? Hips don't lie? She knew a full-on view of her ass would bring that night in Apollo's Temple back to him. She kept on walking.

"Wait!" he cried.

She turned and lowered her eyes. "Yes?"

"Pardon me. I know this must seem like a strange question, but . . ." He took in every aspect of her face.

"Yes?"

"Do you know if that is the only topiary on the balcony?"

What the—

"Yes," Magnus's voice replied. "That is the one."

Darcy gave his cousin an embarrassed nod. "Thank you. I shall return to my, ah, station."

Darcy ducked back out the door, and Magnus, who had appeared out of freakin' nowhere, gave Flip and her hips a withering glance.

"That is just the sort of behavior," he said with equal parts menace and intrigue, "that not only reminds a man there's a debt of honor to be paid, but quite inclines him to call in the chit posthaste." He flexed his hands.

The migratory wave of blood that flew from her brain to points farther south left her light-headed. "How typical," she sniffed when she'd urged her tongue into something like obedience. "A man taking advantage of a woman in an inferior position."

Magnus laughed, a quiet, untamed noise that made her wish someone else would appear in the hall.

"There are a number of positions I could imagine you in," he said in a low voice. "Inferior is not one of them."

She put down the pot before she dropped it.

He caught it and pulled her along with it into the nearest room, which turned out to be a supply closet of some sort, complete with linens, rags, pillows, lotions, soaps, a bottle marked COOK'S BRANDY and something that looked suspiciously like a bucket full of oatmeal. Towels, blankets and other sorts of bedclothes were stacked high on shelves that towered over a sturdy worktable.

"Why do we have only until morning?" he demanded.

Flip cringed. "There seems to be an expiration date on the changes."

"Oh, thank God. They go away?"

"Not exactly. They, ah, stay forever."

He slapped his palms against his eyes and rubbed. "This can't be happening. Forever, you say?"

She slunk back a step. "Yep."

"In every book?"

"Every edition, book or volume. Yep, that's the deal."

He returned to rubbing his eyes. "Holy Christ."

"But you've made progress, yes?" The room, like the hallway, was dark, but it had a small window, and when Magnus turned into the moonlight, she gasped. "What happened to your lip?"

"What? Oh, this." He touched his mouth, abashed. "I impugned Elizabeth's honor."

"The man who won the National Book Critics' Circle award for his work on Jane Austen impugned Lizzy Bennet's honor?"

"Not intentionally, of course. But it had the effect of moving Darcy in the right direction, thereby attempting to preserve both Austen's reputation and my own, not to mention restoring at least a modest opportunity for me to actually win the prize you continue to credit me with already possessing. And yes, I have made progress. With any luck at all, Darcy and Lizzy will be reunited within the hour, no harm, no foul. I must admit," he said, gazing abstractedly into the distance, "it is remarkable to feel a part of this story, to persuade the hero to take his hero's place, to sense Austen's hand in every detail—well, almost every detail."

"If you'd been any more persuasive," Flip said, turning his chin toward the window, "we might have to call a surgeon."

"Very funny. Darcy has a remarkable hook for a man of the aristocracy. I must look up pugilism when we return. I was not aware it had any widespread use as a form of exercise except perhaps in some parts of the navy. Mc-Naughton's work on urban Georgian recreation mentioned something on—"

"Hold on, let me fluff up one of these pillows here before you begin."

"You are not lessening my inclination to call in that debt, you know."

"Hold still, would you?" She pressed his lip very gently to see if the blood was fresh. It was, and she rubbed it away with a skim of her finger that caught not only slick wetness but the bristle of day-old beard and the warmth of softly padded lips.

She was holding the finger in the air, considering her next step, when he caught it and lightly sucked the blood away.

The touch of his tongue unleashed an exquisite ball of pain inside her that roared with such ferociousness she swayed. Clutching the edge of the table she said, "Hey, and I was just going to ask if you'd been tested for HIV." She made a nervous laugh.

"I have," he said. "Regularly, recently, and always clean."

As pickup lines go, it wasn't going to end up in any romance novel. Nonetheless it made that ball of pain feel like she was riding a very enthusiastic horse.

He put his arms around her and kissed her deeply. "You?"

"After J-Jed," she began, but with the taste of him on her tongue no more words would come.

"After Jed you had a test?" he offered.

She nodded.

"And it was clean?"

He had brought his hands to the curve of her hips, and her jaw fell slack. She made a small, struggled puff.

"I'll take that as a yes," he said. "And since?"

She wanted those hands to be rougher. The delicate swirls he was making across parts of her skin that had no right to be so sensitive were torture. She closed her eyes, trying to think past the delicious scent of soap and wool with which he filled not only the room but all her conscious thought, and forced out a barely audible "No."

"No, you've had no need of one since Jed?"

She nodded her agreement, no ego left.

"I see. I shall have my work cut out for me then."

She gasped, and he stopped the noise with his mouth.

But there was something in the practiced nip of her lips after a long moment that made her pause.

What? the voice inside her cried, highly indignant. *What are you doing? Since when is "practiced" bad?*

"Practiced" was nipples plucked to a deep, elemental rhythm. "Practiced" was an irresistible noise in her ear. "Practiced" was curled toes and grasping fingers and enough time to explore every variation in unhurried, languorous turns. "Practiced" was long, hard orgasms that turned her bones to jelly and her mind to satisfied mush.

But "practiced" was also Jed. And "practiced" had a way of valuing occasions over connection. Before Jed she had never minded occasions. Cherished them, in fact. But now . . . She thought of those girls in the school uniforms.

"I need to finish the roses."

"Later." He gave her another kiss and looked into her eyes.

Practiced, the voice said.

"I-I—No." But she raised her mouth for another kiss, and the request was immediately obliged. Then he lifted her skirt and fished his hands beneath it, flexing them into a firm readiness against her ass.

So practiced.

"I intend to satisfy myself with this tonight." He gripped his prize tightly. "Right here. Right now. Your only choice is whether I use two hands"—he pulled her close enough to feel every lascivious detail under those breeches—"or one." He spread the fingers of his right hand, and she could feel the coiled strength in that palm.

Either was going to blow her into a fireball bigger than the sun.

"Choose," he commanded.

"If I choose two," she said in a voice so small she sounded like some pocket-size version of herself, "will the debt of honor be paid?"

"No." He picked her up and put her on the tabletop.

Her mouth was exactly level with his, and that ball of pain, stripped of all burlap and linen, was in direct contact with the business end of those trousers. He couldn't in any decency wear them outside again, she thought. He'd simply have to strip them off and—*Oh God, help me!*

He leaned in close and kissed the place where her hair met the back of her neck. "I haven't heard your choice."

Two hands, the voice said. *And then one.*

"Two," she whispered.

"Excellent."

He loosened a hand and tugged at a ribbon Flip hadn't even noticed. The burlap fell open. One more tug and the chemise released its hold as well. This time he was the one who gasped.

Her ass was forgotten. His thumbs fanned unhesitatingly over her nipples, hardening them instantly.

"Bloody brilliant," he said hoarsely, and she melted.

Screw tomorrow, screw an hour from now. He liked her breasts. She was screwing him now.

"This table is amazingly well placed," he said as he scrabbled at his breek buttons.

She was trying to keep enough oxygen flowing to her brain that she didn't pass out or begin to spout a list of old boyfriends or something. "Do you think this was one of those master–servant things—you know, 'Come here, young lady, for you shall know the sting of my rod, ha-ha-*ha,* or you shall be turned into the streets!' " She twirled a nonexistent mustache.

Magnus stopped long enough to give her a look. "You've spent too much time with your nose buried in romances. Remind me to put together a reading list for you when we get back."

"It's not just in romances. Masters took advantage of their servants all the time. Hardy's Fanny Robin in *Far From the Madding Crowd.* His Tess. Susanna in *The Marriage of Figaro.*"

He raised a brow, impressed. "I withdraw my comment." He lifted her chin and skimmed her nose, lids and forehead with his lips, then inserted a hand between her legs.

The shock knocked her back onto her palms, but the gentle, rhythmic plying unloosened her like two quick shots of tequila, numbing every muscle and instantly casting the outside world into a pleasant, unfocused oblivion.

"It is possible to imagine," he said, "a woman, even a servant, choosing this voluntarily, is it not?"

Nothing about the warmth beginning to lick her limbs and cheeks felt voluntary, though nothing could have induced her to stop it, either.

"God," she croaked, "does anything keep you from being pedantic?"

He began to answer but Flip emitted such a stark, primitive sound that the response died on his lips.

He buried his face in her neck, tasting her shoulders, her collarbone and the hollow of her throat with a growing urgency. "Are you ready to admit that larking with the master like this," he said, "with no fear of pregnancy, no threat of disease, nothing but fevered joinings in dark closets and garden bowers, could not only be benign but salutary and even advantageous?"

Every flicker of his finger brought her knees a little higher and her back into a more exquisite arch, and now she moved with him in a hard rhythm, riding the perfect, tumbling pressure.

"But no man . . . would be satisfied with just this," she choked out. "Not enough. . . ."

Her breasts were beating in tight little bounces against her chest, and he watched her, eyes sparkling. "Any man who wouldn't is a fool."

He spun her 180 degrees, so that her back was against him. Now a towel-filled shelf served as a foothold, and she wrapped her hands around his neck as his fingers and thumb took her in turns. Faster and faster the maelstrom spun in her. Nothing could contain the swirling rush, certainly not the flesh being teased into heart-stopping tension. She bucked hard, and he pressed his length even harder against her back. He plucked one nipple after another, and when she moaned, his breath came in hot, ragged puffs in her ear.

"Now, now," she demanded.

"You're a demanding vixen," he murmured. "Is all of this to be for you?"

"Yes," she whispered. "Yes!"

He slowed his strokes. "How will you serve me?"

"Any way you like."

He brushed a thumb over her lower lip, which she immediately suckled. "Tell me," he said.

"With my body."

"Oh yes. But no pregnancy, remember? You're not taking care to consider your chambermaid's future."

"With my mouth."

"That's right. With those luscious lips and that practiced tongue. And when we finish, if I find you are too practiced, I'll turn you over my knee and teach you to regret your immodesty."

"What, no larking save with the master?"

"None."

She snorted. "The sort of woman who does this remains loyal only to the most able hand—or tongue."

His hand faltered. "Whore."

"Let us see if you have what it takes to master me."

He yanked a handful of towels from the shelves, thrust her on her back and brought his mouth between her legs. Her moans quickly turned to cries as his tongue seesawed over her bud.

"Quiet, wench."

But nothing could contain her.

"If there have been other men," he said, "you'll have to pay."

"Dozens," she taunted.

"Like this?"

She met his eyes, daring him to exact his revenge. "And worse."

He turned her so that she rested on her elbows and knees, and smacked a searing hand across her ass. The crack sent a hot, bone-tingling jolt from her belly all the way to her fingers and toes. The shocking pleasure left her speechless, and she thought she might faint, but the flames of pleasure kept her anchored in the present.

"So you sell your loyalty to the ablest hand, do you?" He slipped his fingers back inside her.

"Damn you." She thrust her hips wantonly, rocking with him.

He clapped his hand across her flesh again, then brought it between her thighs. The split-second sharpness lifted the maelstrom to a furious, muscle-snapping tsunami. She buried her face in a towel, unable to breathe or think or do anything except let herself ride the immense wave that was going to smash her into a million, freeing bits.

"Then I suppose we'll have to ensure my hand is the ablest."

One more stinging crack and his fingers were back, this time with his thumb adding a delicious line of harmony, and she bit the towel as the delicious numbing earthquake shook her knees, unhitching her from her thoughts, her bones and the universe entirely, from everything but the virtuoso plucking that drew the shudder over such an extended moment Flip thought the world would stop.

She flopped to her side, lifeless. She was addicted to this man, this body, this mind, those hands—those exquisite hands. She had never experienced such explosive, mind-altering release. She wanted to die each day under the control of those hands and have them teach her, in long, excruciatingly drawn-out lessons, the sort of pleasure she could bring him.

He lifted her from the table, and her liquid legs unfolded as he brought his mouth to hers. The salty-sweet taste of her on his tongue was ambrosia, and his kisses stirred her still-humming ardor. He slid her down his body, treating her to every tempered inch of his inflamed desire, until her knees reached the thick rug at his feet.

She caressed the taut, sleek wool of his breeches, letting her palms ride the deeply flexing muscles of his thighs, and brought her lips to the mountainous terrain below his waist. She smiled when he groaned, taking in his musky, clean scent, and she nipped and kissed each inch along his iron length.

She must look a tramp, she thought—hair undone, dress open to her waist, on her knees and grinning foolishly—but she didn't care. He nudged her away, and she folded her arms behind her head, watching with pleasure as he began the slow, four-button striptease that would at last reveal him to her.

The door behind them swung open, and Flip flung her arms across her chest. Lizzy Bennet's eyes cut from the state of Flip's dress to the carefully perched hand of Colonel Fitzwilliam on her chambermaid's head.

"I beg your pardon!" Lizzy closed the door and immediately reopened it. "Colonel Fitzwilliam!" she added in sharp rebuke and closed it again.

"Hell." Flip yanked her dress closed and jumped to her feet. "I'd better go to her and explain—"

"No!" Magnus howled.

He was swaying a bit—undoubtedly from lack of blood, Flip thought, smiling.

"C'mon." She caressed his neck and gave him a quick kiss. "We can pick this up later. In fact, I know a little trick—"

"It's not that!" he cried. "It's the topiary!"

She gave him a long up-and-down look. "You have a name for it?"

"Good Lord, no," he said firmly as he stuffed his shirttails back into his breeches, adding in a low grumble, "though a separate passport may be in order after this. I was talking about Darcy. He's waiting behind the topiary on the balcony for Elizabeth to appear. For the second marriage proposal that with any luck will put this horrible miscarriage of fiction to bed."

Flip flew to the window and peered out. "You talked him into an apology?"

"An apology? What does he have to apologize for? I talked him into action. That's what the woman needs. Any fool can see she's wound tighter than an Eastern Bloc Jack-in-the-box. One touch and she'll be on her—" He caught himself when he saw Flip's face.

"On her what?" she said.

Flat-out terror appeared in his eyes. "Er . . ."

" 'Er?' I don't think the Cambridge debate coach would be pleased. Let's try a little harder, shall we? Back? Knees? Best behavior?"

"On her *way*," Magnus lit upon with evident relief. "Her very immediate way, I might add, to accepting his proposal."

Flip harrumphed. "Without a frank admission followed quickly by an apology on Darcy's part, I hardly think—"

"*Shhh.* There she is." Magnus cracked the window silently. Lizzy came into view on the balcony, clutching a wrap around her shoulders and staring distractedly into the night. Flip could hear the *shush-shush* of her slippers on the balcony tiles.

"Watch," Magnus whispered. "Watch and learn."

Darcy cleared his throat and stepped out of the shadows.

Lizzy halted, obviously discomposed.

"I beg your pardon," he said, bowing, "I hope I did not surprise you."

"Nothing would surprise me, sir." She dipped a chilly curtsy in return. "It has been a very odd night."

"Odd?"

She glanced in the direction of the storeroom, causing Flip and Magnus to duck. "I have seen things that puzzle me most peculiarly." She rubbed her temple as if trying to interpret a challenging Egyptian hieroglyph. "I-I . . . Well, 'tis best to say only that I have a number of questions I hope someday to have answered."

"Might I be of assistance with them?"

Lizzy flushed, stole a look at Darcy's imposing figure, swayed a bit and closed her eyes. "I think not. The questions are of a somewhat sensitive nature and, in any case, there is one in particular I'd prefer not to think about."

"Are you certain? I think you'll find wrapping yourself around a particularly hard one can be most satisfying."

Lizzy clasped the railing for support. "Truly?"

"And you know I should go to a very great length to serve you, a very great length."

"I thank you, sir, but no." She unhooked herself from the marble. "I shall importune you no longer. It is late and I—"

"No."

Darcy caught her arm, and Magnus squeezed Flip's waist. "Here it is," Magnus said.

"There is a matter," Darcy said firmly, "we need to discuss."

The rise and fall of Lizzy's chest quickened. "Indeed?"

"Indeed, madam. What stands between us—"

"Is her."

"—is not her, madam, but you." He pulled Lizzy closer. "Can you deny what's between us? Can you deny the heat of this touch?"

Lizzy struggled a bit but relented. "I have no need to deny it. But heat is hardly a rare commodity, sir. Even rutting pigs generate it. Your own experience is proof of that."

Darcy brought her so close only the toes of her slippers touched the ground.

"Elizabeth, I intend to possess you—with a wedding band on your finger or without. And I shan't wait another day."

"Now," Magnus whispered from somewhere deep in Flip's hair as he watched his ersatz cousin.

Darcy lifted Lizzy's mouth to his and consumed her—hungrily, wantonly and with such a lack of restraint Flip almost averted her eyes.

At first Lizzy hung limply, a passive, empty vessel, and then a warm, receptive animation began to stir her limbs, and she threaded her arms fast around Darcy's neck. For a long, long moment she, too, took part in the ambrosial feast, then, just as Magnus voiced a triumphal "Yes!" she lifted a lithe, supple knee, slipped it sensuously between Darcy's legs and jerked it sharply into his bollocks.

Darcy's eyes bulged, and he made a choking noise, as if he'd swallowed part of his tongue. Lizzy released her hands and slid down to standing.

He folded onto the balcony like a top-heavy origami crane.

"I'm afraid any possession involving you shall have to wait another day at least," Lizzy said, and brushed her hands on her skirt. "Though I can assure you, I haven't the faintest intention of adding my name to your list of conquests—whether on a marriage registry or the tongues of every ha'penny gossip in town. Good night," she said severely, and strode off.

Flip groaned. Impounded chaos—with little more than eleven hours to go.

Magnus's arms fell to his side. "The wedding . . ."

"What did you expect?" Flip whispered angrily. "I told you to tell him to apologize."

"For God's sake! He shared a rowdy midnight boff with some overheated society matron months before the thought of Elizabeth Bennet was even a twinkle in his eye. He might as well apologize for sneezing. Liaisons of this sort mean nothing in the course of things. A woman who shares a stolen hour with a man to whom she has no reasonable hope of attaching herself legally or emotionally can hardly be a threat to a woman like Elizabeth Bennet. They may as well be different species. Why can't she see Lady Quillan is no more than the manifestation of a pleasurable but essentially meaningless biological urge?"

Flip felt the sharp, mood-shattering kick of classification—on behalf of Lady Quillan, but also as the most recent object of Magnus Knightley's urges. Despite being two centuries and three thousand miles removed, she realized with a start she'd just been added to Magnus's Rare Book Room collection.

Magnus must have sensed the sudden change in temperature for he quickly added, "I didn't mean you."

"Why not?" she said lightly. "As manifestations go, it was a doozy. Just what the doctor ordered. Let's have a go at it again sometime, eh?"

The openness on Magnus's features disappeared, replaced with a pleasant but bland politeness. He said only, "It would be my pleasure."

Flip felt the joy of the moment hiss away like the helium from a balloon, but she knew she owed it to Austen to put her feelings aside. She called up the game face she had thought only a moment ago she might never have to wear with Magnus Knightley. "Perhaps," she said, "we should join the fighters in their respective corners to see if we can straighten this mess out? There is, as I'm sure I have no need to point out, little time to spare."

Magnus rubbed his temple. "Remind me to ask Madame K to remove *Pride and Prejudice* from her reading list. Then there'd still be the hope, however small, of my having a career after today."

"Look," Flip said, "you're not the only one who's affected."

"No, I'm sure Jane Austen's lying down with a warm compress too."

"I mean me."

"You? My career will be over."

"Yeah, well mine's not going to look too golden either. They'll know it was me."

"How?" he demanded. "How will they know?"

Flip shifted under his granite observation. "Um, it seems I'll become a player in the book, and you will too."

His shoulders relaxed. "A maid and Colonel Fitzwilliam? I've got news for you, Flip. We're already in the book."

"No, I mean us. Magnus Knightley and Flip Allison, by name." She waited for the explosion.

"With . . . that as our literary debut?" He pointed to the towel-covered table, now perched at an odd angle from the wall.

She gave him a "Who knows?" shrug of her shoulders. "And, um, we only have until morning to fix things."

He made a strangled, choking noise. His eyes went from the scattered towels to the frustrated protagonist retching like a fraternity pledge out on the balcony. "You really know how to motivate a team, Flip. Cornell doesn't know what they're missing."

Chapter Twenty-three

Exasperating, provoking, maddening, unyielding—

Pelting down the darkened hallway, Magnus ran through every word he could think of, but none seemed to capture the essence of the gorgeous, ball-tinglingly fuckable, supremely infuriating wench who was in the process of ruining his life. Even now, with Austen's masterpiece laid out before him like one of those horrid E. coli–infested eighty-four-item buffets Americans insist on patronizing, he could barely keep his mind off the faint coconut scent of her hair, the inebriating stiffness of those nipples under his tongue and the lovely, guttural noises rumbling in her throat as she arched and wiggled to his whim.

So why had her invitation to "have a go at it again sometime" made him feel like he'd been insulted, he wondered as he jogged toward the door that led to the balcony. Why, he thought as he turned to steal one last glance at that tight, high ass before it disappeared from view, had he not simply lifted her back onto the table, spread those tan, firm legs and pummeled her until any hint of guardedness or regret on her face had been replaced by something far more satisfying?

He didn't know the answer, and, as he turned back, he noticed far too late that the lintel here was a good ten or twelve centimeters lower than those of the rest of the doorways in the house.

He felt a brain-rattling crack, then the night went pitch-black.

Good God, Jed thought as the old woman rolled his shoulders nearly off both the massage table and his skeleton, I'm glad she ain't going after my cock this way. Looking Glass sure didn't dole it out the way they did in his fantasies of Asian massage parlors.

The woman had said he could imagine himself in his favorite book, and in his mind he had happily dusted off his favorite Penthouse letter—the one involving the twins and the abandoned digital camera—only to have Io whisper *"Pride and Prejudice"* meaningfully when the woman's back was turned. How *Pride and Prejudice,* that yawn-inducing DVD Flip and her friends used to drag out every year, related to a cloned passenger pigeon, he had no idea, but if it meant Io might take that pretty, little pout later and wrap it around his—

"Vhould you like some ointment for de rash?" the woman asked.

"Man, yes. That'd be great."

He sat up while she dug in her cabinet and rearranged his sheet. At least a partial Pose could be struck with the right draping. Io took a deep gulp from the bottled water and handed it to him. He wondered while he drank if Flip and that English dude were having sex in the other room.

"Here." The woman returned to the table, waving a small tube at medicine. "Take off your gloves. I'll do your hands; you can do the rest." She smiled.

The goop was clear and slippery, and the tight circles

she made on his palms were heaven. "Damn, woman, you're good."

"Are you thinking of a book?"

He closed his eyes. *Pride and Prejudice,* eh? Of course, he had usually run long before the DVD player was even turned on, but he did remember one scene with a woman in a slip straddling some guy's lap. *All righty. Let's see. Dark hair. Long. This time I'll try a virgin. Oh yeah.* His palms started to tingle, and it wasn't just the goop. Not just a virgin, he thought, feeling the old woman's brisk movements rocking him to sleep, a *struggling* virgin—subconsciously eager to be introduced to the world of Jed-propelled pleasure, but consciously fighting it as hard as her jiggling tits would allow. *Mmmmm . . .*

"Christ, Jed," Io chided with some embarrassment, wondering if he'd lost his mind. The sheet had risen like a circus tent over his hips.

"It's nothing," the masseuse reassured with a small smile when Jed didn't answer.

Io snorted, thinking, She doesn't know how close to the truth she is.

"Your turn next, young lady."

Flip didn't have to look far to find her quarry. In fact, her quarry had been looking for her.

"I am to request your immediate attendance upon Miss Elizabeth Bennet, no matter the hour," Codsworth said, holding a small beribboned Yorkshire terrier in one arm and a covered tray in the other, "while I deliver the most curious combination of melted butter, salt and a large empty bowl to Miss Jane Bennet's bedchamber." He gave the delicate porcelain clock on the hall table a long look and sighed. "Does anyone remember exactly how much coffee was served after dinner this evening?"

Flip laughed. "How's the dice game?"

"Luckiest night ever," he said with a beleaguered smile. "Haven't lost a shilling yet. And the roses?"

"Like pigs in sh—er, hot water."

"Wonderful."

"Say, those vases are hung in a pretty odd pattern. I can't quite figure it out. Do they spell 'Bingley loves Jane' or something?"

"Better. 'Bingley bestows on Jane the orb of his heart.' "

"Wow. Nothing too over-the-top for our master then?"

"I believe the Pilgrims are consulting. Oh, before I forget, there's a note here for Miss Bennet." He handed Flip the dog, moved the tray from his right hand to his left and fished a sealed letter from his waistcoat pocket. "Please insinuate, if possible, that the messenger has gone to sleep for the evening and that all correspondence, save deathbed expresses for the physician, should be held until daybreak, which should only be five or six more labors of Hercules from now."

"Will do." She took the letter, mustering every ounce of control not to turn on her heel, duck into the first open door and rip it open. "Well, I'll just be off now—"

"Drumstick, please."

"Drumstick?"

He pointed to the small fur puff in her arms, causing it to oscillate like her favorite vibrator. "Oh, right." She handed the dog back, thinking he'd be quite the hefty drumstick, which instantly made her stomach growl, and she was reminded she hadn't eaten anything since that biscotti at the café half a day ago.

"Oh, um, one more thing," she said to her colleague. "Colonel Fitzwilliam has requested a large sandwich—lots of bread, lots of butter, turkey, ham, sausage if you have it, definitely some cheese—anything but cheddar—lettuce, onion, the usual stuff, a large glass of milk, an apple and, ah, maybe something chocolate—just a bite. Watching his weight, you know. Oh, and maybe some pickles on the side—delivered to his room as soon as you can. I'd do it myself but . . ." She waved the letter for Lizzie and shrugged helplessly.

"Right. Turkey, ham, cheddar—"

"No cheddar."

"Codsworth, man." Sir William's head and shoulders emerged clothesless from what Flip hoped wasn't, say, the library. "Fetch me a bottle of champagne, a bowl of berries and a scuttle of sugar, will you."

"Immediately, sir." Codsworth bowed as Sir William withdrew. "Let's see now, turkey, ham, no cheddar, berries on the side—"

"Pickles on the side," Flip corrected.

"Pickles on the side, lots of butter and sugar—"

"Codsworth?"

Another door had opened. Caroline Bingley gave Flip a fleeting white-hot glare, then smiled deeply at the manservant. "Codsworth, I seem to have a chill tonight. Would you mind tending to my fire then drawing me a bath?"

"Actually, milady—"

"You have such a fine touch with dry wood."

He lifted his brow in Flip's direction. "Certainly, milady."

"And, Dolly," Caroline purred, "how are those clothes coming? I hope nothing has derailed you from your assignment. You can be sure I'll be giving my brother a full account of your work in the morning—all of it."

"You are too kind, m'um." Flip curtsied, holding each tuft of skirt with an extended-middle-finger grasp.

"He is not above taking the crop to servants who shirk their responsibilities," she added with a dripping smile, "though in this case perhaps the colonel would be better equipped to handle such a task."

Codsworth raised a decidedly higher brow at Flip, who swallowed, remembering exactly how well equipped the colonel had been.

"You will not find me lacking, m'um," Flip replied. *Because with any luck you won't find me at all, you old bag.*

"Codsworth," Caroline added, "don't forget the lemons for my elbows."

"Codsworth?" another feminine voice enquired.

Jane was peeking from her doorway down the hall, grinning like a fool, clutching the front of her dressing gown and rocking a major case of bed hair.

"Is that my butter?" she asked. The smell of fresh popcorn wafted from the room. Caroline narrowed her eyes and sniffed, and Jane dropped the smile and closed the door behind her as far as she could.

"Indeed it is, milady." Codsworth bowed.

Jane said, "I should like some grated cheese as well and two glasses—that is, I mean to say one very large glass of beer." She jerked as if she'd been pinched, tittered and clapped a hand over her mouth to stifle the noise.

Codsworth bowed again. "Certainly, Miss Bennet. Just allow me to finish—"

Jane giggled again, ducked inside and slammed the door. Caroline did the same.

"—with Miss Bingley's fire."

Jane opened the door and, swallowing laughter, said, "Leave everything outside the door, thank you. Oh, and two more candles, please." She whooped and disappeared.

Codsworth's shoulders sagged.

"If it's any consolation," Flip said, giving him a supportive pat, "it's a beautiful night. I expect the game will go on for hours."

"Ah, to be a mere stable hand again," he said.

"I'll take care of the note for Miss Bennet."

"And I," he said, "everything else. Turkey, champagne, fire, cheddar, berries, lemons, pickles, beer, sugar, candles . . . I know there's something I'm forgetting."

"Fire?" Flip offered.

"Have that."

"Chocolate? Just a bit—"

"Right. Watching weight. Have that too." He squinched an eye, combing the memory banks.

Drumstick let out an enthusiastic bark and piddled down the front of Codsworth's coat.

Flip bit her lip. "Walking the dog?"

Codsworth made a long, put-upon noise and trudged down the hall.

As soon as he disappeared she ducked around the corner, cracked the seal on the note and read.

I received your message, the correspondent had written. *Yes, yes and yes!*

Flip felt her stomach drop. Oh God, she thought, if 'Yes, yes and yes!" were the answers, please let the questions from Lizzy have been "Did you know about the wedding?" "Can

I give your regards to the happy couple?" and "Is northern England cold this time of year?"

She folded the note and stuffed it in her pocket. Now she had to face some extraordinarily awkward and admittedly justified censure from Lizzy while at the same time convincing her to marry the person whose balls she had just driven farther north than the Scottish border. Whoever thought writing a PowerPoint presentation on "Bird Density and Diversity in Clear-cut Oak Forests" was a challenging assignment?

Lizzy stood in her dressing gown gazing out the window when Flip entered. Lizzy turned and crossed her arms.

"Sit down, Dolly," she said sternly. "We must talk."

Chapter Twenty-four

"Bloody hell, that hurt." Magnus groaned. He rubbed his palm against his forehead.

"Vhould you like me to vurk on your calves instead?"

Magnus's eyes shot open, and he lurched up to his elbows. No more Darcy, no more topiary, no more—Oh God! "Where's Flip?"

"Shhhhh." Madame K put her finger to her lips and pointed to the sheet-clad form an arm's length away, whose heart-stopping ass shifted under its snowy mantle.

Flip's eyes were closed, and he could see her back gently rise and fall. He frowned. "She's—"

"Resting. Vuz your visit restful as well?"

"Like Ophelia in *Hamlet.*" He hopped off the table clutching the sheet, and fished *Pride and Prejudice* out of his jacket pocket.

"Is everything all right?"

He flipped to the end. No double wedding. Jane and Bingley are married, oh yes, but not happy. Not with Jane's beloved sister Elizabeth—Christ Almighty!—pregnant and abandoned by— "Wickham?!" Magnus clapped his forehead, which only made his head hurt worse. "Send me back," he demanded, hopping onto the table. "Right now, send me back."

"It doesn't vurk like that, Mr. Magnus. You cannot go back."

"Oh, right. This is a bloody mess," he said, waving the book. "Ruined. Start to finish. One of the greatest pieces of fiction in the world. Whatever is happening there"—he jerked his thumb over his shoulder and into the past—"is changing what happens in *Pride and Prejudice*. It cannot be, do you understand? It cannot be."

"But—"

"What part exactly do you play, madam?"

Madame K hesitated, caught by surprise. "Vhy, I . . . I . . ."

"Yes?" He gave her the DEFCON version of his professorial glare, and she paled.

"You cannot hold me responsible for vhat you've altered."

"*I* did not alter anything. *I* landed in breeches and coat in a world that already had been taken by its ankles and turned summarily on its head. And since then Flip and I have been busting our—"

"Miss Allison?" she whispered, staring at the motionless form on the other table, horrified.

"Yes. According to Flip, the book changed after her first visit."

Madame K's hand flew to her mouth. "Her *first* visit?! She told me she had been imagining, well, it wasn't literature as I had hoped. I suppose you'd call it a racy romance novel, and— Oh, my heavens!" Madame K's eyes widened. "Oh dear, this is very bad."

"Bad, I'm clear on."

"You cannot return to a book you've already visited."

"Apparently you can."

Madame K closed her eyes, clutched her heart, and a fevered stream of words ran silently across her lips.

"We must *do* something," Magnus said. "Panic isn't going to help. Believe me, I've already tried it."

She rubbed the center of her forehead. "I'm thinking."

"Think harder."

"What has changed?"

"What hasn't changed? Darcy aligned himself with the wife of an acquaintance, not just publicly but exceedingly publicly; Elizabeth has punctuated her latest refusal of Darcy's marriage proposal with some sort of Courtney Love move; Sir William Lucas is galloping though the upper floors of Netherfield like a corpulent, unhinged stud horse; and Jane and Bingley—well, I hesitate to characterize that particular relationship except to say that they at least will be marrying in the morning."

"And you," she said, looking at him closely, "what have you changed?"

"Nothing," he said fastidiously.

"Nothing at all? Life has taken no tangents, small or large, because of your actions?"

He thought of Flip and the kiss in that billiards room, but he certainly wasn't going to share that with the masseuse. "Nothing, madam."

"*Hmmm.* Then we may be able to help."

She pulled a heavy red leather book from her shelf and opened it on the table.

Magnus took a tentative step forward, trying for a closer examination, but Madame K thrust her not insignificant back between him and the book, neatly blocking his view not only of the volume, but of most of the bookshelf as well.

She shuffled through the pages quickly and stopped on one near the very end. Her finger flew over the words, back and forth, back and forth, as she read.

"Oh dear." She stopped reading and looked at the clock.

"What is it?" He looked too.

"You are, ah—how do you say it?—screwed."

"Madame K—"

"Not returning is the second rule, but the first rule is that you cannot imagine vhat can't or shouldn't happen in a book. Vhat did you say was the precipitating event here—the first domino that knocked over the rest, so to speak?"

"Darcy, the imprudent fool, swiving some accommodating and, may I say, highly imaginative noblewoman on the railing of the Temple of Apollo as if he'd never heard of an out-of-town inn or even the back of a hay wagon. For God's sake, it's like he was the hero of some semipornographic romance novel—"

He stopped. Both of them turned in unison to the table beside them, where Flip inhaled and exhaled in her unperturbed sleep.

Magnus felt like he'd taken a three-point kick to the gut, and for a moment he struggled to catch his breath. *Flip* had been Lady Quillan. *Flip* had been on that temple railing. He had no right to be jealous, of course, given that the tryst had taken place before the erotically soaked Flip had exploded into his office like something out of a blue-collar version of *Maxim,* and in any case, jealousy might as well be consumption or leprosy for as much relevance as it had in his life, right? Nonetheless, he wanted to take her by those bronzed, damnably independent shoulders and drag her to the nearest flat surface and hammer the thought of Darcy out of that bewitching head.

And Darcy . . . The improvident, short-attentioned scrub. Seeking Magnus's help with Elizabeth, was he? Like an over-sexed bee flitting from pistil to pistil? Had he no idea what gentlemanly behavior was? Christ, even in today's broad-minded world—

"Mr. Magnus?"

He realized Madame K had said his name several times. "Hm, pardon?"

"I said there's not much time. If you can at least throw Miss Bennet into Mr. Darcy's arms—"

"We tried that without much success."

"I meant figuratively, not literally, though if you can accomplish both, all the better—who doesn't love a happy ending? But if you can bring those two together, I believe that, with a little work on my part, I can fix almost everything else. And everything will be forgotten."

"Courtney Love, the stud horse, everything?"

"Everything."

"Thank God. And though I will certainly be giving Flip a firm talking-to when all this is over, I feel certain that at some point in the distant future—er, the far distant future—we may actually, well, if not laugh, then at least reflect upon it without raising my blood pressure past the boiling point."

"No, Mr. Magnus, you vill neither laugh about it nor grow upset. You shall be unaffected in every vay for vhen I said everything vill be forgotten, I meant everything. Neither you nor Miss Allison vill have any memory of anything that's happened since this afternoon, vhen she first set foot into the book, nor will anyone else who has become too closely entangled in this. It will be as if today never happened."

Magnus faltered. "Oh."

Losing his memory of the Temple of Apollo would be an

excellent thing, he was embarrassed to find himself admitting, but losing his memory of those obliging legs as they tilted the chair back at the café or that alluring blue, practically nonexistent bra or the cool silk of her hip as he tugged those panties loose or the coconut smell of her hair or the tang of her mouth or the exhilarating half simmer he felt whenever she looked at him with that provoking irreverence? That would be devastating.

"I-I think," he said slowly, "we should proceed with some care—"

"Vee don't have time for care, Mr. Magnus. The clock is ticking. You must do what you can to fix the book now or suffer the consequences. There is no middle ground."

He thought of that lush middle ground that had writhed and wiggled under his command only a few short moments ago. Then he thought of Austen's beautiful novel, of which he had grown to think of himself as ultimate caretaker.

"I'm afraid," he said softly, "I shall suffer the consequences in either case."

"Excuse me?"

"Nothing."

She patted the table in invitation, and he settled back with a long, woeful sigh.

"Proceed," he said.

Chapter Twenty-five

Snatched from his sleep like a muzzy, unwilling toddler, Jed blinked awake in time to see his hands, directly before him, inexplicably clutching moonlit wisteria vines. Jed opened his fingers, confused, and at once this new world, which in the few split seconds of his experience had appeared dependably unmoving, now loosened its grip on him, dropping him backward as he flailed manically, searching for a hold, until he hit solid, unforgiving ground.

"What the fuck?"

He groaned, rolled onto his side, eyeing the unforgiving cobbles of the empty courtyard. Looming over him was a vast wall of vines and windows interspersed with hundreds of what appeared to be copper tins, the whole thing lit from the bottom and top by regularly spaced, smoky fires.

God, this is worse than the dream where Angelina Jolie came after me with a sickle, then turned into a three-headed version of Grandma Hughes. Where's the dark-haired virgin? This imagining stuff is bullshit.

He climbed to a knee and spotted the paper.

It must have fallen out of his coat. It bore only the word PRIVATE in an elegant script. He snagged it, unfolded the sheet and read.

I thank you for your letters, Wickham. They have comforted me in this awkward time, and I agree, we should meet.

Jed clapped his thigh in delight. "Woo-hoo. I wonder if 'ol Miss Awkward has dark hair too?"

You know where I am for you are aware tomorrow will be a day of great happiness for my family. With the sudden arrival of a certain gentleman, however, my time here has become somewhat trying. My room is the first set of French doors on the right of the upper floor. Outside is a sturdy set of wisteria vines that the factor's children use to scale the building when they think they are not being observed.

Jed stopped reading long enough to take a look at the vines that rose an extraordinary distance above his head, the vines he'd apparently already been in the process of climbing. This was going to be more work than a dream should rightly require, he considered, thinking of the interlude two nights ago that had needed no more than Jessica Biel, a jar of Skippy Super Chunk peanut butter and the hot tub at the Airport Marriott.

I tell you this because I think we could talk tonight if you are willing. Do you agree? Are you willing to risk a brief rendezvous? Will you come tonight when the clock strikes one?

Jed snorted. "Oh, I'll come, darling."

* * *

Flip slunk into Lizzy's bedroom chair and tried not to look too much like a woman who had just allowed herself to be spanked into nirvana by a man she'd known for half a day in someone else's storage room at the turn of a far less open-minded century.

"Dolly," Lizzy said, "we need to talk about what just happened."

"Yes, m'um." Flip lowered her gaze.

"So . . ." Lizzy fiddled with her bracelet nervously. "What happened?"

Flip's head popped up. "Pardon?"

"I mean, I could tell it was *some*thing untoward, the way Colonel Fitzwilliam was yanking at his buttons, but I just don't understand—" Lizzy shifted, obviously distressed. "Were you helping him with his boots?"

Flip nearly swallowed her tongue. "Er, yes," she answered, coughing.

"He was *making* you help him?"

"Why, yes—yes indeed."

"As a precursor to something else, something . . . wicked?" Lizzy's face was half horror, half desperate, unquenchable curiosity.

"I think so, m'um." Flip tried to appear both terrified and confused as she hoped that might allow her to plead ignorance to any further questions. "He was holding my ear quite fierce."

"Oh, the horrid, horrid man! The villainous cur! Abusing a poor servant girl! You are not unprotected, you know. Bingley can have him turned from the house! I shall—" She stopped and clutched her heart. "He did not ruin you, did he, Dolly? He did not . . . before I arrived . . . ?"

"No, m'um, no. But you mustn't have him thrown from

the house. He is a good man, I think, when he isn't drinking, of course. Them Cambridge lads have a right high opinion of themselves, you know—the colonel especially," Flip added with a private roll of her eyes. "And it's worse when they're in their cups, but he has always been kind to me. I do not think it will happen again."

"Are you sure, Dolly? I had in mind to speak to Mr. Darcy."

"Mr. Darcy?" A lightbulb went off in Flip's head.

"Yes. He is Colonel Fitzwilliam's cousin and particular friend, you know, and could easily set the colonel straight as to the proper behavior of gentlemen, but if you're certain . . ."

"I'm not!" Flip, seeing the great potential in Lizzy conferring with Darcy, jerked her story into reverse with an Oscar-worthy sob. "Colonel Fitzwilliam made me promise to come to his room tonight. Oh, milady," she wailed, throwing her face into her hands, "I don't know what to do! If I go, I shall surely be ruined. If I don't go, a single complaint from the colonel will cost me my job! Oh, please, if you and Mr. Darcy think you could do something to help . . . ?" Flip peeked at Lizzy through her fingers.

Lizzy wrung her hands, evidently considering. Cripes, Flip thought, what needs to be considered? That damned colonel with his proud, magnificent boots was going to force me to do more than a quick spit and polish. *React!*

"May I ask you a question, Dolly?"

"Certainly." Flip prayed for no further treks down the ear or button road.

"I-I couldn't help but notice a certain, er, vivacity on your face when I entered. Now, Dolly, don't protest. There is nothing wrong with a woman enjoying the attentions of a gentleman. I used to think there was, but now . . . now I see that it is a perfectly natural occurrence and not to be fought—which is not to say," she added quickly, "one must succumb. One must stand firm, but the feeling itself is quite, er, invigorating and should be enjoyed. What I mean to say then, Dolly, is this: Is it possible you have some special regard for Colonel Fitzwilliam?"

"I-I—" Flip felt the warmth blossom on her cheeks. "Why, no, but—"

"Enough. I have embarrassed you, and Fitzwilliam has embarrassed you. You deserve the privacy of your thoughts. We shall see things set to rights." She gave Flip a benevolent smile and nodded toward the door as a signal of release.

"But you—you shall speak to Mr. Darcy? I am most concerned—most uncommon concerned—about the promise I've made."

"What time are you to meet the colonel?"

Flip looked at the clock. "Er, one o'clock."

"One o'clock?"

"Yes, m'um."

" 'Tis a somewhat inconvenient time," Lizzy said, mostly to herself, "but . . ." She furrowed her brow and bit her lip, deep in thought. "I tell you this, Dolly. You shall keep your one o'clock appointment—"

"But, m'um—"

"Keep it, Dolly, but do not succumb. If you must help him with his boots or his watch fob or whatever else he might require in the way of valet services, do so. Just ensure you find yourself in his arms—deep in his arms—at a quarter past the hour. Mr. Darcy and I shall take care of the rest."

"I-I—" The realization of what Lizzy appeared to be planning passed over her with a jolt. It was positively the most cold-blooded, calculated, fantastic plan she'd ever heard. She'd never look at Elizabeth Bennet the same way again. "As you say, miss." She curtsied and made her way to Magnus's door. Only when she assured herself no one was watching did she knock.

No reply.

She tried again, then opened the door. Empty. Maybe still with his cousin, she thought. But Darcy's door sat ajar, and there was no one in there either.

Codsworth ran by her in the hall. He carried a load of firewood and had changed into a clean coat. "The roses," he called. "The roses."

Cripes, the roses.

She decided on a note for Magnus and ran to the library to find pen and paper and scratch out a plan. When she uncorked the inkwell she heard Caroline's voice in the hall demanding to see Dolly.

As quickly as she could, Flip wrote.

Lusty assignation. Your room. Quarter past one. Be ready. Undress. Eyes will be watching. —D.

She folded the note, waited until the hall was silent and slipped out.

One-eyed Bobby climbed the narrow servants' stairs with the same careful stride he always employed on matters for the master or one of the master's guests. Care is as care does, his mum always said, and he aimed to please as far as he was able. Things had never come easy for him, so he listened to his orders closely and took care to repeat them, first to the upper servant who made the assignment, then, as frequently as he could, to himself, often in a singsong voice as he carried them out. He longed—how he longed!—for one of those gold-laced footman's uniforms.

He dragged the first of what would be a dozen metal urns filled with boiling water from Mrs. Jellaby's kitchen, up the back stairs to make a bath for Miss Bingley. Codsworth had repeated Bobby's assignments three times and had promised to repeat them again whenever Bobby reappeared. But tonight Bobby had been especially clearheaded. He hoped, with the master's wedding tomorrow, that there might be the reward of silver or promotion for the servants after the breakfast feast. If so, he intended to show whoever might be paying attention that Bobby Mitford could shine like the noonday sun. To that end, he had bundled several other deliveries into a small sack tied across his shoulders.

"Sandwich for the colonel," he sang to himself, "water for the lady, champagne for milord, cheese for the lady—oh dear, two ladies! Let's see. Cheese for the pretty one, water for the . . . hmmm. 'The ugly one' won't do—no, no, not at all. Cheese for the pretty one, water for the tall one. There. That's better. Though 'tall' is not so flattering as 'pretty,' to be sure, and the lady could take it as a slight, of course. Perhaps cheese for the pretty one, water for the fancy one? Bit of a stretch, aye, but fitting the song rather handsome.

He emerged at the top of the stairs and began again.

"Cheese for the pretty one, water for the—"

"The colonel is not in his room," Dolly, the new upstairs maid with the golden hair, said in a low whisper. "Have you seen him?"

"No, not a speck."

"I have to hurry to tend to the roses. Can you give this to him?" She shoved the note into Bobby's pocket. "As fast as you can." Then she ran to the stairway and disappeared.

He tried to remember his song, but it was gone. He dredged his brain for his orders, looked at the urn and began again.

"To the colonel, to the colonel," he sang, dragging the water down the hall. "Just as fa-ast as ye ca-an. To the colonel, to the colonel. Just as fa-ast—" He stopped. Dolly was right. The colonel's room was empty. And a pox on Codsworth. No one had set up the hip bath. Where was he to pour the water?

He sighed, righted the urn, exited to the storage room— odd that the towels were all a-hoo—and returned with the second best copper tub, set it up nicely beside the bed and poured in the water.

Scratching his head, he paused. There was something else he was supposed to be giving the colonel . . . But what?

He opened the pack across his shoulders and looked. Sugar scuttle. Bag of sugar. Champagne. Cheese. Nothing looked especially colonel-like. Finally he decided the sugar and bottle went nicely together. He placed the scuttle in a pretty way on the table by the bed, filled it with sugar and put the bottle of wine beside it. Then he retied the pack and headed back to the kitchen.

For an instant when Magnus awakened, he was unsure where he was. Then he heard a faint, wheezy retch and a deeply woeful, "My aching balls."

The beauty of sterling prose, Magnus thought. The classics never fail to please.

He sighed, heaved himself to his feet and, head pounding, made his way across the balcony to his cousin, Darcy.

Flip grabbed the rusty handrail and was just about to start up to the roof when she heard a shuffle through the vines just over the balcony ledge below her.

Wow, she thought, that's either the biggest raccoon I've ever heard or someone's coming over the— Oh, shit!

In breeches, boots, tailcoat and a beret that looked like it had been in a paintball battle came the unmistakable form of Jed Hughes. He paused, wiped his forehead, then scanned the doors across the balcony. When his eyes came to rest on Flip, his brows shot skyward and then his whole face relaxed into a gratified smile.

"Hey, sugar." He gave her dress a close examination and stuffed something into his pocket. "Hell of a dream, ain't it?"

"How did you get here?!" This was a freakin' disaster!

"I dunno, the old broad hypnotized me or something, but it's great." He looked up in awe at the house's grand prospect, took off the beret, ran a hand through his hair and put the hat back on. "I wasn't exactly expecting you, but, well, what the hell, you know? We always had a sweet groove when we put our minds to it. Say, is that what virgins wear in this place?"

"What in God's name are you talking abo—" Then it hit her. Jed thought he was in a fantasy. Worse, Jed thought she was in it too.

"No, this is not what virgins wear," she whispered furiously. "Get your mind out of the gutter. And take that stupid beret off. You look like an effing idiot."

"Oh, I get it," he said, grinning. "It's like when we always did it after a fight. Sweet! Is that the door to your bedroom down there at the end?"

"Jesus, who are you supposed to be?" Was Jed from her story of choice or his? Could he actually be someone from *Pride and Prejudice?* Or was he like a shooter from *Halo* who'd taken a wrong turn?

Jed frowned for a second, then his face lit. "Oh, right. Sure, no problem. I'm, er, Lord Laycock and you've been a very naughty schoolgirl—"

"Jed, stop it."

"No, no, no, milady," he said, placing a firm hand on Flip's hip. "You'll not attempt to lure a gentleman to your bed-chamber and not face the consequences. You knew exactly what you were after when you sent me the note."

"I sent you a note?"

"To meet me in your room? For a little talk? At one?"

Flip gasped. Lizzy's note to Wickham. "It's not from me, you idiot, it's from Lizzy Bennet. Let me see it."

Jed's eyes narrowed. "What's my reward?"

Flip was saved from having to give Jed a taste of a reward Lizzy Bennet–style by a familiar *coo* flying right past their heads.

Flip turned and so did Jed. A gorgeous, squat passenger pigeon came to a flapping stop on the railing beside them.

Jed whistled. "Well, godd*amn.*"

"Jed, you can't."

He brushed her aside and took a step toward the railing. He reached a tentative hand toward the bird, preparing to grab it. The bird tilted its head pleasantly as if it were about to hop onto Jed's finger, then bit him instead and flew off into the night.

"Ow!"

"Oh, for God's sake, it isn't like you haven't been bitten before. Serves you right, in any case."

Jed sucked on his finger, frowning. "You know what? This doesn't really seem much like a dream to me."

"Of course it is. Why else would I be here"— she did a twirl—"in this?"

"First I fall hard enough to bruise a rib and now the bird bites me. And neither time did I wake up. I think this is something more than a dream."

"What are you talking about?"

"Look, I don't know what you and that creep are trying to pull, but if this is how you get little dead passenger pigeons, then I'm getting them too." He rubbed his hands together and looked around the park. "Now, where do you roost, you sweet little moneymaker?"

That's when Flip saw it—about two seconds before Jed did—the distinctive round shape of a dovecote at the end of a walled-in courtyard to the east of the house.

"Bingo," he said.

"Jed, please, this is already complicated enough. I only have a few hours. Please."

"It's not complicated at all, sweetcakes. If you're getting rich, so am I." He lifted a leg back over the railing just as the clock in the drawing room struck one.

Oh, cripes! She had to get to Magnus's room.

Jed cocked his head. "Is it one o'clock?"

"Quarter to."

"Hmm." He stroked his chin and pulled the note from his pocket. "Now the question I have is, is there really a nice young lady waiting all by herself for Mr. Wicket?"

"Wickham."

"Whatever."

"Don't do it, Jed. You'll never—"

The sound of footsteps approaching made her stop.

"Go," she whispered fiercely. It could be Lizzy with Darcy. It could be Caroline Bingley. The last thing she needed was for anyone to find either of them here.

But he didn't move. "What does it matter if it's a dream?"

"Jed!"

The footsteps were nearly upon them.

"Christ Almighty!" She ran through the drawing room doors and ducked.

One-eyed Bobby hauled the second urn up the narrow stairs, his night happily back in order thanks to a new infusion of orders from Codsworth.

"Water for the hip bath, lemons for the lady. Water for the hip bath, lemons for the lady."

He poured the steaming water into the growing pool in Colonel Fitzwilliam's tub and headed for Miss Bingley's room, as clearheaded as a bloodhound.

When no one answered his knock, he entered. "God's teeth," he said to himself. "Is no one in their room tonight?"

He stacked the lemons high on the nightstand and laid a sharp knife beside them, just the way the lady liked. He was just admiring his work—*Quite the artist, you are tonight, Bobby, with the lemons in here and the bottle and sugar in the colonel's room*—when one of the lemons rolled off the table onto the floor.

He stooped to retrieve it, and a note fluttered out of his pocket.

"Sainted Mother of God!" he cried, picking up the sheet.

"Who is this for?" He scratched his head and tried to recall Dolly's instruction, but it was lost in a blur of hot water, Codsworth's questions about the dice game and the smell of Mrs. Jellaby's breakfast biscuits, now rising in the kitchen.

He laid the note on the center of the pillow, "The note must be for Miss Bingley, else why would I be here?"

Chapter Twenty-six

Flip ducked into the kneehole of the desk just in time, for immediately upon her heels came Darcy and Magnus.

"Not to be unsympathetic, Darcy, but I do think I've heard enough about the unfortunate state of your, er, extremities. I admit the topiary was a regrettable suggestion on my part. I apologize. May I get you a drink?"

"Thank you, yes." Darcy limped to the sofa and lowered himself onto the cushion. "The worst part, though, is that it did seem to be working—" He caught himself and cleared his throat. "Naturally it isn't a gentleman's place to discuss such matters. However, I must say, the lady did appear to be, well, moved by my argument."

Flip was out of sight of most of the room except the far corner, though she could see a good deal of what was going on reflected in the wide, gold mirror over the mantel.

"I'm glad to hear it," Magnus said as his legs came into view. "And that in itself gives us hope, though I think it's time to try a different tack." He went to a small bar in the corner upon which three cut-glass decanters and several fat tumblers sat and poured red liquid, filling one glass nearly to the brim and the other halfway. He gulped down a large portion of the liquid in the first, turned, visibly startled when he spotted Flip, then swallowed even more.

She put a finger to her lips.

"What?" Darcy said. "What new tack?"

Magnus handed his friend the second tumbler, dropped into a nearby chair, and lifted his glass. "First, let us toast. To happiness. May each of us find it."

Darcy looked at the portion in Magnus's glass. "So little, my friend? Have you turned over an abstemious leaf?"

"Aye, that's me." With a quick toss, Magnus finished what remained. "For tonight, though, I will indulge with you."

He returned to the decanter and generously refilled his glass. This time when he turned, he did not meet Flip's eyes. In fact, though the bar sat in an alcove into which Darcy could not see, Magnus seemed, in fact, to purposefully avoid her.

She frowned.

"The different tack is an apology," Magnus said as he settled back into the chair. "For the Lady Quillan incident."

Darcy's face cooled considerably but Magnus pushed on, unaffected. "While I don't suppose you regret the interlude—what man would, after all?—there is a suitable way to handle it insofar as the next lady is concerned."

"Is there?" Darcy raised an antagonistic brow.

"You have offended Miss Bennet's vanity, her sense of *amour propre*—"

"Oh, her sense of *amour propre* is quite healthy and intact, I can assure you."

"Lovers, my dear Darcy, are delicate and changeable creatures. They live or die on a single word from their beloved. Silence is death, and your implacability on this topic—admirable might it be so far as society is concerned—has cast your relationship with Miss Bennet into a grievous state from which it may never recover. You must acknowledge your deed, shine a light on your actions. I know it is painful, but given that she found out about it before hearing a single word from you—"

"Bah!" Darcy dismissed his friend's advice with a wave. "She found out about it because the woman in question confided in her confounded friends."

Magnus's gaze grew severe. "You know this for a fact?"

Darcy shifted. "Well, no, but how else—"

"Darcy, the event took place on a hillside in full view of anyone who chose to look. I fear you are tempted to place blame because of the tenuous moral position in which you find yourself."

This was more than his imperious friend could bear. The guarded expression slipped away, and Darcy lashed out with disdain. "The woman—"

"Take care how you proceed, cousin. 'The woman,' as you term her, has friends." Magnus's eyes were hard as steel.

Darcy let out a long, pained sigh, and his shoulders sagged. "You are right, of course. I-I am unused to this sort of scrutiny. And the woman—Lady Quillan . . . Fitzwilliam, have you ever met her?"

Magnus looked at his drink, and Flip would have sworn a wave of pain flickered over his face. "No."

"Well, she is quite beguiling, with thick moonbeam hair and fine pale eyes, and the mouth—oh, the finest mouth I have ever seen."

Flip almost grinned but the dour look on Magnus's face as he heard this stopped her.

"We knew each other as children and then again as young

people," Darcy went on, "but the woman she has become . . ." Darcy swirled his drink and smiled. "Like a fine instrument. She is an adventurous, high-spirited creature with a quick wit, so the melody has always been that of an engaging, energetic flute solo. But that night, it was a whole concerto— dark and stormy, with betrayal and tears and hammering of fists. Her husband, you see, had taken a mistress."

Magnus sat up, his face changing instantly, and his eyes flickered anxiously to the glimpse of Flip in the mirror. "Oh?"

"Not his first, you understand, and he had thrown Lady Quillan from their marriage bed, do you see?"

Flip cringed in embarrassment.

"I appreciate your honesty," Magnus said, "but courtesy would suggest such details be kept—"

"Which would not wound her overly, I think, except she has only one desire."

Don't say it, Flip begged. Don't say it.

Magnus leaned forward. "You say too much."

"It is a woman's fundamental desire," Darcy continued, "though for my part—"

"Enough, my friend."

But Darcy was lost in the memory. "It has to be the lowest blow for one of her sex," he said. "Quillan would not sire a child upon her, and while she did not plead overtly—"

"Enough!" Magnus's fist came down on the table.

Darcy bridled visibly under the censure. He gave his cousin a peremptory, challenging look and finished his thought. "She did not plead, but I saw the soul-shaking thirst in her eyes. And I was going to slake it."

Flip felt as if she'd been stripped bare and staked in the town square. She wanted to run from the room.

Magnus paced to the fireplace, his back to Darcy, and did not speak. Flip watched him fight to gain control of his features.

"And the child is yours?" Magnus said at last.

Darcy rearranged himself on the sofa fastidiously. "It could as easily be Lord Quillan's. He has returned to their marriage bed, you know."

The muscles in Magnus's jaw flexed. He returned to the table, swallowed what remained in his drink and spoke directly to his cousin.

"I think Lady Quillan has been sadly used. Acknowledge your actions to Miss Bennet, apologize for the pride that fueled your silence until now and beg—beg—for her forgiveness.

Then Magnus put down his glass and left.

Chapter Twenty-seven

Jed edged slowly into the darkened room, waiting for either a cry of alarm or a sultry "I've been waiting" to determine both the pace and direction of his next movement, but no sound came.

He found the bed and patted it down. Empty. Shit. He considered stripping down and hopping in, so that Flip or whoever slept here might find him swaying at attention when she lit the candle—Pose number two—but the last time he'd tried something like that, he'd awakened with a gaggle of Dominican cleaning women surrounding him, laughing.

He was just deciding whether to ditch the assignation for now and head to the dovecote when the door opened.

A red-haired servant with much bigger tits than Flip opened the door. Now he was sorry he hadn't undressed.

"Who do you think you are?" she demanded, "hiding in Miss Bennet's room like this?"

"I dunno." He gave her his winningest Jed Hughes smile. "Who do you think I am?"

"Why, Mr. Wickham, of course. You know they'll have you run from the house if they find you here." She put down the polished shoes she carried in her arms. "Though

for my part, I don't see what they don't like about you."
She smiled.

He was Mr. Wickham? Well, he certainly didn't want to
disappoint the young lady waiting for him. He tossed himself against the stack of pillows and crossed his arms behind
his head. "And what's your name?"

"Peg."

"Peggy?" called an old, deep-voiced man from the hall.

Peg jumped. "I have to go. That's Sir William. I am
needed in the orangerie."

"An orangerie? This place has an orangerie too?"

"Indeed, the long, green building to the south—the one
with all the windows."

"And what do you have to do in a silly ol' orangerie this
late at night?"

"Sir William requires my attention there."

"I'm sure he does," Jed said, disheartened. "Be sure to
leave some for me."

The woman dimpled. "Now remember," she said as she
ducked out, "don't get caught."

Not a chance in hell.

Io reached the top of the grand staircase. This was a hell of
a dream, she thought. Like PBS on acid. It reminded her of
when she'd pretended to be Belle or Sleeping Beauty when
she was little. But not even a two-hundred-dollar costume
and a private birthday party at the restaurant in Cinderella's
castle had made it seem as real as this. And they'd certainly
treated her like a princess here, the servants waving her in
from the courtyard and calling "Oh, Miss Lydia!" and "How
glad your mother will be to see you!" Now she just needed to
figure out what Jed had been doing up on that balcony.

"Hey," she cried. "What are *you* doing here?"

Flip's boyfriend, the Englishman with the bedroom eyes, who looked like he'd been drinking, gazed at her like she were a ghost.

"You cannot be serious," he said.

"Hi, stranger." Amazing pants. Prince Charming never had pants like that.

"How did you get here?"

"I want to know everything you know about passenger pigeons. And," she added with a giggle, "I'm willing to sleep with you to find out." What the hell? A dream, right?

He held up a hand. "Totally unnecessary. But I'm afraid I have nothing to tell. I'm a literature professor. Birds are Jed's thing, not mine."

He seemed surprisingly lucid for a dream character. "Jed thinks you guys are hiding something."

"Why don't you ask Jed, then?"

"I'm asking you," she said sharply. She was still smarting from that "totally unnecessary" crack. "I want to know what you and Flip are hiding."

He snorted. "Or what?"

Those soft eyes held a surprising amount of menace, she thought, swallowing. But she could handle menace, the same way she'd handled that jerk-off chemistry professor who threatened to fail her.

"Or I will scream 'rape' as loud and as long as I can."

Knightley let out a decidedly non-literary oath, took her by the arm and pulled her roughly into an empty closet.

Caroline Bingley picked up the folded note from her pillow and frowned.

"What's that?" her sister demanded.

"I don't know." She opened it and read.

Lusty assignation. Your room. Quarter past one. Be
ready. Undress. Eyes will be watching. —D.

Caroline clapped the note closed, then opened it again
and read.

"My goodness, Caroline, you're positively crimson. What
does it say?"

"I-I— Here!" She thrust it into her sister's more experienced hands.

Louisa read it and whooped. "From Darcy! At last you
shall have him," she cried, and added pragmatically, " 'Tis not
a bad way to catch a husband, after all. It's the way I caught
Charles." She read the note again and giggled. "Heavens, my
dear. You have engendered quite the passion. Have you been
flirting as I instructed?"

"Yes, of course, at the Traymores' ball. But that was weeks
ago."

"Well, I'm sure he's been doing a slow boil ever since.
It's funny how men are. Half the time one can't get them to
pay the slightest attention, and the other—watch out!" She
laughed but stopped when she saw the look of sheer panic
on her sister's face.

"Now, dear," Louisa said, "it is nothing. One simply closes
one's eyes. Mummy told me to think of the fox hunt—
that bouncing and sweat, you know; quite animalistic—
but I find simply planning my outfit for the next day to
be equally diverting, and I do believe the look on my face
then is more pleasing to Charles. He has often commented
upon it."

Caroline didn't look convinced. "But the first time . . . ?"

"Oh, there's a pinch, to be sure. But think of Darcy's house and his lovely ten thousand a year. That should be balm enough. And let me get something from my room that will help." She ran out and returned with a large glass of sherry.

Caroline took a large swallow, followed in quick succession by a second and a third, and reread the note. "What do you suppose he means? There, at the end?"

Louisa gazed over her shoulder. " 'Undress'? Come, my dear, I think that should be clear even to—"

"Not that. The 'Eyes will be watching' part."

Louisa frowned. "Hmmm." She snapped her fingers. "I know it! Oh, that unrepentant hound!"

"What? What?"

"It is a bit naughty, Caroline, but, I promise you, you can do it."

Caroline took a deeper gulp. "Oh God, what?"

"Charles sometimes— Well, you see, when he was younger, his uncle once took him to a somewhat, er, notorious exhibition in a Paris club. Ever since then, when the mood strikes, he begs me to, er, disrobe for him while he hums the music he remembers from the show."

"Louisa!"

"It is nothing, Caroline. I must disrobe in any case. I only add a bit of a sashay, and half the time it averts something worse. You see—how shall I say it?—the show ends for Charles a long time before it ends for me. Why, sometimes I have done no more than remove a glove before I hear the familiar gasp and know he will be asleep before I take off my slippers."

Caroline looked as if she had just been smacked. "That's all well and good," she said, appearing as if she felt exactly the opposite, "but Darcy is not here to watch!"

"Oh." Louisa tapped her chin, thinking. "You're right." She perused the note again, then stepped to the French doors. She looked out upon the night.

"Out there," she said.

"What?" Caroline cried. "I need to disrobe out there?!"

"Don't be a simpleton. Darcy is out there. I saw a movement near the stable."

"Where?" Caroline looked. "I don't see anything. It's black as pitch."

"He is watching the window. I'm certain of it. You need to stand right here"—Louisa pulled her sister beside her—"and take off your clothes. Darcy will wait until the end and then come to claim you."

"But my stays! My buttons!"

"For heaven's sake," Louisa chided, pulling at the buttons so hard several went flying across the room, "you must make do. Now, don't forget. Everything adds to the effect including jewelry and hairpins, and you must go very slow."

Louisa paused when she reached the door. "Oh, my dear, I am so excited," she said, grinning fiendishly. "And if you wriggle enough, you may catch a husband without losing your virginity—and that would be an immaculate deception indeed."

Her laughter echoed down the hall.

Caroline slumped for an instant, the now-loosened sleeves of her gown slipping off her shoulder, but the thought of Darcy's house and its glorious bedrooms and marble and gold plate brought her strength. She lifted her arms to her head, rolled her hips like she was stirring molasses with them and plucked the first hairpin from her hair.

"But why are they so important?" Io demanded. "I mean, aren't there fucking passenger pigeons everywhere?"

Magnus rubbed his temple. All he wanted to do was enjoy his last few hours with Flip before Madame K worked her black magic and they'd have no more notion of each other than a bear and a bacterium. But instead he was facing this snarling post-punk annoyance and remembering ever so clearly why he hated teaching freshmen.

"That's a very good question," he said. "You see, most only lay a single egg in a lifetime, and the shell is used to make a very expensive ingredient in the finest perfumes—an ingredient that is still considered an aphrodisiac in certain cultures."

"Really?" Io said uncertainly.

"Oh, indeed," Magnus said, wondering exactly how much of this crap he could shovel in her direction before those kohl-lined eyes would begin to narrow. "The passenger pigeon is very rare, which is why Flip and Jed both have a great interest in it."

"For the money," Io said.

"No, my dear. To protect it. They're ornithologists, *hm*?"

"So, the dead bird. Is it worth anything?"

"Sadly, no," Magnus said. "Dead pigeons hardly ever lay eggs—even the most determined."

Io stewed on this. "So why are they 'passenger' pigeons? What does the 'passenger' mean?"

"Do you speak French?"

"No."

"It's from the French," he said, adding to his lies." *Passengé*.
It means turquoise." He pointed to his eyes. "Their irises."

"Oh." She nodded, impressed. "Are there more around
here?"

"Yes, but they mix in with the other pigeons. It's very
hard to tell them apart unless you examine their tail feathers.
Those with at least two black next to at least three white—
they're the ones."

"Where can I find them?"

"Just to look?" he enquired politely.

"Of course," she replied. "They're very rare."

"Well . . ." He gazed out the storage room window and saw
the distinctive beehive-spaced dovecote silhouetted against
the eastern night sky. "There's the pigeon house there." He
pointed directly south.

Io shoved her way to the window. "I don't see anything."

"It's well beyond the parkland, almost over the border
into the next estate."

"Great. Now point me back toward the staircase."

"Actually, there's a servant's stairway just around the corner that should serve you pretty ably. Remember now," he
called as she disappeared out the door, "just past the end of
the parkland."

He hoped she didn't stop until she reached Land's End.

"You there."

Peg froze on the stairs. It was her master's sister, Louisa.
She had hoped to slip from the house unnoticed. "Yes, m'um."

"I would like to have my bed turned down and a warm
water bottle brought in," the woman commanded. "Oh,
and my sister is having a bit of trouble sleeping. If you could
bring her a bottle of claret I would be most appreciative. Er,

do not disturb her, though, on any account. Just knock once and leave it on the floor outside her room."

"Yes, m'um. M'um?" Through the entry hall window, Peg saw Sir William padding across the courtyard.

"Yes?"

"Might I deliver it in half an hour or so? I am supposed to be picking oranges for tomorrow's breakfast."

"How very diligent of you, Peg. You may certainly return to your harvesting once my bed is ready and that bottle of claret is delivered."

Peg curtsied. "You are too kind."

Chapter Twenty-eight

Lizzy swallowed hard, murmured, "Maddening man," and automatically checked her hair. This was a grim task, she thought as she stood before Darcy's door, but she felt certain he would agree that Colonel Fitzwilliam needed to be brought down a peg. A servant girl! And he a guest in someone else's home!

She would be brief and to the point. Something must be done, and the man was Darcy's cousin, after all. Nor would she deign to an apology for their earlier contretemps, of course. Even a man like Darcy knew when his bollocks had been savaged for a just cause.

She paused, intending to reflect upon that artful jerk of her knee, but her mind flew instead to the moment before the snap, to that imperious, demanding mouth and those shockingly discourteous hands. Why, she could almost feel the muscled shoulders under her fingers and that fine, sleek torso urging her to—

The door cracked.

Lizzy jumped, but not before realizing her mouth had been open in a somewhat suggestive shape.

"Oh," Darcy said, surprised. "I wanted to talk to you as well, but I felt certain it was too late."

He was stockless and his shirt hung open halfway to his waist, revealing a broad expanse of iron-hard chest. Lizzie felt her eyes irretrievably drawn to the gleaming curve of pectoral peeking from the linen. "I-I—"

"I do beg your pardon," he said, hurrying to button himself. "I was just retiring for the night. Care to join me? I mean," he said with a shake, "would you care to step inside so that we may speak in private?"

Lizzie found her voice. "Forgive me, Mr. Darcy. I was inexcusably rude to you earlier, and I should like nothing more than to—"

He turned away to button the remaining buttons, and Lizzy's gaze fell upon the powerful, curved line of his breeches just below his back. A shiver went through her.

"You should like nothing more than to . . .?" he prompted.

Lay my hands across those intriguing curves, and feel the tight, springing energy—

"Madam?"

"Sorry. Yes. To make my amends."

"No," he said, turning. "It is I who must apologize. I should be horsewhipped for what I did outside on the balcony."

"On the balcony?" She tilted her head, wondering if she was confused or if the sandalwood scent of his skin was making her thick-headed. "I thought that was on the railing of the Temple of Apollo?"

"Oh." Darcy colored. "That." He took her hand. "Dear Elizabeth, I did not mean to do you or anyone harm. It happened, of course, before I met you, but that does not excuse it. Lady Quillan deserves my support, which I shall gladly give if she seeks it. But it would be impolitic for me to approach her now. Her husband . . ." His voice trailed off.

"Yes," Elizabeth murmured, understanding. The touch of his skin made her breath catch. "I do not think you need to," she said, smiling. "I am told she is, in fact, quite happy with the situation. It has served to teach her husband that she is a force to be reckoned with."

"That she is." He smiled too.

Lizzy chewed at her lip. "Though I must admit, I should not like to have to resort to something like that to teach my husband anything."

"I think," Darcy said with unguarded warmth, "you should never have to worry about that, Elizabeth."

A noise in the hall made them both jump, and their hands fell away. Reduced to awkwardness again, Lizzy said, "But I have come here for another reason."

"Another reason?" Darcy lifted a brow, and Lizzy swore she saw his gaze cut for a split second to the bed. He realized he'd been caught and cleared his throat.

"Er, yes," Lizzy said, laughter in her voice. "It seems your cousin suffers from the same familial condition."

"What? Is he in love with you too?" Darcy demanded, and Lizzy's heart swelled.

"No," she said at last. "I assure you, no. I found him in a most improper pose this evening with Dolly, the servant girl."

"Dolly?" Darcy rubbed his chin as if plucking the girl's face from the vast inventory of Netherfield servants in his memory. "She is rather odd, is she not?"

"Is she?"

"I think. I am somewhat surprised . . ." He stole a cautious glance at Lizzy's face. "By 'improper' I take it you mean, er—"

"Yes." Lizzy nodded solemnly.

"Shocking behavior in a gentleman. To disport with a willing gentlewoman in such a manner is one thing—"

Lizzy saw the struggle he fought to keep his eyes from the overstuffed mattress.

"—but with a servant girl who depends on the goodwill of her master and her master's friends," he went on, "is insupportable."

"She is a good girl and kind. I am most unhappy to see her misused. Especially because I believe her feelings for him are quite . . . genuine."

Darcy fingered the link in his cuff and sighed. "I admit I am deeply disappointed in my cousin. Be assured he will very soon feel the sharp sting of a rebuke from me—the very sharp sting. And as far as Dolly is concerned, you have my word she need not have the slightest fear for her position—"

"Well . . ." Lizzy said.

"Well?"

"Well, I have a somewhat different plan."

Chapter Twenty-nine

Having grown tired of waiting, Jed shimmied down the wisteria vines and dropped to the courtyard only to discover Io, too, had a supporting role in this dream. She was scurrying toward the main gate in one of those Southern belle gowns he was growing to admire.

"Well, now, this is the sort of coincidence every man hopes for."

Io turned, surprised.

"Where are you running off to," he asked, "looking so goddamned luscious?"

He wondered what women wore under that stuff and realized for the first time that the rash wasn't bothering him anymore. *Damn. How much magic could the old woman produce?*

"Nowhere, actually," she said. "Just taking a walk."

"Well, would you like to join me in the dovecote?"

"Doo-coat?"

"Dove house, love. It's where the pigeons roost." He pointed to the large round-domed building behind her and thought, now there's a chubby to write home about. He wondered if the dream might bring him similar *Alice in Wonderland*–type proportions.

"*That's* where the pigeons live?" she demanded. "That's not what I was told."

His balls jumped into his abdominal cavity. Why did she sound so pissed? "You bet it is. Shall I fetch you a lovely pair of passengers?"

Her face relaxed, and so did his balls. "With an egg?"

"If you'd like. I'll see what I can do."

"If you bring me an egg," she whispered in his ear, "I will definitely make it worth your while."

"Oh, baby, how many eggs do you want?"

She brushed his cheek. "One for every fantastic inch."

He hardened instantly.

"How long will it take?" she said.

About ten seconds if you lean over right now. "Five minutes. Three if I'm lucky."

"Be lucky." She looked around, then pointed to a low green building made almost entirely of windows. "I'll see you there. Three minutes."

He trotted off toward the dovecote. "Alice, don't fail me now."

When Codsworth opened his first hand of cards and spotted both black aces, both black kings and a jack, he wanted to kiss someone. By the time he'd arrived at the stables, most of the dicers had long since swept up their money or their hopes and dispersed. However, there were three similar-minded grooms just arriving, fresh from sleep, whose responsibility it was to prepare the wedding carriages for the early procession to the church and who were more than happy to strike up a game of quadrille, ha'penny to the point.

"Quite the tireless party, I hear," said Aaron, the oldest groom and most devout, tilting his head toward the house.

"Bedlam," Codsworth said, "without the geniality. Who starts?"

Aaron made the lowest opening bid. "Is our master preparing himself for tomorrow's sacraments?"

"Oh, indeed." Codsworth quickly counted his tricks. "I believe you will find him deep in scripture even now. Michael?"

Michael rubbed his cheek glumly and moved his stool closer to the makeshift table. "Pass."

"Vole," Codsworth said, uttering the game's impossible-to-top bid triumphantly. "Black is trump."

"But I haven't bid," whined Tad, a young mole-faced man who had come to Netherfield after an unhappy stint as an apprentice to a Northumberland smithy.

His colleagues waited.

Tad wriggled under their impatient gazes and readjusted his cards. "Pass."

Codsworth shoved the bowl that served as the kitty toward the grooms. "That's three pennies from each of you, gentlem—" he began, then Michael's face made him stop.

Michael's jaw, slack from the start, had dropped nearly to his chin. "I-I think that's Miss Bingley."

Codsworth turned, expecting to see his master's sister striding toward him with more orders, but the courtyard was empty. "Where?"

Michael lifted a meaty finger toward the third set of double doors on the house's balcony. There, lit by a month's salary's worth of candles, stood Caroline Bingley, barebacked, looking over her shoulder in their direction, and grinding her hips like a drug-addled Cleopatra into a towel slung low across her thighs.

"Holy Mary. She's lost her nut."

Miss Bingley was by no means a beautiful woman, but this violent, half-naked rolling of hips in a woman usually dressed to the teeth was so horrifically spellbinding no one spoke for a full half minute.

Then she dropped the towel.

Tad made a noise like the badger Codsworth had once surprised in the pantry and slipped backward off his stool.

Aaron began to mouth something Codsworth recognized from yesterday's service, and Michael's finger hung limply in the air.

"Stop pointing," Codsworth commanded, turning his back to the scene and waving his arms. "Good God, all of you, stop looking." But the commotion only served to rouse the grooms that had been sleeping.

Suddenly Aaron paled, and Codsworth feared the worst.

"Her-her p-pips!"

Codsworth hazarded a terrified glance only to discover Miss Bingley's pale breasts heaving in time to an obscene rhythm heard only by their owner.

The newly awakened men began to laugh.

"Stop! All of you!" Codsworth cried. "Recall yourselves. She is our mistress." He saw the futility of his attempts and ran toward the house.

Io scanned the room, looking for the best prospect. She did love shocking Jed, and with half a dozen eggs, she'd be set. The story of the year and money to boot. That was worth a heroic fuck. She bent over the worktable, hiked her skirts over her ears and hoped Jed's heart didn't stop.

Jed found them—dozens of them. Lovely, ruby-throated creatures with dark gray tails and shimmering iridescent bodies, gurgling and cooing and flapping and landing on his arm.

They took his breath away. He laughed and sunk to his knees, wondering for the very first time if the ivory-billed woodpecker might live on, too, if only in the dreams of euphoric ornithologists.

Sir William's heart leaped in his chest like his horse, Horace, when he took the first hedge at last week's foxhunt.

Peg had eluded him all night, touching and teasing until he thought he would expire, but still he'd been like bread dough. But now, there she was. Plump and pale and split down the middle like a ripe peach disgorging its sweet nectar, Peg's arse wriggled in invitation, and Sir William's flagging member responded in kind.

"Oh, what a girl," he thought, and burst into the orangerie.

"I want it fast, hard and without another word," the girl's muffled voice demanded, and in an instant he was a randy lad of twenty.

He had a vague longing to see well enough to determine if her ship's paint scheme matched that of her pennant, but for the most part he was supremely satisfied to slip his oft-disappointing manhood into her cozy port, grab those delectable orbs and pray for a fitting end to this finely fitting start.

Chapter Thirty

Despite his small but gratifying triumph with the preternaturally annoying Io, Magnus made his way toward his room depressed.

The book was a disaster. He could see no possible way to straighten out the mess Flip had started and he had worsened. And Darcy had been more of an officious ass than he could have imagined. To have bedded Flip was one thing—and Magnus would have to be considerably drunker to begin to think about Darcy doing that—but to talk so offhandedly about a woman's closely guarded secret was unforgivable.

He heard a noise and turned. But it was only that red-haired maid being ordered about by one of Bingley's demanding guests, his sister Louisa, by the sound of it.

Magnus's shoulders sagged and he entered his room. A lamp on the wall cast a meager circle of light. When he turned it up, he saw the wine bottle, glasses and sugar bowl arranged neatly on the far side of the raised bed. For an instant his heart rose, and he turned to see if she was here in the room, waiting. But the room, unlike his thoughts, was empty. He tossed himself on the bed.

No more Flip. That's the worst part of all.

No memory, Madame K had said. None.

He reached for the bottle, uncorked it and drank.

Champagne, he thought, though it was sweeter than the champagne of his time, and the cool liquid reminded him of a marvelous bottle of Château d'Yquem he'd once drunk with a colleague after a conference. It had cost them seventy quid each, but, oh, it had been worth it.

Flip, he thought, was not unlike that d'Yquem. Velvety, full-bodied and long, lingering on his tongue and in his memory well past the last savored sweetness. But Flip offered so much more. The rich scent of her hair. The stiff, upturned nipples and the easy weight of her breasts. The unforgettable sound in her throat when she laughed. The devastating sound when she moaned. He'd never forgotten the wine. How could he possibly forget her?

Have another go at it, Flip had said. She had no idea how much those words had hurt as she had no idea those words were the classic Magnus Knightley sign-off. It didn't take a literary critic to recognize poetic justice.

He took another swallow.

A bottleful of forgetfulness, he thought. That's what he needed. Something to erase the memory of that knee-shaking first kiss and the cool, silky skin at the base of her spine with its lubricious hint of firm mounds below.

Christ. This wasn't helping.

He dropped the bottle on the table and for the first time saw the tub.

Between the bed and the hearth beyond, a hip bath had been set out and filled halfway to the brim. The scent of oranges wafted from its shimmering surface. He went to it and dipped in a hand. The water was neither hot nor cold, just refreshing enough in the warm room to be inviting. With a tug, he drew the light curtains across the opening of the French doors, removed his clothes and got in.

He might have enjoyed the warmth if he'd taken the time to consider it, but the bottle was within arm's reach. He grabbed it, leaned back and drank.

For laying down. That's what they said about new vintages when they were the sort that would continue to grow and improve every year. What he had with Flip was like that— only a day old but holding the promise of so much more.

If Darcy and Elizabeth managed to sort things out by morning and Madame K wiggled her nose or waved her wand or whatever the hell it was she did, he'd wake up tomorrow to find himself exactly as he'd been yesterday—nearing the end of his book and at the top of his profession—with no memory of anything that had happened since Flip first exploded into Austen's plot like a meteor out of literary hell. And there was no guarantee he'd ever see her again after this debacle ended. Guarantee? He snorted. There was no *chance* they'd see each other again. They'd have exactly one shared memory, that of their ugly meeting at the café, a situation that would certainly ensure they'd never speak again, even if they beat the odds and happened to run into each other.

He tipped the bottle high and swallowed until his lungs screamed. Then he closed his eyes and drank more.

Flip looked both ways, then slipped into Magnus's room and quietly closed the door.

He was in a bath of some sort across the room, resting. This was her first real look at him unclothed, and he put

Darcy to shame with his broad, tough shoulders, a lightly furred chest and taut biceps and forearms.

"Magnus?"

His eyes, curious but unfocused, opened immediately. "Flip."

She had expected him to be in bed, but this worked beautifully, too. He'd clearly gotten her note and set the scene. It felt odd, this mock seduction, after so heated and unplanned an interlude in the storage room, but if that's what it took to bring Darcy and Lizzy together, then so be it. In any case Flip had come to suspect theatricality played a fairly large role in all of Magnus Knightley's liaisons. And she hadn't forgotten how he'd reduced their joining to mere mechanics.

"Lusty assignation, right?" She hurried toward the window, refusing to be flustered by his gaze. "Do you mind if I open the curtains a bit? You haven't heard anything, have you?"

He didn't reply, and when she had finished her adjustments and turned back to him, the expression on his face had grown considerably more guarded.

He opened his mouth just as Flip heard footsteps on the balcony outside. *"Shhhh,"* she whispered.

The sound stopped outside the French doors. If she and Magnus were going to be caught in an indelicate pose, now was the time. She looked hesitantly at the tub. Apparently naked was the plan. Well, she was game if he was. She moved silently across the carpet, waiting for him to squawk, jerk into a ball or wave her off. Those eyes never left her face, and he made no move except to clasp the neck of the bottle he was holding a little tighter. She grabbed a stool from the corner and took a seat beside him.

Well, I think we have indelicacy covered.

She cleared her throat, attempting to keep her eyes off the magnificent pale object resting casually across a mass of mahogany curls, and said, "Darcy and Lizzy are ready to go. Let's get to it, shall we?" She bent to kiss him.

The kiss was automatic, clinical even. Nonetheless, Flip felt her breath catch. His tongue flicked hers expertly, and a hot whiplash of pleasure snapped through her. He tasted of honeyed wine, and the scent rising from his skin reminded her of summertime.

Magnus pulled away and looked at her. The topaz in his eyes had grown almost black. She could tell he'd been drinking—taste it, too—and for an instant she saw the look of a wounded animal in his gaze, but then it was gone. He kissed her again, deeper and longer, with none of the detachment he'd shown a moment earlier, and Flip found herself feeling the same earthshaking shudder of connection she'd had when they'd kissed in the storage room. The trick, she realized, wasn't going to be getting the happy couple to believe what they witnessed was real; it was going to be keeping her from believing it too.

He brought her hair to his nose, inhaling deeply.

There was no mistaking what was happening, even beneath the delightfully distorting lens of the water, and Flip felt the electric charge of control.

"I'm going to have to get in there, you know." She ran her tongue along the salty rim of his earlobe. He shivered, and the shadowy blue depths stirred.

Spank her, would he? For his punishment he could enjoy a few uncomfortable minutes exposing his desire to the world.

She kicked off her boots and purposefully lifted her skirts past her knees. He groaned, almost fearful. Her eyes raked his body slowly and deliberately, and she knew he saw she was taking her fill of him.

She stepped across him and began to lower herself.

He caught her hard by the waist. "No."

"No?" she said, surprised. His grip was like steel, and though she knew with a single movement he could have her pinned, he held her above him.

"No."

She had only toyed with the idea of turning their mock performance into something real. Nonetheless, she harrumphed and lowered herself, pressing his erection flat across his stomach.

The water was warm, and her skirts puddled around her waist. He drew his fingers through her hair, letting them trail over her cheek, and his eyes searched her face, as if he were trying to memorize every detail.

"You're Lady Quillan."

It was a statement, not a question, and though he spoke without a hint of accusation, the words knocked the wind out of her. She nodded.

"Did he hurt you?"

"No." The look on his face was so grave, she laughed to dispel it. "No, not at all. It was"—how to explain it?—"stupid and hot and totally meaningless."

"Like us."

But that was wrong, and gravity, however guileless, would not make it so. "Not like us," she corrected.

His shoulders relaxed a degree, and he gave her a grateful caress, but Flip still read misery in his eyes.

"How much of that," she asked, tilting her head toward the bottle, "have you drunk?"

"Enough."

"Enough?" she asked.

"Enough to know this will never be enough."

She drew herself forward slowly and nipped his cheek. "It doesn't have to be enough. It only has to be the start of enough."

He made a tortured noise. "Flip . . ."

She ground her hips against him, amazed at the singular tensile mass beneath her, and with a heavy exhale, he closed his eyes and ran a tongue over his lips. She could see his heart beating in the hollow of his throat, but still the traces of woe were visible.

Dammit, she thought, I can make those disappear.

With two determined tugs, she freed herself from the sleeves of her dress, leaving only her thin chemise. Then she bent forward, dipping her nipples in the water as she plied his chest with an eager tongue.

He groaned, and she could feel the great animal strength as he stiffened against her wiggling rump.

A sound—a cough? a bird?—came from beyond the doors.

"C'mon." She sat up and let the wet linen frame her taut flesh. "You have to do more."

"I don't think we should."

She laughed. Magnus Knightley with scruples? She could feel the raw lust beneath her. Who was he trying to fool?

She gave him a haughty look and moved slowly and firmly along his length.

He grasped the sides of the tub and groaned, a low, aching sound whose reverberations rumbled through her thighs. She felt giddy and wicked, and she crooked an arm languorously over her head, waiting for his reaction.

Eyes flashing like a panther's, he grabbed her chemise and tore.

The act shocked her, and he sat up, unbalancing her as well. His eyes were wild and dark, and he drew them over her as if he might never see her again. Then he pulled her hard by the waist and took a nipple in his teeth.

Lightning strikes of pleasure shot through her. The other nipple stiffened, and he twisted it as he sucked, ignoring her choppy gasps for air.

He uncorked his mouth and examined her breasts with a raw lasciviousness that made her cheeks warm.

"Harder," he said like a painter pondering a far-from-satisfactory canvas. "And sweeter."

He pressed her away from him and raised the bottle, drizzling its chill, effervescing contents over her chest. Immediately her nipples peaked, and he laughed, a deep, aroused laugh that sent a blaze between her legs.

"Lift your arms," he commanded, and when she did, he lapped the circles of sensitive flesh, licking the liquid clean. Every moment of his tongue made her squirm, and he growled when he had to chase her.

He wrapped his hands around her ribs and lifted the soft weight of her breasts as he suckled. With an excruciating tug, he pulled away and said, "Sweeter still."

More cool rivulets were poured down her chest, sheeting into the bathwater at her hips with a lush tinkle. Then he reached for the bowl on the nearby table. The bowl was low and wide, with a colorful pattern of flowers and exotic birds that reminded Flip of a South Sea island. He pressed it into her hand, and she stared at him, confused. With an ungentlemanly movement, he tipped her hips up, pushing her forward until her cheek was by his mouth.

"Sugar them," he commanded.

A firecracker of heat pinwheeled through her body. The look on his face challenged her to demur.

Did he think he, the man of strip Scrabble and library assignations, was more daring than Flip Allison? Ha!

She lifted the bowl, feeling her heart pound in her chest and belly. He stared at her brazenly, as if he had paid for something sinful and expected to get every dollar's worth. Even without his observation, however, performing this task wasn't easy. To keep the bowl level, she had to bend deeply, and at the same time she had to raise herself up, a movement that freed his cock, and she felt it bobble impressively against her thighs.

The sugar grains were fat and brown with sharp edges, and she felt the prick of a hundred little knives as she dipped her straining flesh into them.

"Both," he said flatly, and stared with unexpurgated interest at her work.

She bent again, and when she did, he grabbed her hips, and she could feel him forcibly restrain himself from plunging them down on top of him.

Both nipples sparked in the candlelight now, and every flicker of light in the room seemed to be accompanied by a far more intriguing throb beneath her. She was terrified: terrified of what he was feeling, which seemed dark and unreadable and not at all in line with this game, which was supposed to be merely a way to bring their unruly charges together; terrified of what she was feeling, which was thrilling and good, as if she were on the verge of some magnificent precipice she'd never conquered before; and terrified of what would happen if Lizzy, Darcy or anyone showed up before she and Magnus finished this.

He pulled the chemise free and threw its wet mass unceremoniously on the hearth. In an instant he was standing up, with her in his arms. He carried her toward the bed, and she prayed for the cover of the sheets, unwilling to risk the mortification of being in full view. Magnus had no fear, though, and he tossed her on the cover, pinning her firmly beneath him.

But he did not enter her. He held her close, his heart beating against her flattened breasts, and looked in her eyes.

"A child, is it?" he asked huskily.

"What?" Her voice was barely a whisper.

"A child," he said. "Is that what you wanted from Darcy in the temple?"

She turned her face, unwilling to let him glimpse the devastating pain in her eyes, but he turned her back.

"I didn't want a child from Darcy," she said, "but Lady Quillan did and—" She groaned as an unwelcome tear striped her cheek, and she swiped at it angrily, ashamed. "And I know what it feels like to want that."

"You, though?" he said. "That's what *you* want?"

She hated to be pitied. Hated it. Everything about her life had been lived to impress others with her confidence and independence. Even in her marriage, when she and Jed had lived apart because of various fieldwork assignments, she'd laugh when anyone asked if that was hard. She could live weeks in a forest by herself. She could climb trees of all sizes, including a sequoia once, where she'd gazed down on the top of the fog that covered the morning earth. Two years ago, she'd finished her fieldwork on the red-cockaded woodpecker in an Arkansas bog and hauled her cameras, tent and kit for two days to reach her car, hobbled by a broken foot. But she couldn't make a baby by herself, and the only man she'd ever asked to help had refused.

"Yes," she said, "that's what I want."

"Jed's a fool," he said and buried himself to the hilt inside her.

He was sizeable, and she gasped, trying to accommodate the inebriating burn that swirled like a brushfire around her hips.

"Stop," she said earnestly, feeling the weight of her indiscretion. "I slept with Darcy. Today. You can't . . ."

"The hell I can't. I know how to make babies," he said, perched above her and thrusting easily in a slow rhythm that began on "can't." "Darcy . . ." He made a dismissive noise. "What does he know? Besides," he said, flicking a tongue over one sugared berry of a nipple, "Darcy impregnated Lady Quillan, remember? He may be the fantasy of every middle-aged woman in the English-speaking world, but I don't think even he can manage two conceptions with a single fornication."

But if someone could, it was Magnus, she thought. Already her hips were urging him on and her hands were clutching his tight, muscled ass, trying with every beat to drive him more deeply into her.

Lost in the thrilling violence to her body, she found the moments slipping away and the rising tide beginning to carry her higher and higher. She tasted the salty sheen of his hard, warm body. The low, earthy noises he made when her tongue found him thrilled her, and she buried herself in the grassy, wet scent of his hair, aware of nothing but the overwhelming fire licking her bones.

"It takes a big finish, do you understand?" he whispered, rousing her from her fevered reverie. His voice was ragged, and his body quivered with the effort. "No holds barred. As loud and as long as you can, do you hear?"

"Yes." She clung to him as his hips accelerated, unsure what he meant, for her finishes were of one flavor only—hot, knee-trembling and exquisite.

Then he pressed her open, almost beyond pleasure, and thrust a finger deep between them, finding the bud of her sex and rolling it hard.

The wave began at her knees, filling her lungs and organs with rich, burgeoning, heat. The rolling stopped, replaced with an urgent pluck that flung her mouth wide and arched her back as the universe began to explode.

"No," she cried. "No!"

"Yes," he insisted, drawing back so far Flip feared she would be torn in two. He plunged with a husky, hoarse cry that mixed with her own primitive wail, and the world shook with such an enormous, upending torrent she gripped the headboard to keep from being thrown to the floor.

He jerked again and again, groaning with the effort, before collapsing upon her.

She clutched his spent body to hers, unwilling to let the moment go. She drew herself to his ear to put words to a gratitude that went far beyond that moment. As she did, the French doors banged open, and Bingley, stern and fearsome, said, "Damn your indiscretion, Fitzwilliam. Breech yourself, and meet me on the balcony."

"You have abused my hospitality," Bingley said to a stone-faced Magnus. Flip hovered several paces behind, wrapped in a quilt. Darcy stood nearby, shielding Lizzy, who clasped his arm with a proud and happy ease, and Jane, who beamed over Darcy's shoulder at her fiancé.

"You have ruined a decent woman," Bingley went on, jabbing the night air with his finger. "You have misused your position. You have acted without regard for anyone but yourself, and I am sorry to say this has become your calling card as of late. What have you to say on your behalf, Colonel?"

Bingley, despite looking as if he'd just rolled out of bed, managed to be the perfect Central Casting villain. Flip was genuinely delighted but hid her smile behind her hand. If he'd begun to twirl one side of a nonexistent mustache, too, she wouldn't have been surprised. Lizzy and Darcy had done their job well, and, because of it, so had she and Magnus. So why was Magnus looking like he'd taken a medicine ball to the gut? Sure, Flip would have preferred being found dressed in something a little less embarrassing than an amazed postcoital grin, but surely a man whose assignations regularly included the chance for a small audience of rare book enthusiasts can hardly stand on scruples on the issue.

"I have nothing to say," Magnus replied. "It's none of your business." The scowl that accompanied his answer would have quieted a room full of stranded airline passengers, but Bingley didn't flinch.

"But it is," Bingley said darkly. "Dolly has no family and is therefore under my protection. You will answer to me on this." He opened his coat to reveal two pearl-handled pistols. "You must fight me or marry her this instant."

Magnus stared at Bingley, dull-eyed. For a man who had just succeeded in reuniting his protagonists, Magnus was taking this far too seriously.

"I won't fight," Magnus said simply.

Bingley turned to Darcy. "Get the archbishop."

The archbishop arrived, muzzy from sleeping, though he was clearly the only one in the house who'd bothered to partake. He was a blinking, long-nosed man in a patterned yellow nightshirt that gave him the air of a large, startled duck. He attempted to find the page in his well-worn book, but without his glasses, the attempt was useless. He gave up and snapped the cover closed.

"Colonel Fitzwilliam," he said, "are you prepared to make this woman your wife?"

Magnus, who had neither moved nor spoken since Bingley had called for the archbishop, squared his shoulders. Everyone on the balcony, including Flip, tensed, waiting for the answer.

A faint but clearly furious wail of "Who the fuck are you?" coming from the direction of the orangerie made all of them pause awkwardly.

Magnus broke the silence. "Yes."

Flip felt an inexplicable rush of happiness at this meaningless bit of playacting, mostly because this was the first instant since their discovery Magnus met her gaze full on. Part joy, part pride, part tongue-tied embarrassment, the feeling threatened to betray her, and she turned to hide the flush.

"Dolly is beneath you in rank and education," the archbishop said flatly.

Flip looked at Magnus, waiting for him to smirk, but he returned to that stiff-shouldered, straight-ahead stare that made her feel as if there were a thousand miles between them.

"I want to hear in your own words," the archbishop said, "that you are willing to overlook these differences. Dolly has been ill-used, and if you take her as your wife, your silence on the difference in your stations—now and forever—is rightful penance, and you must be willing to pay it."

"Would that it were the only penance I must pay," Magnus said.

The archbishop ignored this, adding, "Your marriage will raise her to a gentlewoman, your equal. You will provide for her. You will cherish and respect her."

"Yes." The edge in Magnus's voice made it clear his patience for reprimand had ended.

"You are capable of all that?"

"*Yes.*"

The archbishop sighed. "Your anger is most troubling, Colonel." He turned to his host and shrugged sadly. "I'm afraid, Bingley, I cannot in good conscience marry them."

"No!" Lizzy's arm fell from Darcy's. "Your grace, think of the girl. We have no choice."

"There are always choices, Miss Bennet," the archbishop said. "Some we simply prefer not to make."

"But . . ."

Darcy touched her shoulder. "Come now, we tried—"

"No." Lizzy twisted out of his reach, and gave him a look of such pained abandonment, Flip's heart jumped into her throat.

Darcy saw his happiness slipping away. "Elizabeth . . ."

Lizzy's eyes glossed with wetness.

Darcy gave Magnus an exasperated look and said to the archbishop, "Your grace, might I have a moment with my cousin."

The archbishop shrugged.

"Fitzwilliam," Darcy said, "don't be a fool." His eyes cut to Lizzy, and he gave her a regretful smile. "I have been one, a prideful, vain, stupid fool. And because of it, I could have—

may have yet—lost everything. If your heart has settled upon this woman, you must act. You must not let anything but the truest nature of your regard guide you in this. Even if your heart hasn't," he added with a gruff cough, "you must act, for it is a gentleman's duty. And if you abandon her now," he said firmly, "I shall knock you senseless."

Lizzy retook Darcy's arm and inclined her head against his shoulder with an adoring smile.

Magnus stared at his feet, and Flip felt as abandoned as Lizzy had a moment ago.

He lifted his eyes to the archbishop. "May I have a moment alone with Dolly?"

The archbishop nodded grimly.

Magnus pulled Flip through the doors into the bedroom.

"What," she demanded hotly, "is up with you?"

He took her in his arms and kissed her with such urgent, heart-wrenching desperation, Flip began to tremble. Then he pulled away and held up his hand to stop Darcy and Bingley, who had taken several menacing steps in his direction.

"You shall hear her if she complains," Magnus said tartly. "Short of that, I should like the uninterrupted moment I was promised." The men backed away.

"We don't have much time," he said to Flip.

"What?" Flip touched his clenched jaw gently. "What is it?"

"Our memories," he said sadly. "Everything will be wiped clean."

"What are you talking about?" The look in his eyes terrified her.

"I knocked myself out." He tilted his head in the direction of the hall. "On the lintel to the balcony door, when I went to help Darcy. It was enough to wake me up, or whatever one calls coming out of this drug-induced version of *A Midsummer Night's Horror.* I spoke to Madame K. She told me she could fix the book, but that we had to get Lizzy into Darcy's arms—"

"Which we did!" Flip cried.

"Which we did," he agreed, "and that she'd fix the rest, but that when she did"—he dropped his head—"we'd have no memory of it."

"Of the *book?*" Flip said, truly frightened.

His eyes filled with indescribable woe. "Of anything that's happened today. Neither you or I will remember anything that's happened since the first time you arrived here, nor will anyone linked closely to the adventure."

She thought of that first shiver, when his imperious, sexy glare from across the café first excited her interest. She thought of his maddening condescension in the library, then his office, and the gentle touch of his hand during that first, knee-trembling kiss. She thought of the fiery, inhibition-shedding lust he'd ignited in her during that amazing Scrabble game. She thought of his thoroughly amusing terror over Scruffy's boisterous greeting, but most of all she thought of those warm, feeling eyes as he'd said, "I know how to make babies."

"But in there . . ." She pointed to the bed.

"I know. I'm sorry. I shouldn't have— No!" His face changed so dramatically, Darcy and Bingley tensed. "I'm not sorry. I shouldn't have, but I'm not sorry. It's what you wanted, and it's what I can give you—perhaps all I can give you."

A child, if she were pregnant, whom Magnus would never know. A child she wanted so deeply. Without debate, without tears, without the torturous negotiations, without the suffocating sense of the chasm between one's hopes and the reluctant, conditional commitment of the man one's hopes had been placed on. It was a generosity she hadn't experienced, and as it shone on her it moved their impending loss from unbearable to utterly heartbreaking.

Her throat tightened. "Oh, Magnus."

He took her hand and ran a trembling thumb across the base of her palm. "I simply must believe," he said slowly, "that magic, however powerful, cannot completely erase our memories if something like this connects us."

"Fitzwilliam?" Darcy waited for Magnus's decision.

"Yes." Magnus took Flip's hand carefully. "We're ready. Tell the archbishop."

Chapter Thirty-one

Flip shifted uncomfortably under Madame's K's stern gaze, though her embarrassment was outweighed by the exhausting sense of trying to savor the last few moments of an intense, fleeting joy. And the reassuring touch of Magnus's knee against hers as they sat chair to chair in front of the masseuse's desk only served to raise the intensity of the feeling almost to pain.

Flip had managed to maintain her composure through most of the archbishop's hurried ceremony, but when Magnus had taken her in his arms at the end and she had seen Lizzy's hand slip assuredly into Darcy's, she had felt such a debilitating mixture of sorrow and happiness she couldn't breathe.

She squeezed the silk-knotted cuff link—lime green— Magnus had handed her in lieu of a ring at the end of the ceremony and tried not to cry as Madame K made her way through the long list of transgressions she had marked with sticky notes in Magnus's copy of *Pride and Prejudice*.

". . . broken china and glassware; dirty vumen's underclothes scattered about the house; obscene and ill-treated roses"—*Obscene?* Flip thought for an instant before being swept back into the scolding—"and shocking vater damage in the ceiling below Colonel Fitzvilliam's room. Of course, that's nothing compared to the more egregious crimes, eh? Darcy KO'd by the most unfeminine sort of behavior; the Archbishop of Canterbury's summer cold and subsequent near-fatal bout with ague; the seemingly upright and dependable Colonel Fitzvilliam discovered in flagrante with an innocent young girl"—Magnus made a small but audible snort—"followed by a shotgun marriage; Sir Villiam Lucas struck by apoplexy in the middle of the orangerie; a salacious note from the rogue Vickham found on Lizzy's bedside table and Lizzy's equally questionable reply found on the floor of the dovecote; Caroline Bingley's shocking pronouncement of her intention to marry a footman; Vickham forcibly wed to the misbehaving Lydia despite her raving and incomprehensible insistence that Sir Villiam had attacked her; and, finally, Sir Villiam's hastily drafted vill leaving half his fortune and two riding crops to a Netherfield maid named Peg."

Flip adjusted her weight in the chair. "You didn't mention Darcy and Lizzy's wedding."

Madame K slipped her glasses back on. "Oh, yes," she said with a sardonic turn of her mouth, "Darcy and Elizabeth join Bingley and Jane in a surprising double vedding at the Netherfield parish church. Thank you for that, Miss Allison."

"If it makes any difference," Magnus added with an aggrieved sniff, "I'm certain Sir William would have named Peg in his will whether we'd arrived in the story or not."

"It does not."

"Six love stories, though," Flip said with a weak laugh. "That's gotta be a record, huh?"

"Yes," Madame K said without a hint of pleasure. "I'm sure Jane Austen is cheering."

Flip cast her gaze to her feet.

"Fixing this vill not be easy," the older woman said. "It's going to cost me every favor I am owed in the Casting Masseuse Society. Every single thing vill have to be reversed. Lizzy and Darcy vill have a new beginning—and so vill each of you." She gave them a glare.

"A new beginning?" Flip said.

"Yes, with a clean slate, at the public dance in Longbourn, vith no trace of Lady Quillan, just as Austen meant it to be," Madame K said, although Flip had been asking about herself and Magnus.

"Yes, ma'am."

Madame K shoved a plate of small, odd-looking cakes toward her guests. Flip could identify the currants dotting the surface easily enough, but the cake appeared to include a spattering of green and red chips as well. Not just plain green and red, but the lime green of Magnus's socks and the ruby red of a passenger pigeon eye.

"Eat this," Madame K said.

"What do you mean?"

"Two vurds, Miss Allison, neither of them difficult. 'Eat,' as in place in your mouth and chew, and 'this' as in—" She waved a many-ringed hand over the plate.

Flip shifted. "And that's when we'll forget?"

Madame K cut a sharp glance in Magnus's direction. "I see you and Mr. Knightley have been talking."

He said coolly, "I wasn't aware our discussion was confidential."

"It vhasn't," the masseuse replied. "Just an observation. May I ask who you vur in the story? I'm aware, of course, Miss Allison vuz Lady Quillan, though, given the unrestrained chaos of the final chapters, I must say it eez strange

there's not a single mention of vhat happens to her ladyship. Vhat, couldn't you manage a striptease on Parliament
stairs or a middle-of-the-night escape with Louis the Four-
teenth on horseback for her?"

Magnus glowered. "I believe Lady Quillan had reconciled
happily with her husband."

"Seven," Flip pointed out.

"And she did send a lovely bronze to the Bingleys for their
wedding. Or so Sir William said," Magnus added.

Flip's head shot up. "A bronze?"

"A male nude, if I recall. You might have seen it in the upstairs hall. Quite impressive. Adonis, I believe."

Flip choked.

"Vith a child?" inquired the masseuse. "They reconciled
and had a child?"

"So I'm told," he replied.

"And your character, sir?" Madame K sharpened her in-
terrogatory gaze on him. "Who vur you, and vhat did you
upend?"

Magnus managed to keep his eyes off Flip and focused on
his cross-examiner.

"A stable hand," he replied. "A mere spectator. No lasting
impact at all."

Madame K looked at Flip, who fiddled with the corner
of a box of incense. "I fear you underestimate yourself,
Mr. Knightley," the masseuse said. She picked up a pen,
returned her glasses to her nose and handed each of her visitors a photocopied list. "Take a look at this, please. Let me
know if I have missed anything. The story may not return
to its exact form if anything has been changed that isn't
listed there."

Magnus returned the list to the table with hardly a glance. "It's complete."

"You're sure?"

"Yes," he said precisely.

"You understand the story may not be exactly the same?"

"Austen will survive a minor alteration or two," he replied. "Let's get on with it, shall we?"

"Um," Flip put in meekly, "can I ask a question first?"

"Vhat?"

Flip turned to Magnus. "I, ah, may not have mentioned Jed appeared to have arrived in the book as well—as Wickham."

Magnus shook his head. "Jesus. Io was there too. As Lydia."

The older woman regarded them unsympathetically. "Ah, vhat tangled vebs vee veave vhen first vee misbehave in our dreams."

"But, um," Flip went on meekly, "can I ask if they're okay?"

Madame K tapped her pen with impatience. "They've been dealt vith, Miss Allison. They have eaten their cakes and left. They seemed to have undergone some upset during their visit to the story, but the cakes did the trick, and they left in far more settled frames of mind than they'd been in vhen they arrived."

Eight, Flip thought. "Did they, ah, by any chance, have any, well, birds with them?"

"Birds?" Madame K's eyes narrowed.

Flip flapped her hands in the air. "You know, *tveet-tveet?*"

"Yes, I'm aware of the meaning. Do you think I vould have allowed anyone in the story to leave vith something they didn't bring in?"

Slinking in her seat, Flip thought of both the bird she had brought through and the tiny potential life in her womb. "No, I suppose not." Not if you knew about it.

Madame K pushed the plate of cakes closer.

"They look a little funny," Flip said.

"Yes." Madame K crossed her arms, waiting.

Magnus met Flip's eyes. She knew what he was thinking— that if it weren't for Austen and her beautiful story, he wouldn't dream of taking a bite. She knew what he was thinking because she was thinking the same thing.

On the same wavelength at last. Great. Just in time never to see him again.

They reached for the plate, and their hands came to rest on the same cake. For an instant they did nothing, then, knowing they had no other choice, they each pressed and the cake broke in two.

Flip brought her piece back to her lap and cupped it in her hand.

"Can I get something to drink with this?" Magnus asked, forehead furrowed. "It looks bloody awful."

Madame K grabbed a bottle of water from the shelf and banged it on the table.

Magnus stared grimly at the strange-looking bite in his hand, but it was the long, sorrow-laden press of his knee against Flip's, out of Madame K's sight, that made Flip want to cry. She was on the edge of jumping up and shouting "No! We won't do it! Find another way!" when, as if anticipating her completely and wanting to avoid something that would be both embarrassing and in vain, Magnus leaned forward, put his fist to his mouth and ate his piece of cake. His face pinched as he chewed, and, with a grunt of distaste, he opened the bottle and drank deeply.

Flip immediately felt the room change. It was as if part of Magnus had been swept away, even though he was clearly there physically. He watched her with empty eyes as the bottle came to rest on his leg.

She wasn't one to linger, even in the face of something as horrible as this. She flipped her morsel in her mouth and chewed. It tasted exactly like the lemon pastry she'd had at her brother's wedding dinner, the same day her friend Eve had been diagnosed with breast cancer—sweet but with an achingly tart sadness. Wetness stung her eyes.

She looked at Magnus, whose tortured gaze never left her, and shared a silent good-bye. The room sparked around the edges like a sputtering candle, then faded to an infinitely empty black.

Chapter Thirty-two

Flip slumped in the library chair, staring at the same freaking page on her screen she'd been looking at for the last hour: "Bird Density and Diversity in Clear-cut Oak Forests: A Modest Proposal."

She put her head in her hands and groaned loud enough for a prim, heavy-banged undergraduate three tables over to give her a look. If this was forgetting, Flip thought, she would have preferred a sharp blow to the head. Maybe she should have eaten the whole cake. Maybe she should have chased it down with about half a bottle of tequila, though the endless cabernet she'd drunk over the course of the last two nights hadn't really helped that much.

The fact of the matter was, there wasn't a single heart-breaking, knees-jellying detail of that single, momentous day that she'd forgotten.

When she'd awakened in her bed two mornings ago, she'd thought she was still dreaming. The last thing she could remember was the sorrow in those chestnut eyes. Then she realized she *could* remember the sorrow in those chestnut eyes! Which meant she could remember the rest of him too. For many long moments, her mind savored the memory of those slim fingers and soft auburn waves and the way his eyes crinkled when he smiled. She could feel the press of that knee, and she rushed to embrace the memories that were like shadows that might disappear in the light. At first she was delighted, cherishing every recalled moment like a treasure. Then she knew what she had to do.

After checking *Pride and Prejudice* and satisfying herself that nothing of their adventure had remained to complicate the book, she'd rushed to campus. While waiting anxiously for the elevator in the lobby of the Cathedral, she'd spotted Magnus deep in conversation with a dark-haired woman by the far entrance.

There had been nothing inappropriate in his manner or hers, nothing that would indicate anything but a shared and animated interest. The woman might have been a colleague or a graduate student or even a university administrator. But whomever she was, Magnus's demeanor as he talked to her suggested someone who had enjoyed the blissful, unremembering sleep of someone with a clear conscience and an unencumbered heart.

And what was Flip going to do? Insert herself between them and say, Oh, by the way, you may not remember, but we stumbled into the plot of your favorite socioeconomic observational novel a couple of days ago, destroyed it, fell in love, fixed it, maybe started a baby and were married by the Archbishop of Canterbury. Wanna sit down for a latte at Starbucks?

So Flip had returned to the library as if Tuesday hadn't been anything more than the day that followed Monday, just as it had been last week, just as it would be next week, and there she'd spent the last two days with nothing more than three meager PowerPoint slides and an empty box of Kleenex to show for it.

She unfolded her fist and looked once more at the small, green cuff link. Two balls of silk connected by a tiny length of cord. It was like her and Magnus, she thought. Each bound in a seemingly endless knot, and the link that binds them together also holds them apart.

God, how she hated French cuffs!

She shoved her laptop into her backpack and dropped the Kleenex box in the trash. The library was no place for a woman in her condition. She waved at Bob on the way out.

"Truffula loraxa," he called, giving her a happy thumbs-up.

Hey, at least somebody remembered her.

She dragged herself down Forbes and climbed up Chesterfield's steep sidewalk. Looking Glass was open, and Flip let herself in.

Madame K stepped out of the backroom when she heard the bell.

"Good afternoon," she said with a bland smile. "Vhat can I do for you, miss?"

"Yeah, we got a problem." Flip dropped her backpack on the waiting room chair. "Not only do I remember you, I remember him."

"Vell, it can be different for women," Madame K explained as she nibbled a carrot stick. She offered Flip the sandwich bag that held a half-dozen more.

"Different, like, not working at all?" Flip took two and ate. It was the first food she'd eaten all day, and she wondered vaguely if she'd end up in Mr. McGregor's garden.

"The cakes are very dependable, but sometimes the heart is stronger than baked goods."

"Words to live by, I'm sure, but what am I supposed to do now?"

"Vhy not ask him out?"

"Well, I'm not sure if he remembers our run-in at the café or not. It happened before I traveled, but if he does, then he hates me. And if he doesn't, well . . . I'm not sure he'd be that interested in dating someone who looks like she could pass for the plant maintenance trainee. He's a little on the highbrow side, if you hadn't already noticed."

"Vun cannot be intimidated by another's first impressions."

"I suppose I could ask. But the thing of it is, even if he does accept, it's not going to be right. I mean, I have all this backstory that he doesn't. I'd feel like I was hiding something. It's not the way to start a relationship, hoping he'll get to the same place you've already been. It's like running a marathon together on two different days. It wouldn't be the same. Worse, it would be dishonest."

"You could tell him the truth."

"Oh, yes. I'm sure that's just the sort of thing he'd love on a first date. A woman who's barking mad *and* wears a uniform. Perfect."

The clock in Madame K's office struck six, and Flip grimaced. She'd come to hate clocks too.

"We could try another massage."

"With the way I'm feeling now, I'd end up at the end of *Titanic.* No, I think it's time for me to get my head out of the clouds and my feet back onto some solid ground."

"Miss Allison," Madame K said with a grave look, "never underestimate the power of a good love story."

"Well, I'll have the chance to test your theory. It's book club tonight. We're doing *Pride and Prejudice.*"

"Mmm." The woman's eyes glittered. "That's a good one, I hear."

Chapter Thirty-three

Flip stood beyond the heavily paneled lobby of Eve's building and jabbed the bell. She wasn't up for this party. Her eyes were swollen, her head hurt, she looked like shit, and she was pretty sure she never wanted to think about Darcy or Lizzy again.

When she'd made it to the hallway outside Eve's door, she applied some Viva Glam lipstick, wondering exactly how much Glam of any sort could be pumped into a woman with bird shit on her pants. Eve answered, looking fabulous and tan in a pair of violet linen shorts and a white silk T-shirt that showcased not only one perfectly upturned breast but the complete absence of the other.

"Hey, where's your bra?" Flip demanded, smiling.

Eve broke into a huge, ZIP code–energizing grin. "Adam prefers the exotic look. Said it gives me a sort of Xenia the Warrior Princess thing. I dunno, Flip. It's a little kinky. Should I be concerned?"

Flip squealed. "You slept with him?"

"Sleeping was the easy part. It was the striptease before that was hard. Adam said he'd limit himself to half his twelve inches if I thought that evened things up."

Flip hooted with delight. "Twelve inches?"

Eve rolled her eyes. "Oh, please. I'm Xenia, not Samantha Stevens. C'mon, the ladies are here."

And they were—Dinah, her red hair loose and grinning like a fool in anticipation of the dive into her favorite heterosexual love story; Claudia, in bottle-green slides and a pair of matching cords, flipping anxiously through the last chapters of her evidently unfinished copy of *Pride and Prejudice;* Seph, Eve's friend from Pilgrim Pharmaceuticals, legs crossed and laughing as she fingered the tie of her sandal; Beth, Dinah's student friend, listening intently to the older women while she knit what looked to be a cozy for a trash can; and Eve's great-aunt, Lucy Kenney, white-haired and regally dressed in a plum suit and a triple strand of graduated pearls. Aunt Lucy, totally cool and sharp as a tack, was a regular at the book club gatherings. She'd never had kids and treated Eve and her friends as if they were her own.

"Ooh, ooh, ooh," called Dinah, waving her arm. "Flip's here. We can start. I get to ask the first question."

"Please. I need a drink first," Flip said, and the women laughed. She took a seat beside Aunt Lucy.

"You look well, my dear," Lucy said, patting her arm. "Lovely high color in your face."

Aunt Lucy wasn't paying her optometrist enough.

"Thank you," Flip said, accepting the cool glass of Pinot Grigio Eve slipped into her hand. "You, as always, put us to shame."

"You young people have so many more choices these days," Lucy confided. "I like to see a little skin on ladies. It looks so healthy."

"Eve looks happy." Flip watched her friend rearrange slices of bruschetta on a plate. "I'm glad. She deserves it."

"Yes." Lucy took a sip of her wine and nodded. "Some adventures are harder than others. Do you remember, Flip, the first book club I attended?"

"Sure."

"I'd wasted so much of my life until that point just traveling and buying things. When I met you girls, I realized how much more fulfilling it would be to devote myself to giving you the adventures you needed." Then, in response to the perplexed look on Flip's face: "You never met my husband, of course. A Romanian. Mysterious ways, those Eastern Europeans have, with their bottles and powders and incantations. When I met him, he owned a shoe store in Squirrel Hill. When he died, he left three factories. But his baby sister's still around, bless her. She's a—oh, what do they call it these days?—a massage therapist, and she was more than happy to help."

Before Flip could question her Eve clapped her hands. "Okay, ladies. This is it. The appetizers are out. Everyone's got a drink." She lifted her glass in toast. "Here's to *Pride and Prejudice*. Who starts?"

"I do, I do!" With the stage presence of a practiced teacher, Dinah leaned forward, slowly meeting each person's eyes. "Darcy," she said with sincere gravity. "Is he capable of love?"

"What?" Eve exclaimed. "From you?"

"Hang on," Dinah said. "It's a legitimate question, and I'll tell you why. After we chatted on Monday, I read the book again and tried to see it through Flip's eyes. Is Darcy driven only by desire?" In response to the rising noises of objection she added, "Think about this and tell me your honest answer. If Darcy and Lizzy had consummated their relationship prior to their engagement—as any of us today might be likely to do—would Darcy have followed up with a proposal? Assuming mores were the same?"

"Lizzy never would have slept with him until he'd grown as a person," Seph said. "God, he was such a stuffed shirt."

Dinah held up her hands. "Okay, post-unstuffing they sleep together. I'll even grant you it's fabulous. Does the wedding take place?"

"Yes," Claudia said. "Sex blinds and absolutely fabulous sex blinds absolutely."

"Is that how you explain your ex?" asked Dinah.

"That was the house in Saint John, sweetie."

The room broke up.

"I see your point," Eve said. "Does a man who's driven by desire lose that drive when the desire is sated? What do you think, Flip?"

Flip considered Magnus's all-consuming intensity as he loomed over her in that Netherfield bed, preparing to lay claim to both her body and her future. So different from that empty blankness in his eyes after he'd eaten the cake. "Well—"

"Not in my opinion," Aunt Lucy put in. "If there's a connection—a real connection—then great sex only makes the connection stronger. If a man and woman are really meant to be together, then nothing can break that link."

"But," Flip said, shifting, "there could be things out of their control. I mean, what about illness or death or a forced separation. What if," she added earnestly, "the man was in an accident and lost his memory?"

"I heard about this guy in a coma," Beth said, pausing in her knitting. "Wakes up. Doesn't remember a thing. The doctor and the wife don't know what to do. Then one day, totally by accident, the wife runs out of the perfume she normally wears, so she digs in the drawer for whatever she can find. Turns out it's the stuff she wore twenty years earlier when they were dating. She walks in the hospital room. The guys takes one whiff, and everything comes flying back."

Perfect, Flip thought. So long as Magnus remembers the smell of bird shit, we'll have no problem.

The buzzer squawked. Eve ran down the hallway. "Come on up," she called into the intercom.

"Adam?" Flip asked when she returned.

"A special guest," Eve said. "From the university."

A tingle ran up Flip's spine. "Oh?"

"A visiting professor. Magnus Knightley. He's an Austen scholar."

With a madly drumming heart, Flip remembered the invitation Claudia had extended to Magnus at her apartment. But that was after Flip's first visit to *Pride and Prejudice,* and if he remembered that, then he remembered everything, or at least he remembered something. Flip could barely contain herself.

She swung to Claudia, who was grabbing a bruschetta slice while scanning a page of *Pride and Prejudice*. "You invited him," Flip said, desperate for confirmation.

Claudia blinked. "Huh?"

"I invited him," Aunt Lucy said, and Flip felt the world shift under her feet.

"I'm quite a large donor to the university, you know," Aunt Lucy explained, "and I heard this nice young man give a lecture on Jane Austen recently. Seemed like he had some interesting things to say, though of course he's quite wrong on a few points. Nonetheless, I called the chancellor to see if he would be a dear and arrange something for our book club. Apparently the fellow said he'd be happy to join us."

This was almost more shocking than waking up in *Pride and Prejudice*. "He said he'd be *happy*?"

Aunt Lucy waved her hand. " 'Happy.' 'Willing.' What's the difference? And I might have mentioned something about finalizing my will in the next month or so, but I hardly think that could have an effect on the situation, do you?" She gave the room an innocent smile. "The fellow's rather an eyeful."

Beth said, "Hey, we can ask him the sex question."

"No!" Every head in the room turned to Flip, who immediately felt her cheeks sizzle. "I mean, it would probably embarrass him."

A knock sounded at the door, and Flip felt her stomach drop about six floors. She wished she'd done more Viva Glam-ming than a simple smear of lipstick. At least she wasn't wearing her Aviary polo shirt. She jumped to her feet, saying something about a refill, and dug the shirttails out of her khakis as she made her way to the relative privacy of the dining room. There, she unbuttoned the top and bottom buttons of her shirt and tied the bottom flaps into a quick knot over her stomach. Then she pulled the silver-beaded elastic off her ponytail and slipped it over her wrist. If she had to look like a plant maintenance worker, at least she could look like an upscale one. She sniffed her wrist, wishing she'd applied more than Lubriderm after her shower this morning.

Eve opened the front door, and Flip heard Magnus say hello. Panicked, she grabbed a lemon from the bowl on Eve's dining table and rubbed it vigorously under her ear.

"What are you doing?" asked Claudia, who had appeared beside her with Dinah and Seph.

Flip jumped. "Um . . . neck crick. Best thing for 'em."

When Flip saw him enter the living room, she wanted to fall down a rabbit hole. The pressure was immense. If he recognized her, her life turned in an entirely new direction. If he didn't . . . well, she had to admit, as a direction, the crapper wasn't exactly new.

He wore tan trousers that draped elegantly over polished tasseled loafers and a crisp white shirt under an effortlessly perfect chocolate blazer that made the smoky brown of his thick hair nearly sear her heart. Eve led him through introductions in the other room as Flip stood, heart fluttering in her throat, waiting for him to turn toward her.

"He's cute," Dinah said. "For a hetero."

"Oh, baby," Seph purred.

Claudia gave Flip a gentle elbow to the ribs. "I'd take a bumpy carriage ride with him anytime."

"And you didn't meet him before?" Flip asked through the cotton in her mouth.

Claudia gave her a strange look. "Have you eaten today? You know what low blood sugar does—"

"Oh, it ain't low blood sugar," Dinah said, watching Flip's face, "though it is low and involves blood."

"Flip," Eve said, suddenly before her with Magnus in tow, "I'd like you to meet Magnus Knightley, a visiting professor at the university. Magnus, this is Flip."

Flip extended a hand, waiting for the shock of his touch, and realized she was still holding the lemon.

Magnus took the lemon, confused, and shook her hand.

Flip felt the familiar localized earthquake rattling up her arm and shooting off M-80s in her ears. "Pardon?"

"I said," Magnus repeated in a voice that sounded to Flip as if it were echoing through a viaduct half a city block away, "you look familiar. Have we met?"

"Oh, cripes, yes!" exclaimed Eve, clapping a hand over her mouth and instantly turning the color of Hawaiian Punch.

"W-what?" Flip's head ping-ponged back and forth between the two them.

"At the café this week," Eve cried. "Don't you remember, Flip? Sitting at the other table. Forgive us," she said to Magnus. "We're not usually quite so obnoxious. God, I'm really sorry. I had no idea you were the same guy, though the 'Knightley' thing certainly should have tipped me off— Oops!" The Hawaiian Punch pink deepened to Twizzler cherry red.

" 'Knightley' thing?" Magnus's eyes went straight to Flip.

"I-I don't know what you're talking about," Flip said.

" 'Thrice.' " Dinah prompted sweetly. "Don't you remember, Flip? I believe that was your best guess as to his—"

"Thank you, Dinah," Flip interrupted. "I'm sure we embarrassed ourselves enough that day. No need to shovel more fuel on the fire."

Dinah shrugged as if to say, "The confusing ways of heteros," and added under her breath, "Beats 'fortnightly,' which is Flip's usual grab-bag prize."

"Mr. Knightley," Aunt Lucy called, "we were just talking about *Pride and Prejudice.*"

"Ah." Magnus rubbed his palms together and made his way to the chair Eve had dragged from the dining room for him. "How can I be of service?"

Flip wandered back sadly and took a seat on a large throw pillow at the edge of the circle. If she'd been hoping for a shriek of recognition or being flung *Officer and a Gentleman*-wise into his arms, to be carried out of the cruel life of a field ornithologist/plant maintenance worker into the far more rewarding world of a supporter in the shadows of a monster-egoed academic, it hadn't happened.

He had shot her a piercing look, not dissimilar to the

one he'd launched her way at the café three days ago. So at least you're generating the same spark, she thought ruefully. Just because it's the sort that detonates cars at gas pumps shouldn't deter you.

But what she had been hoping for—a tiny irrepressible flash of recognition, the triumph of connection over circumstance—had not occurred. The past was lost to them. Her job now was to believe, in the absence of compelling evidence, that recreating that connection was still possible, and to formulate the field plan that would get her there. No different, she thought, than the plan to find the ivory-billed woodpecker.

Eve said, "I think for Mr. Knightley's sake we should table the previous line of discussion and open the floor for a new topic."

"I've got a good one." Beth's needles clacked like she was responding to the conversation in Morse code. "Jane is the pretty sister—and clearly kind—but arguably vacuous. Is she capable of truly loving Bingley?"

Seph sucked a speck of tomato off her pinkie. "I thought of them as the Brad Pitt–Jennifer Aniston of their day. You know, kindly holding the mirror while the other adjusts his or her hair. A mile wide, a quarter-inch deep, that sort of thing."

Dinah laughed. "I'm thinking more Paris Hilton." She rapped her forehead with her knuckles. "Hellooooo. Anyone in there?"

"Oh, no, you're wrong," Flip said with heartfelt emotion. "Jane's very much in love with Bingley. She really is. And he, her. They play to each other's strengths. It's like you're seeing Bambi and Falene getting twisted up on the ice when they're together. There's a heavy undertone of sexual attraction, of course, which you'd expect in a newly paired couple, but it's just totally sweet and ador—" The looks on her friends' faces made her stop. "I, ah . . . I mean, that's certainly what I'd imagine, wouldn't you?"

Magnus regarded her curiously, tapping a thumb on his knee. "You seem to have built an extraordinary connection with the characters while you were reading."

"I, er . . ." She searched his eyes for some sign of shared insight but found only the same mild bemusement he'd had when they'd talked in his office.

"I guess you had to be there, eh, Flip?" Seph said.

Nettled, Flip grabbed a handful of almonds and popped one in her mouth. "Yeah."

"How about that first proposal scene, huh?" Dinah asked. "That's a scorcher."

"God, I know," Beth said. "Lizzy lays out Darcy's failings so plainly. It's like she's trying to tell him there will never be any more falsehood between them. It's just so ballsy. I'm sure that's the reason Darcy behaves like he wants to take her by the ear and slap her."

"Of course," Eve laughed, "that's probably also the reason he behaves like he wants to take her by the hips and fu—" Her eyes widened and she buried the last word in a noise that sounded like she was choking on an unwieldy cheese ball. "Focus her," she said at last, and gave Magnus a nervous smile. "I'm sure he thought Lizzy was, ah . . ."

Seph offered "Missing the thrust of his argument?" and the rowdy laughter of the women, including Aunt Lucy, who hid her mouth behind a napkin, filled the room.

Magnus's face began to take on that look of Vesuvius before it taught the Pompeians a lesson. Flip, mortified, tried to regain control of the discussion. "Look, I know it's easy to fall into the trap of looking at *Pride and Prejudice* as *Beauty and the Beast* for grown-ups—"

"God," said Dinah, "I love that look on the Beast's face when Belle catches him slurping his soup."

"—but I think we're doing Austen a disservice," Flip continued. "Her landscape was broad and her hand capable. It's a story of manners and change, in a time when the usual stratified societal castes were being thrown over for the beginnings of a world in which meritocracy could take root—"

"Societal castes? Meritocracy?" Magnus repeated sharply. "Who put the downers in your Chardonnay? Darcy clearly had more on his mind than the start of the Industrial Revolution. He wanted Elizabeth, as simple as that, and if we, the present-day reader, see a sexual side to his quest— didn't Freud call libido the primary motivating force in the mind?—I'm sure Austen would allow for changing interpretations in a changing world."

Flip's mouth fell open, and she stared at him full in the face to see if he was joking, but he was gazing at a spot somewhere in the center of his now-empty wineglass, oblivious to her surprise.

"I have a somewhat different interpretation of Darcy," Aunt Lucy said. "I find him a man more to be pitied than admired."

"Darcy's hopes rest on the resolution of Lizzy's pique," Aunt Lucy said. "Why doesn't a man who's capable of carrying himself through all manner of social interaction address this straightforward, albeit uncomfortable, point? Because he's scared. If he opens up to her, he'll know at once if they share that tiny irrepressible flash of connection."

Flip's head shot up.

"But instead." Aunt Lucy went on, and Flip followed the point of her finger as if the rest of the sentence were embossed on the tip, "he lets the days go by, watching from a distance as the world closes the door on his dream. What can we say, Mr. Knightley, about a hero who allows himself to be defeated by circumstance?"

Magnus's silence lasted so long Flip wondered if intended to answer at all.

"Darcy uses the time to change and grow," he said at last, raising his head. "And he does win Elizabeth Bennet's hand in the end."

"Months later!" the older woman cried. "And only when luck intervened to throw him in Lizzy's path at an opportune moment to play the hero. I do not call that courageous or heroic."

Claudia, confused, leaned toward Flip. "Opportune moment?"

Flip whispered, "Lizzy's sister Lydia runs off with the evil Mr. Wickham. Lizzy knows her family's reputation will be destroyed if they don't marry. Darcy works behind the scenes to make it happen. Honestly, you really should read the book."

"But—"

"Shhh." Flip wanted to hear Magnus's reply.

"No, perhaps it is not courageous or heroic," he agreed. "But if the choice is between waiting and hoping, and witnessing the destruction of all hope, the path he chooses may be the only one he can endure."

Aunt Lucy's bright blue eyes rested on him a moment. "Bah," she said. "Love is wasted on the young."

After that, the rest of the evening flowed easily, and much later, in the middle of the spirited debate over whether in fact Darcy could have made the offer of his hand in some way that would have tempted Lizzy, as Magnus dutifully analyzed, interpreted and challenged, Claudia bent toward Flip, still clutching her open book, and whispered, "I don't understand. Am I the only one curious about the baby?"

Flip bobbled her barely touched drink and said, "Pardon?"

"I mean, it's pretty obvious."

Flip laid a casual arm across her lap. She certainly wasn't sure she was pregnant, despite Magnus's confident declaration, and even if she were, she couldn't possibly be showing. "It is?"

"Yes. I know I'm not done with the book, but even I can guess Lady Quillan is going to be knocked up higher than a Las Vegas hotel. And anyhow, what's up with doing it on the railing of a temple? I like hot sex as much as the next person, but is there something wrong with a nice abandoned bower or at least a blanket behind the temple? I mean, think of the poor neighbors. You're going to be seeing these people at the dry goods store for the rest of your life and— Hey!"

Flip had grabbed her arm and was dragging her out to the kitchen.

"Gimme that book." She snatched it out of Claudia's hand and tore through the pages. Lady Quillan perched on the temple railing. Lizzy flattening Darcy on the Netherfield balcony. Sir William Lucas tipping Lydia over the greenhouse workbench. Huh? Caroline marrying a footman.

"This isn't the right book," Flip nearly shouted, wondering if her heart was gonna stop.

Claudia blinked. "It's the one you dropped off for me."

"I dropped off for you?"

"It was on my entry hall table on Tuesday."

"Holy crap." Flip realized Claudia had no memory of that Monday at Flip's apartment. She, like Magnus, had been affected by Madame K's memory reversal. Magnus had said it would affect anyone tied in to the event. Apparently, visiting Flip's apartment and meeting Magnus had been enough to tie Claudia in. But somehow the book she'd picked up had not been wiped clean.

Flip spotted another copy of *Pride and Prejudice* on the counter and jerked it open to the end. A double wedding, nothing more. Relief washed over her. Claudia's copy seemed to be the only one with the problem.

"This," Flip explained, holding up her friend's copy, "is what's called a parody."

"Really?" Claudia lifted a brow. "It's not very funny."

"I didn't say it was a good parody."

"So you're saying I read the wrong one?"

"This one"—Flip held up the copy she'd found on the counter—"is real. No sex. No bastard babies. No Temple of Apollo."

Claudia retrieved her copy from Flip's clutches. "So you're saying I read the right one."

Flip couldn't help but remember with a rush of pride the Olympian adventure atop that Stourhead Garden hill. "That good, eh?"

"Up till two."

"Then you'll lend it?" Flip held out her hand.

Claudia squinted an eye, reluctant. "I guess. Sure. Let me just peek at the end—"

Flip jerked the volume back. "No point. You know how these things end. Hero and heroine marry. No unwanted pregnancies or abandoned brides. Ha-ha-ha. That would certainly not belong in a romance, right?"

"No." Claudia looked at her strangely. "And it didn't appear to be happening in this one either. Flip, are you sure you've read this? Everything I've heard about Darcy and Lizzy suggests they'd be in each other's arms, happy as clams, at the end. And they are together, having conspired to get that pathetic, whimpering maid married off to Colonel Fitzwilliam—"

"Pathetic seems harsh."

"—but they still seem rather hesitant in their affection, unsure of where they really stand with each other."

"Really?" Flip looked at the book in Claudia's hand, confused. "But they marry?"

"Yeah, but I'm imagining them with the same stunned 'how did I get myself into this?' look I had on my face when I married Bernie. You've seen the photos. I looked like my name had been drawn out of a hat."

"No, they're supposed to be very happy at the end. That's how romances are."

"Well, they're happy," Claudia said, "but not very confident. I don't know, Flip. You should read it. There's not a clear happily ever after there."

Seph stuck her head into the kitchen. "Ladies, Professor Knightley has to be off, and Dinah and I have to run too. I have an early flight tomorrow."

"Paris?" Flip asked. She knew Seph's boyfriend lived there.

Seph nodded, smiling.

"Yeah, well, I should go too." Flip tucked Claudia's book under her arm and said her good-byes to Eve and Aunt Lucy.

The women streamed into the elevator with Magnus, who clutched his leather bag. Flip inserted herself beside him, hoping one last whiff of Lubriderm and lemon might spark something. But the only people affected by smell appeared to be Flip, whose knees trembled at Magnus's familiar clean, soapy scent, and Dinah, who sneezed through most of the trip down.

Flip lingered casually, to see if she could attach herself to Magnus for the short walk to the subway, but he stood by Seph, for whom he had offered to hail a cab.

There was, Flip decided, no way their worlds would ever reasonably overlap. What they had shared was a random cosmic collision, electrons that had bumped and parted. If there had been any true connection, they would have emerged connected and changed forever, like hydrogen and oxygen when they make water.

This was not like the ivory-billed woodpecker. Hope was not enough.

She turned back for one final look. If she had needed a sign, the vision of Magnus with his back to her, oblivious to her departure, was it. She tucked Claudia's copy of *Pride and Prejudice* into her backpack and made her way to the train.

Chapter Thirty-four

The subway, a cavernous, gleaming underground, snaked through downtown and across the Monongahela River to the base of Mount Washington. Flip emerged from the train hoping the cool night breeze would clear the sadness from her head. She shouldered her pack and made her way the block or so it took to reach the Monongahela Incline for the ride up the mountain. She flashed her monthly pass at the attendant.

Pittsburgh, a city of hills, had once been served by dozens of these charming inclined trains, edging their way up the steep urban slopes that horses and then cars had struggled to overcome. The Monongahela Incline was one of the two that remained, each like a bookend at the east and west edges of Mount Washington.

The incline's car was set up with three rows of stadium seating, each level holding one bench facing forward and one facing backward. Flip climbed the little staircase in the station to the highest level, entered the car and sat down.

Usually the two-minute ride lifted Flip's spirits. The view of the city's twinkling skyline as the car rose three hundred feet never failed to bring a smile to her face, even at the end of a long day. But tonight she'd been willing to trade privacy for the view. Only the first row had a full view of the city.

Flip closed her eyes and waited for the gears to lurch into motion.

Other travelers boarded, though Flip paid little attention. At this time of night, if they weren't residents of Mount Washington, they were lovers, making use of the quick round-trip to clutch each other warmly and share a kiss.

Flip heard two children arguing in the lowest level, and several teen boys shoving and laughing their way into the middle one. She relaxed, certain her row, with the least appealing view, would be ignored. But just as the "Watch the doors" announcement was made, a couple of riders tromped in and sat down. Flip adjusted her backpack without opening her eyes. Apparently luck did not feel any need to smile on her today.

The car pulled away from the station, beginning the climb upward. The passenger beside her adjusted his foot against the empty bench across from them. As he did, a barely noticeable scent of soap made Flip slit her eyes. Resting on the opposite bench was a black-tasseled foot under a narrow swath of lime.

Her heart hiccupped, and even before she turned her head the amperage that passed from his wool-twilled hip to hers was enough to scorch her flesh.

Magnus said, "Hello. I hope you don't mind me tagging on, so to speak. I have an engagement up the street."

"Heck, no." She laughed nervously. "Free country, right?"

Heck, no? Free country? What? Now you're the village idiot?

He coughed politely. "Indeed."

She wiped her palms on her pants. Everything about him was sexy and dark and utterly magnetic. The cells in her body strained so hard toward him her skin literally ached. What could she do to build an unbreakable connection with him in the next sixty seconds that wouldn't either get her arrested or terrify him?

"It was very nice of you to come for Aunt Lucy," she said, then added with a nervous laugh, "I mean, it was very nice of you to come for all of us. *Pride and Prejudice* is such a good book." The words began to pour from her mouth like five pounds of M&M's from a bag at ten feet and with much the same precision. "Not just for the love story, of course. I mean, there's the whole socioeco-landscape thing going on there too. And what a landscape it is, eh?" She barked a laugh, then added seriously, " 'Landscape' meaning that particular period of time, not like a garden or something. After all, there isn't any garden stuff in the book, right?" Another laugh. "Well, except that bit of wilderness next to Lizzy's house." *God, will you please shut up.* "Austen's writing is all so interior. The mind of the man. But exterior as well. A man of his age and all that. She's just so . . . observant." Flip clasped her hands. "Marvelous."

Thank you, NPR.

"I suppose." He sighed, gazing past Flip toward the narrow city view framed by the curlicues of the car's wrought-iron window frame. "Though on many levels I think it's a just a damned fine love story."

Her jaw nearly hit the floor.

"That's not how you read it?" he asked.

"Well, yeah, I mean, sure."

"With all the lovers happily united at the end?"

Was he sending her a message? She searched those warm whiskey eyes for some glimmer of knowledge. "All?" she said.

"What else, Flip?"

Her face must have contracted for he said quickly, "It is 'Flip,' isn't it?"

"Oh yeah. No, you got it right." No message. She tried to shove the overwhelming disappointment aside but it was more than she could manage. "Short for Philippa," she added, distracted. "As in the wife of Edward the Third."

"Pardon?"

She waved her hand. "Philippa of Hainault. You know, the mother of the Black Prince."

"Really?" he said. "It sounds like the name of a three-legged poodle to me."

Her heart jumped so hard into her throat she could barely speak. "Magnus?"

He swept her in his arms, low and tight, burying his searching mouth in her hair and behind her ear.

"Oh, Flip."

They kissed. It was not just a kiss of desire, though Flip could feel the burn that ran down her spine and shot like a firecracker out her toes and fingers—it was a kiss of loss and sorrow and of such soaring relief she felt the emotion was almost suffocating.

"Magnus, how . . . ?"

"I didn't eat the cake, and I damned you to hell for eating yours."

Now he tipped her back, kissing her so hard it was as if he were pulling that connection out of her, unwilling to stop until everything, everything was whole and reaffirmed between them.

The car stopped and people left and more got on, but neither Magnus nor Flip let go.

"I did eat the cake," she whispered somewhere on their next trip up, "but I didn't forget. It was too . . ."

"Traitorous, ungrateful, wicked, wicked woman." He pulled the tiny knotted silk she hadn't even realized she was holding out of her hand. "This means something," he whispered fiercely. "Did you forget the promise we made?"

She hadn't. The flush that covered her face was evidence enough of that. But she also hadn't forgotten that picture on his office credenza.

"You're separated." She fought hard to hide the quaver in her voice. "The ceremony meant nothing—technically. And you have a girlfriend." She stole a sidelong look at his face. "And children."

"Children?" he squawked. "No, Flip, you are quite mistaken. I do not have children."

She thought of those plaid skirts and jumpers. "But the girls on your credenza—"

"Are my nieces." Flip's heart did an exuberant backflip. "Cara, Jill and Kendall."

Kendall. The grad student with big tits and a trust fund. Damn, when Flip was wrong, she was Milky Way–sized wrong. She thought back to that call and Magnus hanging up then laying tiles on the board. "You play Scrabble with Kendall by phone, do you?"

"Yes. She's thirteen going on twenty-seven, and smart as a whip. Beating me appears to be her greatest pleasure in life."

Flip shifted in his arms. "I, ah, withdraw the objection about a girlfriend, then, too. But that doesn't change the fact you're married—"

"*Separated.*"

"—and that ceremony at Netherfield meant nothing."

"That ceremony," he said, placing the cuff link back in her hand, "meant a great deal. And so might I add did the ceremony that came just before it." He tipped her chin up. "Are you pregnant?"

"I don't know."

"You will be eventually—if I have anything to do with it. Is that your only objection, then? That I'm separated?"

"Yes." Her voice sounded as small as a lark's, she thought, but, oh, how this lark soars!

"We've been separated eight years," Magnus explained. "She's been living with her new boyfriend for seven. It's simply a matter of filing the paperwork. I have it in my desk," he added to silence Flip's newly erupting argument. "Then you and I shall find the nearest prelate—

"Oh, how eminently British," she said, giddy from joy and lack of oxygen.

"—and repeat the ceremony."

"Which ceremony?" She made a sly giggle. "I'm not sure what the Church of England is like, but in America prelates would not look on one of them very kindly."

"The repetition is but a detail." He took her face in his hands and looked so deeply into her eyes she felt her toes sizzle. "That ceremony with the archbishop stands."

"Yes, sir," she began to say, but her reply was buried in a long, eminently British kiss.

As the car reached the bottom of its second roundtrip, her phone buzzed with a text, and she pulled it out of her pocket and read it.

"Come with me," she said, taking his hand as she stood. "I need you for something."

He gave her a sexy smile. "I believe I need you for the same thing."

"Not that," she said, "*yet.* But I have something almost as satisfying."

Chapter Thirty-five

"Stand right there, and close your eyes." Flip moved Magnus against the railing of the walkway that overlooked the pond in the Aviary's soaring rainforest habitat.

Magnus gave her a narrow look and put down his book bag. "The last time someone said that to me, I got a whopper of a measles vaccine and cried for two hours."

"I promise you won't cry."

"I see. So a shot's not out of the question."

When Flip had Magnus situated, she ran to a large cage strategically hidden behind a curtain of palm fronds. She'd been so overjoyed on the Incline, she would have been happy going up and down all night. Though, she thought with a giggle, *I suppose that's going to be happening soon in any case.* But this opportunity had been too good to pass up.

"Your eyes are shut, right?"

"Have you heard of British honor?"

"Yeah, yeah, yeah." She opened the cage and Scruffy strode out. He cocked his head, sending that gorgeous crown of tipped feathers rippling backward, and immediately headed toward Magnus.

"Now lift your pant cuffs."

"No. Oh, no." Magnus grabbed the railing behind him, eyes still scrunched shut. "You cannot be serious."

"I am. Not every man has Day-Glo pheromone-infused socks. Now lift."

Peeking through the elbow he'd folded across his face, he said, "They are not Day-Glo. They're Ted Baker apple green, and at ten bloody pounds a pair, I'll thank you to remember that."

"Ten pounds. Got it. Lift."

Magnus sighed and delicately raised the left cuff of his pants.

Scruffy's crown feathers stiffened as if he'd heard a distant battle cry. Then his bright blue wings began to beat, his head began to bob like a boxer's, and his bass drum rumble filled the room.

"Perfect!" Flip cried. "Don't move."

"Bloody Christ, there's nowhere to go but over the railing into the swamp."

Scruffy was pecking furiously at Magnus's feet now, and Magnus was doing a manic sort of tap dance in order to avoid being pierced and, at the same time, appear to be co-operating. Flip ran to a second cage on the opposite side of the walkway and unlatched it.

"This is Vicky," she said. "She was very glad to see her favorite friend return to the Aviary yesterday."

Vicky, a second Victoria crowned pigeon, emerged peering around Flip's calves toward Scruffy nervously.

"Burned before?" Flip said under her breath to the bird. "I know the feeling. Ya gotta keep at it, though. See that guy over there? All mine."

Vicky nodded, impressed, took an uncertain step and made a hesitant trill.

Scruffy stopped mid-peck and spun around. Vicky's head tilted left. Scruffy's head tilted left. His chest expanded. He ducked his head in a courtly bow.

"That's it, man," Magnus said. "You've got to charm them first."

Vicky circled to Scruffy's side. Scruffy lifted his head and made an impressive wing flap. Their eyes met.

"Time, gentlemen, please," Flip whispered to Magnus. She picked up her backpack and jerked a thumb toward the door. Magnus tiptoed out behind her into the winding hallway that housed the desert bird enclosures, leaving Scruffy and Vicky looking as happy as, well, two lovebirds.

"Thank God for hormones." Magnus lowered himself onto a children's viewing perch shaped like a massive rock and wiped his brow.

"Truer words were never spoken."

"And speaking of hormones . . ." He pulled her across his lap and gave her a scorching kiss.

"Do you think," Flip asked when the tingle subsided, "they'll be happy?"

"How exactly can you tell when a bird is happy? Do they skip? Buy the next round? Update their blogs?"

"I meant Lizzy and Darcy."

"Ahhhh." He nodded professorially. "Yes, I do."

"There you are, Fli— Oh, God, I'm sorry."

Vera, the community outreach ornithologist appeared, and Flip jumped out of Magnus's lap.

"Vera," Flip said, blushing, "this is Magnus Knightley."

Vera extended her hand, smiling. "My goodness," she purred to Flip. "You've netted a big one."

Flip cleared her throat. "Thanks for keeping an eye on Scruffy tonight."

Vera waved her hand. "No biggie. I'm working on a grant application. I knew I'd be here late. Did you get my text?"

"About Scruffy being ready? That's why I'm here."

"No, the other thing."

"What other thing?" Flip demanded. "There wasn't another thing. You said, 'Come to Aviary. It's important. Scruffy's primed.'"

"I said, 'Come to the Aviary. It's important *&* Scruffy's primed.' Totally different. Gotta watch your ampersands, missy."

Flip crossed her arms. "What is it?"

"Go listen to your voicemail. You got a hell of an interesting message."

Flip's eyes went from Vera to Magnus anxiously. Christ, it could be anything from Jed blackmailing her over passenger pigeons to Madame K offering her a cameo in *A Farewell to Arms.*

Magnus shrugged his shoulders as if to say let's get to it. He stood. "Your office?"

Flip led the way. When they arrived, Flip gave Vera a look. "Maybe it's better if I hear this in privacy."

Vera leaned against the doorframe. "Honey, I've already heard the whole thing. It came in while I was finishing up out here."

Great. This might require lies improvised on the spot.

Flip lifted the handset, pressed the buttons and listened. She couldn't believe what she was hearing.

"I got the fellowship!" she cried as she hung up. "At Cornell! I'll be going out to look for the ivory bill!"

Vera clapped, and Magnus swung Flip in a circle, nearly knocking a stuffed penguin off its mounting. "That's wonderful!" he said.

Flip could barely breathe. Too much was happening in one day. "He said—the man from Cornell—I wasn't their first choice. But their first choice—one Jed Hughes—withdrew his name after a late night call earlier in the week accusing the committee of allowing their decision-making to be swayed by the receipt of sexual favors."

Magnus laughed. "Jed's just sorry it isn't an all-woman panel."

"Wait. It gets better. He also said he's filing a complaint with the Association of Field Ornithologists," Flip howled, clutching her sides.

"Oh, Cornell's going to love that." Magnus said. "When do you go?"

"Monday."

"Monday?" He looked like someone had slipped a knife between his ribs.

"Uh-oh," Vera said. "That's my cue to skedaddle. Congratulations, Flip. You deserve it. Find that bad boy." She swept out.

"Monday?" he repeated again.

"Only for a couple of weeks. We'll be readying the observation posts in Arkansas. I'll be back for a few days here, then spend a week for orientation with the team at Cornell. Then it's off for the big hunt. We'll have cameras and video stations and recorders set up everywhere we can in this huge tract of forest. We'll be fanned out, in boats and on foot, waiting, looking and listening. It will be the definitive, pull-out-all-the-stops search! I can't believe I'll be part of it."

He took her in his arms. "I'm thrilled for you."

She looked at the picture tacked over her desk, from the last confirmed spotting of the ivory bill, and felt the tears well in her eyes. "If that lovely, mistreated bird is there, we'll find it. Think about it. We'll be bringing a miracle back, a miracle. Oh, Magnus."

"I know." He hugged her tightly, then pulled back a little and met her eyes. "May I ask you something?"

She nodded.

"It strikes me that finding the ivory bill means something more to you than just an ornithological miracle."

Flip felt like he'd turned the key in something she'd kept locked away for so long. The emotion that swelled in her, urging her to allow him to share her secret, both scared and thrilled her. What if he scoffed? She gathered her courage.

"Eve—our hostess tonight—has some pretty aggressive breast cancer. When she was first diagnosed, we all pulled together, went with her to chemotherapy, helped any way we could. And she fought hard. But the first scan after that, the one that showed the cancer had begun to shrink, happened the same day they announced a reported sighting of the ivory bill in Arkansas. It was just one ornithologist, and not everyone believed it. But that day changed everything—for Eve and for the birding world." She lowered her eyes, afraid to see his reaction.

"Ah. And you, I suppose, see this as a sign?" His voice was flat and unreadable.

Flip inhaled, feeling he was about to cross a line from which they wouldn't be able to recover. If he dismissed her determinism as misplaced superstition, she'd never be able to open herself fully to him. "Yes," she said, almost afraid to speak.

Those sharp brown eyes cut across her face.

"Then find that bird," he said, pulling her close. "Find it for Eve. Find it for you. Hell, find it for us."

Her heart filled with a joy so full and light, it felt like it might fly out of her.

"But come back, dammit," he added fiercely, and cupped her head next to his shoulder. "Be my falcon, leaving to hunt, but returning when I call."

"To that fine, hard hand." She giggled.

"Which reminds me." He slipped one hand down her khakis, connecting with an electric charge to the rise of her ass. "I'm still owed a debt of honor."

"That debt of honor was paid," she said.

"Half paid," he corrected. "I want you over my lap for a good thirty seconds and a bed with a strong footboard nearby."

Now the hand had a firm grip on both cheeks and the other was making significant inroads at the top of her fly. In another minute her pants were going to be around her ankles.

He said, "The correct answer is 'Yes, Magnus, as soon as we get to my place.' "

"No," she cried.

"Here then?" He shrugged. "If you insist."

Spanked in her office? The metallic grind of her zipper letting go sent a comet of terror through her.

"No!" she squeaked. "I mean yes. My place. As soon as we get there."

"Yes, *Magnus,*" he corrected.

"Yes, Magnus," she repeated.

"Excellent."

Her heart fluttered to a livable thump. Getting discovered bare-assed where she was supposed to be a model of responsibility for the junior ornithologists was not exactly the way she wanted to launch herself into the fellowship at Cornell. And in any case, she thought, looking around at the sterile, sharp-edged furniture, she, too, had some interest in a soft bed being close at hand. Which reminded her . . .

"Hey, I've got a question."

"There'll be a moderate sting." He rezipped her pants. "But it's the visual I'm going for. It's what comes after that will really elicit a reaction."

"Not that," she said after her lungs unfroze. "The Rare Book Room."

Caught off guard, he looked at his watch. "It's locked, but I suppose I can try to raise the key."

"No, I'm wondering how it's done there. The, ah, coiting, that is. There doesn't appear to be an accommodating surface. I've been wondering ever since we visited."

"Ah." He finished with her trouser button and stepped back, clasping his hands professorially. "Interesting question, actually. Allow me to demonstrate."

In a move as smooth as a dancer's, he spun her in a circle and pulled her against his lap as he came to rest against the desk-height filing cabinet. "We're leaning against the book-viewing table," he explained.

"But the angle doesn't seem right at all," she said, and gasped happily as he cupped her breasts.

"Imagine this"—he hooked a Navaho basket filled with reference books with his foot and pulled it in front of her—" is the lowest shelf of the dictionary stand." He directed her to put her feet on top of it. "And this"—he bent her at the waist and drew her hands around the water pipe that ran from the floor to the ceiling about two feet in front of them—"is the security grill over the window above it."

She was now bent at a 45-degree angle, ass tilted invitingly, with enough anchoring power in the pipe to withstand several hundred newtons of hammering force.

He slipped his hands up her shirt and thumbed her nipples. "Do you see?"

She thought of the windows of the law school directly across from the Rare Book Room. "Yeah, and so does everyone else."

"For a field researcher, you're not very adventurous."

"For a professor, you're not exactly a trustee of your student's best interests."

"Clearly you've never spent an hour bathed in the light of the law school. The torch of enlightenment shines brightly. And a woman who first dropped her towel to kiss me then dusted her nipples into a diamond-tipped fury doesn't have a lot of room to talk."

She gasped. "You saw that? You never said anything!"

"Talk? It was all I could do to keep upright."

She gave him a sly grin. "I believe I've got an idea that might help with that."

He stood up, bringing her up with him, and drew his arms around her so tightly she could feel his chest rise and fall. The friendly mocking in his voice had transformed into unalloyed regard. "Can we go home, Flip? I really, really want to lie next to you."

Home. "Yeah, sure." Grinning crookedly, she kissed him. When they finished, she drew back reluctantly, letting her cheek come to rest on his chest. "Falcon, huh?" she said with more than a little pride.

He squeezed her. "I promise I won't be an overly demanding master."

A noise in the outer office reminded them they weren't alone, and Flip and Magnus parted.

"I guess we should go." Then she remembered. "Oh, wait. The last scene in *Pride and Prejudice*."

"Oh, no." Magnus held up his hands. "Not more."

"It might be important. Have you read the book since we got back?"

He gave her a thoroughly British look. "Word for word. My copies and every other copy I could get my hands on."

"Did you notice anything different?"

"A few tiny bits here and there. Nothing to cause any notice."

"Claudia—my friend at the party?—she read the copy I gave her this week, and, well, maybe you'd better look." She delved into her backpack, fished out the copy she'd convinced Claudia to lend her and handed it to him.

He opened the book hesitantly, scanned the page, raised his brows and met her eyes. "Remind me to look for the sugar bowl when we get to your place."

"Not that." She grabbed the book, flipped to the last pages and read it with him.

"See," she said when she'd finished. "They're not quite certain they've made the right decision. They don't seem as happy as they should. Claudia was right. I wish there was something we could do."

"But it's only in this copy," he reminded her. "I've checked dozens."

"But still. It's Lizzy and Darcy. Shouldn't they be blissful?"

His eyes flickered to his book bag. "I can't believe I'm about to say this. I actually kept the rest of the Drink Me water from Looking Glass. It's in my bag."

She looked from the bag back to him. "Do you think we should?"

He sighed. "Have a seat, Flip. Those shoulders of yours are looking tense."

Chapter Thirty-six

Lizzy clasped her husband's arm hesitantly as the carriage cleared the last bump in the country road, turned through the wide stone arch and delivered them onto the relatively smooth gravel of the drive leading to Netherfield. She was tired, slightly hungover, headachy from the surprised well-wishers at the church, and terrified of the night ahead. The exuberant, energizing giddiness of newfound love, richly tinted with lust, had begun to wane in the morning light, leaving her half certain that allowing Darcy's signet ring to be placed on her finger had been a dreadful mistake.

The rest of the wedding party had tarried at the church, but her husband had hurried her out, and now Darcy gave her an aloof sidelong glance that shook her hard.

As the carriage approached the crest of the drive, Darcy said, "Oh dear."

"What— Oh!"

In the bright morning light, the Cadiz roses, some of them at least, had bloomed to life, and the flowers, which were to have spelled out "Bingley bestows on Jane the orb of his heart," now appeared to urge simply, "B-l-o-w J-o-b."

"Not exactly the sort of wedding wishes one is accustomed to receiving," Darcy said.

"No." Lizzy had to cover her mouth with her hand to keep from smiling.

"Leave it to Bingley to emphasize the obvious."

Despite everything, Lizzy giggled. And when she did, a broad smile broke out on Darcy's face.

"Oh, my love, it is such a relief to hear you laugh."

"You have heard me laugh almost since the moment of our meeting."

"True. Mostly at my expense. And I have heard it as a siren's call when any other sane man would have run with his tail between his legs."

"Perhaps sanity is not a requirement of a good marriage."

"I might assert it is only a hindrance."

"I see you've met my parents."

This time they both laughed. When the carriage slowed and Lizzy saw they were about to enter the courtyard of Netherfield, she felt a mild dread overtake her.

"Oh, no," she said with a hitch in her voice, "I cannot face any more people congratulating us today."

He opened the window and banged on the frame of the carriage. "Driver," he called, "turn here. Take the path around the park. Then . . ." He returned his head inside and looked at her. "Derbyshire, London, or the closest inn in Meryton, milady?" He bowed his head solemnly. "The world is yours."

"Well . . . Perhaps not the *closest* inn." She bit her lip and blushed. "I should like to grow a little more used to this feeling. Do you mind?"

"Not a whit." He redirected his voice to the driver. "Then on to Harpenden," he called. "We shall take our lunch there."

Their fingers laced. His hand was cool and dry. It

sheltered hers without binding, and Lizzy found that she enjoyed the feeling.

"Harpenden is two hours, at least," she said after a long moment. Her gaze was focused on the distant woodland on her side of the carriage just as his was focused on the small lake on his.

"Indeed it is, milady."

"Would you wait forever?"

She could feel him smile.

"I would," he said.

"But Harpenden will do?" She grinned at her shoes. The declaration of her interest in the unknown pleasures of the wedding bed was as plain as she could make it.

"I would wait forever," he replied gravely, "but Harpenden will be quite satisfying."

Lizzy brought her face up without thought, and Darcy, with a seemingly similar lack of premeditation, kissed it. After an interlude covering a good quarter mile, they each took a breath while still clinging to each other like new kittens.

"Magnus," Flip whispered, resettling herself on the carriage seat. "This is all her. I'm not saying any of it."

"Nor am I," he whispered back. "Seems Austen didn't need our help, after all."

Flip nodded, still fingering one of the silky chestnut locks that hung below his collar. "Perhaps just a little longer, though."

"I'm in for Harpenden," Magnus said, and Flip felt the world settling slowly, properly and astonishingly into place.

Epilogue

Madame K placed the red queen on the black king. Ah, love stories, she thought. Even in solitaire.

"Yes, ov course," she said into the phone. "I told you, you could count on me. They are set . . . It might not have looked that way to you, but sometimes you have to trust, *ja*? . . . Yes, yes, yes. I am vurking on the rest. It's not a simple matter of snapping my fingers, you understand— Oh! Got to go. My bell's ringing."

She hung up and hurried to the waiting room. A young woman with pigtails and a bright orange backpack stood peeking in the door.

"I hope you don't mind," the student said. "I saw your light on."

"No, not at all. Sit, sit. I'll be right with you."

Madame K returned to her office and picked up a large towel. "Now you two vill be okay, *ja*?" she whispered. "Vee have company. You know, like that man with the beret who brought you here and his little girlfriend. You must be very quiet. Can you do that? Of course you can. Now don't be worried about the dark. It eez a cool night, eh? See vhat you can do to remedy that."

The two passenger pigeons stared at her, clearly daunted,

as she draped the towel over their cage and fixed it with a binder clip.

Madame K shook her head and sighed. "All in good time, I suppose. And speaking of time . . ." She looked at her watch and counted down, "Three . . . two . . ."

The bell rang again.

She ducked into the waiting room and stopped, wringing her hands. "Oh dear. Two ov you. Do you mind if you share a room?"

The young woman looked at the slightly plump, red-bearded young man who'd just entered. "Sure. Why not."

The young man held out his hand. "Great, thanks. I'm, ah, Bob McTaggert, by the way."

"Oh, I know you," she said. "You work at the library."

"Yeah. You, ah, take out a lot of Brits. Er, writers, I mean. Books." Splotches of pink climbed up his neck.

"Yep." She grinned. "That's me. I'm Beth. Beth Olinsky."

"Vonderful," Madame K cooed as they shook hands. "Now that the introductions are out of the way, let me ask. Are either of you familiar with our specialty here—imagining yourself in a book?"

They looked at each other blankly and shrugged.

"I'm not," Bob said. "But it sounds sort of cool."

"Vunderful." Madame K clapped her hands. "Now raise your hand if you've read *Gone With the Wind*."